EARTH'S BLOOD

DYSTOPIAN URBAN FANTASY

ANN GIMPEL

Edited by
ANGELA KELLY
Illustrated by
FIONA JAYDE

CONTENTS

EARTH'S BLOOD

EARTH RECLAIMED, BOOK TWO

Dystopian Urban Fantasy
By
Ann Gimpel

BOOK DESCRIPTION: EARTH'S BLOOD

Clinging to their courage in a crumbling world, Aislinn and Fionn vow to save Earth, no matter what it takes.

In a post-apocalyptic world where most people have been slaughtered, the Celtic gods and a few humans with magic are all that stand between survival and Earth falling into chaos. The combination of dark sorcery leveraged by the enemy is daunting. Destruction is all but certain if the small enclaves of humans who are left can't get past their distrust of the Celts.

Captured by the enemy, Aislinn Lenear wonders if she'll ever see her bond wolf or Fionn, a Celtic god, again. She's had nothing but her wits to rely on for years. They haven't failed her yet, but escape from her current predicament seems remote.

An enticing blend of dystopian urban fantasy and romance, this second volume of the *Earth Reclaimed* Series provides fertile ground for Aislinn and Fionn's relationship to deepen. Headstrong and independent, the pair run up against each other's demands time and time again. Fireworks spark. In the end, they learn to savor every moment in a bittersweet world where each day may well be the last.

you better connected to the wonderful world that has been created. Just as the first book this one grabs you from the start and pulls you into a wonderfully created world with a tension filled plot, beautiful descriptions and easy to love characters. Book Bliss Blog

ionn tumbled through a gateway and leapt to his feet. Something was decidedly wrong. The wolf and raven were right behind him, but he'd lost all sense of Aislinn's presence in the traveling portal. It made him half-crazy with fear, but there was nothing he could do until the spell spit him out. Mouth dry, heartbeat thudding in his ears, he waited to see who would follow him out of the ragged hole he'd left in the ether.

For the love of the goddess, please let me be mistaken about this.

Rune emerged. A howl split the still air. *"Where is she?"* the black and gray timber wolf demanded. He reared up and plunked his paws on Fionn's chest. *"What happened to my bondmate? I cannot feel her anywhere."* He howled again. It was a mournful sound, full of grief.

Fionn wrapped his arms around the wolf, but Rune dropped to the ground, apparently not interested in comfort.

"Yes, where did Aislinn go?" Bella demanded, bouncing forward with her awkward avian gait. Ever cantankerous, the raven was bonded to him, so Fionn was used to her moods. She spread her large wings, took to the air, and cawed her displeasure.

He stared after her and struggled to manage a mounting sense of panic while balling his hands into fists. Both bond animals knew the truth: Aislinn had disappeared somewhere between Ely, Nevada and wherever they were now. He barked a word to close off his magic. The place they'd rolled out of shimmered and disappeared.

He loosed a string of Gaelic curses. "What the fuck went wrong?" he muttered. Fionn drew magic to augment his night vision and gazed wildly about for clues. They were in the midst of rubble that could well be Salt Lake City, so at least that part of his casting had been true. *No,* an inner voice corrected him, *I doona know that. This could be anywhere.* He shoved straggling strands of blond hair out of his eyes and sent his magic spinning outward to gather data. His heart beat a worried tattoo against his ribcage.

The air to his right took on a pearlescent hue. Bran and Arawn leapt through a portal in a flash of battle leathers, the snug-fitting garments indistinguishable from Fionn's attire. Arawn barked a command, and their gateway winked shut. His midnight gaze scanned the small group. "Why is Gwydion not here?" he demanded. "He left afore any of us."

Rune threw his head back. Another desolate howl split the night.

Bran's coppery eyes narrowed. "Aye, and where is the lass?"

"And that Hunter scum, Travis," Fionn growled. He spread his hands in front of him. "I havena felt Aislinn since a few moments after we entered the portal. Join your magic to mine so we might figure out what has happened."

Bran nodded curtly. "Aye, Travis must have lied to us, but to what purpose?"

"To save his own sorry hide, what else?" Fionn snapped. "Or mayhap because he wanted Aislinn for himself."

The air took on an iridescent waviness. Gwydion stumbled out of the odd-looking place. Tangled in a welter of blue robes, he clutched an intricately carved staff; blond hair swirled around him. "Be gone, I say—Wait, what happened to—?" He took in the tableau as he lurched unsteadily to his feet. Fionn almost heard wheels turning as Gwydion tallied who was missing. The warrior magician pounded the end of his wooden staff into broken asphalt. Lightning crackled from the end of the staff, betraying his annoyance.

Something snapped in Fionn. Bright, brittle anger lanced through him, and he launched himself at Gwydion, driving the other Celtic god to the ground. "Bastard," he screamed. "Ye were in charge of Travis. What? Ye couldna control a simple human? Look what your slipshod seeds have sown!" He raised a fist and drove it into the side of Gwydion's face. It was more satisfying than using magic. Closer and more personal.

Rune jumped into the fray and sank his teeth into Gwydion's leg. Bella cawed her disapproval. She tangled her talons in the mage's long hair and pulled as she pecked at him. Gwydion bellowed in pain. The air thickened and developed an electric quality as he reached for his magic.

Fionn had just cocked his arm back to hit Gwydion again—before his fellow Celtic god shielded himself—when strong arms closed about him and dragged him back. Magic surrounded him, forming a barrier.

"That willna help," Arawn, god of the dead, revenge, and terror, said, his voice stern with command.

"Aye, it willna get your lass back," Bran agreed. God of prophecy, the arts, and war, he often had a gentler approach than the other Celtic deities.

Gwydion rolled to a sit, looking dazed. He placed his hands on the wolf and raven, muttering in Gaelic. After a time, both animals retreated. He touched the bloodied places on his thigh; the flesh mended quickly. The master enchanter and god of illusion didn't make any move to get to his feet. He settled his blue gaze on Fionn, bowed his head slightly, and said, "I am most sorry. Ye are right to be angry with me. The lad came at me flanked by Lemurians. I never even knew how many. When I sent my magic spiraling out to find Travis, he was gone beyond my reach."

"Why didn't ye tell me?" Fionn growled.

"How?" Gwydion countered, sounding weary. "Communication isna possible in the portals."

Fionn groaned inwardly. He knew that. Where were his brains? *Taking a wee holiday,* a sarcastic inner voice suggested. Fionn jerked against the magic holding him. "You can let me go now," he told Arawn and Bran. "I've returned to my senses."

He stepped forward and extended a hand to Gwydion, who grasped it. "I'm sorry I lost my temper."

Something sparked from the mage's blue eyes—compassion laced with pity. Gwydion stood and then brushed off his robes; dust flew in all directions. He bent to retrieve his richly carved staff. It glowed blue-white when he touched it, and he arched a brow at Fionn. "See, the staff knows battle lies ahead. The important thing is what we do now. A good start would be not tearing one another to bits."

Though Fionn agreed, he secretly wondered if Gwydion might have tried harder were it not for the bad blood between them over Tara, Aislinn's dead mother. As a MacLochlainn, Aislinn was bound to him, just like her mother had been. But Tara had loved Gwydion. To avoid marrying Fionn, she'd given herself to a stranger and run away to America, effectively severing an age-old bonding. Tara MacLochlainn had been an Irish queen. Under laws of blood and dynasty, she should have belonged to him, Fionn MacCumhaill, Celtic god of wisdom, knowledge, and divination...

Guess she had other ideas about that. What a fankle. Mayhap one we're still paying for. Fionn forced his mind to stay in the present. No point in dragging old bones out and chewing them half to death. Rune's large black and gray head rammed his side. The wolf bared his fangs and growled.

"I understand." Fionn settled his blue gaze on Rune. "We have to find her. And we will."

"Let us go over what we know." Bran stepped closer. Blond braids were tucked into tight-fitting battle leathers. He had a dreamy look about him, but Fionn wasn't fooled. The god of prophecy's mind was sharp as a whip.

"Good idea," Arawn echoed. Dark hair cascaded down his leather-clad shoulders. Looking as grim as the dead he commanded, his face etched into harsh lines. Eyes, so dark that iris and pupil were indistinguishable, flashed fire.

"Let us ask the goddess's blessing," Fionn intoned. A weight like a cold stone settled into his guts. They couldn't afford to make any mistakes. Aislinn's life depended on them getting this right the first time. *And my life right along with it.* Fionn thought about the next thousand years without the only woman he'd ever truly loved, and his soul shriveled. He cursed his immortality. Life without Aislinn wouldn't be worth very damned much.

Gwydion began a Celtic chant. The other three joined in at proscribed intervals, punctuated by Bella's shrieks and Rune's barks, whines, and howls. Night yielded to a sickly orange sunrise as they sang.

"I believe we are ready," Gwydion murmured.

"Aye, I feel a goddess presence," Arawn spoke reverently. "'Twill provide a balance point against all our male energies."

"Let us return to cataloging what we know." Fionn gestured impatiently. Though he understood the wisdom of securing divine assistance, he wanted to get moving before something lethal happened to Aislinn. A vision of her being tortured—long limbs splayed over a rack—rose to taunt him. He muffled a cry, but his mind wouldn't clear. Blood ran down Aislinn's face and blended with the red of her hair. Her golden eyes were glazed with pain. He bit down hard on his lower lip, feeling powerless. Adrenaline surged, leaving a sour taste in the back of his throat.

Bran nodded. "We are, indeed, ready."

Fionn latched onto the sound of Bran's voice and let it pull him out of the black pit his mind had become. He crooked two fingers. "Talk, goddammit."

Bran inhaled sharply. "The Hunter, Travis, sought us out. I dinna try verra hard to test his words, but there was enough truth in his tale to satisfy me."

"And I, as well," Gwydion agreed. "So mayhap his small group of humans truly was set upon by Lemurians—"

Fionn snapped his fingers. "I have it. That putrid poor-excuse-for-a-human cut a deal to save himself. Mayhap part of it was designed to wrest Aislinn away from me since he was in love with her, too. She told me—" The words curdled in his throat. He couldn't bear the thought of Aislinn fucking anyone else. She'd been with Travis once.

If she was telling me the truth... Mayhap she was with him many times and softened the telling to spare me.

Arawn cocked his head to one side. "Even though ye stopped midstream, what ye did say made sense. Travis agreed to serve as bait in exchange for his life—and mayhap the life of his bond animal, as well. If he had his eye on the lass afore all this, well, the pot would have been all the sweeter."

Fionn waved him to silence. "Ye say ye felt Lemurians?" He looked at Gwydion, who nodded. "Well, then, she must be in Taltos. Where else would they take her?" Relieved to have a destination and something to do, Fionn pulled magic, intent on leaving immediately.

"Hold." Gwydion put up a hand.

"What?" Annoyed, muscles strung tighter than a bow, Fionn locked gazes with him and sparred with a pair of blue eyes nearly identical to his own.

"Ye canna go off half-cocked. There are not enough of us." Gwydion hesitated. "As the god of wisdom, knowledge, and divination, Fionn MacCumhaill, I would think ye would know that without me having to tell you."

Frustration fueled rage. Fionn opened his mouth to tell Gwydion what he really thought of him. "Why you sanctimonious—"

"Never mind that," Bran spoke up. "We need a strategy."

"And mayhap more of us," Arawn added.

"Aye, and what about Dewi?" Ignoring Fionn's bitten off words and the challenge beneath them, Gwydion furled his brows.

Fionn blew out an impatient breath; his anger receded. The others were right. Dewi, the blood-red Celtic dragon god, was linked to the MacLochlainn women. She'd also spent centuries in the tunnels beneath Taltos, spying on the Lemurians. Yes, they definitely needed the dragon.

"All right," he ground out through gritted teeth. "I get it. I agree we need Dewi and probably more of us as well."

"We must return to Marta's house. As soon as we can."

The wolf's voice startled Fionn. He turned to look at Rune. The wolf padded closer. *"I have been to Taltos both ways,"* the wolf reminded him, growling low. *"It is much easier and more direct if we enter through the portal in Marta's basement. That way we maintain the element of surprise. The Mount Shasta gateway is akin to going to their front door and ringing a bell."*

Fionn kicked himself. *Even the wolf is thinking more clearly than me.*

Rune had been bonded to Marta and knew her secrets. She'd been onto the Lemurians, delving deep into the extent of their lies. Before they killed her, she'd managed to figure out that the war against the dark gods was a sham. The Lemurians were actually in league with the dark. They were the ones who'd masterminded cracking the veils between the worlds to allow the dark ones access to Earth. An ancient race, the Lemurians understood they were dying. They'd needed an infusion of magic, so they cut a deal. Access to Earth in exchange for—

Fionn filled his lungs with air, blew out a breath, and did it again. He had to get hold of himself, or he'd be less than useless hunting for Aislinn. *That will not happen. Focus, goddamn it. Pull it together.* Fionn pushed the ache in his heart aside and buried it deep. He couldn't afford emotion. Or mental forays into Lemurian treachery. Not now. When he'd met Aislinn, she'd been a foot soldier in the Lemurian army, branded so she couldn't use her magic against them.

Voices flowed over him. When words fell into coherent patterns again, he heard Gwydion ticking off a plan on his fingers. Apparently one the others had formed without any input from him. *How dare they?* Anger flared hot and bright. Fionn welcomed it like a drowning man might grab a spar. He needed the energy to find the woman he loved.

"…agreed, Bran will hunt for Dewi. Arawn will return to the Old Country to muster as many of us as he can find. Fionn, the bond animals, and I will return to Marta's house. We will sneak into the tunnel a time or two to see what we can discover, but we will not move to rescue the lass until you arrive with reinforcements."

Gwydion nailed Fionn with his blue gaze. "Aye, and ye have returned to us. Did ye hear—?"

"Aye." Fionn cut off Gwydion's next words. "Let's get moving."

The master enchanter inclined his head. "As ye will."

Fionn looked at him and wondered if it were mere coincidence that Gwydion would end up babysitting him. He decided to test those waters. "I really would be fine with just the bond animals. Feel free to join either Arawn or—"

"Pah!" Gwydion interrupted. "Not on your life. I know you, Fionn MacCumhaill. If ye returned alone, ye would turn Taltos upside down to find your lady love. Then the rest of us would have two to search for."

Arawn moved forward and laid a hand on Fionn's arm. "Remember," he said, "the Lemurians came from Mu. They may still have a way to retreat there. If they do so, we willna be able to follow. Or they might strike a deal with the five remaining dark gods and go to one of their worlds if they feel threatened. We can travel to the border worlds, but it isna pleasant. Nay, if they have truly taken Aislinn to Taltos—and we doona know this as a fact—it is imperative they remain there. So doona do anything foolish."

"I understand." Fionn clamped his jaws shut. Thoroughly chastised, he felt like a child again. He hadn't considered either of the alternatives Arawn just outlined. Apparently they'd come up in the part of the conversation he'd missed while wrestling with himself.

"I know ye do." Arawn favored him with a rare smile. "Bran and I are leaving." The words had scarcely left his mouth when the air around both mages took on a numinous quality.

Fionn locked gazes with Gwydion. "Are ye ready?"

"I am." Rune took up his traveling position next to Fionn's side.

"As am I." Bella settled on his shoulder in a flutter of wings.

Fionn stared at the bond animals. They'd returned to audible speech; that must mean they'd gotten their anger under control. *If they can do it, so can I.*

Gwydion nodded slowly. "I doona believe there is aught else to be done right now, so the answer to your question would be aye."

The air thickened as Gwydion drew magic to open a portal. Blessedly numb inside, Fionn added his own to the mix, buried a hand in Rune's neck ruff, and stepped through.

After they returned to Marta's house in the ruins of Ely, Nevada, Fionn spent the next hour rattling through it, looking for clues that might help them. He started in the bedroom, but Aislinn's scent, a mix of honey and musk, clung to everything and nearly undid him. When he caught himself pulling her pillow to his nose, he threw it against the wall and stormed out of the room they'd shared.

The rest of the house hadn't yielded anything. Fionn didn't bother going up to the attic. Marta's parents were there, trapped in a state of suspended animation by a strong spell. Best leave them to their rest, since they held the gates between the worlds open.

Because there wasn't anything else to do, he settled at the kitchen table with a bottle of mead and nearly emptied it. The anesthetic effect he hoped for hadn't happened, though. At least not yet.

"Would ye like to talk about it?" Gwydion's melodic voice interrupted Fionn's bleak thoughts.

He swiveled his head to look at the mage standing in the doorway, flanked by Rune and Bella. Dirt clung to his robes; Fionn wondered where he'd been. Gwydion had told him where he was going, but Fionn hadn't paid much attention.

Hmph. Even the animals deserted me.

I'd have deserted me, too, a different inner voice inserted dryly. *The way I banged around in here wanting to kill something—anything—if only it would bring Aislinn back to me.* Fionn understood at a level beyond reckoning that if he ever laid eyes on Travis again, the Hunter would be dead before he saw what hit him.

He tipped the bottle in Gwydion's direction. "Not sure what there is to say," Fionn mumbled.

"Och, and there is much to be said between us." Gwydion clomped to the table, hooked a chair out with one of his perpetually bare feet, and sat heavily. "For example, we havena ever truly talked about Tara—"

"With good reason," Fionn snapped.

Gwydion shook his head. "Ye doona trust me. I sense your hesitation. We must clear the air."

Fionn opened his mouth, but Gwydion shook his head. "Hear me out. That empty place inside you? The one ye're trying your damnedest to ignore—or drown with spirits? 'Tis akin to how I felt when Tara fled Ireland to escape having to choose you or me. She wanted me, but the ancient bond demanded she wed you."

"I know all that. I still doona see—"

"For the love of the goddess, would ye stop interrupting?" Gwydion's blue eyes flashed dangerously.

Fionn subsided against the back of his seat.

"'Twas no skin off your ass when the lass left Ireland, yet I mourned her loss every day. It's been years, but I miss her still. 'Twas a gift to see her once again in the tunnels under Slototh's lair —even if she was already dead."

Something in Gwydion's words penetrated the desolation surrounding Fionn. He'd known Gwydion cared for Tara, but he'd never appreciated the extent of his loss. Truth hit home, and shame washed over him. When Gwydion waved it in front of his nose—no, make that shoved his nose right in it—Fionn recognized kindred pain. He drew his brows together. "Why were ye not angrier at me? We had words, but it seemed we made things up soon enough."

"Nay, I simply buried my resentment. What would've been the point in holding a grudge? I tracked Tara to America. By then, she'd wed another and made it painfully clear she wanted nothing to do with you or me—or the dragon—ever again."

"At least part of that was my fault. I could've—"

A bitter laugh bubbled past the close-cropped red-blond beard on Gwydion's face. "Aye, ye see it now. Ye dinna see it then. All ye could see then was that she was the MacLochlainn. *Your* MacLochlainn."

Fionn looked at his hands. What Gwydion said was true. He hadn't loved Tara, and he'd known she didn't even like him, yet he'd insisted on pressing forward with marriage. Of course, there was the niggling problem that he already had a wife, so he'd been finagling a divorce. Tara, finally eighteen, took matters into her own hands and left Ireland.

"I really am sorry. I should've been more considerate—of both of you."

"Och, aye." A thread of magic forced his gaze to meet the master enchanter's. "I forgive you."

A corner of Fionn's mouth turned downward. "The question is whether I can forgive myself."

Gwydion held out a hand for the mead. Fionn passed it to him. Eyeing what was left of the bottle's contents, Gwydion said, "There never was a drink that offered enough oblivion to purge Tara from my thoughts."

"Wasna working for me, either." Fionn snorted. "I should know this. Ye told me, but I wasna paying attention. Where did you and the animals go?"

"We did the same outside as ye were supposed to be doing within. That would be hunting for clues Travis may have dropped while he was here."

Fionn waited. Instead of talking, Gwydion tipped the bottle and drank until it was empty. "Did ye find aught?" he asked after it appeared the other mage wasn't going to say anything else.

Gwydion's forehead creased. He shoved blond hair over his shoulders, pulled a leather thong out of his robes, and bound it out of the way. "It was odd," he murmured. "At first we all"—he gestured toward Rune and Bella—"thought we sensed Old Ones—ah, I meant to say Lemurians. When I looked more closely, though, whatever had been there was gone." He shrugged.

Something tugged at Fionn's internal alarm system. Attuned to danger, it rarely failed him. "Do ye suppose they were after Marta's parents?"

For a moment, Gwydion looked confused, but then his features smoothed. "Och, ye mean the Lemurian-human hybrids ensorcelled in yon chamber." He waved a hand over one shoulder. "Mayhap. There is little else here to draw the Old Ones."

Fionn thought about the genetic manipulation that must have gone into hybridizing the couple in the attic and shuddered. Did the Old Ones want Marta's parents' blood so they could do the same thing to Aislinn?

"At least Aislinn is likely still on this side of the veil," Gwydion muttered.

Fionn looked sharply at him, realizing the other mage must have read his thoughts. He dragged a hand down his face. "Aye, we all hope that."

Something sharp closed over his calf. Rune had bitten him. "It is time. We should go into Taltos. I must see for myself whether my bondmate still lives."

"Can ye feel her?" Fionn asked.

The wolf's amber eyes gleamed in the dim kitchen. "No, but if she is in Taltos, I will know once we open the gateway and I cross over."

"They might've her shielded in some way—" Fionn cautioned.

"Enough words." Rune nipped Fionn again. As if to support her fellow bond animal, Bella landed on Fionn's shoulder and dug her talons deep.

A wry smile split Gwydion's face. "It would appear the animals have spoken."

"We did tell the others we'd do a reconnaissance." Fionn stood.

Gwydion followed suit. Both men went to the corner of the kitchen with the hidden trap door. Fionn kicked the rug aside and tugged the door upward. When he looked back, he saw Gwydion's staff glowing with a blue-white light.

Fionn worked his way down the ladder, helping the wolf. It was awkward. When Aislinn had gone into Taltos without him, she'd used magic to transport the wolf to the gateway. The thought of her seared his soul. His throat felt thick. A pulse pounded behind one eye, promising a mother of a headache if he didn't focus magic to soothe the inflamed blood vessels.

At the bottom of the ladder, he strode to the section of wall holding the gateway and began the incantation from Marta's journals. Gwydion's energy vibrated next to him. Stones scraped against one another as the gateway swung open. Fionn bent to give Rune instructions, but the wolf bounded through the opening and disappeared into the dark.

"Damn it." Fionn swore softly. "Ye stay with me," he said to Bella.

"I am not going past this doorway," the bird informed him. She fluttered from his shoulder to a chair and perched on it. "Fewer of us, less chance of discovery. Safer for Aislinn."

Fionn couldn't help but agree with her. His bird had warmed to Aislinn, much to his relief, since she'd taken a perverse delight in making all the other women in his life—including Tara—miserable.

"Mind speech," Gwydion said sharply. *"And precious little of that."*

"I suppose we follow the wolf. He gave us little choice."

"After you."

Fionn stepped through into a dark tunnel. Careful to mute his magic in case the Lemurians had posted guards nearby, he turned left and trailed after Rune. Guts tight, barely breathing, he moved beneath Taltos, the city built by Lemurians deep inside Mount Shasta. Desperation thrummed through him.

I have to find her. Failure is not an option.

CHAPTER 2

*A*islinn sat on a dirt floor, grateful for the heavy material in Marta's green work pants and jacket. As she thought about things, she was grateful to Marta, period. The woman had been Rune's first bondmate and was a true visionary, seeing through the Lemurians' chicanery long before it became obvious.

She shook her head, feeling like a fool. The Old Ones had gotten aggressive after striking the bargain that allowed the dark gods entry to Earth. *I wonder if they knew the cracks between the worlds would draw bright magic, too. Sorcery tuned to a frequency humans could use.* She wrapped her arms around herself to quell a shudder. Most of modern civilization lay in ruins. In the midst of destroying things, the Old Ones had managed to convince a few select humans they were Earth's salvation.

"I can't believe I was so stupid," she muttered. "Christ! They killed millions of us while pretending to be my friend because I had Mage and Seeker abilities." Aislinn inhaled raggedly. She could almost hear Metae's voice dripping with compulsion as the Lemurian patiently explained why humans without magic had become superfluous—a drain on valuable resources.

And now I'm their prisoner. No more pretending good will on either side...

Aislinn shivered and zipped her black wool turtleneck up to her chin; she tugged her jacket closer about her. Pale light filtered through cutouts high on the walls. Assuming she was in Taltos, deep under Mount Shasta, the light had to be generated by magic. Not that there was anything to see. Her cell didn't contain so much as a bucket. The thrum of alien magic pounded against her—not sounds exactly, but a subliminal grating that set her nerves on edge.

She'd expected Regnol, Travis's Lemurian mage lord, to kill her on the spot, or right after dragging her to Taltos so the others could observe her death, but it hadn't happened. She hadn't even seen any other Old Ones before being whisked to this small stone cell. She'd tried to break and run, understanding Regnol's intent to imprison her, but the contest was laughable. She'd made it about six inches before her limbs froze in place. After that, he'd simply picked her up like a stiffened version of a rag doll and dropped her in this stark room. It had taken a while before she could move again.

Time passed. Her terror ebbed and flowed in waves. She removed her backpack, got a drink from her water bottle, and dug her black wool watch cap out. Aislinn had no idea how long she'd been in her cell. The light level never fluctuated. She tested all five of her magical skills: Mage, Seeker, Seer, Hunter, and Healer. While she could maintain her warding, sending magic outward was another story. No matter what she tried, her spells bounced back hard. It was as if the Lemurian magic holding her captive thrived on an infusion from her. After the last time, where she'd deployed Hunter magic in a desperate effort to link with Rune, she gave up. The backwash had been so violent, she'd nearly passed out from the pain.

Wonder if they'll just starve me. Or let me die from dehydration. My water bottle's nearly empty. Maybe I'll sink into madness from their infernal chanting. Now that she'd had a chance to absorb the sound beating against her, that was exactly what it sounded like: the clicks and clacks of the Lemurian tongue loaded onto an endless tape loop.

Something brushed against her mind. At first, she threw up wards, but there was something familiar about the feel of whoever wanted in. Aislinn clamped her lower lip in her teeth. She chinked the tiniest space in her mental armor and readied herself to slam it shut immediately.

"Mistress." The mind voice was barely a whisper.

Tears welled. One dripped down her cheek; she ignored it. Fear for her bond wolf dug deep. *"Don't try, Rune. They'll get you, too."*

A muffled howl rose. She could picture the timber wolf, his muzzle thrown back.

"Is Fionn with you?"

"Aye." Fionn's voice resonated in her head. Bottomless relief reverberated in that one word, and her heart took flight. *"No more talk, both of you."* Even though he tried to sound stern, he couldn't mask his joy that she was alive.

Rune merged with her and looked through her eyes. It was only for a moment, though, and then the wolf was gone. Hope flared, so intense it was almost painful. If her bond animal could figure out where she was—

Aislinn dropped a chiaroscuro curtain over her feelings, just in case. The Lemurians were intelligent, but their intelligence was different enough from human that she'd never had much trouble tricking them—at least for a short time—so long as she kept her thoughts cloaked. Human enemies would never have let her keep her backpack. The Old Ones hadn't even bothered to look through it, let alone take it away from her. Also, they weren't quick thinkers. Most decisions seemed to depend on some sort of hive mentality and required at least three of them clicking and clacking away at one another.

"Tears will not help you."

Aislinn jumped at the sound of an Old One's voice and shored up her wards. She scrambled to her feet and peered at the door.

Which one of them would come for her? It didn't matter. Not really. She'd never be able to talk a Lemurian into letting her go. *Is this when they sacrifice me to that god of theirs?* Thoughts of Rune and Fionn and rescue flitted through her mind; she muffled them. Lemurians were excellent mind readers—if they chose to focus their hive magic. No point in giving them ammunition.

"Get moving," the disembodied voice instructed.

Aislinn scanned her quarters, but didn't see a way out.

As if *that* thought registered loud and clear, the voice continued, "The door will open when you get close to it. Turn right and walk to the end of the corridor."

Aislinn sucked in a ragged breath. "What happens if I just sit here? Or if I turn left?"

The braying sound that passed for Lemurian laughter raked across her. "Try it and see, *child.*"

She winced. *Child* had been Metae's pet name for her, but her Lemurian mage lord was dead. *Yes, dead because I killed her.* She told her inner voice to shut up, goddammit. No point in making her captors any angrier than they already were.

"You needn't remind us of Metae," the metallic voice grated on. "She is missed. We have not forgotten."

I'll just bet you haven't.

Aislinn got to her feet and shouldered her pack. She walked through the heavy wooden door—which had, indeed, opened—and stopped. The magical thrum receded as soon as she stood outside her cell. She didn't realize how accustomed she'd grown to it until it wasn't there anymore. Its absence was a tremendous relief. She blew out air as she sifted through options, trying not to miss anything that might buy her freedom. *Wonder if my magic will work again?* She considered testing it, but decided not to. Better if the Lemurians thought her thoroughly cowed.

She gazed down a long stone passageway with inward curving walls. It stretched as far as she could see in both directions, broken by an occasional door. Unlike the dirt floor of her cell, the corridor was tiled with interlocking paving stones. The walls were gray brick. Light came from the same cutouts that had been in her cell. Deciding it would be stupid for her to ignore the Old One's directions, she dutifully turned right and started walking very slowly. Maybe if she dallied, it would give Rune and Fionn a chance to locate her.

"Come now. We did not injure you. Surely you can manage a quicker pace."

"How do you know you didn't hurt me?" Aislinn added a slight limp to her gait. "No one's bothered to check on me since you dumped me in that cell."

Silence.

Guess they're not going to answer.

"Another right, then through the open door just ahead." Rather than metallic, the voice was multi-tonal, which told her the Lemurians—or at least the one speaking to her—had to be close. They couldn't project that particular voice quality over distance.

Aislinn slowed even further. She had a feeling something horrible was going to happen once she entered wherever they were directing her. Her skin crawled. Throat tight, she faked a stumble and came down hard on her ankle. Annoyed with herself—after all, she hadn't meant to make it *that* realistic—she crashed to the floor.

"Oooph." She gritted her teeth. It wasn't hard to look as if she were in pain. Heat lanced up her leg. She wondered how badly she'd damaged herself and waited for someone to chastise her, but no one did.

Aislinn pushed herself upright and reached outward with magic to steady herself. She didn't think first; she just did it. Having lived with magic for years, using it was almost subconscious. Excitement blazed when she realized she could tap into the reservoir that held her power and project it without consequences. An open doorway loomed ahead. She was certain the room would extinguish her link to her power, just as her cell had.

It's now or never. Cursing herself for a fool for having injured her ankle, she bent and rubbed it to buy herself another moment. The spell she'd just cast needed time to build momentum. *Please, please don't let them notice. Let them be egotistical enough to assume I'd never go against them.*

One last quick breath. Aislinn threw her power wide open, diverting some to shield herself. She funneled the rest into a wild sprint away from the gaping maw of a door. Pain lanced up her leg, but she ignored it and urged her muscles to greater speed. She needed to free up at least a three-minute lead so she could jump herself out of there. Portals took time to form, so she was vulnerable at the start of traveling jumps.

Her lungs burned; the ragged sound of her own breathing echoed off the walls. Where were Rune and Fionn? Throwing caution to the winds, she called for Rune. Maybe he could find her. *If he can do that, he'll lead Fionn to me.*

A high-pitched shriek filled her ears and built to where it was unbearable. Her leg wasn't the only thing on fire. Her eardrums ruptured. Hot fluid ran down the sides of her face. A wave of dizziness threatened to flatten her, but she didn't slow. It had taken the Lemurians a few precious seconds to react to her disobedience. She prayed it would give her enough time to escape.

The air in the corridor shimmered fifty feet ahead. Desperate, she looked for a side tunnel, an open doorway, anything she could duck into. It would be just like the Old Ones to cut off her escape from all sides.

Noooooo, a voice in her head screamed. *I do not want to die here.*

The brightness intensified. *It may not matter what I want,* a different inner voice muttered dourly. She snuck a peek over one shoulder. The air looked funny there, too, but it was different somehow. Bleaker.

"Lass, drop your shielding." Fionn's voice sounded in her head. *"Ye must, or I canna jump us out of this hellhole. Hurry, or they'll have you from behind."*

She wondered if it was some kind of insidious trap. She tried to sense Fionn, but couldn't. He'd be warded as well, but still... She risked another glance behind her. The ocher-tinged air was, indeed, closer. It smelled like the reptile exhibit at the zoo her parents used to take her to when she was a child: musty and rank. A few more steps, and the brilliance ahead surrounded her. *"Now, lass. Now."*

Fionn's unique energy pulsed against her. Practically sobbing with relief, Aislinn pulled magic from her wards. The second she did so, he closed his arms around her. The gut-wrenching sensation of jumping when someone else controlled the spell pummeled her. Even if it made her puke, she'd never felt anything quite so welcome.

"Rune?"

"He's fine. Hush. I need to concentrate. This was a much narrower margin than I'm comfortable with. We're not out of the woods yet, leannán."

Her ears throbbed. Her leg ached. She didn't mind being quiet. Not when Fionn's arms were around her. She could stand just about anything so long as they were together. Travis's sneering face filled her mind, along with an impotent rage.

I'm going to kill that bastard if I ever see him again.

"Only if I doona get to him first," Fionn snapped.

She considered complaining because he was in her head again— without her permission—but choked on a snort. After today, Fionn MacCumhaill could spend as much time as he wanted in her mind. Hell, he could take up residence there for all she cared.

The familiar walls of Marta's kitchen rose around her. Snarling and snapping came from the study, followed by Gwydion's Celtic brogue. "There now. She is back. 'Tis a stubborn creature, ye are. Ye dinna believe me. Go."

Rune galloped into the kitchen, his claws skidding on the wooden floor, and launched himself at Fionn in his eagerness to get at Aislinn. "Put her down," the wolf demanded.

Bella flew into the room right behind the wolf, quorking, "Yes, put her down." The bird landed on Fionn's shoulder.

"Be careful," Fionn cautioned. "She's hurt. Doona be too exuberant. Bella, watch your talons."

"I know how Aislinn feels," Rune said indignantly. "After all, she is bonded to me."

"Och aye, I hadna forgotten." Fionn rolled his eyes and chuckled indulgently, while ruffling Bella's dark feathers.

Aislinn lowered herself to the floor and closed her arms around Rune. She gloried in the feel of his rough outer coat and the soft fuzz beneath. Fionn and the hard, muscled planes of his body would keep. In spite of everything that had happened, desire forked through her at the thought of his lips on hers, his hands stroking her naked flesh, and his hardness buried deep inside her.

"Soon, lass." Fionn winked at her. He added a vision of her mouth locked around his shaft and quirked a brow.

She laughed and raised her gaze to meet his intensely blue eyes. "No secrets, huh?"

"Never, lass. It may not be a Hunter bond like ye share with the wolf, but our pledge, one to t'other, runs just as deep."

Bella took flight, landed on Aislinn's shoulder, and rained love pecks on her head. "Don't be listening to my bondmate. He always had a honeyed tongue."

"Really?" Fionn stepped close enough to mock-swat the raven.

"No secrets," the raven cawed scornfully.

"Point taken. Come here." Fionn held out an arm, and Bella fluttered to him. The two bent their heads together. Aislinn figured they were probably talking in their private mind speech.

The wolf howled and then whined and licked every inch of skin he could find. "Hurt? Where are you hurt, bondmate?"

"Ankle and ears. It's nothing. Aw, Rune. I never thought I'd see you again." Gratitude swelled inside her. Her throat thickened until it was hard to breathe; tears rolled down her face. The wolf licked them up.

Still cradling Rune, who was bound to her through the Hunter Covenant, Aislinn glanced around the kitchen. Fionn and Gwydion sat across from her on the wooden floor, passing a mead bottle back and forth. Bella perched on Fionn's shoulder. "Why aren't you at the table?" She jerked her chin toward the round oak table, with its comfortable chairs, in a corner of the kitchen.

Fionn shrugged. "I doona know. We just ended up here—right along with you."

Aislinn held out a hand for the mead. "Hey." She winced against the ringing sound in her ears. "I need that more than you do."

"The lass speaks true." Gwydion smiled and then handed the bottle over.

"Aye, and if she's asking for spirits, I figure she'll survive." Fionn grinned. "Of course, I've an idea or two that might speed the healing."

Gwydion poked him with his staff. Fionn laughed. Aislinn took a large swig of mead and looked hard at the two of them. Something had changed. An ease lay between them that hadn't been there before. She wondered if they'd finally found a way to let her mother's ghost rest.

Hope so. Maybe if they can let her go, I can, too.

"Lass?"

Aislinn looked at Gwydion, alerted by something in his tone. "Sorry, did I miss something?"

"Aye, I asked you what happened. Ye had this vacant look. What were ye thinking about?"

She shook her head and twisted her features into a grimace. "I wasn't thinking about anything in particular except how grateful I am to be back here. As for what happened, it's simple enough. Travis sold us out. That fucking prick had the nerve to tell me, 'You belong with humans.' Right after that, Regnol told him he'd done well, and then Travis and his bond civet left. So it was all a setup."

"We intuited as much," Fionn muttered, using American English for a change. Aislinn found it fascinating that he could drop in and out of Celtic brogue at will. "But we weren't certain."

"He's mine if we ever find him," Aislinn growled.

Rune snarled. "No, he is mine. I want to tear his throat out."

"Looks like we have ample candidates to annihilate Travis." Fionn scanned the homey kitchen, with its warm oak cupboards and stone countertops before settling his gaze on Aislinn and Gwydion. "My, what a bloodthirsty lot we are."

"'Tis kill or be killed." Gwydion looked grim. "Ye know that better than any. 'Tisn't only the Lemurians that need killing. Doona forget the dark gods. Travis was nothing but a pawn. The lad is scarcely worth wasting a jot of energy."

Aislinn rubbed the sides of her face. The conversation sounded as if it were coming from the bottom of a well.

"Would ye like for me to Heal you?" Without waiting for an answer, Gwydion scooted next to her, displacing Rune. The wolf snapped at him. "Still angry with me, laddie?" Gwydion stroked Rune's head. "I had no choice. Fionn couldna take you with him. He barely made it back here with Aislinn as 'twas."

"But it was me who found her," Rune protested. Bella flapped around the kitchen, cawing her support.

Fionn beckoned the wolf over and laid a hand on either side of his head. "Aye, and I couldna have found her without you. Were it not for you, Aislinn might be dead now. I dinna know what I might face in Taltos. I had to split my power to both shield us and bring us back. I wasna certain I'd have enough for three of us. As 'twas, we barely escaped. Another second or two, and I doona think we would've made it."

Aislinn's head snapped up. *Ach, Christ. It was that close.* A shiver ran down her spine. It wasn't easy to chase the might-have-beens away.

"I could have found my own way back." Rune jerked his head out of Fionn's hands.

"Mayhap," Fionn spoke evenly. "Mayhap not. Imagine how Aislinn would have felt to be safely returned with ye missing."

"Aye"—Gwydion, who'd been chanting softly over Aislinn, half-turned to look at the wolf—"and we would have had the explaining of why we dinna keep a closer eye on you."

Rune snapped his jaws shut. Bella fluttered to his shoulder, and the two of them stalked out of the room.

"Rune," Aislinn called after him. "When I tried to use my Hunter magic, it bounced back at me. I couldn't find you, and it made me so sad, I almost couldn't stand it."

The wolf didn't answer.

Aislinn met Gwydion's gaze. His eyes were nearly midnight from the Healing magic running through him. "He'll get over it," she murmured. "He was just scared."

Fionn made a sound midway between a snort and a grunt. "*He* was scared? If ye wouldna have dropped your wards—"

Aislinn rolled her eyes. "I wasn't sure it was you."

"And who else would it have been?"

"Stop." Gwydion held up a hand. "Fionn, go draw a bath, or turn down your bed or something. Let me finish here. I need her still, not trading barbs with you."

"Hmph." The sound of Fionn's footsteps receded as he moved down the long hallway that led from the kitchen to the back of the house.

Aislinn closed her eyes. Whatever Gwydion was doing felt wonderfully soothing. Her ears didn't hurt anymore, and her ankle was about halfway back. "God bless magic," she mumbled.

"Aye, lass. Except I am using goddess magic. Best ask her blessings, too, but quietly. 'Twill go more quickly if I can concentrate."

She tried to follow the spells Gwydion wove around her, but gave it up for a lost cause. They were far more sophisticated than any of her workings. It was easy to lose herself in the peaceful cocoon that supported her while it mended her injured places.

Her warm, dreamy drowsiness lessened as Aislinn felt the spell recede. She eyed him speculatively. "Did you and Fionn, ah, bury the hatchet around Mother?"

The mage's gaze latched onto hers. "And why would ye be asking that?"

She shrugged. "The air between you seems cleaner. That's all."

"Aye and we did." Fionn's voice sounded from the hall. "Are ye about done with my woman?" He strode into the kitchen. No longer in battle leathers, he'd changed into a faded pair of jeans and his tattered *Go Bears* sweatshirt. Blond hair hung to his shoulders. His blue-tinged mage light hovered off to one side, illuminating the strong bones in his ageless face. Concern radiated from his sky blue eyes.

Aislinn cocked her head to one side. "Are we done?" she asked Gwydion.

His full lips curved into a salacious grin. "Aye, off with you." He flowed to his feet in a supple motion and dropped a hand on Fionn's shoulder. "As a favor to you, I will take first watch. Ye'd not be worth a damn since all ye can think about is sinking yourself into yon lass."

Fionn nodded his appreciation, his eyes twinkling warmly, and helped Aislinn to her feet. Once she was standing, he wove an arm around her waist.

She weighted her foot and smiled. "Thanks," she said to Gwydion. "Feels much better." Something he'd said registered. "First watch?" She looked from one of them to the other. "I don't get it. We're safe. Why don't we all get some sleep?"

Gwydion's eyes looked sad. "'Tis war, lass. None of us are safe. Nor can we afford the luxury of believing we might be. Mayhap the others will be here tomorrow. Hopefully with Dewi."

A growl, punctuated by a snarl, sounded from the hall. Aislinn sighed. Rune didn't like the dragon. He saw her as competition for Aislinn's affections. "Do you mean Arawn and Bran?" She realized she hadn't asked about the other two Celtic gods. Hadn't even realized they were missing. She chided herself for being sloppy and unobservant. Sloppy got you killed.

"Aye." Gwydion inclined his head. "Plus any reinforcements Arawn could scare up in the Old Country."

Reinforcements? Aislinn's blood chilled a notch or two. Fionn was close to a thousand years old, Gwydion probably much older. If they were that worried, they must have good reason. "Since we're taking turns," she said, "I want to be in the rotation. Rune can watch with me."

The wolf bounded to her side and licked her hand.

Bella landed on Fionn's shoulder. "Yes, yes." He turned his head to look at his raven. "Ye can watch with me as well."

"That willna be necessary tonight, lass," Gwydion said. "Tomorrow, after ye've had a good rest, then ye'll be part of the lineup."

CHAPTER 3

ionn tightened his arm around her waist. Aislinn leaned into him as they navigated the hall. Her musky, wildflower scent surrounded him, making his groin tingle in anticipation. He nuzzled her neck. The weight of her against him felt so good, he flirted with dragging her to the floor and taking her right there. She had a dreamy, otherworldly quality, though, rather than sensual. Probably a byproduct of Gwydion's healing.

Rune was right behind them; he bumped his snout into Fionn's legs. Bella's talons flexed against his shoulder. She had moods, his bird. He'd gotten fairly adept at reading them through the tension in her claws. The raven was worried about something. He'd tried to ask her about it earlier, but she hadn't been inclined to confide in him. Though Fionn didn't want to dwell on it, he had his own set of qualms. He and Aislinn had escaped the Lemurians by the skin of their teeth. He wished there'd been an opportunity to chew things over with Gwydion because he was nearly certain it hadn't only been Lemurians chivvying them in Taltos.

Fionn moved aside to allow Aislinn through the bedroom door. Once the wolf was in, he kicked it shut. Bella fluttered to a nearby chair. Silent for once, she tucked her head under a wing.

Aislinn turned to face him, her heart in her eyes. "You took an incredible chance in Taltos—"

"They canna kill me."

"No, but they could imprison you. Or torture you. Or force you into that place in the *Dreaming,* where you go so deep, you trap yourself." She pounded a closed fist into her other hand; her troubled eyes never left his face. "I thought I'd lost you in the labyrinth beneath Slototh's lair. I never want to go through that again."

Fionn cocked his head to one side, unsure of what to say. He was unwilling to placate her with a soothing web of lies. He'd figured they'd simply fall into one another's arms the second he got her alone, but apparently she needed to talk. "Aye. I took a chance. I would do the same again, *mo croi.*"

A tear rolled down her dirty cheek. "I couldn't bear it if anything happened to you or Rune." Aislinn averted her gaze and swallowed hard. "Especially if you sacrificed yourself for me. How could I live with myself, knowing you'd bartered your freedom for mine?" Her golden eyes blazed; fury mingled with hopelessness was mirrored in their depths.

He held out his arms, but she shook her head. "Not yet. I need to know how close it was in Taltos."

"Why? What earthly difference will that make, lass?"

Aislinn folded her arms over her chest. Tears flowed freely, but she didn't wipe them away. She snuffled. "I... I don't know. It's just... Shit, I don't know what's wrong with me. I'm a maudlin mess."

Fionn kicked off a pair of slippers that had probably belonged to Marta's husband and sat on the edge of the bed. He patted the coverlet next to him. "Sit, *leannán.* I will tell you...things." The bedsprings shifted as she settled next to him. He turned toward her, reached out, and tilted her chin so she had to look at him. "Once I am done, ye have two choices."

"And they are?"

Thank Christ, she's smiling. "Ye will take off your clothes and bathe afore we make love—"

"Or?"

A corner of his mouth turned downward. "Ye can skip the bath."

"I pick door number two." Warm laughter washed over him. She scrubbed her jacket sleeve across her wet face and then bent to untie the laces of her boots so she could tug them off. Her socks followed, landing on the floor next to her worn boots. She looked at him and furled her brows. "Start talking. I'd like to get to the bedding part before Gwydion comes to collect you."

"Good to hear. For a moment there, I was beginning to wonder." He cupped a breast through her jacket and sweater and leaned in for a kiss.

"Uh-uh." She shook her head and pushed his hand away. "Come on, Fionn. There's something you're not telling me. I deserve to know. Lovers share everything. Not just their bodies."

"Guess I doona know much about that part…because I've never been in love before." Listening to his words fill the silence of the room, Fionn wanted to say them again and again. He wanted to shout his love to the skies and to the netherworld. Though it seemed a weak substitute, he settled for, "Ach, *leannán*. I love you with every fiber of my being," and then grinned like a besotted fool —but a happy one.

"I've never been in love before, either, but that's neither here nor there." She smiled fondly at him and gestured with two fingers for him to spill what had truly happened in Taltos.

He pushed his tongue against his teeth, wondered where to begin, and mentally threw his hands up. *Best to plunge right to the heart of things.* "We were agreed to wait until everyone was here to attempt to free you—"

"Who's we?"

"Och aye, and ye're going to interrupt every thirty seconds?"

"No, only when I need to know something."

"We is Gwydion, Bran, Arawn, and me. Bran went after Dewi. Arawn went in search of more Celtic gods. The plan was to meet here, draft a plan, and then go after you. Gwydion and I had only thought to do a small reconnaissance—to assess the lay of things, ye understand—when your wolf bolted."

"Ingrate," Rune growled from the corner where he'd settled. "The minute I was fully into Taltos, I sensed my bondmate. I had to find her. Good thing, too—"

"So you and Gwydion followed Rune?" Aislinn drew her brows together into a worried line.

"Aye, that we did. Not that we had much choice in the matter." Fionn glared at Rune.

The wolf snarled, his hackles at half-mast. "Be sure to tell her what happened next," he muttered through a growl.

"I was planning to." Fionn inclined his head. It was a struggle not to oust the wolf from the room. *It's no wonder he and Bella get along so well. They're cut from the same cloth.*

He turned back to Aislinn. "The wolf located you almost at once. I understood ye were being marched to some sort of interrogation chamber. For once, Gwydion and I agreed we couldna afford to wait for the others. So he took the wolf—"

"Against my will," Rune noted stiffly. "That will *not* happen again."

"—and I went after you." Ignoring the wolf, Fionn sucked in a breath. The ground they'd just covered was the easy part. He turned over the next bit in his mind.

"You're trying to sugarcoat something," Aislinn snapped, sounding nearly as surly as her wolf. "Just spit it out for chrissakes."

He nodded. "All right, then. Keep in mind, I doona know any of this for a fact. 'Tis all conjecture. I suspect the reason ye were able to run from them is because the Old Ones had discovered my presence and turned their attention away from you. I sensed something dark behind their group intelligence orchestrating things. Mayhap Perrikus. Mayhap D'Chel—"

She gasped, and then her mouth formed a hard line. "I knew it. I couldn't figure out why they sat back and let me pull magic so I could run from them. They had the power to flatten me. To kill me where I stood. I've seen them do it..." Her voice ran down. The hand she laid on his arm shook ever so slightly.

"Aye. If the dark god—whoever it was—instructed them to target me, that would explain things. And lass, it was close. I felt their magic closing about me. We had seconds to spare. If ye had hesitated the second time I told you to drop your warding..."

A shudder ran through her. Fionn pulled her against him and buried his lips in her hair. Love welled within him, along with a savage protectiveness. "*Mo croi*. If ye're gearing up to tell me I should have run when things got dangerous, save your breath. I was *not* leaving without you."

"You should have." Her voice sounded muffled against his chest.

"Hmph. Not a chance."

"Because I'm the MacLochlainn?"

He pushed away from her and laid a hand on either side of her face. "Nay, *mo croi*. Because ye're you. I love you. I doona think being a MacLochlainn has aught to do with it. After all, I dinna love your mother. I couldna, no matter how hard I tried." He twisted his mouth into a crooked smile. "There were no other MacLochlainn women for me to practice on."

The corners of her mouth twitched. "Borrowing from your earlier conversation with Bella, point taken."

She slid off the bed and started shucking clothes. When she was down to silky wisps of panties and bra, he said, "Not that I'm complaining, mind you, but I thought ye wanted to talk."

She waved her hand nonchalantly. "You've told me everything important."

Surprise wafted through him. "How can ye know?"

"Two can play that mind-reading game." She shot him a smile worthy of one of the Sirens. "What? Isn't the sight of my near nudity driving you crazy? I know I probably don't smell all that good, but there was a time—"

His feet hit the floor. He pulled her against him, bent his head, and settled his mouth over hers, desperate for the taste of her, for the feel of her against his body. She sucked greedily on his tongue when it parted her lips. He inhaled the scent of her like a drug, drawing it deep. She tasted of honey and wildflowers, spicy, exotic, and alluring. Aislinn wove her arms around him; her fingers clutched his shoulders. The peaks of her nipples pressed into his chest. He pictured them, strawberry circles tipping her full breasts. His cock hardened and throbbed where it rubbed against the junction between her belly and thigh.

He dragged his mouth from hers. "I assume this means no bath?"

She laughed, a husky, passionate sound. "Told you that earlier. Door number two."

"I dinna know what ye meant."

"That, my love, is because you probably never watched television."

"Och, but I—"

She rolled her eyes. "Never mind." She plucked at the waistband of his jeans, undoing them with nimble fingers.

His throat was dry. His heart thudded so hard it echoed in his ears. *Och aye, I'm like a lad about to lose his virginity.* Fionn stopped thinking. Nothing beyond their bodies twined together mattered. He helped her push his pants down, and then he stepped out of them. She closed her hands around his cock. He groaned from the pleasure of her touch. Electric, it sent jolts of pleasure to every nerve ending.

He unclasped her bra and had just bent to take one of her nipples into his mouth when she slithered down his body, running little, lapping kisses across his chest. When she trailed her lips down his stomach, all his muscles tightened in anticipation. He didn't have to wait long before the heat of her mouth closed about his shaft, and she began a slow, sensual licking around the head of his cock while sliding her hands up and down him. The sensations were so incredible, it was all he could do not to come. He got harder and harder until controlling himself was almost painful.

Without warning, she moved her hands behind him, grabbed his ass, and pulled him farther into her mouth. Fionn pumped his hips and thrust deeper. He buried his fingers in her hair and heard himself cry out. An orgasm spooled deep inside his belly, past the point of no return. She pushed a finger between his legs and rubbed the base of his balls. They tightened against his body, and control fled like so much fairy dust. His climax developed a mind of its own and raced outward in burning jets as he drove into her again and again.

The sound of his ragged breathing was loud in his ears. Cock still buried deep in Aislinn's mouth, he gazed at her hair cascading down her shoulders like a curtain of living flame and was overcome by how much he loved her. Tenderness nearly overwhelmed him. Hot tears pricked behind his lids, and he tightened the fingers twined in her hair.

Apparently feeling his gaze on her, she moved back, releasing him. The sensitive skin of his cock felt cold where her mouth had been. "So." Her eyes twinkled as she looked at him. "Was that what you had in mind earlier?"

"Nay." Seeing her worried expression, he hurried on. "'Twas a million times better than my imagination."

Fionn smoothed her hair back from her face and reached for her. He lifted her easily and placed her on the bed, then bent his head to kiss her, tasting himself on her tongue. The salty tang of his semen made him hot all over again. She arched toward him. He flicked his tongue into her mouth, withdrew it, and teased her lips with nibbling kisses.

She pulled away. "Come here." She wrapped a hand around his cock and tugged. "Or are you going to stand over my bed worshipping me from afar, like a vestal virgin?"

"What would you like, *mo croi*?" He loved looking at her. With her long legs, flared hips, and full breasts, she was as close to perfect as a woman could be. He took a strand of her wonderful silky hair and let it play through his fingers.

She captured his hand and guided it between her legs. Her

panties were soaked. Liquid slicked her thighs. He pulled the lacy fabric down and settled next to her. Fionn lay on his side, propped on one elbow. He took a nipple in his mouth and sucked, while cupping her pussy under his hand. The heat of her seared him. Her hips bucked. He knew what she wanted, because he wanted her the same way. Their lovemaking always ended up the same, bodies crashing against one another, frantic with need.

She mewled low in her throat and spread her legs wide. Aislinn pushed insistently, positioning him to enter her. Fionn knelt between her legs and drank in her beauty. Sometimes, like now, he wanted her so much, it humbled him. As hard as if he hadn't just come, his cock jutted in front of him.

She snared him with her golden gaze. "Now," she cried. "I need you now."

He touched the head of his shaft to the wet, magical spot between her legs. She wriggled against him, and he sank slowly into her while she wrapped her legs around his waist and dug her hands into his shoulders. Her back arched as her hips ground against him, and she sank her teeth into his neck.

Fionn threw back his head and laughed. "Bella pecks me. Ye bite me. Must be something ye picked up from the wolf."

"I resent that," Rune growled from his corner.

She twisted her head toward Rune. "I'm sure Fionn didn't mean anything by it."

The wolf muttered something, but Fionn couldn't make it out.

Aislinn locked gazes with him again. Her muscles pulsed around his cock, and her hips writhed in an age-old dance of passion. "Move, damn it."

He knew her well enough to understand how close she was. He drew back so only the tip of him circled her entrance and held himself there. Her panting breath rasped between them. She pulled down hard on his hips, but he just smiled at her. "How much do ye want me, *leannán?*"

"Not the time for this. You came. I want to. Have to." She moved a hand from his body, placed it between her legs, and rubbed her clit. Her head fell back against the pillows. Her lips parted, her cheeks flushed. He felt her climax build in the tension of her muscles.

Fionn grabbed her hand, shoved it away, and slammed into her hard. He did it again and her body liquefied around him as orgasm pounded through her. She cried his name and told him she loved him while her pussy contracted around him. Because he didn't expect it, his second climax took him by surprise. Carried on the wave of her arousal, he pumped into her, draining himself.

Fionn collapsed on top of her and covered her face with kisses in between crooning to her in Gaelic.

"Watch it," she murmured, her voice still thick with passion. "I understand most of that."

He rolled off her onto his back. "Good. Then ye know I think ye are the most wonderful, the most beautiful, the most amazing—"

"You can stop now." She reached for his hand and squeezed it. "I get the picture."

"Most women like to hear their virtues extolled."

"Fionn." She repositioned herself so she was on her side, facing him. "This is not the sixteen hundreds. I'm not a pampered female whose self-image rises and falls on the basis of some man's opinion of me."

"What would ye like to hear from me?" Truly curious, he turned so he could watch her face.

"Only that you'll treat me as an equal partner in all things. That we'll stand together. Make our decisions as a team." She held up a hand. "Think carefully. I'm not certain your fellow Celtic gods would approve of including me in what they probably see as men's business."

Fionn opened his mouth and then closed it. She was right. While the occasional goddess was included in critical things like strategizing a war against the Lemurians, he was fairly certain it would be an uphill battle to get Aislinn a permanent seat at the table. Then he remembered Dewi. The dragon regarded herself as bonded to the MacLochlainn as surely as the wolf did. It was why Rune hated her. He saw her as competition for Aislinn's affections.

Dewi was sacred to the Celts.

"It may not be as difficult as ye think," he began, picking his words carefully. She furled her brows, and he said, "Now stop that. I'll always support you, Aislinn. I doona see you as less than me because ye are a woman. I canna control how the others react to you, but Dewi will be your ally."

The wolf growled.

Fionn got off the bed and walked over to him. He hunkered on his haunches so they were at eye level with one another. "Ye stop it, too. I know ye doona trust Dewi and that ye see her as a threat to your bond with Aislinn."

The snarling rose in volume.

Fionn laid a hand on Rune's muzzle. "Ye willna like to hear this, but Dewi's claim to Aislinn predates yours by a thousand years or better. That dragon has always been linked to a MacLochlainn woman—if one was alive for her to bond with. There were a good many years without any MacLochlainn females. If Aislinn and I have a daughter—which isn't likely, since males run in the MacCumhaill line—Dewi will be bound to protect her, too."

"If that's true," Rune said huffily, "why didn't Aislinn know about her?"

"Because Mother hated the dragon," Aislinn replied. "She fled to America and spent the rest of her life hiding from Dewi. The dragon finally gave up on Mother and spent centuries waiting for me in the tunnels beneath Taltos. I'm still not certain how she knew I'd show up there."

"Oh." There was a protracted silence before the wolf added. "Would you rather be bonded to her?"

Aislinn sprang off the bed in a flash. She knelt next to Fionn and Rune. "No. Don't ever think that." She sank a hand into his neck ruff. "I know I made a fuss about not having Hunter magic when you and I first met, but I've accepted the bond. You and I are bond-mates. Until death."

The wolf whined and licked her knees. "That is how it should be. Thank you. I will try to tolerate the dragon."

Fionn thought it enough of a concession. And a good place to stop. "Thank you," he told the wolf. Turning to Aislinn, he said, "How about that bath?"

She yawned. "Not sure. I'm pretty tired…"

"I already drew the water. All I need to do is heat it."

"In that case—" she smiled "—I'm all over it. I can smell myself. And I can still smell that rotten reptile stench the Lemurians exude."

Fionn rose to his feet. He walked into the adjoining bathroom and dipped a hand into the water while chanting. Marta's house still had running water from a gravity feed spring out back, but electricity was a thing of the past. Steam was just starting to rise when Aislinn joined him.

"Is it ready?"

"Uh-huh." He pulled his hand out of the water, and she lowered herself into it, sighing with pleasure. "Thanks for picking up on my cue back there."

She cocked her head to one side. "What cue?"

"'Tis always best to stop when things are going well—"

"Oh, you mean with Rune."

He'd just nodded when the bedroom door flew open. Fionn whirled and raised his hands to call magic. Gwydion burst into the bathroom, brandishing his staff. It glowed a deep, angry red, which could only mean one thing: extreme danger. "Ye must come now, man. We're under attack."

"*Cad a tharla?*" Shocked the Lemurians had converged on them so soon, Fionn lapsed into Gaelic to ask what happened.

"Something reanimated the hybrids."

Not Lemurians after all. At least not directly. Fionn thought of the ensorcelled pair in the attic room above. They held the gates between the worlds open. What would happen if he and Gwydion destroyed them? Would the dark gods be trapped on Earth forever?

The warrior magician spun and took off at a dead run.

Fionn dragged a robe off the bathroom door, threw it around himself, and raced after Gwydion. He called back to Aislinn. "Ward yourself."

CHAPTER 4

$\mathcal{A}$islinn's mouth dropped open. Weary from thirty hours without sleep and still tingling from sex, she stared after Fionn, fixated on the empty spot where his body had been moments before. Her mind felt slow and stupid. She dragged her hands down her face, then slid forward and dunked her head all the way under the water. When she came up sputtering, Rune stood in the bathroom door.

"We need to fight," he informed her, ears pricked forward. "Why are you wasting time in that bathtub?"

Aislinn rolled her eyes and blew out a breath. She gripped the sides of the claw foot tub and pushed to her feet. Water sluiced down her body. She grabbed a towel and draped it around her head. Once she was standing on the tile floor, she wrapped herself in the other terrycloth robe, figuring it would soak up the rest of the water. She'd hoped immersing her head would help clear it, but so far, it wasn't working.

"Hurry," Rune urged.

She eyed him. "Hurry where? Fionn told me to ward myself."

"Well"—the wolf nailed her with his amber gaze—"so far, you haven't done that, either."

Aislinn pushed past Rune and walked into the bedroom. She reached for her magic. It was sluggish and slow to respond. She needed rest and food to recharge. Her Seer skill was strongest of the five magics. It was also the one she was least familiar with. Before she'd met Rune and Fionn, she'd seen herself as a Mage with weak Seeker skills. In the few months since meeting up with the wolf and the Celtic god, she'd discovered she had access to all five abilities. Healing came easily as had her Hunter bond with the wolf. The Seer talent—which allowed her to both see into the future and manipulate it—was much harder to control. It also let her go backward in time and make certain changes.

Wouldn't it be convenient if I could simply erase the last hour? Maybe, if we'd had more warning...

After several frustrating minutes, Aislinn gave up on deploying Seer magic. She was just too tired. Instead, she summoned her Mage gift to ward herself and the bedroom. Inspecting her work, she shook her head, feeling disgusted. It was one of the worst wards she'd ever built. Amateur and full of holes, it was so weak a six-month-old kitten could have punched through it.

"Sorry, Rune." She reached a hand to the wolf. "I'm pretty tapped out. Let me try that one again."

The next ward was better. Not good enough for her to risk falling asleep, but... A crash sounded from above her. Then another, louder one. Something shattered. Rune's hackles rose along his spine. He drew his lips back into a snarl.

What the fuck is happening up there? A couple weeks ago, she'd attempted to unravel the spell binding the two creatures in their caskets. Later, she'd realized it was fortunate she'd failed. Gwydion had figured out the couple were brother and sister, as well as Marta's parents. Product of some macabre science experiment, they were human-Lemurian hybrids. Where they'd embraced Lemurian culture and were allied with the Old Ones, Marta had taken the opposite track. She'd ensorcelled her parents to take them offline. Her journals suggested she hadn't killed them outright because they were guardians of the gates between the worlds. Gates that had gotten kicked open the night Aislinn's father was murdered high in the Bolivian Andes. If they closed, there might not be a way for the dark gods to return to their realms.

Aislinn shivered. The dark gods were so beautiful—and so sensual—they were nearly impossible to resist. She'd injured one of them, maybe even killed him, though Fionn and the other Celts thought otherwise. Unfortunately, her success meant they'd lost the element of surprise. The five other dark gods would be far more difficult to catch off guard.

Hell, if what Fionn sensed under Taltos is accurate, they're not even bothering to wait for us to attack. They're coming after us.

Another crash. More breaking glass. A shout from Gwydion. Fear blasted through Aislinn, souring her stomach. She tasted bile in the back of her throat, but the adrenaline rush was welcome. It perked her up enough that she stopped feeling like an extra from *Night of the Living Dead.* She dropped the towel and robe to the floor and bent to rummage in Marta's dressers for something to wear. She couldn't bear the thought of putting her Taltos clothes back on. They still stank of reptile. Under the Old Ones' layers of illusion to make them look human, they were nothing but large reptilian-esque creatures. They could marshal magic to alter their appearance, but not their smell.

Aislinn slipped into black sweatpants and a black sweatshirt. A thick pair of red woolen socks provided a buffer between her feet and all the holes in her boots. She made a knot out of her long, wet hair to keep it out of her face and let the ends trail down her back.

The racket upstairs hadn't abated.

Aislinn stared at the door and muttered, "Should I?" Fionn obviously expected her to wait for him.

"What about all that talk between you two?" Rune asked.

"Huh?" She wrenched her concentration away from what sounded like heavyweights duking it out at Madison Square Garden.

The wolf padded over and shoved his head under her hand. "Remember? When you told him you wanted to be equal and all that."

"You eavesdropped."

The wolf made a snorting sound that could have been laughter. "You were right next to me. I have excellent hearing, so I did not need to *eavesdrop*. Besides, there are no secrets between bondmates."

He's right. I took a stand with Fionn about being included in everything, and here I am, hiding behind a door.

"Glad you see it that way." If the wolf could have smirked, he would have.

"Awk. Get out of my head."

A spate of desperate-sounding Gaelic rang out. She understood the language from her Irish mother. Fionn and Gwydion were losing ground. She turned to Rune. "Okay. We're going up there. You will do exactly as I tell you. No heroics. And no taking off like you did in Taltos. Understand?"

He just looked at her, nostrils flared and tail high. "I will not make empty promises. I will do what I think needs doing. I am no one's lackey. Not even yours, *bondmate*."

Aislinn winced at the sarcasm. "Have it your way. Just try not to get sucked through a vortex into some other world."

She laid a hand on the door and sent magic spinning outward until she felt Gwydion and Fionn. Woven into a complex pattern, their magic was clean. The other power made her suck in a breath. It was so murky and dark, she couldn't recognize it, but it didn't feel like the dark gods or the Old Ones. For a moment, her resolve faltered. *What am I walking into? And what if Rune gets hurt...?*

"Stop thinking."

"Christ. You sound like Yoda." Aislinn glared at her wolf.

"I'll take that as a compliment. I loved *Star Wars*. Marta had me watch it with her on DVD."

"Gawk! Just stay out of my fucking head. I have enough to worry about without you picking up some stray thought and overreacting."

She pulled her magic close. No point in protecting a room she was about to leave. The ward was easier to reassemble with just her and the wolf at its center. She drew in a deep breath, then another, and blew out any uncertainties standing in her way. The centering exercise had always worked for her. It muted any lingering reservations and helped her focus on staying strong.

No time like the present. Aislinn turned the knob as silently as she could and let herself into the carpeted hallway. The noise level doubled as soon as she opened the door. It sounded like she was underneath a bowling alley. Because she needed her hands to work magic, she wound a few tendrils of her warding in front of her ears to protect them. The staircase leading to the attic was directly across from the bedroom door. Light flashed from the stairwell. Rune's warmth hugged her side. Even though he was being subtle about it, she felt him in her mind.

For a moment, she wished Arawn, Bran, and the dragon were there, and then she cleared her thoughts. *Got to work with what I have. No point wasting energy wishing for the impossible.* She waited for Rune to make a snarky comment about Dewi, but it didn't come. Perhaps even the wolf understood that the dragon's ancient power —never mind her extensive knowledge—would be useful right now.

She crossed the hall and started up the stairs. Her mouth was dry. Sweat dripped down her sides, despite chilly air that was doing nothing but getting colder as she mounted the circular staircase. She slowed as she neared the top so she wouldn't turn into an easy target and make things more difficult for Fionn and Gwydion.

One more step, and I should be able to see something...

Rearing up on tiptoe, she peeked over the top riser. Gwydion was locked in combat with the thing that had been Marta's mother. The hybrid's long gray hair was wrapped around the mage's throat. The woman had her teeth buried in his arm; she swiped at his eyes with her broken, yellowed nails. As Aislinn watched, horror turning her guts to water, the thing circled more hair around the master enchanter's neck. The greasy strands seemed to have a life of their own.

Her gaze shifted to Fionn. Buck naked, his golden skin gleamed in light that emanated from the empty coffins. He and Marta's father moved around one another warily. Magic flashed between them. From time to time, Fionn's worried blue gaze swept toward Gwydion. Aislinn could tell he was trying to maneuver himself close enough to help, but the hybrid blocked him every time.

A gagging, wheezy sound came from the master enchanter. Aislinn pulled magic, intent on sending a killing blow at Marta's mother. Something dark streaked past her. It took a moment to register that it was Rune. He launched himself at the hybrid, canines sinking into her neck.

An ungodly, high-pitched shriek filled the low-eaved room. Yellow ocher flowed from the hybrid. Gwydion, obviously recognizing opportunity, didn't hesitate. With his hands freed from holding the hybrid, he pulled a knife from his dark blue robe and severed the hair that was choking him.

Aislinn felt Fionn's disapproving gaze burn into her. She strode into the attic and threw him a defiant *what are you going to do about it* look before turning her attention to Rune. The hybrid writhed under him, but wasn't anywhere close to dying. Since the wolf had severed her carotid artery, it didn't make sense, unless...

"Aye," Fionn panted, "ye canna kill these things. They died long ago. The power filling them comes from the Old Ones."

"But I thought Marta left them in suspended animation," Aislinn said.

"Aye, and there is much we doona know, lass. Tell yon wolf to let go." Gwydion's voice was rough. "The problem was the hair. I have things under control."

"Rune, to me."

The wolf, looking immensely pleased with himself, sidestepped away from Marta's mother. His snout dripping yellow gore, he trotted to Aislinn with his tail swishing from side to side. The hybrid made a hideous groaning noise and scrambled to her feet. The groan morphed into a shriek, and she hurled herself at Gwydion.

Aislinn wrapped her arms around herself, wishing she'd put on a coat. It was freezing in the attic. Her breath plumed in the air in front of her. "If we can't kill them," she asked, trying to keep her teeth from chattering, "how can we put them back to sleep?"

"If we knew that"—Fionn feinted left to avoid a jolt of magic—"doona ye think we would have done it afore now?"

"You managed to with Bran and Arawn," she began.

"Aye, but neither of them are here," Gwydion spat, breathing hard. He and the undead thing circled one another. She seemed more aggressive than Fionn's opponent. Muddy brown eyes gleamed with cunning intelligence as she tried to pin Gwydion into a corner.

"Lass," he said, "try the unmaking spell. Do ye know it?"

She nodded. She'd used it a time or two to rid herself of small numbers of Bal'ta, apelike minions of the dark gods. Near as she could tell, it simply scattered living molecules to kingdom come. Except these weren't living creatures. "Are you sure it will work?" she asked dubiously.

"With a few twists, mayhap," Fionn answered. "We were close, but the female is strong. We thought she was bound, but she broke through. There are three of us now, though." Coarse laughter burst from him, and he sent magic skimming toward the male hybrid. "The odds have improved."

"Four," Rune corrected.

Aislinn looked around for Bella, only just now realizing the bird's absence. "Where's—" she began.

"Asleep downstairs," Fionn muttered. "I dinna wish to bring her into danger." He looked pointedly at her for a second before returning his gaze to the hybrid, who was trying to run him through with a rusty saber, apparently having given up on magic for the moment. "At least she stayed put."

"Only because you cast a spell over her," Aislinn retorted tartly.

"Enough. We have bigger problems." Fionn jumped out of the saber's path.

Gwydion wove his hands in a complex pattern and chanted. A spell plaited itself around his opponent. Aislinn threw her magic into the mix and felt Fionn direct some as well. He couldn't pull all his magic away from the fight. If he did, the creature would have him. As it was, a blast of power from the male hybrid—after the saber clattered to the attic floor—had been far too close for Aislinn's comfort.

She dragged her concentration away from Fionn and poured everything she had into the unmaking spell. Rune chivvied the female hybrid and forced her to stay in the midst of the net working its way around her.

Gwydion's expression was grim. The hard line of his jaw twitched as magic geysered from him. A wild, Celtic whoop filled the air. "Aye, a bit more and we'll have this one corralled. I doona plan to make the same error we made last time."

He tipped the writhing hybrid into one of the coffins. Aislinn raced forward and slammed the lid. The tenor of Gwydion's chanting changed. While she didn't recognize the incantation, Aislinn figured he was sealing the casket. Rune walked casually over to the coffin and lifted his leg. A stream of urine sprayed against the polished metal.

Gwydion brayed laughter. "Aye, and that will surely keep her contained if my magic should fail."

"You're welcome." Rune sashayed to Aislinn's side.

She turned her gaze to Fionn. He looked like the old world god he was, all hard muscled flesh, blue eyes glinting dangerously. "Well?" she asked Gwydion. "Are we ready to do the same thing again?"

"Eager one, aren't ye?"

"Not particularly. I want to get this over with so I can get some sleep." While she'd gotten used to killing, Aislinn had never reached the point where she actually enjoyed the process. Only the results.

"Nay, ye're just wanting that one back in your arms. Can't say as I blame you, lass."

"Well..." She shot him a crooked smile. "Now that you mention it—"

"Would the two of you stop fucking nattering and help me?" Fionn sounded beleaguered. He jumped over another jolt of magic.

"Oh, I doona know." Gwydion smiled broadly. "Mayhap, we'll just leave you here while the lass and I—"

With a growl worthy of the wolf, Fionn loped away from his opponent and planted himself squarely in front of Gwydion. "Would ye now?" His gaze shot blue darts at the other mage.

"Fionn!" Aislinn screamed.

The creature launched itself at Fionn's unprotected back. Rune hurled himself against the male hybrid, sank his teeth into its neck, and the two of them crashed to the floor. The hybrid put his hands around the wolf's neck, trying to choke him.

Not waiting for the two Celtic gods, who seemed engaged in a testosterone-laden standoff, Aislinn sent killing magic spinning toward the hybrid. To hell with trying to corral the damned thing. It was going to kill her wolf if she didn't do something. Running wide open, she hit what was left of Marta's father with all she had. He didn't so much as blink. She pulled the knife she always carried in a sheath strapped around her waist and rushed the creature, stabbing his hands. That got his attention. The chokehold on Rune loosened. Aislinn drew fire from the earth and funneled it so the hybrid's flesh began to smoke and then burn.

A putrid smell filled the room, but the damned thing's hands fell away from the wolf.

"Rune. Get up."

He just lay there. Aislinn dragged him a few feet from the hybrid, who seemed focused on his melting flesh. "Do something," she shrieked at Fionn and Gwydion. "I've got my hands full." She'd just sent her magic into Rune to find out what was wrong so she could Heal him, when she felt Fionn and Gwydion's magic build.

"Take care of yon wolf, lass. We will finish this," Fionn cried.

Their magic flowed around her. She sat next to Rune, infusing Healing magic to repair the wounded places in his neck. The injury wasn't too serious. Some lacerated tissues and torn blood vessels. It wasn't nearly as bad as the time wargs had attacked him and torn out his throat. That was when she'd discovered she could Heal with magic.

Yeah, it was the first time in a long time I cared enough about someone that I wanted them to live.

She withdrew her magic about the same time she heard the second casket lid clank shut. The wolf stirred beneath her hands, and then lurched to his feet. "Ssssh, it's all right, Rune. You can lie back down."

He sank to a shaky sit, panting.

Aislinn rolled to her hands and knees and then got up. She was so tired, she was surprised she didn't collapse next to her wolf. Her head spun crazily, and she shifted from foot to foot, trying to find a balance point.

Arms closed around her from behind. "*Mo croi.*" Fionn's voice was soft. "Ye were supposed to stay below."

"Aye, and had I done that," she returned, aping Tara's brogue, "ye might be the Old Ones' prisoner now." Her eyes narrowed and she returned to her usual English. "Once they had you, they'd have come back for me."

"Over my dead body," Rune growled, having found his voice again.

"Well, and none of that happened." Gwydion spoke with a brisk asperity that revealed how drained he was.

"Do you think the gates are still open?" Aislinn looked from one to the other of the Celts.

Fionn shrugged. "I doona see why they should not be."

"We did change the quality of the spell binding these two,"

Gwydion pointed out.

"Okay, next question. Do you think Slototh went back to wherever he came from after I, ah, wounded him?"

Another shrug from Fionn. "We doona know that, either, lass. The dark gods are nearly impossible to kill. As the god of filth and all that's discarded, Slototh would be particularly difficult to do away with, since he could hide behind all the memories he's stolen."

She glanced at Gwydion. He nodded agreement and mimicked Fionn's shrug.

"Christ, what good are the two of you?" she blurted before dropping her head into her hands. "Ach, sorry. It's just, I'm so tired I can barely see, let alone think straight."

She looked up in time to see something subtle pass between Fionn and Gwydion. Though she couldn't quite interpret it, it alarmed her.

Fionn herded her toward the stairs. Rune shambled to his feet and took his place on her other side.

"Where are you taking me?"

"To bed, *leannán*."

"The trouble's not over, is it?" She stopped and turned, locking gazes with him.

"Nay, lass. Not now. Mayhap not for a verra long time ahead, but ye need rest. And food once ye are rested."

"Aye." Gwydion's voice sounded from behind her. "Despite Fionn trying to shield you, ye were a great help here. Yon wolf, too. We need your magic. Ye must care for yourself so 'tis available to us."

She felt Rune preening in her mind and sent loving thoughts his way. He was so brave and so selfless, it made her feel petty by comparison. *I'm lucky to have you.* She buried her hand in his fur.

"Yes," he agreed, *"you are."*

She would've laughed, but she was too wiped out.

Sandwiched between her wolf and her lover, Aislinn found her way back down the stairs. She didn't even remember crawling into bed.

CHAPTER 5

"*W*ake up!" Dewi's mind voice blasted Aislinn out of a deep sleep.

The fucking dragon.

Aislinn rolled over. *"I'm tired. Leave me alone."*

"I am many things, too, but it does not excuse me from duty. Get up and get out here. Now."

Aislinn threw a pillow across the room and focused her bleary brain. *Must mean Bran is back, too. Thank God we have reinforcements if those things upstairs get out of control again.*

Forcing her gritty eyes open, she rubbed them to get some of the irritating particles out. She could've slept several more hours. Her entire body ached. Rune was curled in his customary spot on the floor. It was the same place he'd slept in for years as Marta's bond animal.

Fionn was gone. His energy was unmistakable and it was conspicuously absent. She reached a hand to his side of the bed. Apparently he'd left quite a while ago because the duvet no longer held any remnants of his warmth.

An imperious tapping sounded at her window. Rune growled.

"None of that," she chided the wolf. "It'll only make things worse.

55

It has to be Dewi. If she could fit inside this house, she'd have rousted me more directly."

Dragon laughter rattled the windowpanes. Aislinn threw back the comforter, pulled on the first robe she saw—which happened to be Fionn's—and padded across the room to pull the curtains open. After a minor struggle, she managed to open a window.

The dragon bent her long, sinuous, red-scaled neck down to peer at her. "You look like hell," she pronounced.

"Thanks," Aislinn muttered.

"You're in luck. I have just the cure for that. Put some clothes on and come ride with me."

The bedroom door slammed open. Fionn's presence pulsed against her back. "She can go riding"—he strode to the window and draped an arm around Aislinn—"as soon as she's eaten."

"A wee bit overprotective, aren't you?" Dewi snorted.

"I do need to eat." Aislinn turned her head and gave Fionn a quick peck on the cheek.

"Get some clothes, *leannán*. There's food on the kitchen table."

Aislinn hunted for the black sweats she'd worn the night before. At least they didn't take any energy to get into. Somewhere between her pants and boots, Rune got up and stretched out each paw, obviously taking his time. He shook himself all over and walked from the room. Bella, who'd been on Fionn's shoulder, flew after him.

"I swear,"—Fionn shook his head—"Bella has a stronger bond to Rune than she does to me. She certainly spends a lot of time with him."

"Has the wolf told you aught about himself?" Dewi asked peevishly.

Aislinn battled irritation, not bothering to glance Dewi's way. "Don't start. I just got him settled down about you." As dressed for the day as she thought she was likely to get, Aislinn linked an arm through Fionn's. "I'm ready for breakfast."

"You didn't answer me," the dragon snapped; smoke streamed from her jaws. Double rows of teeth gleamed in the midday light.

"How about if we delay this conversation until our ride?"

"Good idea." Fionn herded her toward the door.

Dewi loosed a spate of Gaelic so archaic Aislinn only caught one word in three. She stopped in the doorway and turned to face the dragon. "I'm sorry if you're not happy with me. I still feel like I'm going to fall on my face if I don't get more rest and something in my stomach. I'll be outside presently."

"Well—" the dragon sniffed haughtily "—I suppose that will have to do."

Yes, you old bag of wind, I suppose it will.

"Watch it." Fionn's voice sounded in her head. *"She reads minds."*

Aislinn stomped down the hall. A headache throbbed behind her right eye. She still hadn't forgiven Dewi for using her as a vehicle to have sex with the Minotaur. It was unfortunate, but she didn't trust the ancient Celtic dragon god as far as she could throw her.

"Nonetheless, ye are bonded to her," Fionn reminded her gently. "Not in the same way as ye are bonded to Rune, but the dragon has a claim to the MacLochlainn. Until we produce a child or two, that would be you."

Aislinn didn't want to think about the dragon. She practically fell into a seat at the table and spooned oatmeal with nuts into her mouth as fast as she could swallow the gelatinous mixture. *No wonder I'm so hungry. It's been around forty hours since I've had anything to eat.* Fionn handed her mead to wash it down.

She looked at the flask dubiously. "Booze? In the morning?"

"Aye. It'll refresh you."

Figuring she needed all the help she could get, Aislinn took the flagon and tipped it back. When she looked in her bowl for more oatmeal, it was empty. "Damn. I'm still hungry." She zeroed in on the stove. "Is there any more?"

"Nay, but I can boil more water. It was a stroke of luck Marta hoarded food." His hand swept wide, encompassing well-filled bins and cupboards in the tidy kitchen. "In the meantime, how about dried fruit and nuts?"

Aislinn nodded. She slid from her chair and opened several canisters to retrieve cashews, walnuts, almonds, and dried apricots. Fionn busied himself at the stove, heating water with magic.

Bran strode into the room from the adjoining study, battle leathers immaculate as usual. The tight-fitting garments showed off his heavily-muscled physique. His blond hair was tightly braided, and his copper-colored eyes looked grim. "In light of what happened here last night, I've been trying to glean something from those infernal journals."

"And?" Fionn eyed him.

"That fucking witch wrote in circles. Every time I think I may be getting close to something important, she veers off topic."

"Don't let Rune hear you call Marta that," Aislinn cautioned. Something he said gave her pause. "Have you considered the journals might be spelled? At least the ones you're reading. The ones I looked at didn't give me any problems at all."

Bran creased his forehead in thought. "Ye may have a point, lass." He looked her up and down. "And might I add, ye're looking fetching this morning." He licked full lips in obvious invitation. "Oh, and have I told you if ye tire of—"

"Yes, I'm quite certain ye have told her that," Fionn snapped. He made shooing motions with both hands. "Aislinn had a good idea. Try a neutralizing incantation."

Bran laughed. "I know a brushoff when I hear one. I'll shout if I find aught of relevance." He detoured past the table to grab a handful of nuts from one of the canisters before disappearing into the study.

Fionn plopped another dish of oatmeal in front of her. She dug in, but more slowly this time, her state of near-starvation partially mollified. "You know what you said about children?" she asked around a mouthful of cereal laced with walnuts. Still busy over by the stove, he turned to look at her and nodded. She laid a hand over her flat stomach. "Well, I don't think we should even consider having any."

He was by her side in a flash. "And why not? Do ye not love me?" He looked so distraught, it shocked her.

"No, silly. That's not it at all. What kind of life would this be for a baby or a child? I don't even know if I'm going to be alive from one day to the next—"

"I wasna thinking about that." He sounded mildly cowed. "I assumed when ye conceived, I'd move you to the Old Country. 'Twould be much easier to care for you and our bairns there. Magic is closer to the surface. Easier to access. Ye'd find that true as well." He favored her with one of his thousand-watt smiles. The kind that made him look like the handsomest man who ever lived.

Anger flared, biting deep. Aislinn struggled to restrain the temper that had always been her undoing. She looked at him through narrowed eyes. "Just when were you going to spring that one on me? Were you even going to ask me if it was what I wanted?" Tears were too close to the surface for comfort. She stuffed some dried apricots into her mouth and chewed to mask her emotions. In some ways, Fionn and the dragon were a matched pair. Both of them assumed they could control her future.

Dewi trumpeted from outside.

Speak of the devil... Aislinn dragged a hand down her face, made a grab for the flask, and emptied it. Alcohol really did help take the edge off things. So what if it wasn't even afternoon quite yet.

Fionn spread his hands in front of him. "I—"

She shook her head. "Don't start. I don't have enough energy for you and her today. Dewi will probably start dismantling this house board by board if I don't report front and center. My bottom line is this: no children until Earth is safe again. What that means is the dark gods and Lemurians aren't a threat anymore." Aislinn dragged herself out of her chair and plodded toward the back door. Maybe if she were lucky, she'd fall off the damned dragon and not have to deal with any of this.

Don't even think that way, an inner voice that sounded a lot like Tara Lenear chided.

The chilly outside air was welcome because it cooled her heated cheeks. Aislinn drew in a deep breath and trotted down the stairs to face the dragon. Dewi stood better than eight feet from the tip of her head to the ground. Leathery red wings folded over her back. Her eyes were whirling dark pools, just like the Lemurians'.

"Well. It took you long enough. Did you polish off every scrap of food in the house?"

Aislinn shook her head. She placed her hands on her hips and looked up at Dewi. "If you're going to give me a hard time, I'm going right back into the house. Last night, I wished you were here. Today, I'm rethinking that."

The dragon cocked her head to one side and blew out a gout of steam. "A wee bit on the touchy side, aren't you?"

"You would be, too, if you'd been captured by Lemurians and had to fight human hybrids, all in the same day."

Dewi crooked a talon. "Come, Daughter. I'll help you up."

Aislinn liked riding. It had frightened her at first, but she really enjoyed feeling the powerful beat of Dewi's wings keeping them airborne. She set a foot on Dewi's knee and let the dragon boost her onto her perch at the base of her long neck.

They'd no sooner left the ground when the dragon said, "Now, about that wolf of yours—"

"You obviously have something you think I need to know," Aislinn muttered. "So go ahead and tell me." Leave it to the dragon to wait until she was a captive audience to bring up something that was likely spiteful.

"It involves Fionn, as well." There was indeed something unpleasant riding beneath the dragon's tone.

"Tell me and get it over with," Aislinn snapped. The usual joy she felt with the wind in her face dissipated. What the hell did the dragon have up her sleeve?

"Bran and Sceolan were Celtic hounds that belonged to Fionn, and Tuiren was the bitch that spawned them. Well,"—Dewi's tone became conspiratorial—"Tuiren was actually Fionn's aunt. See, she was transformed into a hound by the Sidhe, and no one could undo the spell."

"Your point?" Aislinn spat from between clenched jaws. She couldn't see how Celtic mythology had any bearing on what was happening today.

"Rune is descended from Bran—or maybe it was Sceolan, I never can get that part straight—so he is rooted in Celtic legend and bound to Fionn just as his ancestors were."

"You told me this, why?"

"Hmph. I'll wager neither of them told you they had a connection."

"No, they didn't. I'm betting they don't even know about it," Aislinn countered. "Why don't we land so we can ask them?" Something batted about in a corner of her mind. Rune wasn't the wolf's real name. He'd been reluctant to tell her what was. Could this possibly have something to do with that?

"It is probable"—the dragon sounded unbearably serious—"that they're just waiting for you to drop your guard—"

"To do what?" Aislinn cut in. "They love me. You should be ashamed of yourself. You've known Fionn for the whole thousand years he's been alive. You're an impossible gossip. Did you know that?"

"I was only trying to help."

"Let's land and ask them. I'm sure this will sort itself out."

The dragon soared higher, scribing large, lazy circles around Marta's house. Aislinn considered asking what she was doing, but decided against it.

"You can trust me. In fact, I'm the only one you should trust." Compulsion flowed under Dewi's words. In Aislin's mind, she heard a reverberating, *trust me, trust me, trust me...*

"I really am ready for us to land," she told the dragon. "You've done this to me before. If you want me to ride you, you have to respect when I've had enough."

"We've barely begun, little magic-wielder."

The anger that had surged at Fionn earlier returned tenfold. Muscles tense, teeth clamped together, Aislinn eyed the ground. No reason she couldn't jump herself back to the house. It wasn't very far, and her spell should work like it always did. Heartily sick of being manipulated, she wove the threads that would free her from Dewi's back.

"What do you think you're doing?" The dragon sounded horrified.

"You won't put me down, so I'm working on another way to leave."

Dewi angled her neck around so she was looking right at Aislinn. "You wouldn't."

"Oh"—Aislinn smiled as sweetly as she knew how—"but I would. I've had it with all of you deciding what's best for me. I'm the author of that. Now either you land, or I'm leaving." Her magic hovered between them. She knew the dragon could feel it.

"Very well. No need to risk yourself." Dewi spread her wings, using them as airfoils to allow them to drift downward. When they were about ten feet above the ground, the dragon asked, "Are you sure this is what you want?"

"Very. Land, goddammit."

The second the dragon touched down, Aislinn didn't wait for assistance. She slid down the spiny hide on Dewi's side, ripping the hell out of her soft pants and scratching the tender skin beneath. Fury thrummed through her. She stalked toward the house, holding the shreds of her clothing together.

The ground shook as the dragon lumbered after her. "Wait."

"Why should I?" Aislinn didn't even bother to turn around.

"I am sorry—"

Aislinn twirled to face Dewi and balled her hands into fists. "So am I. This proves I can't trust you. That was the last time I will ever get on your back. You've heard the old saying, 'fuck me once, shame on you. Fuck me twice, shame on me?'"

"No, I can't say as I have. Look, Daughter, be reasonable."

"Sorry, I'm not in the mood." She raced up the porch steps and slammed into the house.

Fionn and Bran were in the study poring over Marta's journals. Located just off the kitchen, it was a cozy room with leather furniture, an enormous glass-fronted mahogany desk, and a generous fireplace, complete with a brass screen and andirons.

Bran smiled when he saw her. "Lass, that was a brilliant idea—"

"Can it." Aislinn threw herself down on a small couch, so angry she was practically beyond speech. "Don't talk to me."

"Och, dragon problems, eh?" Bran patted her arm before returning his attention to the thick volume that lay open in his lap.

"What happened?" Fionn moved to sit next to her.

She considered asking snappishly what part of "don't talk to me" he hadn't understood, but bit her tongue. "I can't trust her," she muttered. "Because I can't trust her, I'm done. I'm never riding her again, no matter how many times she apologizes. She does what she wants and doesn't pay a whit of attention to me."

Fionn shrugged. "Aye, that's likely true. She's been like that for thousands of years. Ye willna change her."

"Well, can I get out of the MacLochlainn thing? Even if I did have children—and I haven't changed my mind about that—the last thing I'd want would be for them to be bound to that dragon."

"She's really not all that bad—" Fionn began.

Something brittle snapped, and Aislinn surged to her feet. "Oh, she's not, is she?" Aislinn paced from one end of the room to the other and back again. She crimped her hands into such tight fists, her nails cut into her palms. "She wanted to get me alone to tell me some crap about a couple of hounds you once owned. I think your aunt or something was their mother. She thinks Rune is related to them...and to you. And that the two of you are plotting something dastardly—with me as the target."

"What?" The distress on Fionn's face had to be genuine.

Aislinn came to a stop in front of him. "I told her she was full of shit. I wanted her to land so we could talk to you—and Rune."

Fionn laid his hands on her shoulders. "The part about my aunt is true. The Sidhe turned her into a Wolfhound as punishment for something-or-other. I kept her in my stables to prevent further mischief, and she produced litter after litter of puppies. I kept two from one of the early batches. 'Tis been so long ago, I doona recall what happened to the rest."

So that part was true. Aislinn's fury shattered around her, leaving her feeling vulnerable. She took a deep breath. "What about Rune?" Her voice was quiet. She twisted bits of Seeker magic into a truth net.

"I doona know about that part. I never laid eyes on him until I met you next to that lake near my underground home."

Fionn's words pinged cleanly off her magic, which meant he'd told the truth. She retreated to her place on the couch, aware of an empty spot inside her. Whenever she got so angry her vision blurred to a red haze, she felt the same hollowness afterward. She'd always supposed it came from understanding how impotent her anger had been to change either her mother's or father's deaths.

She cleared her throat, hoping for a return of control over her emotions. "Rune told me he had another name."

"What is it?" Fionn looked intrigued.

"I have no idea. He'd never disclose it."

"Well, mayhap we should find him and ask what it is," Bran suggested. "Afore we do that, I think I may have found what I was looking for." He tapped a calloused index finger on the page open in front of him.

Aislinn glanced at the book in his lap. "What language is that written in?"

Bran quirked a brow. "Greek."

"Hmph. Handy you've been alive for so long. I suppose you know Latin, too, just like Fionn?"

"The interesting part," Fionn inserted before Bran had a chance to answer, "is Marta knew both languages well enough to keep journals in them."

"Quiet." Bran's tone was deadly serious. "'Tis nigh onto a miracle you are all still here. Marta's parents built this house at the conjunction of psychic fault lines. My guess is the Lemurians told them exactly where to put it, but Marta doesna go into that part."

Aislinn scrunched her brow in concentration. "Translate, please."

"What he means"—Fionn jumped to his feet and moved to peer over Bran's shoulder—"is that this house could serve as a gateway to another world—or mayhap more than one." He scanned the page. Apparently not finding what he was looking for, he reached a finger to turn it.

"Doona bother." Bran slapped his hand away. "What ye seek is here." He riffled the pages, flipped a few backward, then pointed at a passage and read Marta's words, "The original plan was for the dark gods to enter Earth from here. I foiled that by trapping my parents in those caskets and setting wards around the gateway."

Aislinn sprang to her feet because she couldn't bear sitting still. "So, all that chanting at power points around the world happened because the dark gods couldn't get through here?" She heard a shrill note in her voice and tried to rein it in.

"'Twould appear so," Bran concurred.

Her father's murder at the hands of two of the dark gods rose before Aislinn's eyes. It played in slow motion like a bad movie she couldn't turn off, and her eyes filled with tears.

"Gwydion!" Bran and Fionn screeched in unison, startling her out of her funk.

"What?" Then she realized she hadn't seen the master enchanter all day. "Where is he?"

"Sitting guard over the hybrids. Damn it!" Bran bolted out of his seat and raced through the door in a flash, calling over his shoulder, "I must tell him to take care with his magic, else the lot of us could end up...elsewhere."

"I don't understand. Why?" Even though she'd asked, Aislinn wasn't sure she wanted to know.

Fionn puffed out an exasperated sounding breath, but he looked more worried than angry. "When ye are verra close to fault lines—think weak spots—betwixt the worlds, it doesna take much magic to fracture them. Bran is right. We could've been sucked through a hole last night. Christ knows we blew through enough magic to bring down half the countryside."

She tried to form coherent thoughts, but her mind felt sluggish. "Ah, where would we have ended up?"

"I doona know, lass."

"What do you mean, you don't know?" Her voice rose, its shrill tone back in spades. Listening to herself set her teeth on edge.

"There are many worlds." He inhaled sharply. "'Tis not like ye learned in school. There are no geographic maps delineating which world sits just where."

"Why not?" She grasped at sand slipping through her fingers, but understanding eluded her.

"Because magical worlds move around."

Sorry I asked.

Aislinn glanced past Fionn. Her reflection stared back at her, captured by the large mirror mounted over the fireplace. She blinked stupidly, not realizing until that moment just how bad she looked. Her face was pale and drawn, with spots of color high on both cheeks. Shadows etched dark hollows beneath her eyes, and her long hair hung in strings around her face. She hadn't gotten a chance to wash it after her ordeal in Taltos. Her quick rinse in the tub hadn't made a dent in the grease gluing the strands into clumps.

Aislinn clamped her jaws together to keep from screaming. She didn't like things she couldn't understand, and gateways into the unknown held a definite creep factor. Fionn opened his mouth. She supposed he was about to clarify what he knew about parallel worlds and how they played off one another. She shook her head because she was on overload and didn't want to hear any more.

"How about if we find Rune?" she mumbled. "At least we can solve that puzzle. Besides, I'd really like to be able to tell Dewi she was wrong."

"*Mo croi.*" Fionn stepped close and wrapped his arms around her. The familiar scent of him, exotic and spicy, filled her nostrils. He felt warm and solid and comforting.

It's illusion. He can't protect me any better than he protected Gwydion last night. I have to take care of myself.

"Aye, lass," he said, obviously having been inside her mind—again. "But doona forget I would move heaven and earth to keep you safe."

For a moment, she let herself cling to him. Then she straightened, turned around, and walked out the door, intent on finding her wolf.

CHAPTER 6

Fionn flung himself after Aislinn. He had no intention of letting her face whatever truths she was about to drag out of Rune by herself. Moreover, he had to admit he was intrigued. He hadn't had any sort of hound since migrating to the new world during the late seventeen hundreds. For a moment, he wondered if Tuiren still lived. She'd birthed hundreds of litters before he left. None of the puppies had inherited her immortality, though. He snorted. His aunt had such a roving eye, it wouldn't surprise him if half the dogs in the world were loosely related to her.

Fionn set his jaw in a hard line. Dewi was a problem. While her highhandedness fit in well enough in the Old Country, where people had more tolerance for magic—and respect for magical creatures—it was a definite impediment here. The dragon would throw a fit if Aislinn carried through on her threat to never set foot on her back again, particularly if there was fighting to be done.

He tried to get his thoughts in rational order as he hurried along, but they weren't cooperating. He actually didn't blame Aislinn for not trusting Dewi. The dragon tended to her own interests—first, foremost, and always. She was used to being treated with absolute deference. He gritted his teeth. Both the dragon and Aislinn had to be irritated by the ancient linkage that bound them. Dewi demanded obedience. Aislinn demanded respect. It didn't seem those two requirements could coexist in the same plane.

Tara had run from the dragon's incessant demands, but Aislinn had nowhere to run to. Besides, having lost Tara, Fionn assumed Dewi would track Aislinn to the ends of the Earth—if not beyond.

"In here, Fionn." Aislinn called from the front of the house.

"Be right there." He wanted to get his feelings under better control. While Aislinn wasn't terribly adept at mind-reading, she could look at his face and intuit what he was thinking without making a trip inside his head. He'd been shocked at her reaction to his casual remark about children earlier in the day. He thought she'd be pleased and he could use it as a springboard to tell her she carried his son… Fionn swallowed hard. She'd probably figure it out soon enough. Fear bit deep that she'd use magic to abort their child, maybe without even mentioning it to him.

He buried his concerns, arranged his face in neutral lines, and walked into the formal living room, which was furnished in nineteenth-century French design. Floral couches with carved legs lined two walls, and large, soft chairs and mahogany tables were scattered about. Cut crystal lighting fixtures, useless without electricity, hung from the ceiling and sat on tables. He twitched a dust cover off an upholstered chair and sat. Aislinn had taken a matching chair. It looked as if she was waiting for him to begin her discussion with the wolf.

Uncharacteristically silent, Rune and Bella faced away from him. The pair stared out an enormous bay window.

"What?" He gestured at their bond animals. "Are they mad at us?"

"I don't know." Aislinn sighed. "They were like that when I came in here, and neither seems inclined to turn around."

Fionn clucked. The raven flew to him and settled heavily on his shoulder. She dug her talons in deep. He winced and reached a hand to loosen her grip.

"Okay, Rune," Aislinn said. "I don't want to have to order you over here. How about if you come closer?"

"Why?" His lush tail swished back and forth, but he didn't turn around.

"We need to talk. Dewi says you're related to Fionn. Do you know anything about that?"

The wolf got to his feet and shook himself from head to toe. When he twirled to face her, fury sparked from his amber gaze, and a low, rumbly growl filled the air. "That dragon has to leave. I can't, so she must."

"You didn't answer me," Aislinn said gently. "I need to sort this out first."

He walked stiffly toward her and stopped about five feet away. Hackles quivered the length of his back. "Yes, I am descended from Celtic lineage. All of us—dogs and wolves alike—spring from Cŵn Annwn."

"Isn't that the Wild Hunt?"

Rune nodded. "But that does not make me any more closely aligned to Fionn than any other wolf." He growled again. "That dragon is a meddling, malicious bitch—"

"Enough." Fionn infused just enough command into his voice to keep Rune from saying any more. For all he knew, Dewi was listening. She had a nasty habit of eavesdropping.

"Wait." Aislinn held up a hand. "I wasn't done." She focused on Rune, meeting his gaze evenly. "Soon after we became bondmates, you told me you had another name. What is it?"

"Why do you want to know?"

"I just do. I have Healed you three times now. Surely that means you can trust me with your true name."

"Three?"

"Outside the ruins of my home in Salt Lake, in the tunnels under Taltos, and last night."

The wolf hung his head. "You win, bondmate. My true name is Cuchulainn."

"After the blacksmith turned warrior?" Fionn asked, thinking this was getting odder by the moment.

Rune didn't answer him.

"How did you find out your name?" Aislinn held her head cocked to one side, brows drawn together.

"Marta used magic to scry it. She told me to guard it well because the dark could use it to trap me." He hesitated. "She discovered my name only a few weeks before she was killed."

Fionn cloaked his thoughts. That was not how any creature discovered its true name, but he wasn't about to tell the wolf. Either the gods graced you with it. Or they didn't. Marta had had something up her sleeve. What the hell was it?

"It's a beautiful name." Aislinn smiled softly. She reached toward the wolf, but he didn't nuzzle her hand. "I swear I will conceal it so well no one will see it by accident in my mind."

"As will I," Fionn concurred. *I wonder if Marta wrote anything about this in those books of hers.*

Rune bowed his head crisply, snapping it up after a moment. "Thank you. Now, about Dewi—"

"I was just thinking about that afore I came in here," Fionn cut in. "She needs something to do. She wouldna cause nearly as much trouble if she were occupied."

"Do you suppose she knew about this house being on fault lines between worlds and unstable?" Aislinn asked.

"What?" Bella squawked. "We've been in danger the whole time we've been here?"

Fionn stroked her feathers. "Ssssh. Aye, but we're all still here, so no harm was done."

"The dragon probably knew," Rune snarled. "It would be just like her to know something like that and not bother to mention it."

Something in the wolf's tone nagged at Fionn. "It's almost as if you knew her from somewhere before." He focused on the wolf and tried to see into his mind, but Rune shut him out. Lacking the

Hunter bond, Fionn retreated. No point in alienating Aislinn's bondmate.

"Marta had several run-ins with Dewi under Taltos," the wolf said after a lengthy pause.

"And?" Aislinn prodded.

"She thought it was the Lemurians' dragon, but it made her life hell. Once Dewi found out about me, she set traps in the yard." Another snarl. "She almost killed me once when Marta wasn't here. I was much more careful where I stepped after nearly being blown to bits next to the garage."

"Oh, Rune." Aislinn looked stunned; her lips pressed into a thin line. "I had no idea. You should've said something." She reached for the wolf, but he turned his head away.

Fionn pounded a fist into his open palm, trying to mitigate his fury so he could think. When he got really angry, all he wanted to do was kill whatever stood in his way. That wouldn't work here. The Celtic gods had proscriptions against killing one another. Like it or not, Dewi was one of them.

Och aye, and doona we have enough problems without an entitled, renegade dragon who thinks it's still the Middle Ages?

"Not that I don't believe you"—he looked at Rune—"but how did you know it was her?"

"Smell, how else? The dragon has a unique scent, not at all like the Old Ones, even though both are reptiles."

Aislinn winced. "Uh, I hope Dewi's not listening. She'll make us all pay. Being likened to a snake would really piss her off."

"Ask me if I care. She needs to leave, because I don't trust her." Rune turned so his butt faced Aislinn.

Fionn made a sound midway between a snort and a grunt. He was surprised by how rude it sounded when it came out. "I need to talk with Bran and Arawn. So that means we wait till Arawn shows up. Besides, then I can take stock of who he brings with him and how much help they'll be."

"Help with what?" Aislinn looked at him.

"With whatever plan we come up with to get enough distance from our present problems so we can go back to trying to oust the dark gods."

"Oh." She narrowed her eyes thoughtfully. "If they keep us busy enough with minutiae, we'll never get back to that little project."

"Smart lass. That may well be their strategy. I'm certain they're all still reeling from the loss of Slototh. They saw themselves as invincible, yet ye outwitted one of them in a single afternoon. 'Tis proud I am. And infinitely grateful ye dinna get yourself killed."

Color rose to her cheeks. "Uh, thanks. I think."

Aislinn slid out of her chair onto the floor and extended her arms. After a long hesitation, Rune turned, walked into them, and let her hold him. It warmed Fionn's heart to see the two of them. A softness shone from Aislinn's eyes, and he imagined the young woman she'd been before the dark gods had robbed her of her family—and her hopes and dreams. Before he knew her well, he'd asked her once where her human parts had gone. Her terse reply was they'd died right along with her father in the Bolivian Andes.

He let his eyes close for a moment. If he had his way, he'd whisk Aislinn to his manor house outside Inishowen in Northern Ireland. He knew it was still standing, because he'd set strong wards about it. Besides, he'd just been there a few months ago, right before he met Aislinn. Bella's talons dug in hard enough to hurt. Probably hard enough to draw blood. Fionn sucked in a breath, about to scold her, but the raven used him for a launching pad, pushed off, and flew out of the room.

Hmmm...mayhap 'tis not only Dewi who's a jealous mistress here.

He got to his feet. "I'm going to look in on Bran and Gwydion."

"Think I'll stay here with Rune." Aislinn stroked his head.

"All right, *leannán*. See you presently. Until then"—he tried for diplomacy, since Aislinn didn't like being told what to do—"it might be best if ye dinna go outside."

"I have no intention of trying to talk with Dewi, if that's what you mean. I'm appalled she tried to kill Rune. And for no reason.

She was just indulging in sport, probably bored as hell wandering up and down that infernal tunnel under Taltos. No wonder she was so excited when I showed up. Even if I hadn't been the MacLochlainn, I was a diversion." Aislinn paused. "Say, why couldn't you give her another assignment? Like watching the fracture lines, or whatever this house sits on."

"That's not a bad idea, lass. Problem is, she'd have to agree. Mayhap there'd be some way to trick her into it."

"Run it past the others."

"I will."

Fionn walked the length of the hall and mounted the attic stairs. Aislinn was right that they had to either secure Dewi's full cooperation not to launch any more mischief, or get her out of the way entirely. He had a niggling hunch Marta had figured out the dragon was Celtic and the name she'd come up with for Rune was an attempt to protect him. The wolf had loved and trusted Marta and would have believed whatever she told him.

Fionn stepped into the attic, started to call a greeting, and froze. Both caskets were open—and empty. Bran and Gwydion stood, hands raised as if to cast a spell, but something was desperately wrong. The air had a putrid feel and a stench like decomposing flesh. If Fionn hadn't been so deep in his own mind, he would've noticed it long before getting to the top of the stairs.

Dark magic surged across the room. Fionn spun, sidestepped, and constructed a sloppy ward. It bought him a few moments, but that was all he needed. Something had opened the gateway. The hybrids were gone, but so were Gwydion's and Bran's astral selves. What he didn't know was if they'd gone willingly, giving chase to whoever had freed the hybrids, or if something had dragged their essence from their bodies.

Strong magic heaved against his warding. Fionn grunted from the force of it. Knowing he didn't have much time—whatever wanted him was incredibly strong—he chanted, generating every protection spell he could think of, and walled the attic off from the rest of the house. Once he'd done all he could, he slammed the attic door and then added more layers of spells to it.

Sweat dripped down his forehead, and the harsh sound of his breath rattled in his chest. With a final exhortation that *this door will hold, goddammit,* he clattered down the steps, taking them two at a time. He closed off the door from the downstairs hall and subjected it to similar treatment.

Fionn raced down the hall. When he stuck his head into the front room, Aislinn was asleep, curled on the floor next to Rune. *"Watch over her,"* he sent to the wolf.

"With my life."

"Doona let her leave this room until I return."

"Why? What has happened?"

"Later. No time."

Fionn ran through the side hall toward the kitchen, leaving a very worried-looking wolf sitting guard over Aislinn. He called for Dewi in his mind before he cleared the back door, but the dragon didn't answer.

At the bottom of the steps, he scanned the yard. No dragon. Her bright red color was impossible to miss. He looked up. Relief surged as she flew toward him, albeit slowly. Thank the goddess for small favors.

"What do you want?"

"Just get down here, Dewi. We have problems."

"I have problems of my own."

Fionn had no intention of biting on *that* conversational gambit. He watched as Dewi got lower and lower. After considerably longer than it should've taken, she landed on the far side of the yard and folded her wings across her back, making it apparent she wasn't going to come to him.

Fionn clenched his jaw. That bitch of a dragon wasn't going to make things easy, but he didn't have any choice, so he strode across the yard and came to a halt right in front of her. Fionn inclined his head. "Thank you, sister god, for coming to my aid." It was an ancient greeting among them and one he hoped would garner the dragon's good will.

"Hmph," she breathed. Flames shot skyward. "You, at least, recall I am your equal. Now, that worthless piece of trash, who unfortunately has MacLochlainn blood in her veins, is another matter. She has forgotten her place."

"Stop." Fionn held up a hand. "I doona wish to discuss Aislinn. I told you, we have serious problems."

"Well, so do I, and her name is MacLochlainn."

Fionn's muscles tensed. He didn't want to get into a longwinded discussion with the dragon about the woman he loved. "This house is balanced precariously between worlds—" he began.

Dragon laughter sprayed fire and interrupted him. Fionn swatted at embers burning through his leather breeches.

"You're just now figuring that out? A bit slow on the uptake, weren't you?"

"Dewi. Please."

Something in his tone got her attention, because the dragon stopped throwing fire around.

He inhaled raggedly. "Thank you. If ye must discuss Aislinn, ye would get further with her if ye treated her as an equal."

"But she isn't." Dewi focused her whirling eyes on him. "The ancient covenant—"

"—states the MacLochlainn and the Celtic dragon god will fight evil as a pair throughout time. It says nothing about Aislinn being your handmaiden or bondservant or any other variation where she has to do what ye tell her."

"That's the way it always worked before," Dewi said peevishly. "Why should it be different now?"

Hope surged. At least Dewi was listening. "Aye. This is partially my fault. I was the one who sent you to spy on the Lemurians a few hundred years ago. In that time, the world has changed—and rather dramatically." Since the dragon wasn't trying to burn him to a crisp or insert her own opinions, Fionn hurried on. "Ye saw what happened when ye played the heavy with Tara. She ran like hell. Couldna get away from you fast enough."

"I just thought there was something wrong with her," the dragon muttered.

"Aye, well, that same *something* is wrong with all modern women." Fionn laughed wryly. "Not that it bothers me. In fact, I appreciate their independence, but somewhere in the last hundred years or so, women came into their own. They no longer do what either men or dragons tell them."

"Oh." Dewi sighed, but only steam billowed from her nostrils. "Here I thought she was simply stubborn, just like her mother."

"It runs much deeper than that." Fionn took a chance. "If ye doona wish to alienate her completely, I suggest ye tell her we had this conversation, and ye would like to begin anew with different ground rules: the first being ye each stand on equal footing."

Silence sat between them for so long Fionn considered what to say next to convince her. The dragon saved him the trouble. Dewi wound her long neck so she met his gaze head on. "I can do that. Thank you for telling me, Fionn MacCumhaill."

"I tried to tell you when we stood outside Slototh's hellhole in Arizona, right after ye'd as much as let the Minotaur rape Aislinn, but ye dinna listen."

"Some messages require more than one telling. This time, I took care to listen with my third ear." The dragon's eyes whirled faster.

Fionn shifted his gaze downward. Things had gone far better than he'd expected. He hoped Dewi's temper wouldn't flare and ruin it all.

"What was that you started to tell me about this house?" The dragon changed the subject abruptly.

Thank bloody Christ, she's moved off talking about Aislinn.

"Ye know about the Lemurian-human hybrids?"

The dragon nodded.

"Well, their coffins are empty. Gwydion's and Bran's bodies are in the attic, but their astral selves are gone."

"Did they go willingly?"

"I doona know."

Scales clanked as Dewi narrowed her eyes. "What did you do?"

"Set wards around the attic. Sealed it. Did my best to separate it from the rest of the house."

"Good."

"Do ye know which world they've gone to?"

Dewi's large head moved up and down. "I believe so. Perrikus's is closest. Then D'Chel's. It is likely one or the other."

Fionn thought about the dark god he'd sensed behind the Lemurians during his foray into Taltos. A sense of foreboding settled in his chest, heavy and unwelcome.

"Where is Arawn?" Dewi asked.

"He should be on his way back here with help."

She nodded. "I am thinking we should wait until he returns. You and I could go, but the odds will improve if we are not two alone against goddess-only-knows how many."

"Unless Gwydion and Bran were dragged from their bodies against their will. In that case, the longer we wait, the greater chance they have of sitting out the next few millennia in the *Dreaming*, severed from their magic."

"I propose a compromise." Dewi tapped his chest with a talon. "We'll wait until midnight. If Arawn hasn't returned, we'll see what we can find."

"Thank you." When Fionn mouthed the heartfelt words, he understood he hadn't really expected the dragon's help.

"You're welcome." Dewi's jaws parted in what could have passed for a smile. "Now, where are Aislinn and that wolf of hers?"

"Aislinn is asleep. Let her be until she wakes, please. She's exhausted." Fionn flirted with the wisdom of eroding Dewi's good will, but didn't see that he had any choice in the matter. He girded himself against a shower of sparks. "So long as ye brought it up, we need to discuss the wolf…"

CHAPTER 7

*A*islinn leaned into Rune's warmth. She hadn't meant to fall asleep, but his body felt so soothing next to hers, she'd let her eyes close. When she opened them, she was relieved light still filtered in from the room's large windows.

"Too much to do to sleep the clock round." She struggled to clear her sleep-fuzzed brain.

"You needed rest." Rune licked her chin, got to his feet, and shook himself from stem to stern. Fur eddied in the air around him.

"How long—" she started to ask and then bit her tongue. Time questions were pointless with the wolf. Aislinn pushed herself to a cross-legged sit. "Where's Fionn?"

"I am not certain. He told me to make sure you stayed here until he returned."

That didn't sound good. Aislinn clanked her teeth together; annoyance vied with fear. "What happened?"

"I do not know. Fionn raced in here like the dogs of Hell were right behind him. All he said was to keep you in this room."

Aislinn sent Mage magic spinning outward. It ran aground when it tangled with wards in the back of the house. She pushed hard enough to recognize Fionn's work before backing off. At first she was confused, and then it came to her that last night's problems must have returned, but magnified tenfold. The attic was just about where her magic hit a dead end.

The bedroom. My things. Crap.

She got to her feet.

"Where are you going?" Rune sounded worried.

"To the kitchen. I'm hungry. I'm also filthy, but apparently that can't be helped right now. This doesn't seem like a good time to take a bath."

"You're not leaving this room. I promised Fionn." Rune positioned himself in front of the door and bared his teeth.

Aislinn fought burgeoning irritation mixed with love. The wolf was trying his damnedest to protect her. Her mind still felt muddy, but not nearly as bad as when she'd fallen asleep. She tried to think of something diplomatic to say that would mitigate Rune's sense of responsibility, so he'd let her leave.

Heavy footsteps sounded in the hall. She was pretty sure it was Fionn—the energy felt like his—but she readied magic just in case. The door flew open, and a disheveled-looking Fionn lurched through, panting. His hair was awry; burned spots smoldered in his battle leathers.

"Thank the goddess ye stayed put." He must've seen questions brimming from her eyes, because he added, "The hybrids are gone."

"Gwydion and Bran?"

"Their bodies are upstairs, but that's about it."

Aislinn felt like someone had kicked her in the guts. "Oh." She shook her head hard and pulled herself together. "Well, what are we waiting for? We need to go after them."

Fionn shook his head. "Not yet. I've been talking with Dewi—"

"I don't want to hear about it."

"Well, ye will listen. Ye as well," Fionn said to Rune. "The long and short of it is the dragon is sorry—"

"We've heard that one before," Rune snarled.

"Yes," Aislinn chimed. "I seem to recall her being *sorry* outside Slototh's lair."

Fionn sighed. He coiled his hands into fists at his sides. "Aye, I told her much the same. And gave her a history primer, as well. She dinna realize—"

"I said"—Aislinn turned away—"I don't want to hear about it."

Fionn thumped his hands heavily onto her shoulders and turned her to face him. "Ye doona have a choice, lass. I will spare you the details, but I believe I got through to the dragon this time. We need her. If Arawn isna returned by midnight, she has agreed to help me search for Gwydion and Bran."

She knew it was childish, but Aislinn was furious Fionn had given Dewi the time of day. It felt disloyal to her. He could be on her side, or the dragon's, but not both. *I've got to get hold of myself.* She forced herself to breathe before she said something she regretted. The pressure of his fingers digging into her shoulders hurt. She moved under his hands.

He muttered, "Sorry," and loosened his grip.

Aislinn raised her gaze to his and tried to forget how absolutely wonderful Fionn's blue eyes were. This was *not* a time to get sidetracked. "There are things I need to know. The first one is what will happen to your friends if we can't bring them back here?"

"That depends on how they left. If they departed of their own free will, chasing after one of the dark gods or the hybrids, things are not nearly so desperate. On the other hand, if their astral selves were forced out of their bodies—"

"If you go, I'm going, too."

"Yes, and you are taking me." Rune padded to where the two of them stood, his tail pluming.

"I doona think that is a verra good idea—" Fionn began.

Aislinn clapped a hand to her forehead. "Shit. It's Dewi inside my head demanding I come outside to talk with her. I really don't want to."

"Then don't," Rune growled.

"Ye should hear what she has to say." Fionn's voice was gentle, but Aislinn recognized compulsion beneath his words.

"You'd ensorcel me to get me to talk to the fucking dragon?" Outrage boiled over, and she bolted from the room.

Fionn's footfalls sounded right behind her. Unfortunately, he caught up to her easily and clasped her arms from behind. "Not ensorcel." He bent so his breath was hot against her ear. "Please, *leannán*, indulge me. If ye doona like what she has to say, ye can leave."

"She doesn't sound one whit different. Same bossy, demanding, entitled—"

"If she does that, neither of us will stay." Fionn moved to her side and linked an arm through hers. "Come on. We'll face this together."

Against her better judgment, Aislinn let him drag her through the kitchen and out the back door. Rune walked by her side, growling imprecations. She didn't have to go any farther than the top of the steps leading down from the back porch because Dewi was as close to the house as she could get.

The dragon settled her whirling eyes on Aislinn before shifting her gaze to Rune. She belched smoke streaked with fire. "Good. You are both here—"

Rune inserted his body between Aislinn and Dewi. "She is *my* bondmate," he snarled, "not yours."

Dewi arched her neck. Concerned the dragon would burn Rune to a cinder for being insolent, Aislinn shoved the wolf behind her.

"Oh, stop it. I wouldn't hurt your precious wolf. I'm willing to recognize the two of you are bonded, even though my link to the MacLochlainn is far older—"

"Stop." Fionn held up a hand. "There is enough of Aislinn to go round. She can hold bonds to both of you without the two of you sniping at one another." He looked meaningfully at Dewi and Rune. "We have a larger enemy to face. If we destroy each other with bitter harping, we'll save them quite a bit of trouble."

"I hate to admit it, but you've got a point." Aislinn blew out a frustrated breath. "I thought the question at hand was whether we fought the dark with her"—she jabbed a finger at Dewi—"or on our own."

"You can't go without me." Shock permeated Dewi's voice. "Furthermore—"

"Oh yes, we could. I don't trust you. There's nothing worse than being in a battle with an ally who might turn on you. Rune told me you tried to kill him when he was bonded to Marta." Aislinn forced herself to hold the dragon's unsettling gaze.

"That was different. Marta was not the MacLochlainn."

Rune's jaws snapped shut. "That does not make me feel any better." He moved between Fionn and Aislinn.

"I apologize." Dewi sniffed. "You take things too personally. Marta was tampering where she had no business. I was merely trying to scare her off. I knew if she made too many trips into Taltos, the Old Ones would capture her. Besides..." She eyed Rune with asperity. "I had no idea your sense of smell was so feeble you wouldn't sense my trap before it nearly blew up in your face."

"I wasn't expecting a snare in my own yard." The wolf growled just before he lunged at the dragon.

Dewi fanned her wings. Smoke plumed from her snout.

Fionn dragged the wolf back, muttering curses in Gaelic. "Ye are supposed to be apologizing," he snapped at Dewi. "Remember our discussion. Humble. Undefended."

"I'm trying—"

"Not verra hard, ye're not. Tell Rune ye are sorry. Try to sound as if ye mean it."

Dewi made a coughing sound. She shut her eyes and then opened them. "I am sorry, Rune. Had I known what the cost of my mischief would be, I would have found another means to warn Marta off."

Rune, who'd been tugging against Fionn's iron grip, relaxed. "Accepted," he snorted and padded to Aislinn's side.

Aislinn paid out Seeker magic, relieved to hear the ping of truth bounce back at her. Despite Dewi's annoying high-handedness, at least she was telling the truth. "All right." Aislinn settled her hands on her hips and kept her Seeker magic deployed. "Now what about me? Fionn says I need to hear you out. If it weren't for that, I wouldn't have heeded your summons."

Aislinn pressed her tongue against her teeth. Despite Dewi's half-baked apology to Rune, she felt her temper rising and clenched her jaws to keep it in check. Bad things happened when her anger got out of control, like running into an electrified ward and dying. If Fionn hadn't been close by to bring her back...

"What do you mean, not heed my summons?" Dewi tossed her head back, and her eyes whirled faster.

"That's just it." Aislinn spun toward Dewi, riding a fine edge of control. "You think you can *summon* me and I'll dance to your tune. Well, think again. No one summons me. If you want me to work with you, you need to ask if it's something I want to do, not just assume I'll drop everything and fall at your feet every time you call my name."

"I think I understand that now."

Aislinn heard another truth ping and blessed her Seeker gift.

"I truly am sorry," Dewi said. "I didn't understand how upset you were—or why—until Fionn drove a few points home."

"Good." Aislinn buried a hand in Rune's thick neck fur. "Because if we're all going after Bran and Gwydion, we'll need to work together—"

"That was one of the things I tried to address earlier, when you said the two of you might go without me." Dewi focused both eyes and words on Fionn, as if the last thing she wanted was another confrontation with Aislinn. "It would be best if the MacLochlainn, untrained as she is, remained here."

He shrugged. "I dinna invite her—" he began.

"No, he didn't," Aislinn agreed. "I invited myself. And then Rune said if I was going, he was coming, too. Seems you could use another couple pairs of hands." She locked gazes with Dewi. "I am not *untrained*. I've had more than three years in the Lemurian-version of military Special Forces preparation."

"It will be extremely dangerous." For once, Dewi didn't sound the least bit patronizing. "You might actually jeopardize our efforts if we have to divert energy to save you."

Aislinn crossed her arms over her chest. "You still don't see me as anything other than a child. And a rather dim-witted one at that."

"Hmph."

"Don't bother denying it. My Seeker magic corroborates what's true."

"Fionn and I are used to working together—"

"Great," Aislinn interrupted, not caring she was being rude. "Then you can get used to working with Rune and me as well."

"Is she always this pig-headed?" Dewi asked Fionn.

He laughed and draped an arm around Aislinn's shoulders. "I'd say so. 'Tis one of her more endearing traits."

"Cripes. I'd like to know what my unappealing ones are," she muttered and leaned into Fionn's warmth. There was something solid and heartening about his bulk next to her. Even Rune seemed to have lightened up somewhat.

"Are we done here?" Aislinn glanced from Fionn to Dewi.

"No." The dragon's sharp tone shocked Aislinn. "What was one of the first things the Lemurians drummed into you about fighting the dark?"

"To follow orders precisely, without question. And to be careful."

Dewi cocked her head to one side. "Exactly." She exhaled noisily, and a plume of smoke curled into the chilly air. "No matter what you think of the Old Ones or the dark gods, they understand battle strategy. We need a plan if we are to have any chance at all."

"Once that plan is formed, we each play our roles," Fionn added, sounding graver than she'd ever heard him. "I doona know if Arawn will return in time, so we must move forward as if we willna have his help."

Something nagged Aislinn. "Where do you think Bran and Gwydion are?"

"In a border world. Either Perrikus's or D'Chel's," Dewi answered.

A growl rumbled in Rune's throat. Aislinn remembered when he'd taken her to a border world so they could discuss the dark gods. A shiver raced down her, curdling her empty stomach. She was grateful she hadn't eaten recently. Suddenly, Fionn's warmth wasn't enough to keep the chill at bay, and icy tendrils froze her from the inside out.

"Ye doona have to come." Fionn spoke low, his lips brushing her ear. "There wouldna be shame if ye stayed."

Aislinn bit her lower lip. "I've faced both of them before. I can do it again."

Fionn didn't say a word. He just looked at her; care and worry competed for control of the sculpted lines of his face.

She dropped her gaze. "I know I'm vulnerable," she murmured, "but I managed to trick D'Chel and Slototh, despite their sexual maneuverings."

"Barely."

"Shit!" She stepped away from Fionn, her spine ramrod straight. "You're supposed to believe in me."

"I do. Yet, I recognize the truth of things, too." He reached for her, but she shook her head.

"All right." Fionn nodded tersely.

"We don't have time for a lover's quarrel." Dewi sounded exasperated. "We need a strategy. Come down here in the yard, all of you, so I can draw what I remember of both those worlds in the dirt." The dragon bent forward and sketched with an outstretched talon.

Rune trotted down the steps, tail pluming. He looked back over one shoulder at Aislinn. "Coming?"

"In a minute." She grabbed one of Fionn's hands. "Look, I'm sorry. I understand how perilous this is. Dealing with the dark gods is so horrifying, I can barely force myself to think about it. Then to hear you say I'm weak—"

"I dinna say that. I merely wanted you to remember what a close call ye had with D'Chel in the forest outside my home and with Slototh in his lair. Caution is your friend, lass. Betimes ye are headstrong and doona think."

There was actually more than one close call with D'Chel, and he doesn't even know about the one with Perrikus...

Heat rose in a whoosh from her chest to the top of her head. "Guess you've got my number." Embarrassment filled her, but she plowed on anyway. "Sometimes, if I stopped to really think things through, I'd probably get so scared, I wouldn't be able to do anything."

He closed his arms around her and touched the top of her head with his lips. "No matter what, *mo croi*, ye must promise ye'll do what Dewi and I say, even if ye doona understand the *why* of it, or if ye think another course wiser." He hesitated. "The dark ones all know by now that ye are the one who laid Slototh low. They will be wanting vengeance. Since ye are determined to come, we will need to disguise you."

"Good idea," Dewi seconded. "Now get down here and look at these maps before we lose the light. We'll need every scrap of magic we have. No reason to squander any on mage lights when we still have the sun."

Fionn furled his brows at Aislinn. Nodding, she trotted down the steps and bent to peer at two drawings spread in the dirt. "Why does this one look as if it's mostly water?"

"That's D'Chel's world. Because he controls illusion, no one really knows what it looks like. I was only there one time, and the trickery he churned up then was water, probably because he wrongly assumed dragons don't care much for it."

"What's this?" Aislinn squatted next to the other drawing. "It looks like you've drawn some kind of fort or collection of buildings with a dragon inside."

Fionn sucked in air loudly enough that Aislinn looked up at him. "What?" But he was focused on Dewi.

"Is that what happened to him?" he asked softly.

"Yes." Somehow, the dragon made that one word into a dirge.

Aislinn intuited the rest. "Your beloved is trapped on Perrikus's world."

"My consort, Nidhogg. I tried to free him, but I wasn't strong enough—and no one would help me." She shot a meaningful glance at Fionn, and a plume of flame rose from her mouth. The dragon shook her head hard enough to spew fire in a large arc. "That isn't our mission this time. If we try to do too many things, we will doom ourselves."

Aislinn stared at Dewi. "Wasn't Nidhogg a Norse dragon god?"

"Aye," Fionn answered. "Nidhogg was *the* Norse dragon god. There is no other. He was Guardian for the One Tree, the Tree of Life. It sundered and died in the years since his capture."

A ray of sympathy made a chink in the armor Aislinn had erected against Dewi. "How long has he been gone?"

"Many hundreds of years. Focus, child, ah, Aislinn. That isn't important." All wistfulness had fled from Dewi's tone. "Look here." She pointed with a talon. "We will enter Perrikus's world first from roughly this point. A dead forest there might provide some cover. Fionn and I will cast illusion to shield you and Rune."

"I don't need to be shielded." Rune's tail swished.

"Ye do if ye doona wish the dark one to know your mistress is close. He will sense her through you," Fionn said.

"If we come up dry in Perrikus's world and end up on D'Chel's, there used to be a good-sized island here." Dewi tapped the ground. "Goddess only knows what we'll find now."

"Um, how will we be able to tell if we're in the right place?" Aislinn looked from Fionn to Dewi.

"We won't until we search for Bran's and Gwydion's energy," Fionn replied. "It'll take time."

The dragon straightened. "You must not eat or drink anything in the border worlds, save what you've brought with you."

"'Twould be best if ye could avoid breathing as well," Fionn said grimly, "but I doona see how that would be possible."

"Things are not as they seem in the dark ones' worlds—" Dewi began.

"—which is why ye must trust what we tell you," Fionn finished.

"What about my magic?" Aislinn asked.

"Use it as little as possible," Dewi cautioned. "It will draw the dark to you like a beacon."

CHAPTER 8

$\mathcal{A}$islinn speared another piece of dried fruit with her fork and stuffed it into her mouth. She followed it with a spoonful of cooked grain. "Blech. I'm stuffed I can't eat anything else, no matter how long I have to live on short rations."

"Ye say that now." Fionn grinned at her. "Ye'll be hungry soon enough."

"Well, it's not as if we won't be taking food with us. Water will be more of a problem. It's heavy and we can only carry so much." She looked up from her bowl. "Do you think it would be safe to go to the back of the house to use the bathtub? Or maybe the one in the hall bathroom."

I doona know why anything would have changed...

Fionn got to his feet. "I'll go see how the energy feels. Even if things seem stable, I doona think it wise to dismantle my wards. Or for you to be where I can't lay eyes on you."

"Never mind." She stood and stripped off the same black sweat top and pants she'd worn since yesterday. "I'll take a sponge bath here in the kitchen at the sink. It's not as convenient, but I can wash my hair and the rest of me fairly well."

He watched the curves and planes of her body emerge, his breath quickening in his throat. Aislinn was the most beautiful woman he'd ever laid eyes on. Her red hair fell almost to her waist, and her golden eyes, like a large jungle cat, gleamed in the semi-darkness of the kitchen. He added a few lumens to his mage light. It flared upward with enthusiasm, just like other parts of his body were doing.

"Want a peep show?" She tossed a vixen's glance over one shoulder, yielding a tantalizing view of half a breast. "If you want to help, come warm the water after I get it in the sink."

His cock was already hard. It pressed against the tight fit of his battle leathers. Damn the woman. She always had this effect on him. They could be standing on the edge of the end of the world, and he'd still want nothing more than to sink himself within her and feel the heat of her body surround him.

"I can warm it from here, lass."

"Now what would be the fun in that?" Aislinn faced away from him, bent over the sink. She shimmied her bare butt, and the firm globes of her ass bounced slightly. He imagined taking her from behind. She was nearly as tall as he was, and while he loved the feel of her long legs wrapped around his hips, he thought he'd like sliding against the cushion of her butt nearly as well.

He cupped his erection and groaned. His breeches, tight to begin with, were almost painful, so he undid the lacings that held them in place.

"Water's still cold."

Fionn got to his feet and stepped out of his pants. Undoing more laces, he kicked off knee-high boots, then moved silently across the few feet separating them and wound his arms around her. His cock settled in the curve between her buttocks.

"I wondered what you were up to." Her voice was muffled by running water; soap sluiced through her hair and down the drain.

"Did ye now?"

Aislinn laughed. "Not really. Your voice sounds different when you want me."

Long, wet hair slapped him in the face as she tossed her head back. "Brrrr, lass. Your tresses are cold."

She turned in his arms. "Your own fault. I asked you to make the water warm." She ran her tongue over lushly pouty lips. "I can tell there's not much point in washing the rest of me until we're through here." Full breasts pushed against his chest; her nipples peaked into hard points of lust. She rubbed the mound between her legs against him and captured his cock in both hands. Her skin took on a rosy glow, and her breathing developed a breathy edge.

He closed his hands over her ass and pulled her close, settling his lips on hers. She always tasted wonderful, spicy and mysterious, like a fine, well-aged mead. She opened her mouth to him, and he sank his tongue inside. She sucked on it. His cock twitched in her hands, where it was sandwiched between them.

"What are you doing? It's nearly time to leave," Dewi's voice sounded in his mind.

"Leave us alone," he panted. *"Just for a few minutes."*

Aislinn pulled away from their kiss. "The dragon?"

He nodded.

She tossed him a grin worthy of Aphrodite. "Let go of me." Turning away from him, she leaned against the kitchen counter, spread her legs, and arched her back.

The invitation was unmistakable. Fionn surged forward and buried himself to the hilt. He filled his hands with her breasts and rubbed small circles around both erect nipples. She moaned and shoved back against him, dropping a hand between her legs. He felt the motion where she fondled herself. It excited him beyond reason. He drew back and thrust himself home over and over. His cock had never felt so hard—or so needy. He heard himself cry her name.

He let go of one breast, shoved her hand aside, and worked her clitoris between thumb and forefinger. Her muscles clenched around him. He knew how close she was by the tension in her body and the ruddy hue dappling her skin. Good thing, because his own orgasm was nearly there. He rode a fine edge of control and rubbed her harder as he plumbed her from behind. She shrieked and drove her ass back into him. Her body bucked, and Fionn let himself go. Iridescent lights filled his vision as he shot into her, stunned by the violence of his climax.

They sank to the floor in a tangle of arms and legs, gasping for air. He stroked wet hair back from her face. "*Mo croi*. I love you."

A crooked smile lit her features. "Oh you do, do you? Here I thought it was just my irresistible body."

"Aye, I love that, too." He ran a calloused palm down her face.

"If I can figure out how to stand, I'll finish my bath."

"I'll get travel packs ready for us. Seems Dewi's anxious to leave."

"It can't be midnight yet." Using his body for a ladder, she climbed to her feet.

"Nay, 'tisn't."

"I thought the whole point was waiting as long as we could for Arawn." Back at the sink, Aislinn wetted a dishtowel and rinsed water down her body, ignoring the puddles it made on the floor.

Fionn snatched up their clothes and piled them on the table to keep them dry. "It was. I'll go talk with her once I—" He snapped his fingers and looked at Rune, curled against one wall. "Where's Bella?"

The wolf glanced at him. "She told me she was leaving for a while."

Fionn narrowed his eyes. "When was that?"

"Before she flew out of the front room this afternoon."

"Were you planning to take her with us?" Aislinn asked. She'd shifted to drying herself.

Fionn shook his head. "Nay. Too dangerous."

"Maybe she knew and it pissed her off."

"Mayhap." Something needled Fionn, but he couldn't quite put his finger on what was wrong. It wasn't like the bird to desert him, even if she was angry. He chided himself for not noticing her absence before now as he shrugged into his clothes and bent to stuff dried fruit, nuts, and water bottles into their travel packs.

Aislinn was half-dressed by the time he blew her a kiss and said, "I'm going to talk with Dewi and try to figure out where Bella is."

"Maybe the dragon knows," Rune said, making a whuffling sound that might've been laughter. "She seems to have her claws into almost everything."

Fionn opened the back door to a cold, clear night filled with stars.

"It's about time," Dewi huffed. "Finally done rutting?"

"Where's Bella?"

"I was wondering when you'd notice her absence."

"Damn it." Fionn clacked his jaws together so hard they hurt. "I doona need a lecture. I need information."

"I'm right here." A darker shadow detached itself from the place between Dewi's wings, where Aislinn sat when she rode the dragon. "I'm going with you. The dragon said I could."

"Ye nearly died at D'Chel's hands when we first met Aislinn," he protested.

"I helped, too." The raven fluffed her feathers.

Not wanting to get into a pitched battle with the bird, Fionn switched gears. "Why do ye want to leave now?" he asked Dewi. "'Tis two full hours from midnight."

"Simple. I don't believe Arawn will return this night. I cannot sense him anywhere near. The more hours of darkness we buy ourselves, the better."

"'Twould be true," Fionn spoke slowly, "if time flowed the same in the border worlds as it does here. But it doesna do so."

"Tonight it will."

Fionn tried to push into Dewi's mind, but found it barred to him. "Ye know things ye're not telling me."

"Yes," she said simply, "I do. It's why I believe it wise to allow your raven to accompany us. If it were just you and me, I might have made a different choice."

"So long as ye brought Aislinn up..." Fionn spoke low and then switched to mind speech. *"If anything goes wrong and I tell you to snatch her and the wolf and return to this world, I expect ye to do so."*

"Has she figured out she's with child?" Dewi's eyes whirled.

"I doona think so."

"Why haven't you told her?"

Well, why haven't I? Fionn felt uncomfortable. *"I just figured it out myself a little bit ago. I've, ah, been waiting for the right time."*

"You're afraid she won't want the child and will destroy it." Dewi sounded smug.

"If ye know so much, why bother asking?"

"Hmph." A column of smoke rose from the dragon's nostrils into the sky.

"Aislinn, always Aislinn. What about me?" Bella sounded indignant.

Fionn cocked his head to one side. *"Since ye insist on coming, I assume ye'd wish to stay close to me, your bonded one. Yet, ye are still atop—"*

A cacophony of squawks cut off his words.

The back door squeaked on its hinges. Aislinn stepped onto the porch, and Fionn moved over to give her some room.

"I'm ready," she said. "I would've liked cleaner clothes, but at least these sweats are warm and serviceable. They're also good for traveling unnoticed at night."

"Excellent." Dewi's bottomless eyes reflected light from half a moon. "Get your things, ward the house against intruders, and we shall depart."

"I'll get Rune and the travel packs." Aislinn disappeared behind the door.

"I doona have a good feeling about this."

Bella landed heavily on his shoulder. Her taloned feet dug into his battle leathers.

"Nor do I," Dewi concurred. *"Yet, we have little choice."*

"What was that? I didn't catch it." Aislinn backed out of the house, dragging both packs. She hefted hers. "What'd you put in these? Rocks?"

"Water. The conversation wasn't important. Ye dinna miss much."

Fionn buckled his pack around his body and then helped Aislinn with hers. He cast a protection spell around the house that was a combination of warding and illusion. Hopefully, a casual passerby wouldn't even notice the house was there. Marta had warded it similarly. As he hurried through small, familiar tasks, he swallowed ambivalence over and over again. His intuition was rarely wrong, and it blasted him with klaxon horns. Each one said Aislinn should stay behind.

He glanced at the wolf. Rune felt something because his hackles were at half-mast. "Mayhap we ought to rethink this—"

"If rethinking translates to leaving me here, forget it." Aislinn hurried down the steps and stood next to Dewi. Rune followed her.

"*Leannán*—"

"We need to leave right now," Dewi said. "The time for talking has past. Now is the time for action."

Air currents shifted around Fionn as the dragon called magic. Bella jabbed him in the neck with her beak. "You heard Dewi. Unless you plan to use our own spell—and maybe come out in a different place—I suggest we join the others."

"Since when do ye call the shots?" The bird could be impossible. He recalled how much effort he'd expended ignoring her over the centuries. Fionn unclenched his jaws, strode down the steps, and placed an arm around Aislinn, taking care to position himself so Bella couldn't reach her. The bird had made every woman in his life miserable. Tara Lenear still hated the raven—and she was dead.

That's not important. I need to focus.

Dewi's magic intensified, and he added some of his own to the mix. He wasn't certain what they'd find and wanted to make the transition as easy as possible—and as safe, if such a thing were even doable.

"*Thank you,*" sounded deep in his mind from the dragon.

A portal edged with flame opened in the air. Fionn tried peering through, but all he saw on the far side was darkness. For just a moment, he wondered if Dewi was engaged in some treachery of her own, but he put a lid on his reservations. *If I canna trust the dragon, I canna trust anyone.*

"I will hold the gate," Dewi announced. "Hurry. This is taking more magic than I thought it would."

Keeping a firm hold on Aislinn, Fionn jumped through into absolute darkness. He felt Rune next to his leg. Bella clung to his shoulder. Rather than anger, the bird's death grip transmitted fear. They fell through an airless void that was so cold, icicles formed on his eyelashes and in his hair. He fanned warming magic to encompass them all, but he couldn't create oxygen where there wasn't any to begin with.

His lungs burned. If they stayed in this in-between place for very much longer, they'd all be dead. Aislinn's hand tightened on his. He wanted to reassure her, but there wasn't enough air to talk. He couldn't divert magic to use mind speech; there wasn't any to spare.

Fionn was just starting to conjure a counter spell to, hopefully, return them to Earth, when the darkness developed gray streaks. He sucked in a breath, gratified oxygen was returning to the atmosphere. It had a way to go, but at least his aching lungs eased a little. Gravity tugged and he fell faster. Fionn diverted the magic he'd called for his counter spell into a casting to weave air molecules together. The lower they got, the more substantial the cushion of air felt.

"Thank Christ I can breathe again," Aislinn murmured low.

"*Mind speech, mo croi.*"

"*Do you think Rune is all right?*"

"*I doona know. What happens when ye feel for him through the Hunter bond?*"

She made a disgusted sound. "*I'm not thinking here. Just a moment.*"

His body touched something solid, but softly, as if gravity were different here. The border worlds were never the same two trips running. Fionn hated them. If he spent too long on any of them, they perverted his magic and made him not care—about anything. He avoided them whenever he could.

"I am here." Claws clicking over granite sounded unnaturally loud nearby.

"Walk softly," Fionn urged.

Aislinn blew out a breath. *"Shit! That was much harder than I expected. Way worse than where Rune once took me."*

"'Tis likely because he dinna take you to one of the dark gods' lairs. There are border worlds other than the ones controlled by the dark."

Fionn looked around them. As Dewi had promised, it was night in this world, too. Dual moons rode side by side in the sky, casting the landscape in an eerie greenish glow. He stood on the edge of a hard-packed dirt plain with deep fissures in it. Behind them was a forest, but most of the trees were either dead or dying. The air held an unpleasant smell, rather like road kill left in the sun to rot.

Aislinn leaned against him. She trembled slightly and reached a hand to welcome Rune. The wolf shook himself, his amber eyes reflecting moonlight.

"Where's the dragon?" Bella asked.

"Hmph," Fionn snorted, his earlier suspicions racing to the forefront. *"Good question."*

"Look behind you."

Fionn spun. It was Dewi's voice, but he hadn't heard her land. *"I doona see how—"*

"Spell of absolute silence. It was why I had so much trouble with the gate and why it took so long to transit the boundary betwixt the worlds. When did you stop trusting me, Fionn?"

He recognized truth in her words and winced. *"Probably after ye coerced Aislinn into fucking the Minotaur. Doona fash, Dewi. I can lay it aside. We must be united, or we shall fail."*

"Agreed. I will shift the silence casting to one of invisibility with Aislinn at its core."

"*What's that?*" Aislinn sounded terrified. She twisted her head from side to side.

The ground vibrated beneath him about the same time he heard Aislinn's panicked mind speech. "*Quick,*" he sent. "*Into the trees. Invisibility spell or no, we canna hide on this plain.*"

CHAPTER 9

*A*islinn swallowed, but her throat was dry and scratchy. It was one thing to fight with just her and another human. Or just her and Rune. Fionn had been right when he'd made a bid for her to remain on Earth. They were too many. She didn't see how the five of them could do anything but fall over one another—and end up dead, or worse, captured. She remembered too late how she'd sent Fionn, Rune, and Bella packing so she could face D'Chel alone. It was easier that way. If she made any mistakes, she'd be the only one to suffer.

She tried to walk as noiselessly as possible, but it wasn't easy. The forest, such as it was, was full of dead, dry branches and choked with dense, crackly undergrowth. She had no idea what Dewi was doing. The dragon was far too large to wend her way through the path Fionn set for them. Aislinn wondered just how far the dragon's invisibility casting could reach.

Visions of Perrikus, with his waist-length auburn hair and green eyes, taunted her. Like all the dark gods, he was so beautiful it was hard to look at him. D'Chel's chiseled features cropped up next, as if to inquire, *what about me? I'm beautiful, too, aren't I?* He'd killed her father on that long-ago night in Bolivia. Silky dark hair flowed around well-defined muscles and bronzed skin. Copper eyes leered at her, and she realized her imagination had cast him naked; his substantial erection rose to mock her with its perfection. Against her will, her body started to respond.

Just like in the forest that day... Aislinn shoved the memory away. She'd come within a hairsbreadth of succumbing to D'Chel, and more than once. Shaken by how close she'd come to being lost forever, she focused on how cold he'd been and the nearly-too-late knowledge she'd freeze from the inside out if he touched her.

"Ooph." She bit off a string of curses and dragged her foot out of a tangle of roots. It throbbed and she knew she'd twisted it. Rune nosed her hand, urging her forward. *That's what I get for not paying attention.* She limped after Fionn and Bella. The pain was welcome because it drove D'Chel's sneering face—and perfect body—out of her mind.

Aislinn glanced around, grateful her hair was tucked under a hat. Dead branches were thick, and the forest had a rotten smell that hinted of dead things layered beneath her feet.

"This way," Fionn hissed. *"Pay attention."*

She stared through the murk. Fionn wasn't ahead of her anymore, and her throat tightened. *"Where?"*

"Half a dozen paces back, then hard right."

Aislinn knew how to follow a track, and she dunned herself for carelessness. Feeble light from the moons illuminated telltale pebble patterns and branch breakage. It was easy to see where she'd deviated from Fionn's route. *"Why didn't you say something?"* she asked Rune.

"I did. It was like you couldn't hear me. I was getting ready to bite you."

Great. Something about this place has me in its grip already. She shuddered. *"Fionn, wait."*

She slid under a thicket, trying to keep long thorns from catching in her clothing. The ground sloped downward until she entered a narrow fissure in a rock wall. The moonlight disappeared. Darkness enveloped her, and she inched forward by feel, hoping she wouldn't fall off the edge of something. She heard water dripping nearby, and the air felt heavy and damp. Fionn had led them into an underground cavern.

The faintest of lights flared ahead, illuminating Fionn with Bella on his shoulder.

"*Where are we?*" She covered the few feet to stand at his side.

"*'Tis a route I took once before. The air feels cleaner to me down here. We needed a place to regroup. I sensed something untoward happening to you, but there was naught I could do out in the open.*"

"*Where's Dewi?*"

Fionn shrugged. "*She can take care of herself. What happened back there?*"

"*My mind was suddenly full of Perrikus and D'Chel. They were all I could think about...*"

Fionn pounded a fist into his hand. "*Damn it all to hell. I was afraid of that. They know ye are here. Something about you draws them.*"

"*You don't know that. Not for sure.*" She felt unaccountably defensive. "*They probably figured we'd come after Gwydion and Bran.*"

"*All right. Then they see you as the weakest link. So ye are their target. Either way, 'tis far from good.*"

"*I thought Dewi made me invisible.*"

"*She probably has her own set of problems. Look...*" He drew her close. "*'Tis every person for himself on these worlds. The dark gods twist things so ye can scarcely believe your senses.*"

Aislinn pulled away. "*The less time we spend here the better. Have you figured out if Gwydion and Bran are even here?*"

He shook his head.

"*Our best bet is to split up. We can cover more ground searching that way.*"

"*Nay.*"

"*I didn't insist on coming to have you babysit me. Rune and I will be fine.*"

The wolf nipped her hand. "*Not so sure about that. You didn't hear me when I tried to tell you something.*"

Aislinn ignored him. *"Did we ever figure out what I felt just before we took off into the woods?"*

"Yes, a perversion of the Cŵn Annwn. The Wild Hunt. 'Tis likely where Dewi is. Drawing them off."

"But I felt the ground shake."

Fionn blew out an irritated breath. *"And just where do ye think the Hunt stays when they're not in the air?"*

"Oh."

"This is why ye canna go off alone. Ye doona know enough—" His blue eyes sparked in the dim light. He looked like he wanted to pick her up, toss her over one shoulder, and have done with any further discussion.

"Okay. Okay." She repressed her aversion to being ordered about. *"We're not accomplishing anything here. Let's get moving."*

"Aye, and we must hurry. Keep me in sight and keep up." Fionn turned and walked deeper into the cave, paying out just enough light for her to follow.

"Where are you going?" Aislinn demanded. She felt unaccountably peevish, maybe because her ankle ached. *"If you don't tell me, I'm not—"*

Bella cawed; the sound bounced off the cave's walls. *"We have been here before,"* the bird said. *"Trust Fionn. He will not lead you astray."*

It would be easier to trust him if he'd talk to me. Aislinn stalked after Fionn. She understood that part of her rotten mood was a manipulation of this place. Maybe Fionn was having the same problem.

She helped jimmy Rune through a narrow gap in the rock. It took her pushing at his hindquarters and him scrabbling at a rocky shelf with his front paws to get him past the barrier. Fionn must have turned sideways to navigate the slender arched opening, and even then it would've been tight.

His light flickered far ahead. She grasped the sides of the fissure, intent on following while she could still see something.

"Got you." An intransigent grip settled around her waist.

"Fionn!"

"Go ahead. Use your real voice. I've muffled your magic and made you invisible to him. He won't be able to hear you." A man chuckled menacingly.

Fear catapulted through her. She writhed against her captor, desperate to turn around so she could see who held her.

Rune howled. She heard him running toward her.

"Hmph. Hadn't counted on that creature of yours."

Hands lifted her; Aislinn flew through the air. She landed hard, breath knocked out of her. Gasping, she lurched to her feet and half-ran toward the opening Fionn and Rune had gone through. A man stood between her and it, faced away from her. His broad shoulders blocked her view, but the long black hair was unmistakable. D'Chel. This must be his world.

Rocks ground against one another as the gap closed. Her skin tingled unpleasantly while D'Chel pulled magic, and she hurled herself at his back. Aislinn clung like a wild thing, scratching and biting. She had to keep Rune safe. The dark god could kill her wolf with a thought. She'd just reached around and dug her fingers into D'Chel's eye sockets when the man's body began to change beneath her.

D'Chel, god of illusion, was shucking his human form, probably in favor of something with scales or a thick coat she couldn't injure. "Noooooo," she shrieked. "Nooooooo."

Reptilian scales thick with slime cut her hands. Aislinn ignored the pain, but slick muck coating the scales did her in. No matter how tight she held on, she still slipped backward, hitting the rocky floor of the cave hard enough to knock the breath from her lungs-- again. Since stealth didn't matter anymore, she leapt to her feet and threw her magic wide open. Despite what D'Chel had said, it burned bright within her. She called up a mage light and set wards about herself. Something that looked like a cross between a smallish dragon and a dinosaur spun to face her. Its scales were black, its whirling eyes copper, just like D'Chel's.

On the other side of the rock wall, Rune howled mournfully.

Thank Christ he's still alive. One less thing to worry about. She squared her shoulders and tossed her hair back. Magic pummeled her ward, but didn't come close to breaking it.

"Not possible," the dragonesque creature snapped. The air shimmered and the reptile turned into D'Chel again. "I muffled your magic."

Aislinn cocked her head to one side. "Well, it appears you didn't do a very good job. Now, what do you want with me?"

His perfect face broke into a smile, displaying very white teeth against his bronzed skin. "I'm not quite certain. Though with your spirit and your magic, you'd make a most excellent mother for my children." He snorted. "Once we abort the one in your belly, that is. Last thing we need is more Celtic god scum mucking up the works."

Her hands flew to her stomach. Shock roiled through her. "Y-You're mistaken," she stammered. "You're just saying that to throw me off guard."

He furled perfectly arched brows. "Since your magic is obviously intact, why don't you check for yourself?"

Aislinn's hands shook from more than fear. Was this why Fionn had asked about children so casually the other day? If what D'Chel said were true, no wonder Fionn hadn't wanted her to come along tonight. She girded herself and sent a tendril of Mage magic snaking inward. Tears flooded her eyes. *A son. I'm carrying Fionn's son. He must have known. Why didn't he tell me?*

"Ah." D'Chel's copper eyes stared right through her. "So you've discovered I speak the truth." He laughed in a macabre parody of mirth. "I don't always, but in this particular instance..."

"Shut up. Just shut up," she moaned.

He inclined his head. "As you will. I do not require talk. You have two choices, human woman. Come with me willingly, or I will bind you with magic and bring you along anyway."

"Where are you taking me?"

"That is none of your concern. Nor is it up for discussion. Your choice?" A flat coldness lay beneath his words, and his tone told

Aislinn now was not the time to try to bargain. No, she'd be well served to keep her options as open as she could.

"I will follow willingly."

He narrowed his eyes; she felt him probe against the edges of her ward and poured magic into it. "As you will," he said again. "No tricks. This is Perrikus's world. I am here at his behest. We knew someone would come for the two Celts we hold prisoner."

"Lead out." Aislinn clamped her jaws together and dug her nails hard into her palms. Seeking a calm center through pain, she pushed everything but the present moment from her mind. It was best that way. If she thought about Fionn or Rune, she'd fall apart. Never mind the child in her womb…

"Loose your ward." She heard the suggestion in her mind. It was seductive and thrummed with persuasion.

"Never."

Magic wove itself into hers. Hot, lusty, sensual magic. It seemed her ward was still intact, but hands settled on her shoulders. Her eyes snapped open. Aislinn didn't realize they'd been closed. D'Chel was inches away.

"Why the rush, little human? See. I remembered. I made my hands warm just for you."

She wriggled in his grasp. Her ward had altered to let him in. How the hell had he done that? "I said I'd go willingly, not that I'd—"

"Oh, but we both know you will. You don't have the strength to resist me."

He moved a hand to her breast. To her horror, her nipple pebbled under his touch. He caressed it through the thick fabric of her top. "See, you know you want me. You wanted me in the forest. I felt your desire. Smelled it just like I smell it now." He settled his lips over hers—warm, savage, demanding—and pressed his tongue inside her mouth.

Rune howled again. It gave her what she needed, and Aislinn wrenched away from D'Chel's grasp. "This will not happen," she spat through clenched teeth. "No matter how hot you make me, it will not happen." Her body vibrated with need. Her clit was on fire, aching for release. She stuck a finger in her mouth and bit down, welcoming the diversion pain created. It didn't quench the flames spiraling through her body, but it muted them a little.

"Look what you're missing out on." D'Chel moved his heavy silken robe aside. His cock, as perfect as the rest of him, curved upward against his belly. Just as in her vision earlier, his bronze skin glowed. He stroked his shaft, copper gaze never leaving her. "You know you want me. Would you like to watch me come? That should heat your blood."

"No." She couldn't look away, though. The sight of his perfect phallus mesmerized her. She wanted to touch it, taste it, feel it inside her body.

He laughed. This time, the sound was intimate and inviting. His hand pumped faster. The sound of his breathing drew her like a magnet. She took a step closer before she knew what she was doing. And then another. Her own arousal notched up. It was all she could do not to shove a hand between her legs.

"Go ahead," he panted. "Touch yourself. I like to watch, too."

Aislinn clasped her hands behind her back. Her pussy muscles clenched and clenched again. She was about to come where she stood, and there wasn't a damned thing she could do about it. Magic spun outward from D'Chel and snared her. His hand on his cock was irresistible. His balls snugged against his body. A satisfied cry and semen burst from him. At the same moment, her own climax rocked her.

Shame heated her face. Even though he hadn't laid a hand on her, she'd still been as good as unfaithful. He hadn't even had to touch her to make sexual heat flare so hot she couldn't make herself close her eyes. No, she had to watch him bring himself off. *Stop. Just stop. Castigating myself won't do a whit of good. This is what he wants. Me. Humiliated and beaten.* Aislinn sucked in a ragged breath. Her crotch was soaked.

"Well. You're quite the little hottie." D'Chel snugged his midnight blue robe around his slender waist and tied it with a blood red sash. He smiled provocatively. "Just think what we could accomplish actually touching one another."

Aislinn bit her tongue. Let him think he had her cowed. She'd bide her time. Fionn would figure some way to find her. So would Dewi. No way she'd let a second MacLochlainn woman escape her clutches.

"You said we were going somewhere. If it's all the same to you, I'd like to see just where that is."

"My, my. Not quite the post-coital talk I'd envisioned." He leered at her. "You're supposed to rave about my cock."

Aislinn gritted her teeth. "Um, yes, it's quite nice."

He sent an appraising glance skittering across the air between them. "If you think you'll outsmart me, human, think again. You caught Slototh by surprise. The rest of us pieced together what must have happened. You waited until he was vulnerable, lost in lust, and trapped him. It won't happen again." His voice rose, no longer sounding honeyed, and his copper eyes blazed with rage. "Bitch. I should kill you on the spot."

"What about my spirit? My magic? The children you want from me?" She struggled to keep her tone neutral, rather than mocking. Alarm and fear sluiced through her. She had to stay alive long enough to escape.

"We shall see." He gripped her arm and shoved her forward.

Aislinn warded her mind. It might not keep him out, but it was all she had. Her thoughts were a mixture of horror and hopelessness. D'Chel's rapid mood shift from sexual to feral was more frightening than anything he'd done from the moment he'd snared her. If she couldn't predict what he'd do next, she'd never be able to second guess him long enough to find a way out of his grasp.

I have to make him believe I won't fight back. It's my only chance.

CHAPTER 10

ionn gritted his teeth. Bella's talons raked his shoulder. Somewhere toward the front of the cavern system, Rune howled like a fey creature. The second D'Chel captured Aislinn, Fionn's mind had cleared. He didn't realize he'd been ensorcelled until that moment. He'd felt out of sorts, but had chalked it up to being anxious about getting in and out of the dark god's world as soon as possible. It was why he'd chosen the underground route he'd stumbled on years before. "Aye, and that time 'twas a safer alternative," he muttered. Fionn castigated himself for not tethering Aislinn to him, but realized he was wasting precious minutes.

"*Rune. Come.*"

The wolf trotted out of the darkness. "*Hurry. We must find a way out of here so we can rescue Aislinn.*"

"*What's wrong with the way we came in?*"

"*Blocked by rocks.*"

Fionn clacked his jaws together in frustration. "*Can ye sense her through the Hunter bond?*"

"*Of course. Can't you with your magic?*"

"*Nay.*" Fionn took off at a jog; he prayed the other end of the cave system was still open. It was a stroke of luck that Rune's link to

109

Aislinn was intact. D'Chel probably hadn't factored that into his plans.

Two more long, looping bends, and he came to a large cavern with an underground lake. The way out was on the far side of the water. He added a few lumens to his mage light, but he still couldn't see the tunnel on the far side that should lead to freedom. The water was murky, and he didn't even want to consider what might be hidden in its depths.

Rune lifted his muzzle and sniffed.

"Can ye smell different air currents?" Fionn asked hopefully.

"No."

"Ye should use mind speech—"

"Why?" the wolf broke in. "They already know we're here. If they didn't, my howling back there would have alerted anyone who wasn't already certain."

"Good point." Fionn stroked Rune's head. "May as well save magic for what's important."

"I'll go look for that way out we used last time." Bella launched herself from her perch on his shoulder and flew across the dank pool.

"Doona be long." Fionn shone his light after her, then remembered her exceptional night vision and dialed it back.

"What do we do if there's no easy way out?" Rune asked.

Well, and what do we do? "I could use magic to move the boulder blocking our egress. It would be faster to jump us out of here, though."

"If you can do that, why are we wasting time hunting for a way out?" The wolf's tone was plaintive.

"Because I canna determine exactly where I will bring us out. I may jump us right into a trap."

"Where's the dragon? Maybe she could move that rock."

Good question. "I doona know."

"Can you call her or something?"

Fionn clamped his jaws together so hard they ached. He considered slapping himself to urge a return of rational thought. *I'm still not thinking straight.* "Aye, Rune. I'm ashamed I dinna already do that."

Bella's winged form flapped toward them. "It's no good. Someone shoved a boulder into that tunnel, too. It happened a long time ago. The earth didn't smell freshly disturbed." She reattached herself to his shoulder.

At least we dinna swim across that hideous-looking water for naught. Fionn threw his mind wide open. *"Dewi!"*

"Where the hell are you?" she asked crossly.

"Trapped in a cave system. Boulders are blocking both exits."

A long hissing sound filled his mind. Dewi was obviously annoyed and trying to keep it under wraps. *"Do you sense where I am?"*

Fionn sent magic spiraling outward. *"Aye."*

"Jump to me."

He buried his hand in Rune's ruff and called the casting. His magic was sluggish now that he asked it to actually do something. Fionn poured double the amount of power it normally took into the spell. He did not want to get stuck in some unspeakable in-between place. The unnaturally still air in the cavern shimmered and then stilled. "Come on, goddammit," Fionn growled. He chanted aloud to strengthen the binding.

After a pause so long he was certain his magic was too weak to transport them out of the cave, the air brightened. Fionn gave it everything he had. In a far corner of his mind, he was horrified it took so much effort to produce a trivial spell. He felt a familiar tightening in his gut and knew they'd be out of the cave in seconds. Whether they'd come out next to the dragon remained to be seen.

Everything went dark for the few moments before Fionn plunged through a portal. Sharp rocks sliced into his battle leathers. He fetched up against something that didn't yield and scrambled to his feet, hands raised to call magic—if he had any left. Defying both motion and gravity, Bella still clung to his shoulder. Barely visible in moonlight filtered by dead branches, Rune rolled out of the opening. Fionn barked a command to close it and scanned a small clearing in the dead forest. It was still night, though he didn't see how it could be, unless nights lasted far longer here than on Earth. Where was the dragon?

"Right in front of you." Her voice dripped scorn. *"You ran into me. I realize this place addles you, but why in the goddess's name did you close off the portal before Aislinn had a chance to emerge?"*

Rune leapt to his feet. He turned in the direction of Dewi's voice. "My mistress has been taken."

"Use mind speech," the dragon snapped.

"But Fionn said—"

"Yes, and his decisions have been so stellar of late that you're willing to follow them?" Steam jetted from a patch of darkness. The dragon had cloaked herself just as she'd said she would. A long-taloned foot emerged from the blackness and pounded Fionn's chest. *"How could you have lost Aislinn? And the child."*

Fionn opened his mouth.

Before he could say anything, Dewi jabbed him again. *"Never mind. Who has her? Perrikus?"*

"D'Chel," Rune answered.

"Pfft." More steam. *"So both those bastards are here."*

Fionn gathered his scattered wits. *"I want you to take Rune and Bella and—"*

Rune's teeth closed around his calf. When the wolf released him, he said, *"I am not leaving without Aislinn."*

"I am not leaving you," Bella chimed.

Fionn rubbed the bridge of his nose between thumb and forefinger. *"'Twould be easier for me were I by myself—"* he began.

"Too bad," Rune snarled.

Bella didn't bother to talk; she just pecked the side of his head.

"You waste time," Dewi said. *"Do any of you have any idea where Aislinn is on this infernal world?"*

"*I know exactly where she is,*" Rune replied. "*The Hunter bond is... different here, but I can still sense her.*"

"*Which way and how far?*" Dewi asked.

Rune inclined his head. "*That way. I have no way to measure distance, but perhaps the time from the sun's rise to when it sits high in the sky.*"

"*She canna be six hours away.*" Fionn's eyes widened.

"*Of course she can,*" Dewi retorted. "*The dark ones use magic to travel, too. All of you, on my back. They already know we're here—*"

Fionn shook his head. "*Nay. No point running off half-cocked. We must have a plan.*" He drew in a tense breath. Aislinn's survival depended on them. If they blew it, she wouldn't get a second chance. He thought about his child and forced his mind away from dangerous territory. D'Chel would kill it where it grew in Aislinn's womb. Mayhap he already had...

"*Stop feeling sorry for yourself,*" Dewi hissed. She hooked a talon through his sleeve hard enough to draw blood.

"*Stay out of my head.*" In a blinding moment of reckoning, Fionn understood how Aislinn felt when he helped himself to her thoughts. He vowed never to do that again and prayed he'd have a chance to follow through.

"*I will do what I think best,*" Dewi informed him. "*In terms of a plan, I already have one. We will jump to within easy striking distance. Once we're there, if I can overfly where Aislinn is sequestered, it will make our task easier. Once we see what we face, we can plan further.*"

"*If they're here, Gwydion and Bran might be able to help, so long as there was some way to reunite them with their bodies...*"

"*I'd considered that,*" Dewi said. "*They're both here, yet I have no idea how to use that to our advantage. The body's owner must summon it. For that, his magic must be intact.*"

"*Let's go,*" Rune shouted. "*We can talk while we travel.*"

"*No,*" Dewi countered. "*We cannot. It will take all my concentration to maintain my invisibility spell and fly.*"

"If I cannot talk with you, how will I be able to tell you where Aislinn is?" Rune asked.

"Come close, wolf." Dewi drew her foreleg back into the murk surrounding her.

Rune whined. He tucked his tail and slithered forward until the darkness around the dragon swallowed him.

"I can't believe you were so stupid as to lose Aislinn," Bella snarked in their private mind speech.

"What's it to you?" Fionn snarked back. *"Ye are so jealous of the lass, your feathers have developed a definite greenish cast. I canna imagine how ye'll be once the bairn comes. There'll be no living with you."*

"I like Aislinn." The bird was silent for a space. *"Since she came into our lives, you scarcely talk with me anymore, unless I ask you to. It's like I've become an inconvenience."*

Fionn opened his mouth to protest and then snapped it shut. Bella had a point. He'd been so entranced with Aislinn, he hadn't paid much attention to his raven. It hadn't helped that they'd been either under attack or on the run ever since he'd found Aislinn and Rune near his home in the northern Sierra Nevada Mountains.

He stroked Bella's feathered head. *"Ye make a good argument, bonded one. I'm sorry, and I will try to do better."* The raven leaned into his touch, which was always a good sign. *"Aislinn likes you. 'Tis not like it was with Tara."* Fionn wisely chose not to remind his bird that the war with Aislinn's mother had been mostly of her own making.

"Thank you." Bella pecked gently at his hand. *"I will try to do better as well."*

Rune materialized out of the dragon murk and stalked to Fionn's side. *"We have a workable arrangement. If I sense we are off course, I have Dewi's permission to tell her to land."*

Dragon laughter sounded in Fionn's mind. *"No, little wolf. You may ask me to land. No one tells me anything. We shall jump the first distance. Come within my shrouding."*

The first task was getting Rune onto Dewi's back. After he'd tried to leap and failed, Fionn stood behind him on Dewi's bent foreleg and pushed. The dragon's scales were sharp. They must've cut into the wolf's pads, but Rune didn't so much as whimper. Finally, Fionn was settled at the base of Dewi's neck, with the wolf sprawled in front of him. "Good job," he whispered into Rune's ear. "Would you like me to send a calming spell into your mind?"

The wolf's body trembled. *"Will it dull the Hunter bond?"*

"I doona believe so. Would ye like to experiment?"

"Oh, please." Dewi sounded exasperated. *"We won't be flying for this leg. It's easier for me to keep track of everyone if you're on my back when we jump."*

"I'll be fine." Rune's voice held a quiet dignity that made Fionn proud of him. *"Let's get going. We've wasted far too much time as it is."*

"There's a piece of wisdom." Dewi snorted and smoke plumed above them. *"Fionn. As you've figured out, magic is sluggish here. Link your mind to mine and share your power. We're going much farther than you did when you brought the animals out of the cave."*

SWEAT ROLLED down Fionn's sides, and he was breathing hard by the time they emerged from the portal. He barely had enough energy to speak the word to close off Dewi's and his combined working.

"Perfect," Dewi crowed.

Fionn gazed about them. *"Which way is Aislinn?"* he asked Rune.

"In line with Dewi's nose." The wolf started to sit and then apparently thought better of it. *"We are closer to Mistress, but not as near as I thought we'd be."*

"Why is that?" Fionn asked. *"I doona understand."*

"You will," Dewi trumpeted in mind speech.

Fionn put his hands over his ears and then realized it was pointless since the sound came from inside his head. The dragon was up to something. He recognized it in the tone of her voice and the set of her head on her long, sinuous neck. He blew out an annoyed breath. *"You've detoured to free Nidhogg. Damn it!"* He pounded the side of Dewi's neck with his fist; her scales stabbed him.

"We are much nearer Aislinn." Dewi sounded indignant. *"We've closed the distance by at least half. We need my consort. He's a magician."*

"Dewi." Fionn chose his words with care. *"For all ye know, he's weakened beyond measure by his years of imprisonment."*

She lapsed into Gaelic.

"Aye," Fionn replied. *"Now ye mention it, I sense his energy, too. All it means is he yet lives."* He shut his mouth before the rest of what he wanted to say leaked out. It wouldn't do any good to argue with Dewi. She'd convinced herself that her course of action was the soul of altruism. For him to point out she was being selfish and putting them all at grave risk wouldn't buy anything but ill will.

He gauged the distance to the ground. It was a long jump for Rune. *"We are getting down,"* he told the wolf. *"If ye wait for a moment—"*

Rune gathered his haunches under him and launched himself off Dewi's back. He landed solidly and loped to a nearby tree. Fionn climbed down, not wanting to waste magic if he didn't have to.

"Wait for me here," Dewi instructed.

"I don't care what you choose to do." The wolf looked pointedly at Fionn. *"I am going after my bondmate."*

"It's best if we don't split up." Dewi, obviously anxious to depart, furled her wings.

"You are the one who is leaving," Rune noted scornfully.

Bella quorked her agreement, but softly.

"Enough." Fionn squared his shoulders. *"Rune is right. We three will go after Aislinn."*

"Understood. Nidhogg and I will find you." Red, leathery wings beat the air, and the dragon disappeared in a cloud of smoke and magic.

"Just as well," Rune muttered. He nudged Fionn with his snout. *"This is why I do not trust her. Follow me."*

"Mind speech," Fionn reminded him.

Bella muttered incomprehensible Gaelic.

"I suppose ye have an opinion about Dewi, too." Fionn glanced at the raven, but she didn't answer. He took off after Rune.

He'd been following the wolf for about half an hour through country so open, it made the fine hairs on the back of his neck stand on end. The countryside was baked, cracked earth. No so much as an insect's life energy pinged back against his magic.

"Rune. Wait for me."

The wolf slowed from a lope to a walk, but didn't stop.

Fionn caught up. *"I doona like this. No cover. Tell me which way, and I'll jump us in small steps. Mayhap we'll find a place we aren't as exposed."*

"Will it be as fast?" Rune's tongue lolled.

"Faster." Fionn remembered his last jump out of the cave and hoped he'd told the truth. No time like the present to find out.

"I thought you said it wasn't safe because you can't see where we'll come out."

Fionn gritted his teeth. He wanted to growl his frustration to the skies. *"This isna safe, either. We could be beset from any side."*

"I would smell them long before they got to us."

"Would the two of you stop arguing and do something?" Bella snapped.

"Ye are correct. This is taking far too long." Fionn pulled magic and visualized them coming out a mile ahead along the same trajectory Rune had set.

The short jumps were harder in some ways. They took just as much magic and far more concentration to focus the spell. Fionn stepped out of a portal, noting with satisfaction that another dead forest rose around him. He turned to help the wolf out, but Rune sprang past him, raced to the base of a tree, and lunged at something. Bella left his shoulder and flew into the trees.

Fionn peered ahead through narrowed eyes. The animals sensed something. Why didn't he? It must be the portal. His magic was tangled up in it. Normally, that wouldn't have mattered, but on this world, it did. He closed his working.

Danger hit him between the eyes. Adrenaline surged. Fionn

grasped at it like a drowning man. He was tired, and he'd take any edge he could get, because something ominous lay hidden in the woods, waiting for them. He raised his hands and lobbed magic at the trees, taking care to avoid Rune. He couldn't see Bella, but the raven could take care of herself.

The dark gods know I'm coming. They'll do everything they can to keep me away from Aislinn. Fionn stalked forward, his mouth twisted into a grimace. Power flowed from his hands. He'd kill anything that stood between him and his love.

Anything.

CHAPTER 11

*A*islinn paced from one side of her room to the other. She supposed D'Chel could have tossed her in a dirt-floored dungeon complete with rats. Instead, she was locked inside a relatively sumptuous, windowless chamber. Tapestries adorned two walls. For some reason, they were hard to look at for very long. Thickly tufted Persian rugs covered most of the stone floor. A tempting bed decorated with a multi-colored blanket sat against one wall. A chamber pot was in a corner. The only other furniture in the room was a table with two chairs. A pitcher of water and a plate of rich-looking biscuits were on the table. Dazed from her capture, she'd actually picked a biscuit up and lifted it to her mouth before she remembered the dragon's exhortations not to eat or drink anything.

"Could be a problem if I'm here very long," she muttered, staring at the biscuits.

She marshaled her magic and tried to jump herself out of her prison—again. It bounced back like a slap in the face. She patted the walls. Her magic seemed intact, so they had to be shielded in some way. She rifled through her travel pack and took a drink from one of her water bottles. D'Chel had been so preoccupied with something, he'd dumped her in the room and taken off without as much as a word. In fact, he hadn't spoken since their exchange in the cave. The magic he'd called to transport them hadn't taken very long, but since she didn't understand the dark god's magic, she had no idea how far she was from where she'd left Fionn and Rune.

Aislinn sat on the floor, leaning against a wall. She needed energy, so she munched on nuts and raisins while her mind raced.

I have to get out of here.

Yes, but how?

She closed a hand over her belly. Aislinn hadn't allowed herself to think about her baby. She tried to tell herself it wasn't a good idea to think about him now, but the door in her mind was already wide open. A rush of love so intense it brought tears to her eyes undid her. It wasn't just her anymore. She was responsible for her son's life as well. The hand over her stomach curled into a fist. She squeezed so hard, her nails cut into her palm.

If Fionn would've told me, maybe I'd have had the good sense to stay behind.

"Oh, stop." She spoke aloud to steady herself. "No point in blaming him. It's my body. I could have figured out I was pregnant." Aislinn blew out a breath, and then another. Pregnancy had never occurred to her. She'd had the occasional bout of unprotected sex before and she'd never conceived. Why now?

Her eyes pinched into narrow grooves as she answered her own question. Though she saw him as human, Fionn was a god. Among other things, that meant he could control things like which of his sperm created new life. Aislinn bit her lip. He'd told her as much before, which clinched it.

He might have consulted me.

Well, he didn't. I need to pull my head out of my ass and find a way out of here. If I want to yell at him for taking one more thing for granted, I have to free myself.

She shook her head, feeling disgusted and taken advantage of. Between Fionn and the dragon, she was just about done trusting anyone. She scanned the tapestries, her gaze drawn to them almost against her will. They weren't as difficult to focus on from a distance. If she tilted her head and aimed a thin beam of Seer magic, runic writing scrolled across them.

Aislinn scrambled to her feet and walked closer. Something about the tapestries gave her a headache. She examined the script. It was an obscure language, one she'd never seen before. The pounding in her head intensified as she got closer, which suggested the runes were spells.

She snapped her fingers. "That's it," she murmured. "I'll bet that's why my magic won't work to get me out of here." She'd just dragged a chair over, intent on pulling the thick, woven fabric from the walls, when she heard movement outside. Rather than standing on the chair, she sat on it and folded her hands in her lap.

The door slammed against its stops. Perrikus and D'Chel sauntered into the room. Fear twisted her gut into a tight knot. The door stood open behind the dark gods, and she gauged her chances of making a run for it. Not very good. She'd have to kill both of them, not an easy task. Impossible if she listened to the Celts or the dragon.

I'll be damned if I let those bastards turn me into a mindless pawn. A plucky part of her raced to the fore, but Aislinn stomped on it. *It's two against me. I need to look cooperative. Throw them off guard. Once they leave, I can—* She warded her thoughts.

"Just as delectable a morsel as you were the last time we met." Perrikus strode to her and ran his hands through her hair. His auburn locks flowed around him. Green eyes gleamed like exotic gemstones. He had an unusual, musky scent that reminded her of incense. He glanced over a shoulder at D'Chel. "I still think we should share this one."

The other god narrowed his coppery eyes and barked something in a language Aislinn didn't understand.

Perrikus laughed, his lush lips framing perfect teeth. "Mayhap she will be a spot more cooperative with one of us to corral her magic while the other enjoys her."

Aislinn jumped sideways out of her chair. She extended her ward so it covered her from head to toe. What were they expecting? That she'd just sit back and let them pass her between them like a trussed goose?

D'Chel rolled his eyes. "Oh, stand down. We're not planning to rape you on the spot." He licked his lips. "Not that we wouldn't like to, but we have other priorities just now. Like the trap we set for that pesky dragon."

"Yes," Perrikus broke in. "If we wait a bit, I'm certain that Celtic god who's besotted with you will show up as well. It will be a clean sweep. Then we can get back to the business at hand."

Aislinn forced herself to face them. She quirked a brow. "And what might that be?"

"Ensuring our dominion of Earth is complete. It's almost the only living world left. The rest of them look much like this one." Perrikus eyed her. "You're intelligent for a human. I'm surprised you didn't figure that out."

Maybe if I can keep them talking...

"The Lemurians painted you as the enemy. They duped the few of us who were left into believing we fought to oust you."

"We're still not entirely convinced—" D'Chel began.

Perrikus silenced him with a glance, but Aislinn understood well enough. "You're wise not to trust them," she purred. "They want Earth for themselves. You were merely a convenience to shore up their flagging power."

"How would you know that?" Perrikus asked.

She shrugged and wove a subtle *believe me* spell into her words. "Simple enough. There's a gateway to Taltos beneath the house I stayed in. I did a lot of eavesdropping."

D'Chel's handsome features twisted into a grimace. "How do we know you're not lying to us? Your mind is closed to me."

Aislinn smiled. "You don't. Here." She chinked her ward enough to allow him to find truth in her next words. "I killed my Lemurian mage lord; my wolf killed two others. I hold no allegiance to the Old Ones." She hesitated for emphasis. "I don't like being lied to —or used."

"We'll keep that in mind." Perrikus closed on her as if her ward wasn't there. She felt his magic weave itself into the fabric of her own, just before he tangled his hands in her hair.

Aislinn wondered if her mind was safe from intrusion, since her body certainly wasn't. She readied herself to pull magic. Anything to keep his hands off her. Fear set her nerves thrumming, and her heartbeat thudded loud against her ears.

"We don't have time for this," D'Chel snapped.

Perrikus moved from her hair to her breasts. The same sexual heat she'd felt with D'Chel rioted through her. He tweaked her nipples through the material of her top. Aislinn sank into a morass of lust. She wanted to chuck her clothes and beg both of them to take her. She could suck one while—

"Nooooo," she cried and whirled away from Perrikus. "No! Don't do this to me." She reached for her magic, intent on dishing out as much damage as she could. Something like an electric charge pounded into her. She flew through the air, hit the wall, and slithered to the floor, dazed.

Perrikus turned to face D'Chel. "Why in the nine hells—"

"Because the bitch was determined to kill you. You were so lost in rut, you weren't paying attention." D'Chel's gaze dropped to the erection protruding from Perrikus's robes.

Aislinn stared, too. The dark god's cock was huge and perfect; his bronze skin contrasted with the deep green of his silk robe.

"Hmph. She seems docile enough now. Mayhap betwixt the two of us—"

"Later." D'Chel's voice held a bitten-off tone. "Once we are certain we shan't be disturbed, we can hobble her magic and take our time." He dropped a hand to his crotch.

Aislinn remembered D'Chel stroking himself to a climax; she

wanted to see him do it again. She bit her tongue hard enough to hurt so she wouldn't cry out and tell him she had to see his cock. A perverse part of her wanted to see both gods naked, just as they'd been the night they crawled out of the earth in the Bolivian Andes. Such beauty should never be under wraps.

She shook her head, feeling sick and dizzy. The stink of their magic hung heavy in the room. They'd ensorcelled her to make her want them. *I've got to find a way to shield myself.*

"Come." D'Chel crooked a finger at Perrikus. "It is enough she realizes she's at our mercy."

"How could she think otherwise?" Perrikus snorted. "We never even bothered to shut the door. She understands escape is impossible." The dark gods lapsed into the language she didn't understand, went out the door, and slammed it behind them.

Aislinn's head ached. Her crotch was on fire. She sucked in a jagged breath and sent Healing magic inward. Thank God nothing was broken and her baby was all right. She got to her feet and took a few tentative steps. Nothing was twisted, either, except her foot from before she'd been captured. Her hand strayed between her legs, but she snatched it back. Maybe they had some way of spying on her. She would *not* give them the satisfaction of seeing how hot they made her.

As a diversion, she focused Healing magic on her injured foot and her throbbing head. She ate a little more and got herself some water before tackling the tapestries. They were attached to the walls by hooks; although, even standing on a chair, she couldn't reach them. She tugged at the fabric as hard as she could, but it didn't give.

Her breath rasped and echoed back to her. Sweat dribbled down her sides. The longer she wrestled with the tapestries, the surer she became that they stood in the way of her escape. Forced proximity to them made her feel ill. She had a knife in her waist sheath, but if she cut through the weave, it might alert Perrikus or D'Chel.

She scanned the room. Of course. She scrambled off the chair and moved the pitcher and plate off the table. It was heavy, but she managed to drag it beneath the nearest tapestry. She lifted the chair atop it and clambered up so she stood on the chair. *Yesssss!*

Aislinn curved her fingers around the back of the tapestry and lifted it carefully from its hooks. She took care to keep it flat while getting down. She'd roll it, but not until she had both of them down and was ready to test her theory. Because she had a system, the second tapestry soon lay on top of the first. She'd been anxious the dark gods would be monitoring the wall hangings, but each minute the door didn't fly open fueled her courage.

She got as far away from the woven fabric as she could and sent a cautious tendril of Mage magic outward. That was the magic she'd need to jump herself out of her prison. It didn't bounce back. Maybe she didn't need to roll the tapestries to cloud their magic.

Aislinn didn't waste time thinking. Heart pounding like a mad thing, she shouldered her pack and called magic, much more than she thought she'd need because of the way this world muted her power. It took two or three minutes to set up a jump. She was vulnerable during that time. If the dark gods caught her, the gig would be up. Her stomach twisted. For half a second, she was certain she'd puke and have to start all over again, since her heaving stomach would cut into her concentration.

Where am I going?

She needed to hold a destination in mind. Because it was the only place she knew on this world—and she would not leave without Fionn and Rune—she held an image of the entrance to the cave where D'Chel had trapped her.

Seconds ticked by. Aislinn was so rattled, it was hard to focus her Mage gift. The air shimmered; the walls of the room started to fade. She let herself hope she'd make it. It wouldn't take much more, maybe another thirty seconds.

In a dim corner of her mind, she heard angry voices shrieking and a door crash open. Then there was nothing but darkness as her jump spell transported her. Aislinn's heart seized. It was too close. They could track her magic and follow her. She had no way to abort the spell mid-jump. She tumbled out into dead vegetation and barked the command to close her portal before her feet totally cleared it.

She dove behind one of the boulders hiding the cave's entrance and hunkered on her haunches. Hands raised, she gathered defensive magic. No matter what came after her, she'd blow it to Hell and back. Throat so tight she could barely breathe, she squatted until her muscles screamed in protest. If Perrikus and D'Chel were going to follow her, surely they'd be here by now.

Aislinn stood and shook out her legs until the pins-and-needles sensation subsided. She dropped her hands and let her magic dissipate. Defensive magic was for use in the now. Holding it in abeyance exhausted her. She shucked her pack, got a drink, and scanned the forest, magic senses on high alert. Nothing. She blew out a relieved breath and then kicked herself.

"Who am I deluding? They can find me anytime they want," she muttered. "It's their world, their home court. My energy sticks out like a sore thumb here."

Where were Rune and Fionn? For that fact, where was Dewi? Aislinn supposed they were hunting for her. She could find Rune through the Hunter bond. If she was correct and the dark gods could trace her as easily as a dog locating a long-since-buried bone, projecting her magic wasn't a risk.

They'll come for me when they're good and ready. Not a moment sooner.

Aislinn slid her pack over her shoulders and walked in a tight circle, hands clasped behind her back. She clicked through what she knew. It had taken a lot of magic to jump and even more to hold a defensive stance as long as she had in front of the cave. If that hadn't drawn the dark ones to her instantly, perhaps the Hunter magic wouldn't, either.

She, Fionn, and Rune were far stronger together than apart. Aislinn paid out Hunter magic. *"Rune."*

"Mistress." His voice in her mind was so welcome, tears gathered.

"I am back at the cave."

"You must come to us. Fionn is injured."

"What? How?"

"Just come."

Aislinn locked the coordinates in her mind, pulled Mage magic, and jumped. She rolled out onto heaps of dead animal bodies.

Rune jumped nimbly over them and licked her effusively. *"Shut the portal,"* he growled, *"then follow me."*

Should've secured it the second I was out.

Aislinn closed her casting and sprinted after the wolf. Bones snapped under her boots. She didn't take time to examine the dead things; it was enough they were no longer a threat.

Fionn sat propped against a tree bole. Bella clung to his shoulder, her sleek, feathered head leaned against him. Blood streaked his face and hands. *"Mo croi. Mo croi. I've been working on Healing myself, so we could go after you, but 'tis been slow going."*

He opened his arms. She dove into them, and they closed weakly around her. Love made her throat thick. She wanted to cling to him and never let go. Tears threatened to spill over, but she squeezed her eyes shut to push them back.

"I am glad you are here." Bella sounded far more formal than usual.

No time for this. Got to move fast before they find us.

Aislinn started to ask what happened, but it didn't matter. Not really. Fionn needed to conserve what little energy he had. The important thing was they were together. She drew back from his embrace and sent Healing magic into his body. The small bone in his right arm was broken. She instructed the bone ends to knit together and did a quickie patch-up job on the worst of his abrasions while Rune sat guard.

"It's amazing they haven't come after us," she said.

"Aye, 'tis the same thing I thought." Fionn laid a hand on her arm.

"Where's Dewi?" Aislinn scanned the sky, which had shaded to a sickly gray. Morning must be coming—finally.

"That meddling turncoat went after her mate," Rune growled.

"She hadn't seen him for hundreds of years," Bella protested, defending the dragon.

"Doona be concerned. We can leave without her, but not without Gwydion and Bran." Fionn got to his feet. *"Thank you, léannan. I feel whole again."*

"What are these things?" Aislinn kicked at the piles of furred bodies.

"I doona know what they are called, but they were out to kill us. As ye can see, they wouldna have been much of a challenge had there been but a dozen or so. When they numbered in the hundreds, they were more difficult to deal with."

Aislinn turned one over with the toe of her boot. It looked like a large beaver, but with double rows of razor-sharp teeth. *"Wonder where they came from? I haven't seen so much as an insect here."*

"It doesna matter—" Fionn's head snapped up; he inhaled sharply. *"Damn it! Aislinn, behind me."* He spun and raised his hands to call power.

Rune faded from sight. The dark gods' trickery pummeled her. She couldn't see them, but they had to be close. Aislinn drew magic and readied herself to fight. She wanted to talk with Fionn about their child, but now wasn't the time.

ionn glanced to see if Aislinn had followed his directions. Not exactly. She was off to one side. He could shield her more effectively if her body was behind him. He set his jaw in a determined line. The odds weren't good if Perrikus and D'Chel both showed up, particularly since D'Chel had tried to claim Aislinn for his.

We're not so different as all that. He sees her as his. I see her as mine. Were it just the two of us, 'twould be a fairer fight.

Bella's claws dug into his shoulder. The bird was frightened, but she'd lay her life on the line for him. She'd done it before. He wanted to comfort her, but couldn't divert his attention. The air fairly crackled with dark magic. It made the fine hairs on his arms stand on end.

"*Ye must do what I tell you,*" he said.

"*Who are you talking to?*" Aislinn's voice held a definite edge.

"All of you. Where's Rune?"

"*He can take care of himself. He has this thing he does where he can hide—*"

"*Sssssht. Enough,*" Fionn hissed. "*Stand ready. They will be upon us verra soon.*"

"There they are." Perrikus's musical baritone boomed from behind Fionn. He whipped about and raced forward so his body was still between Aislinn and the dark gods.

"And just as stupid as they ever were." D'Chel flickered into view. "Squandering power on mind speech. Tch. Tch. As if we couldn't locate alien magic on our own world."

Fionn bit his tongue and locked his gaze onto the two dark gods. Arrogant and overconfident as usual. There had to be a way to use their conceit to his advantage.

Perrikus strode forward. "A bit on the quiet side today, Celt. Something bothering you?"

Fionn spat into the dirt. "This whole world bothers me. Ye've managed to kill it. Last time I was here, at least a tree or two still lived."

"Really?" Perrikus shrugged. "I hadn't noticed."

"Ye will once there's nothing left to breathe. The air's already depleted."

"No concern of yours. There are other worlds if I choose to abandon this one."

Fionn shifted from foot to foot. Perrikus was up to something. It wasn't like him to engage in idle conversation. He pushed against the dark god's mind, not surprised to find it shuttered.

The god's green eyes blazed. "Do not anger me, Celt. You will regret it. The only reason you yet stand is because I—rather we"—he gestured toward D'Chel—"offer you a bargain."

Fionn drew himself up and squared his shoulders. He had a feeling he knew what Perrikus had in mind. He hoped Aislinn had the sense to ward herself, but didn't want to chance mind speech. "I doona bargain with evil."

D'Chel barked a wicked laugh and glanced at Perrikus. "I told you this would be a waste of time. The lot of them are too stubborn to recognize when to stand down." He moved next to his fellow god. "Let's get this over with, so we can see which ship will leave port."

Fionn's lips curled into a sneer. "Let me guess. The offer is Gwydion and Bran in exchange for Aislinn."

"Now that you mention it"—D'Chel rubbed his hands together —"that's exactly what we had in mind. Simple, elegant. No blood. No one gets hurt—"

"Bullshit." Aislinn's clear voice rang out. "I will die before I spend another second with you."

"You liked me well enough when I had my cock out in the cave." D'Chel grinned and licked his finely chiseled lips. "Couldn't tear your eyes away, as I recall." He shifted his attention to Fionn. "Why, she was so excited watching me, she even came. She smells so sweet. I can hardly wait to—"

Pressure built inside Fionn's chest until he could scarcely breathe. The thought of Aislinn engaged in any sort of intimacy with that monster was intolerable. Magic flew from his fingers and bounced off D'Chel and Perrikus.

"Bit of a short fuse, eh?" Perrikus nudged D'Chel, who laughed. He chucked his auburn hair over his shoulders and turned to Fionn. "This is why we offered a bargain. We could stand here for hours trading pot shots. Eventually, D'Chel and I would prevail because we are stronger, but why waste the energy?"

"I'd much rather save it for the woman." D'Chel winked lewdly at a point behind Fionn's shoulder.

"What about the dragon?" Fionn shifted gears. He needed to buy time so he could think. Perrikus was partially correct. A pitched battle would last for a long time and end in a stalemate at best.

"What dragon?" Perrikus asked. "The one you brought with you won't be a problem quite soon."

"Nay, the one ye've held prisoner these long years."

"Ah." D'Chel nodded. "He means *that* dragon. No, he's not part of the bargain."

Truth hit home. "You've been draining his energy to maintain yourselves here." Fionn sent a faint prayer Dewi's way. Mayhap she'd been wise to go after Nidhogg after all. If she was successful, his absence would weaken the dark ones' toehold on this world.

"Would ye consider adding him to the deal?"

Aislinn's energy burned behind him. He wished he could reassure her he was engaging in a stalling tactic, but her hot temper beat him to it. "If you all think I'm just going to stand here while you haggle over me like a tethered piece of meat, think again," she bellowed.

The air currents canted crazily. Aislinn was about to engage the dark ones in a full-out war. *"No!"* Fionn screamed. *"Doona—"*

"For all the help you've been, you can damn well shut the fuck up," she snarled. Killing blows flew from her hands. One missed him by an uncomfortably narrow margin.

Fionn dropped back to her side. The die was cast. There was no going back. He'd stand by Aislinn's side until they won. *Or until the two of us are dead.* He joined his magic to hers, grateful she didn't waste power shutting him out. Aislinn's temper was a thing to be reckoned with.

Dark magic sizzled against his wards, and he strengthened Aislinn's. "Don't bother," she panted. "Both of them can penetrate my wards. Besides, they want to fuck me, not kill me. Save your magic to defeat those bastards." Light erupted from her hands. "Earth magic is weak here. Quick. What do I do?"

"Use air. Blend in fire." Fionn experimented with different proportions to see which would be strongest. No matter what he hurled at Perrikus and D'Chel, it bounced off their wards. Nothing constructed from materials on this world could injure them.

Fionn maneuvered Aislinn and himself a few yards away so the dead forest was at their backs. He wondered again what had become of the wolf. Bella hadn't left his shoulder, which was good. Enough magic boomeranged through the air to kill her if she left the protection of his wards.

"This isn't working." Aislinn heaved more magic. "We'll be worn out, and they'll still be standing there grinning at us like a couple of gargoyles."

"Not necessarily—"

"I'm going to try something while I still can." Fionn clamped a hand around her wrist. "Don't you dare get in my way." She twirled away from him, her golden eyes on fire.

He wiped blood off his forehead. A trickle of the dark gods' magic had seeped through his wards. It was only a matter of time until the four of them dropped their shielding and got down to the business of annihilating one another.

Aislinn pranced to one side. What the hell did the lass have in mind? She smiled coquettishly at D'Chel. "Come on, sweetie." She crooked a finger at him. "Want to have a little fun?"

The dark god's features clouded with confusion. He must have suspected Aislinn was up to something, but his arrogance got the better of him. He swaggered forward. "Come to your senses, have you, human?"

"Maybe. Not much point in slugging it out until all of us are trashed."

D'Chel stopped a foot from Aislinn. "I pointed that out quite a while ago. Does this mean you're ready to come with me?"

"What about the bargain you offered?" Aislinn edged closer.

Fionn's attention was glued to her, so he nearly missed a huge blast of magic that would have decimated his wards. He jumped to the side just as Perrikus's destructive power cut a swath two feet wide through dead trees. The racket nearly deafened him as they crashed against one another.

The dry grassland before him erupted in sparks. Aislinn had done something. D'Chel grappled with his throat as if he couldn't breathe. Rune raced from somewhere and knocked the dark god to the ground. Aislinn stood over him, hands raised, shrieking words in Gaelic.

Her accent was off. It took Fionn a moment to understand she was exhorting something to burst. *Och aye, she's doing the same thing she did to Slototh, trying to burst a blood vessel.*

Perrikus raced to the pair. A well-aimed kick sent Rune flying. Before Fionn could react, the auburn-haired god gripped Aislinn's shoulder and shook her hard. She dropped to the packed earth like a stone. Rune whined and crept toward Aislinn on his belly. He laid his body atop hers and snarled at the dark gods.

"If ye've killed her," Fionn screamed, "I'll not rest until ye're dead."

Perrikus sneered at him, bent, and laid a hand on D'Chel's head. The other dark god scrambled to his feet. "Stupid of me." Hate radiated from his copper eyes. He rubbed the side of his neck. "Bitch nearly had me."

"Yes, she did." Perrikus steadied D'Chel with a hand. "We killed her father. I remember the smell of his blood. It was the night we claimed Earth for our own."

"Interesting." D'Chel smirked. "We've expended far too much time on this little project. I say kill them now and be done with it. I don't need the woman. She's too much trouble."

Aislinn hadn't stirred. Fionn sent magic spinning toward her. *Thank bloody Christ, she's alive!* Inexpressible relief and a fierce protectiveness thrummed through him. He threw his body between her and the dark gods. By all that was sacred, he'd fight them with every resource he had. Gaia avoided the border worlds, but he called on her for help anyway. There was always a chance she'd hear him and come to his aid. Power flashed from his hands. D'Chel wasn't warded. His body vibrated from the impact; he swayed, but didn't fall.

Perrikus growled something in a guttural language. D'Chel pulled magic to shield himself.

Fionn heaved more power at them. For every blow he landed, two hit his wards. Sweat ran into his eyes and down his sides. The harsh sound of his breath was loud in his ears. Two against one was not good odds. *Doona think about that. Just fight.* He longed to go to

Aislinn, to hold her close, but he couldn't drop his guard. *"Take care of her,"* he told Rune.

"Should I drag her into the forest?"

Fionn considered it. *"Nay. We doona know how badly she's injured. 'Tis best not to move her until we know more."*

"Damn it." Perrikus's head swiveled. He gazed into the distance.

Fionn chucked power, dialing up the intensity. Maybe, if he could catch the dark one unguarded... Perrikus chanted in a language Fionn didn't know. A fiery portal opened. The dark god jumped through. As quickly as they'd appeared, the flames winked out. Fionn inhaled sharply and wished the air in this world were cleaner. His lungs felt dirty and constricted.

D'Chel eyed Fionn. "Looks like it will be just the two of us for a bit. Cozy, eh?"

"Why?" Fionn had a feeling he knew, but he needed a breather. Engaging D'Chel in conversation would kill two birds with one stone.

"My, um, colleague has gone to address a different problem. It would appear your Celtic dragon didn't cooperate with our plan."

Yesssss!

Fionn was exultant. He sent a silent prayer for Dewi's success. She was more than a match for Perrikus. "Really?" Fionn quirked a brow. "She doesna confide in me. I had no idea where she was."

"Lies," D'Chel hissed. "More lies. We"—he tapped his breastbone—"are supposed to be the cheats and liars, but we're slackers compared with you Celts."

"Hmph. I'll take that as a compliment."

Rune whined. Bella flew to him and bent her dark head over Aislinn.

"Is she worse?" Fionn asked.

"I don't know. It's hard to tell. Finish this, Fionn, so you can take her home." Anguish ran beneath the wolf's words.

A blast of sorcery grazed the side of his head, catching him by surprise. Fionn tried to pour power into his ward, but quickly realized he didn't have enough to both fight back and shield himself. In a split-second decision, he dropped his warding and went after D'Chel, magic running wide open.

Cuts opened all over his body. Blood dripped into his eyes. At least D'Chel looked as ragged as him. *If I could only disable him for a few minutes, I could jump all of us to safety.* It worried him that Aislinn hadn't moved. What had Perrikus done to her?

Fionn cast about for a solution. He had a small window of opportunity. Once Perrikus returned—assuming he did—the gig would be up. He'd be imprisoned right along with Bran and Gwydion, and Aislinn, and the animals were as good as dead.

D'Chel screeched something incomprehensible. He shook his fist at the sky and launched himself at Fionn. "It's just you and me, Celt," he growled. "Die."

Fionn twirled from his grasp. He redirected power and resurrected his warding. Hope burned bright. Dewi must have injured Perrikus. "I have no intention of dying," he snarled and raised his weary arms to direct magic. They were both near exhaustion. Maybe, just maybe, he'd get lucky.

CHAPTER 13

*D*ewi flew as fast as she could and still remain relatively hidden. The dark gods could scry where she was if they tried. Her lungs filled with tainted air. Until now, she'd taken care to keep the bottom half of her chambered lungs clear of what passed for an atmosphere, but the time for caution had passed. She would sacrifice herself if it meant Nidhogg could fly free.

Her hooded eyes flooded with sudden tears. They were the last of the dragons. She'd been warming a clutch of eggs when Nidhogg left on what both of them thought was a trivial mission. He'd merely planned to overfly the border worlds to help Gwydion map the location of each of the dark gods—and make certain none had escaped the boundaries of their worlds. Weeks passed. When he didn't return, she tried to contact him telepathically. He never answered.

Dewi snorted and steam plumed upward. It would be visible if anyone was looking, but she didn't care. She'd begged Gwydion and a few of the other gods to go after Nidhogg. Since no one could contact him, they were convinced he was dead and refused. It got harder and harder to spend her days sitting on her eggs. Young dragons took the better part of a year to hatch, which meant she had a couple more months to go. By then, Nidhogg might truly be dead.

One desperate spring day, Dewi made a decision that still haunted her. She'd left her clutch, knowing her brood would die, and gone in search of her mate.

It had taken years before she finally found him, alive but in a sort of stasis. When she'd tried to free him, the dark gods nearly captured her, too. Sore and weary, with rents in both wings, she'd made her way back to Inishowen. Surely the other Celts would return with her and help free her love. They hadn't. The Crusades had been in full swing, and non-Christian sects were under fire. Gwydion, Fionn, and the rest were fighting for the right to exist outside the *Dreaming*. They'd told her they were extremely sorry, but they had their hands full.

Fire streamed from her mouth. She was still angry with all of them. They had lovers and children; she had nothing and never would. She'd returned to her clutch of eggs. No one had disturbed them. Oh, how she'd keened over those eggs. Dewi's heart had broken when she looked inside each shell with magic; she'd castigated herself for abandoning her children while she ran off on a fool's errand. If she'd had even one youngling, it would have made such a difference.

She'd kept to herself for hundreds of years. It was a relief when Fionn assigned her to spy on the Lemurians from beneath Taltos… With a quick shake that rattled her scales, Dewi dragged her thoughts from the past.

She narrowed her eyes and peered intently ahead. Though still quite distant, Nidhogg's prison came into view. She remembered it well. The structure looked like an American fort out of their Old West. Built from large logs, it must've been constructed before all the trees on this world died. She reached out with her magic, but couldn't get near enough to sense how Nidhogg was guarded. She'd have to fly closer. The spell that hid her presence was a real power hog. It was hard to hold it in place and do much else.

She eyed a grove of dead trees and furled her wings. She needed to scope out what she faced before she marched in and tore Nidhogg's prison to toothpicks. If she made the same mistakes she'd made last time, she may as well have remained with Fionn, Bella, and Rune.

A flutter of worry for Aislinn nagged her, but she pushed it aside. The MacLochlainn had a competent warrior, a raven, and a wolf to rescue her. Dewi landed, settled her wings, and lumbered deep into what remained of an evergreen forest. It wouldn't do a very good job hiding her bulk, but she couldn't be choosy.

She dropped her shielding and sent a cautious spray of magic outward. Nidhogg's energy pulsed against it. Dewi's mind raced. *Maybe there's something I can do from here to destabilize the spell holding him.* She focused her magic and looked closely at the weave of the casting surrounding her love. It was much weaker than it had been a thousand years before. She clamped her double rows of teeth together. The dark ones probably hadn't so much as looked in on Nidhogg for a very long time.

She blew out a breath, careful to keep smoke and fire to a bare minimum. Fionn had been right about one thing. If it were possible to revive Nidhogg, he'd need food and water and time to regain his strength. Truth dawned. Assuming she could free him, her best bet would be to jump both of them back to Earth—immediately.

Damn it! I don't like those choices. It's much the same as when I left my younglings to go after my love. Fionn and Aislinn need me, too. She thought about the wolf and raven. They were self-sufficient creatures. No reason to waste time worrying about them.

Dewi sheathed her magic. She had what she needed. Her next move would be to dismantle Nidhogg's two prisons: magical first, then physical. She readied a casting and then hesitated. Abandoning Fionn and Aislinn didn't sit well. She didn't want another mistake like her clutch weighting her conscience for the next few hundred years. Options flashed through her mind. It might have been better to rescue Aislinn first. Then all of them could have freed Nidhogg and left this accursed place.

She shook her head; scales rattled. It would take too much time to go back, find Fionn, and do this over again. *No help for it. I will do what I can to free Nidhogg, transport him to safety, and then return here.* It was a relief to have arrived at a decision, though it felt flawed. The only way her plan could work was if Perrikus and D'Chel didn't attack. She was as vulnerable by herself as Fionn and Aislinn were. Dewi sent up a prayer to the goddess to watch over them all.

She crept closer to the building. At one point, the forest had butted against its back wall. She wanted to be as close as she could get. Once she severed the first thread in the weave holding Nidhogg ensorcelled, it would alert someone. She'd have very little time after that. Her ancient heart pounded in her scaled body.

I must do this right. I won't get another opportunity.

Dewi threw her magic wide open. She plowed through the casting holding Nidhogg and called to him. He didn't answer, but she hadn't expected he would. Fire blazed from her mouth. The dry timbers caught like a well-oiled torch. Fire wouldn't hurt Nidhogg. It might even help him remember what he was. Dragons had been conceived in fire when the Earth was young.

Dewi strode through the burning building. She kicked open the door to the back room where Nidhogg had been. Her second eyelid was closed to protect her from smoke, but she saw at a glance that the chamber was not only empty, but hadn't been occupied for eons. She trumpeted her dismay. *Where is he? I sense him. I unlocked the magic surrounding him. He must be here.*

An answering trumpet sounded weakly from below her. "What?" she shrieked. "Those bastards buried you?"

Dewi focused magic and blew a hole in the timbered floor. She kicked shards of wood out of the way with her powerful hind legs and sent more magic after her first blast. After a few tries, the opening was big enough. She fanned magic around the burning building. She wouldn't be able to fight while she was in the tunnel she'd just made. The dark gods must know what she was about. Why hadn't they interceded yet?

"Dewi." Nidhogg's dear voice, a voice she never thought she'd hear again, sounded deep in her mind. *"Do not come down here. I will crawl out."*

She tried to answer, but her emotions were too close to the surface. All she managed was, *"Hurry."*

A taint of evil cut through the smoke and fire. At least one of the dark ones was closing in on them. *"Hurry,"* she repeated. *"They come."*

Nidhogg snorted. He'd been a master of dry humor. That he could dredge it up now gave her hope. *"Of course they're coming. They laid this trap to snare you long ago. The only reason we've done as well as we have is because they're lazy bastards and didn't bother to renew the spell."*

A black-scaled snout came into view. Dewi bent and touched it with hers. She scrabbled in the hole for his taloned forelegs and tugged. *"I'm jumping us to safety."*

"Don't tell me. Goddess's breath, just do it." His green eyes whirled. *"I'm too weak to be much help in a fight."* Nidhogg dragged the rest of his body out of the hole. He tried to rise on his haunches, but fell back to the ground.

Dewi forced her gaze away. Her heart ached. Nidhogg's once robust form had shriveled; he was a third his former size. *"Fire is our friend. The dark ones will not be able to get too close."*

A blast of magic rocked her. How the hell? And then she realized the dark gods must be targeting them from outside the burning building. It wouldn't be hard to zero in on their energy. She summoned magic to jump them out of the inferno. She didn't need long, but there would still be an interval when they were vulnerable to attack.

"What are you waiting for?"

Dewi didn't answer. She clamped her long jaws together. There'd never be a better opportunity to injure whichever of the dark ones was close. *"Can you hold the traveling magic?"*

"Yes."

She shoved it off to one side, pleased when Nidhogg gathered it close. Dewi waited until the next jolt bounced off her scales. She judged its trajectory and sent a killing blow back along its path. She didn't hold back. She hit the dark god with everything she had. Part of her wanted to see what damage she'd done, but that was foolhardy. It didn't matter. He wasn't dead. No one killed the dark ones, but if she'd injured him, it would help Fionn and Aislinn.

She opened her mind to Nidhogg's, reclaimed the magic to jump them to safety, and set the traveling spell in motion. Soon, the smoke and fire fell away. The airless vacuum between Earth and the border world clawed at her lungs. She hoped Nidhogg was strong enough to withstand the journey, but there hadn't been any choice. Not really.

They rolled out into Marta's yard. Dewi had picked it because she hoped Arawn had returned. She'd stay just long enough to fill him in and get him to take care of Nidhogg. She wanted to screech her triumph to the skies. Finally. After long years and against steep odds, Nidhogg was free.

Arawn loped down the back steps before she had a chance to close off her traveling portal. "What's this?" he began, and then his dark eyes widened. "Och aye, and ye've brought Nidhogg home after all this time." Arawn bent over the dragon; his long dark hair mingled with Nidhogg's black scales. He laid gentle hands on either side of the dragon's head. "Aye, and he'll be needing food and water and Healing."

Relief made Dewi weak. For once, she'd guessed right. Someone would care for her love. "I must return," she said and hurriedly sketched out what had happened.

"I should go with you," Arawn murmured. "'Twill even the odds."

"Did you bring other gods from the Old Country?" Dewi scanned the empty yard.

"They are coming, but aren't here yet." Arawn thinned his lips into a hard line.

Nidhogg raised his head. Shakily, he used his forelegs to push himself upright on his haunches. "I understand, my love." Eyes like green pools shone at Dewi. "My safety is meaningless if you die on that world we just left. I would return with you, but I'd be naught but a liability." He inhaled deeply. "The air here is clean, clear of taint. If you could but settle me near fresh, clean water and perhaps lay a bit of food nearby, I will be fine until you return. Or until the other gods come."

Arawn nodded. "Let's do that. A spring is verra close. Ye will be comfortable there. The grass is soft and fragrant. I doona know about food." He eyed Dewi.

"Meat," she said succinctly. "He needs meat."

"Simple enough. I shall beg the goddess's pardon this once and use magic. Game is plentiful here."

It took a while, but between the two of them, Nidhogg rested comfortably next to water, with several dead deer near to hand. He bent his head and drank long and deep, then looked up. "By the time I work my way through what you've left for me, I shall be strong enough to hunt on my own." His second eyelid covered one lambent eye. It took her a moment to understand he'd just winked at her.

"I love you," Dewi murmured. "Grow strong."

"I never stopped loving you," he said simply. "Or hoping we'd find a way to be reunited."

"Enough talking." Arawn raised his hands to call magic. "We must hurry. If Gwydion and Bran are not reunited with their bodies soon, they willna be able to effect the merger."

Dewi dragged her gaze from Nidhogg. Her soul ached to remain with him, but Arawn was right to hustle them along. She crooked a talon at him. "Come close. We will travel with my magic, since I know where we're going."

She brought them out near where she'd left Fionn and Rune.

Arawn looked about them. "'Tis quite barren here. I sense Fionn's presence—and Aislinn's wolf as well. What plan did ye have?"

"I thought we could track them."

"'Tis as good as any other. I doona have a good feeling about this, though. Mayhap, 'twould be best—"

"No one has good feelings here," she interrupted, not liking her peevish tone. *"We should use mind speech."*

"Why? They know we're here."

"How could you possibly know that?"

Arawn shrugged and settled his battle leathers more firmly about himself. "I just do. Give me a moment."

Power radiated from the god of the dead, revenge, and terror. It was so potent, it surprised her. He opened his eyes. They were dark as night, whirling and bottomless like dragon's eyes. "They are beset. Join your magic to mine."

Dewi recognized the urgency in Arawn's tone. For once, she didn't argue. She'd given the Celts a hard time because of her anger over their refusal to help free Nidhogg, but the time for fury and retribution was over. She opened her mind to Arawn so she could see through his eyes.

Fury rattled her scales. Fionn bled from a hundred places. Aislinn lay on the ground behind him. Rune stood over her like a sentinel. It was clear both would die before they'd give her up. "How far?" Dewi asked.

"Minutes. Shall we?" Arawn opened a portal and they jumped through.

Dewi rolled out of their gateway moments later, fire spouting from her mouth.

Arawn raced to Fionn's side. "Need a wee spot of aid, brother?"

"Why would ye be thinking that?" Fionn managed a lopsided smile. The two gods stood shoulder to shoulder and lobbed deadly magic at D'Chel. The dark god was adept at sidestepping and redirecting, but his margin of safety shrank as he tired.

Too bad it's not ten against one, Dewi thought sourly and added a few blows of her own to the fray.

She focused her magic. Perrikus was nowhere in sight. A small satisfaction burned in her heart. That must've been who stood outside Nidhogg's prison. Maybe she'd hurt him worse than she thought. Fionn and Arawn had things under control, so she reached for Aislinn's energy. The girl was so still, Dewi worried she might be beyond help. Rune raised his hackles and growled at her.

"I understand you're worried, but I'm not going to hurt her," the dragon reassured him. She focused an envelope of magic around Aislinn while searching for signs of life. *Yes!* Dewi was exultant. Things were getting better and better. *The MacLochlainn lives.* She wanted to race to Aislinn's side and check her more closely—or better yet, bring her back to Earth—but that would have to wait.

"So." Dewi stepped to Fionn's other side and aimed her words at D'Chel. "How's Perrikus these days?"

D'Chel twisted his handsome features into a grimace and snarled, "He'll live, no thanks to you, you meddling reptile."

"Meddling reptile, is it?" *To hell with magic.* Fire roared from her mouth.

The dark god's robe smoldered and burst into flame. D'Chel slid out of it and batted at his long tresses. The stench of burning fabric and hair filled the air. He raised his hands.

Dewi warded herself and waited, girding herself for the blow she was certain would come.

"Doona bother," Arawn spat. "The dirty yellowbelly is leaving."

"Guess he dinna like the odds," Fionn snarked.

Sure enough, the air flickered; black light shot through it. When it cleared, they were alone. Fionn raced to Aislinn's side, dropped to his knees, and clasped her against his chest, crooning in Gaelic.

Her eyes fluttered open. She wound her arms around him. "I'm sorry—"

"Time enough for that later," Arawn snapped. "Get moving, Fionn. We must see to Gwydion and Bran."

"Aye, I hadna forgotten." Fionn kissed Aislinn's forehead tenderly and murmured, "I love you, *mo croi*. Dewi will see you safely back."

"I will go with them." Bella flew to Rune and settled on his back.

Fionn snorted. "Good call." He straightened and strode to Arawn's side. Magic sweetened the stale air. It shone brightly, and the two Celts disappeared.

Rune limped to the dragon. "Take us home."

"Indeed. I will take us all." Dewi bent, picked Aislinn up, and cradled her between her forelegs and her scaled chest. The dragon furled her wings and eyed the wolf and raven. "Stand next to me, against my body. It would be easier if you were on my back, but I can manage."

"I can fly there." Bella floated to the junction of the dragon's neck and shoulder.

Love, an emotion Dewi had denied forever, surged through her. These were her people, her family. A rush of fierce protectiveness warmed her as she called the magic that would transport them to safety.

Something about the MacLochlainn was different. It took the entire journey home before Dewi realized Aislinn's womb was empty.

CHAPTER 14

*D*ewi's warmth soothed Aislinn. She leaned against the dragon's comforting bulk and tried not to think, but it was a losing proposition. Her mind jumped from topic to topic, none of them pleasant. Perrikus had tried to kill her. If he hadn't been so intent on murdering her child, he might've succeeded. By the time she'd felt the life within her flicker out, the dark god had moved on. An unpleasant thought jabbed her. Perrikus must've thought she was dead right along with the child; otherwise, he'd never have left her side.

Her lungs burned. Her vision grayed at the edges. Travel between Earth and the border worlds was brutal. She turned her face toward the dragon. A few air molecules were trapped within her ruby scales. Just when Aislinn was certain unconsciousness was imminent, the air improved. Tears filled her eyes. They'd be home soon.

No. There is no more home. We'll be back on Earth at Marta's. And I'll be alone.

Guilt stabbed mercilessly at her. Aislinn hadn't wanted the baby, not really, but she would've done her best to love and care for it. It was a shock when D'Chel had rubbed her nose in her pregnancy.

Things happened so quickly after that, she hadn't had a chance to warm to the idea. Grief mingled with a healthy jot of self-blame now that the child was no more. She laid a hand over her abdomen and murmured, "I'm sorry."

She'd tried to draw the dark gods away from Fionn—and done her damnedest to kill D'Chel. *Yeah, I was chock full of hubris and bravado, and look where it got me.* Worry for Fionn raced through her. He and Arawn were far from safe. It would be a miracle if the four Celts returned from the border world intact. The tears that had threatened earlier spilled over. If she lost Fionn, Aislinn swore she'd lay waste to the world. Her heart retreated behind the protective shell she'd erected after her mother's death.

Never should have taken it down. Hurts too much.

Dewi's forelegs tightened around her. *"Hush, child. I know you mourn your loss, but you must be strong. There will be more bairns."*

"Not if Fionn doesn't come back, there won't."

The dragon didn't answer. Aislinn hadn't expected her to. Heartache and fear for the future soured her stomach. She reached for the wolf through the Hunter bond. *"Rune?"*

"I am fine. The dragon encased me in some sort of magic. At least I can breathe this trip."

Dewi trumpeted. A gateway opened and she marched through into Marta's yard.

"You can put me down," Aislinn said. Dewi bent and set her gently on her feet. Every part of her body ached, but it was nothing compared with the parched wasteland in her soul.

A shimmery ball next to Dewi broke open. Rune trotted out and made a beeline for her side. He rubbed his lush pelt against her leg and whined. "Mistress. I was so worried. You lay as if dead for far too long." He hesitated. "I am sorry about the pack puppy."

"As am I." Bella fluttered to Rune's shoulder and latched onto it.

"Holy Christ." Aislinn put her hands on her hips and glared at dragon, bird, and wolf. "Am I the only one who didn't know I was pregnant?"

Rune whuffed softly. "It would appear so."

Dewi lumbered toward the far side of the backyard. "Come," she called over her shoulder. "There's someone very special I'd like you to meet." Something bittersweet in the dragon's tone caught Aislinn's attention. She'd never heard the dragon sound quite like that before.

Though she was so weary all she wanted to do was fall on her face and sleep for a hundred years, Aislinn plodded after Dewi. Rune paced beside her with Bella on his back. It was easy to keep up. The dragon was so large, she didn't move very fast on land.

Aislinn's gaze landed on another dragon. "Oh my." Her hand flew to her chest; fatigue slid away.

Nidhogg's dark scales gleamed in the afternoon sun. The Norse dragon was elegant, with such an unearthly beauty it was hard to look right at him. Green eyes whirled at her. He inclined his head in greeting.

"I am Nidhogg, the Norse dragon, feared amongst all seven seas—"

"Beloved, oh beloved." Dewi broke into Nidhogg's introduction and settled on her belly in the dirt next to him. "You are looking stronger—and larger than when I left." Aislinn could've sworn Dewi was smiling.

"Hmph. Never did let me finish my sentences. I ate everything you and Arawn left. It was a start."

Aislinn moved close. She forgot her own pain. Compassion for Nidhogg burned deep. "How did you manage to survive for so long in that hideous place?"

Steam streamed from his nostrils. "The dark ones wanted me alive. They fed off my energy, so they made sure I had just enough to eat to keep me on this side of the veil. I knew eventually—" he harrumphed and leveled his gaze at Dewi "—someone would conjure a way to free me."

Dewi wrapped her forelegs around him. He twined his neck with hers. Tears flowed from her dark eyes; they turned into gemstones when they hit the ground. The dragons breathed steam into each other's mouths.

"No need to get maudlin, woman. I'll live," Nidhogg said gruffly and disentangled himself. "I could use more food, though. Mayhap we could do a spot of hunting."

"If you're sure you're strong enough..."

Aislinn stared at Dewi. The dragon sounded positively maternal, her tone soft and tender.

Nidhogg rolled his eyes. A creaking sound that might have been laughter rumbled from his throat. "If I'm not, I'll come right back and wait for you to serve me." He turned and eyed Aislinn. "Hmph. Another MacLochlainn. We need to watch it, you and I." He lowered his tone conspiratorially. "There'll be no living with that one"—he hooked a talon at Dewi—"once she has both her mate and the ancient MacLochlainn bond at her beck and call."

"I'll be sure to keep it in mind." Aislinn smiled in spite of herself. Nidhogg was impossible not to like. He wasn't imperious or haughty like Dewi.

Rune trotted closer and sniffed cautiously.

"You don't have to be so tentative." Nidhogg edged closer to the wolf. "I don't bite."

"No, but you command fire."

Nidhogg sat back on his haunches. Steam billowed from his mouth. "If what the dark ones told me is true, it has been long since dragons roamed the world, but we never injured bond animals."

"It's my fault, beloved." Dewi mirrored Nidhogg's posture, but didn't meet his twirling gaze. "If I hadn't gone in search of you—"

"Stop. We start anew today, Dewi. No recriminations. If I hadn't been so arrogant, I'd never have let those bastards trap me in the first place. Shall we?" He straightened his rear legs and furled his wings. "By the goddess, it's good to be free."

Aislinn watched as the two dragons took to the skies. Dewi waited until her mate was inscribing lazy circles in the air before joining him. "I'm happy for them," Aislinn told Rune and Bella. "It's not often a love story has a happy ending after such a long time."

"Come inside." Rune walked toward the house and then turned to make certain she was following him.

"I'm not sure I can." Fionn's scent and feel was all over the inside of Marta's house. For one self-indulgent moment, she considered jumping back to the border world to help him and Arawn. Aislinn shut her eyes.

I'm too tired. I'd be a liability.

Fluid dampened her crotch. Blood. Something else to attend to.

She plodded up the back steps and into the house. Aislinn stopped just inside the kitchen door and sent her magic spiraling outward. She was tired, but there was no point in walking into something unexpected because she'd been too slipshod to check. She thought about the house being unstable because it was situated on psychic fault lines. They'd need to move their base of operations once the Celts returned.

"If they don't come back, it won't matter," she muttered.

"Of course Fionn will return." Bella sounded indignant. "I swear, that man is like a bad penny. He always turns up."

Aislinn bent and ruffled the bird's feathers where she perched atop Rune. "I hope you're right." She ran a hand through Rune's coarse fur and gazed about the kitchen, bleary-eyed. Her search for anything malevolent came up dry. Since the hybrids had escaped their coffins, she wondered if the back of the house would be safe again.

More blood dripped between her legs. She set her jaw, her teeth clacking together. She needed a bath and a place to lie down so she could reach inside with her Healer gift and repair her womb. She unbuckled her travel pack and dropped it in a corner of the kitchen.

The wolf sprang between her and the door leading to the hall-way. "Where are you going?"

"To the back of the house to take a bath and lie down."

He growled at her. "You can bathe in the front bathroom or kitchen sink and rest in the living room. Fionn said—"

She put her hands on her hips. "Fionn's not here. Who are you bonded to? Him, or me?" She blew out an impatient breath. "I checked. I think it's safe. Besides, I really should go to the attic and look in on Gwydion and Bran."

"We can do that," Bella cut in. She pecked the side of Rune's head. The wolf narrowed his amber eyes. He looked as if he wanted to say something, but Bella pecked him again, and he turned and trotted down the hall.

Aislinn warded herself, just in case. When she tapped into her magical well, she wasn't surprised to find it nearly dry. She'd need rest and food to recharge. She moved cautiously down the hall after Rune and Bella. Fionn's warding on the attic door was intact. It was too complicated to take the whole thing apart, so she only focused on the part of it that kept the door locked. Panting with effort, she finally tugged the door open for the animals.

Her eyes fluttered from weariness, and her hands shook. *I need food before I tackle the bedroom warding.* Aislinn traipsed back to the kitchen, stood over the canisters, and shoveled dried fruit and nuts into her mouth. She turned on the kitchen tap and drank from it. She was just about to go back down the hall when Rune and Bella trotted into the kitchen.

"Well?" She eyed them.

"They feel about the same to me," Rune answered.

"Yes. Alive, but not. We're hungry, too," Bella added.

"If you can spare me for a while, I would like to hunt." Rune swished his tail.

"Of course." Aislinn made shooing motions with both hands. "I'll be fine. About all I'm going to do is sleep."

She trudged down the hall and reached toward the casting holding the bedroom door closed. Fortunately, Fionn had used similar magic, so it didn't take her nearly as long to dismantle as the first one had. Her gaze scuttled from bathtub to bed. She finally decided on a compromise and grabbed a towel from the bathroom so she wouldn't bleed all over the sheets.

Aislinn undid her pants and let them slide down her hips. Her eyes widened at the amount of blood staining the fabric, but then she reminded herself that bloody wounds nearly always looked worse than they were. She turned back the bedcovers, spread the towel, and lay on it. The room was cold, so she pulled the blankets over herself.

She swallowed, but her throat was dry and the tissue rubbed against itself. This next would be hard, but it had to be done. She marshaled what magic she had left and probed her injured womb with Healer energy to help the thickened lining slough off. Her embryo was gone. She found the place it had been attached and layered magic over ruptured blood vessels. Her heart ached. Maybe she was destined to lose every single thing she'd ever loved.

Clear and cold, the voice of reason intruded. *Be honest. I didn't love it. That's why I feel so wretched.*

Only because I didn't know about it. Her cheeks were damp with tears; she scrubbed them away with grubby fingers.

Oh, Fionn. Why didn't you tell me?

Realization nearly wrecked the concentration she needed to Heal herself. He'd tried to broach the topic that last day in the kitchen, but she'd been so high-handed, the conversation died before it could even get started. She attempted to picture the look on his face when she'd said flatly that she never wanted children, but it wouldn't come into focus.

"It's just as well," she murmured, finishing up with her ministrations. She might bleed for a day or two, if at all, but other than the searing emptiness in her soul, there'd be no lasting scars.

Dragons trumpeted loudly. She rolled off the bed and moved to the window. At first she couldn't see anything, but then two forms—one black, one red—came into view. Their bodies were twined together, and she realized they were mating. The trumpeting escalated, radiating joy and possession and love.

Even though Aislinn felt she was intruding on a private moment, she watched their graceful, aerial ballet, her eyes hot and gritty. She needed to cry, but was empty of tears right along with magic. A leaden dullness sat heavily in her chest.

I've got to get hold of myself.

Aislinn gritted her teeth. Self-pity wasn't her style. She left the window and fashioned a rag out of a scrap of cloth. That done, she pulled on her panties, and settled the rag between her legs to soak up her flow, in case there was any. She looked longingly at the bed, but knew she'd sleep better and waken stronger if she ate more.

Aislinn clung to small tasks to keep herself from shattering. Every time she thought about Fionn, she felt like a tennis ball. On one side of the court, her life would be over if he didn't return. When the ball bounced to the other side, she was furious with him for not discussing something as important as a pregnancy, which would impact her body for months, before he sent his sperm to settle in her uterus. Because the dichotomy was ripping her heart to shreds, she forced herself to focus on one thing at a time, walked slowly to the kitchen, and made herself eat and drink.

She chewed and swallowed mechanically. The food was tasteless. It may as well have been sawdust. After a last slug of water from the tap, she found her way back to the bedroom. Aislinn crawled into bed, pulled the covers over her body, and closed her eyes. She was so exhausted, she assumed sleep wouldn't be a problem. Her entire body ached. Heart sore and weary, she willed sleep to erase everything for a while. Instead, Fionn and Arawn rose behind her closed lids. It took a moment for her to realize they were in the same place Perrikus had held her prisoner.

Fionn started. He spun and looked right at her. *"Nay, leannán. Doona try to return here. Not with your mind or your body. 'Tis dangerous for you to even be within my mind. D'Chel still wants you. He hasna given up."*

"Fionn." His name tore from her in an anguished howl. "You have to—"

The vision winked out as quickly as it had come. Sour-smelling sweat poured from her body and pooled beneath her. What was going on? Had they been taken captive as she'd been? She raised both forearms under the covers and slammed her hands down on the mattress. Frustration battled an impotent rage.

I couldn't take on a field mouse in my current state. I have to sleep.

Rune padded into the bedroom, claws muted by the carpet. He jumped onto the bed and licked her face. The anguish pouring through her quieted under his touch. After a time, he lay next to her, and the warmth of his body lulled her into an uneasy sleep.

CHAPTER 15

Fionn glared at Arawn. "Do ye have any more bright ideas?" He snapped his fingers a few times. "Quick. I need them afore Aislinn throws caution to the winds and comes after us."

"Aye. I have one, but it might be the death of Gwydion and Bran. Mayhap us, too."

Fionn clamped his jaws together. His mage light knocked gently against Arawn's, where the two globes were suspended off to one side. He scanned the underground room where they'd found Gwydion's and Bran's astral selves contained within glowing cylinders. The dank chamber looked like an impromptu dungeon with stone walls and an iron portcullis for a door. Water dripped down slime-covered walls. Not so much as a rat had shown up to pump for information. Fionn shook his head to clear it. He wanted to return to Aislinn so bad, it got in the way of his concentration.

He laid a hand on the glass chamber with Gwydion's essence locked inside. It brightened. The master enchanter spoke into his mind. *"I wish to hear Arawn's idea."*

Fionn lifted a brow. "Did ye hear that?"

"Aye." Arawn nodded. "'Tis a small enough boon, but I doona

believe Aislinn was held in this space. Did she tell you how she managed to free herself?"

"Nay. There wasna time. I'd been injured." The glass warmed beneath Fionn's hand. A corner of his mouth turned down. "Gwydion is impatient, and rightly so. Ye changed the subject at hand."

"That I did." Arawn drew his dark brows together. "'Tis because I am still thinking, but I can see why he'd be edgy. He must find his body—and soon." Arawn strode across the small space. Something that sounded like bones crunched beneath his boots. He laid a hand on the other side of Gwydion's cylinder. *"Can ye hear me when I am not touching you?"*

"Yes." Gwydion's mind voice sounded exasperated. *"Ye doona even need to stand nearby. Bran and I can hear. We just canna talk unless ye are touching us."*

Fionn started to ask how they'd let themselves be captured, but now wasn't the time. "If ye have an idea"—he locked gazes with Arawn—"spit it out."

"Shield us."

Fionn cast a ward to encompass all of them. Their magic worked within the stone walls of their prison, but they'd been unable to project it outside. It was almost as if someone had woven heavy iron bands into more than just the portcullis. His body had grazed it on the way in, leaving a burn across his shoulders. At the time, he'd thought it a shade too easy to sneak into the dark gods' lair.

Aye, and now I know why.

They'd barely gotten inside the room when the portcullis dropped like a boulder, shaking the stones in the walls. Fionn had spun and called magic to halt the gate, but it hadn't helped. He'd grasped it with his hands, and the iron seared his palms. It had taken precious time and magic to Heal them.

Arawn drew an arm across Fionn's back and pulled him close. "Thicken the ward. I doona wish to be overheard."

"The dark ones had no problem penetrating Aislinn's warding."

Arawn made a sound between a snort and a grunt. "Mayhap because she used her body as a lure in the past and they learned the pattern of her energy. I will use mind speech. Betwixt that and your ward, we should be able to converse. Besides, the iron that dampens our magic should be a two-way street."

"How so? If it weren't so thick, we could blast past it."

"Aye." Arawn set his lips in a hard line. "Because 'tis so dense, 'twill help keep our conversation private." He placed a hand on Bran's cylinder. It flickered and brightened. "*Afore I describe what is a verra chancy escape route, bear with me. What do we know about where we are?*"

"*When we try to cast magic beyond here to escape, it bounces back at us,*" Fionn said.

"*Aught else?*"

"*Even if you are successful freeing yourselves,*" Gwydion said, "*there's still the problem of breaking the enchantment that holds us within these cylinders.*"

"*One thing at a time,*" Fionn muttered. His brow creased. "*Would freeing you sever the enchantment and allow you to return to your bodies? Or is there something we've overlooked?*"

"*What do ye mean?*" Arawn asked.

Fionn locked gazed with him. "*Will breaking the enchantment free their astral selves from the glass chambers, or do we need to do something additional? I doona wish to miss anything.*"

"*If this were Earth, simply freeing us would fix things,*" Bran said.

"*I believe it's worth a shot,*" Gwydion cut in. "*I have a feeling I know what Arawn has in mind. You will do best unburdened with our essences.*"

Fionn hadn't stopped staring into Arawn's dark eyes, but reading his thoughts was difficult. "*What think ye?*"

The god of the dead tightened his jaw. "*If we pull enough magic to free them, we will surely alert Perrikus and D'Chel.*"

"*I've been wondering why we haven't seen them yet,*" Fionn muttered darkly.

"If ye work a spell atop another, it just might work," Bran said. *"That would free us at the same moment the two of you make a run for it."*

Fionn nudged Arawn. *"Spill it. Once I know what ye have in mind, I'll be better able to assess if we could pull both magics off."*

Dark hair fell across Arawn's face as he leaned forward over both glass chambers. Even his mind voice was the barest whisper. *"If 'tis only Fionn's and my magic—"*

"Nay." Gwydion interrupted. *"Ye need all our minds to ensure our best chance. Once we're free, Bran and I will return to our bodies—assuming they havena died and can still pull us back to them."*

"Right as usual." Arawn sucked in a breath. *"My plan was to use the paths of the dead. 'Tis my realm. They accept me."*

Fionn tightened his muscles until they threatened to cramp. He'd walked the halls of the dead—and more than once. They gave him the creeps. *"How will we get there from here?"*

"The dead are not of the Earth, as ye may think."

Fionn clamped a hand around Arawn's wrist. They were wasting precious minutes. *"Then where?"*

"The realm of the dead is everywhere. It knows no boundaries."

Fionn pushed his tongue against his teeth in frustration. *"That isna helpful."*

"The risk," Arawn continued as if Fionn hadn't said anything, *"will be getting from here to there. I'm not certain how the architecture of this particular border world fits with the country of the dead."*

"The risk," Gwydion murmured, *"is you would be trapped in an airless void until it squeezed the life out of you and forced you into the Dreaming forever."*

Fionn inhaled raggedly. *"The odds?"* he barked before realizing he'd spoken aloud.

Arawn shrugged. *"I doona know. I've never tried to do this afore."* He spread his hands in front of him. *"Surely at least fifty-fifty."*

Fionn wanted to scream that wasn't good enough. He had Aislinn to consider. He owed her an apology—and a lifetime together.

Bran's cylinder flickered. *"Ye must decide quickly. I feel them closing on us."*

Arawn faced Fionn and clasped his forearms. *"I wouldna have suggested it if I dinna believe it was almost our only chance. Otherwise, we sit like tethered pigs, awaiting the pleasure of the dark ones."*

"We could hold them off for a long time—"

"Aye, but not forever. 'Tis their world. We will weaken here over time."

Fionn projected magic to search for Perrikus and D'Chel, but came up dry. It was a wonder Bran could feel them through the iron in the walls. Maybe it had to do with not being burdened with a body. He balled his hands into fists. Any chance was better than none. *"All right. I'm in. Let us decide who will do what."*

"No decision to be made. We lay hands on the glass chambers so Gwydion and Bran can help. Ye must free them while I open a pathway for us. Is everyone ready?"

Fionn nodded.

"We begin now. Doona tarry. I canna feel beyond these walls, but I trust Bran."

Fionn called earth and fire. Earth was sluggish, but fire responded with alacrity. Once he held a mix he was certain would be more than sufficient, he inundated Bran's glass chamber. It shattered. The room brightened and Fionn did the same to Gwydion's prison. Magic flashed so bright, Fionn shielded his eyes. The air sizzled, smelling like ozone.

"Say a prayer for them," Arawn murmured. "They are off. Come on. Perrikus and D'Chel are nearly—"

"No nearly about it, Celt," Perrikus snarled. "I am here. Whatever you have planned—"

"Is accomplished," Arawn shrieked. He grabbed Fionn's arm. A rush of magic buffeted his body and roared loud in his ears. Perrikus grabbed his other arm. For a long, awful moment, Fionn felt as if he were being ripped in half. Dark magic bombarded his body like a sledgehammer.

Wards. I need wards. Fionn poured fire into a shield to stymie Perrikus before D'Chel turned up to help.

"What are ye doing?" Arawn screeched into his mind. *"I need your magic to get us out of here."*

"Trying to stay alive long enough to escape." Fionn didn't bother with mind speech. He didn't have the power to spare.

Smoke rose from beneath Perrikus's hand; the stench of burning flesh thickened. The dark god jumped back, nursing singed fingers. "Fucking Celt," he growled and lunged for Fionn again.

"Now." Fionn redirected everything he had into Arawn's casting. A boom rocked him. The walls wavered and disappeared. *"Christ, but that was close."*

Arawn's hand clutching his arm tightened. *"Och aye, we are just at the beginning. 'Tis a long journey from here to Earth. Link your mind to mine."*

A LOUD THUNK jarred Aislinn from sleep. Disoriented, she bolted upright, eyes wide and staring, and gathered her wits. Rune was nowhere in sight. A glance at the window told her it was night, but she had no idea how long she'd been asleep. Was it the same day, or had she slept the clock round and then some? Her mouth was dry, her eyes gritty. She untangled herself from sheets and blankets and traveled the few steps to the bathroom, where she stuck her hands under the tap and splashed cold water on her face. Cupping her hands, she drank some, too, and then powered her mage light so she could see.

Head a little clearer, she turned off the water and straightened. She was just about to pull magic to scan for what had wakened her when Rune burst into the room with Bella right behind him. The raven fluttered to the top of the door and curved her talons around it. "You need to come," Rune said.

"Yes, and quickly," the bird added.

"Why? What's happened?" Aislinn's heart sped up. She hoped her magic had replenished itself, since it was looking as if she'd need it. She grabbed her pants from off the floor, ignoring that they reeked of blood.

"Never mind those. Follow me." Rune loped out the door and turned hard left and up the risers to the attic.

"Daughter." Dewi's voice sounded in her mind. *"Gwydion and Bran are returned, but they are very weak. Link with me once you are next to them. I will do what I can to help."*

She may have brought me back from the border world, but it'll be a cold day in Hell before I link with her again.

Aislinn vaulted up the stairs, taking them two at a time. Her mage light floated ahead of her to brighten the way. *"Where are Fionn and Arawn?"*

"I do not know the answer to that. Mayhap, if the other two do not slip into the Dreaming, they will have answers."

"What's wrong with Gwydion and Bran?"

"You're wasting time. Hurry." The dragon's old, imperious tone was back in force.

Aislinn bit her bottom lip so hard it hurt. She catapulted through the door and took in a scene from hell. Fionn hadn't described how the attic looked after the hybrids escaped, so she had no way of knowing what damage had happened then and which was new. Furniture was tossed about like wooden toothpicks. The walls had holes in them, and yellow ocher smeared the floor and open caskets. The stench was reminiscent of a charnel pit; she gagged and clapped a hand over her mouth. Fionn's warding must've kept the smell from permeating the rest of the house. Thank God she'd only dismantled enough to get the door open for the animals. If the rest of the house smelled like this, there'd be no living in it.

Gwydion and Bran lay on the floor. Their faces were gray, eyes closed. Rune licked frantically at Gwydion. Bella pecked Bran's head, but softly. Aislinn closed the distance and dropped to her knees. She laid her hands on Gwydion, sent her Healer gift into him, and ran into the same wall she'd found in Fionn when he lay unconscious beneath the Arizona prison where they'd found Slototh. She moved her hands to Bran and found the same barrier.

"They are closed to me," she told Dewi and then mentioned that they felt the same way Fionn had when he'd retreated to the *Dreaming,* a last retreat for the Celtic gods. Once they barricaded themselves in, it took more magic than she possessed to get them out again.

"Damn it. I feared as much." There was a long pause. *"Um, would you trust me to link my mind to yours?"*

At least she's asking.

The last time the dragon linked with her, Dewi had used her body as a conduit so she could have sex with the Minotaur. A shudder ran down Aislinn's back, right along with a tongue of flame. It had been the darkest, kinkiest sex she'd ever had, but the experience had eroded her faith in Dewi almost beyond repair. If Aislinn were totally honest, she hadn't exactly forgiven the dragon for that particular betrayal.

"Daughter. Time is wasting. They sink farther from us with each passing moment."

"I am standing by," an unfamiliar voice said. *"I will see that my mate doesn't get out of line."*

Nidhogg.

"I hope I get a chance to know you better," she told the Norse dragon. *"I think I'd like you."*

"The MacLochlainn belongs to me," Dewi protested.

"You're wasting time," Nidhogg pointed out.

"Daughter?"

"Oh, all right. But if you fuck me this time, Dewi, it will be the last time. MacLochlainn or no, you and I will be done."

The dragon didn't bother answering. She slammed into Aislinn's mind, leaving her reeling from the impact. She blinked and tried to catch her breath. The dragon had such a rich bevy of memories from her thousands of years of life, it was hard not to get lost in her complex mind. Last time, she'd been inside Dewi's body. This time, Dewi was in hers.

"Relax, child. Give me control of your body. If I have to fight you, it will dilute my magic."

"Done."

Aislinn unclenched her jaw and watched from the sidelines as her hands moved to Gwydion's face. Magic blasted through her. Dewi's power even brightened her mage light so it looked like a small sun. Her hands moved slowly down the Celtic god's sides. More magic jolted through her at intervals. Color returned to the mage's face, but so slowly that it was hard to notice at first. Aislinn thought she heard Dewi give a small *phuff* of satisfaction, and then her hands shifted to Bran.

It's like being a conduit for a lightning rod. Because she hadn't fought Dewi or used any of her own power, Aislinn wasn't drained when the dragon abruptly withdrew.

"See." Her tone was smug. *"I didn't harm so much as a cell in your body."*

Aislinn stared at Gwydion and Bran. They still weren't moving, but at least she could see the rise and fall of their chests. *"What do I do now?"*

"They are back on this side of the Dreaming. Now you can Heal them."

Aislinn thought she heard the dragon mutter about the MacLochlainn being brain-damaged, but didn't rise to the bait. Rune and Bella had switched positions, with Rune licking Bran. She placed a hand on each of the Celts and sent magic spinning into them. Bran seemed slightly better, so she turned her attentions to Gwydion. Her Healer gift didn't find anything particularly wrong within him, beyond scrapes and bruises. His mind had gone deep, though. It took a great deal of coaxing to persuade him to return.

Finally, his blue eyes—eyes so like Fionn's they nearly stopped her heart—fluttered open. "Och aye, lass. Had I but known 'twas you..."

"Save it." She turned to Bran.

It didn't take nearly as long to lure him back to the surface. His coppery eyes crinkled in the corners as he smiled at her.

Aislinn rocked back on her heels. She was too anxious to be subtle. "Where's Fionn?"

"Somewhere betwixt the border world, the halls of the dead, and here," Bran replied.

Aislinn rolled her eyes. "That tells me less than nothing."

"Sorry, lass. 'Tis all we know," Gwydion said.

Rune padded over and licked her. Bella flapped to one of the caskets and perched on it.

Aislinn pushed to her feet and paced from one end of the attic to the other. Her feet were bare, so she watched where she walked. "Can we go after them?"

"I doona see where we will have much choice if they doona return fairly soon." Gwydion flowed to his feet in one graceful, catlike motion. His tattered robes settled around him. He picked his staff up off the floor and turned for the stairs.

"Where are you going?"

"Downstairs to get something to eat." The master enchanter looked over one shoulder and eyed her shrewdly. "Unless I miss my guess, ye could do with a spot of Healing as well."

Bran shoved his blond hair over his shoulders and groaned as he pushed to his feet. "By the goddess, my entire body hurts. Is there any food made, lass?"

"When would I have had time?"

Dragon laughter shook the house. *"That's my Maclochlainn. Feisty as ever. Bet your eyes are on fire, child."*

"Stay out of my head, goddammit."

"Lass." Bran looked at her with an odd expression on his face. "It sounded like there were two dragons laughing out there."

She snorted. "There are. Dewi rescued Nidhogg from the border world."

"Excellent news." Gwydion clattered down the spiral stairs.

"Indeed." Bran sprang after him.

"Why? What difference does it make?" Aislinn glanced down at herself and realized all she had on was a filthy shirt and blood-stained panties. She blew out an exasperated breath and followed the men and animals down the stairs. Her mage light looked dim now that Dewi wasn't powering it.

She thought about trailing after them to the kitchen, but decided on a bath and clean clothes first. Gwydion and Bran could keep watch. It was obvious none of them were going anywhere until after they'd eaten. She had lots of questions, like what had happened to them in the first place and how the hybrids had escaped. Gwydion's enthusiasm for Nidhogg's freedom seemed a bit overboard, too.

Maybe, if I give them a few minutes, they'll actually cook something. I can ask all the questions I want while I'm eating. She shut the bathroom door and turned on the water. Her heart and arms ached for Fionn. Her womb ached for the child that would never be. If it hadn't been for her foolishness trying to take on D'Chel, she wouldn't have been injured, she and Fionn would never have separated, and the baby would still be safe within her body.

Why couldn't Fionn have been one of the ones to return? I need him.

She pushed her panties down her hips and rinsed out the blood-spotted rag she'd placed between her legs. If Fionn were lost to her, having his child would have been—

Stop! Just stop. I will never give up on finding him. Not until I know he's beyond my reach.

She stepped into the half-full tub and pulled magic to warm the water.

CHAPTER 16

*A*islinn plaited her wet hair and dug through drawers in Marta's bedroom. Though the woman had been as much of a packrat with clothing as she'd been with food, there wasn't much left that was clean. *If things ever slow down, I'll rinse out a few things.* She pulled on tan sweatpants and a nondescript black top. A green sweater with moth holes in it provided some warmth. Aislinn crossed the room and peered out the window. Stars scattered across a black sky. Dawn was still a few hours away.

She stuffed her feet into scuffed slippers and tromped down the hall to the kitchen. The smell of cooked grain greeted her before she pushed open the swinging door. Rather than mage lights, the men had lit a couple of fragrant candles. They sat at the kitchen table spooning food into their mouths and passing a mead bottle back and forth. She latched onto it and took a deep drink before filling a bowl from the pan sitting on the stove. Given the absence of gas and electricity, magic did a fair job filling in.

"Thanks." She spoke around a mouthful of barley and dried vegetables and then pulled out a chair and sat across from the men.

"Well"—Bran winked at her—"'twould have been far better had there been a kitchen wench to see to the cooking."

"I agree." She winked back. "I overheard some of your conversation coming down the hall. You were discussing the reinforcements Arawn went to the Old Country to find."

"Aye." Gwydion nodded, and his forehead creased into worried lines. "I doona understand why they're not here yet."

"Maybe everyone was busy?" Aislinn raised a brow and kept eating. She held out a hand for the mead bottle.

"Nay." Bran gave her the honey wine. "It doesna work that way. If one of us asks for help…" His voice trailed off and he shrugged.

"How the hell did the two of you end up in Perrikus's world?" She passed the mead back to Bran.

"Miscalculation," Gwydion muttered.

"Aye. It dinna help that we nearly lost the entire house in the process."

Her spoon stopped midway to her mouth. "What?"

Bran looked chagrined. "Things happened verra fast. The coffin lids flew open. The hybrids weren't sluggish at all this time. They sprang out and attacked us—"

"We might have managed," Gwydion broke in, "except I felt the house slipping toward the border worlds, so I had to divert my attention."

"When he did that—" Bran took another swallow of mead "—the female hybrid jumped him."

Gwydion made a face. "Aye, I can still feel her fingers cutting off my wind. Magic didn't make a dent in her chokehold on me."

"We couldna figure it out until D'Chel showed up."

Aislinn swallowed hard. "D'Chel was *here*?"

"And why would that surprise you?" Bran asked. "The dark ones can travel as easily as us now. They couldn't afore the Old Ones cast the mischief that let them escape their lands, but that happened over three years ago."

"Mischief is too kind a word. Allowing that scum to invade Earth was the worst kind of treachery." She blinked back tears. "It feels like the worst kind of violation to have D'Chel so close."

"Lass." Gwydion leveled his blue gaze right at her. "Nowhere is safe. Earth is under attack. There is the best of chances we may lose it to the dark gods and your buddies, the Lemurians. Unless..." He hooded his eyes.

"Unless what? And they're scarcely my buddies." Aislinn scraped the bottom of her bowl with her spoon. She was surprised she'd polished off what had been a generous portion. *Guess I was hungrier than I thought.* She looked at Gwydion, waiting for him to answer her, but he didn't. "Unless what?" she prodded.

The back door snicked open. Rune and Bella trotted in.

The raven flew to Bran's shoulder. "When are you going after my bondmate?" she demanded.

Bran ruffled the bird's feathers. "We'll give him and Arawn until mid-morning. It will take us that long to come up with a strategy."

Aislinn dropped her spoon into the bowl and held out her hands. Rune padded over and sniffed her from feet to crotch. "What are you doing?" She batted his nose away.

"Making certain you are better."

"Thank you. It's good to be cared about." She buried her hands in his black and silver coat and smoothed it.

"Out of the mouths of wolves." Gwydion got to his feet and walked to her side of the table. He placed a hand on her head and the other on her abdomen. Aislinn felt magic thrum through her like a mild electric shock. "Hmph. Did a spot of Healing yourself, did ye? I added to it, but ye were verra close to well."

Aislinn nodded. "I thought I took care of..." She shook her head. It was hard to talk about the baby that wouldn't be out loud. "Besides," she hurried on, "you never told me what happened after D'Chel showed up."

"Och aye." Gwydion straightened and rolled his eyes. "Things fair went to hell in a handbasket."

"And damned fast." Bran got up and pulled cups from the cupboard. "Tea, anyone?"

"I'd like some," Aislinn said.

"Aye, for me as well. It dinna take long afore it was abundantly clear if we dinna follow behind D'Chel, he'd pull the entire house into his world."

Aislinn's eyes widened. She sucked in a breath. "He's powerful enough to do that?"

Bran snorted. "Lass, Gwydion and I could do much the same. This location isna stable. But if D'Chel had done that, 'twould have put the entire area for miles around at risk. Rather akin to setting up a vortex or a black hole."

"Och aye, we couldna chance it. I doona know how many still live in this region, but 'twouldn't have been fair to them."

"One of the things I've been thinking about is that we really ought to move from here if it's that unsafe," Aislinn began.

The kitchen window rattled. Her head snapped up.

Dewi's snout pushed against the glass. "Come outside. All of you."

Gwydion laughed. "Same old Dewi."

"And ye were hoping for...?" Bran handed steaming mugs all around.

Gwydion shrugged and took his tea. He grabbed the mead bottle and poured some into his cup.

"Grand idea. Ashamed I didn't spike it myself," Bran said and held out his mug to Gwydion.

"Me, too." Aislinn took a sip of the steamy alcoholic mixture and headed for the door with Rune at her heels. She glanced over one shoulder. "By the way. What happened to the hybrids?"

"I have no idea." Gwydion shrugged and followed her outside.

The air was cold and still. She filled her lungs with its tranquility. Nidhogg was a few feet from the house. Dewi lumbered over to stand next to him. Both dragons glowed against the blackness of the night.

Bella flew to Dewi's shoulders and perched. Elaborately carved staff clutched in one hand, Gwydion pushed past Aislinn and down the steps with Bran close behind. Both Celts stopped a few feet in front of Nidhogg and bowed low.

"I am grateful the goddess has seen fit to return you to us," Gwydion said once he'd straightened.

"What a crock." Dewi leaned forward and batted his chest with a taloned foreleg. "I rescued him just like *we* could have if you'd only—"

"Enough." Nidhogg's voice cut like a whip. "I told you, Dewi. We start fresh. No recriminations."

Flames flashed from Dewi's mouth. She turned her head, but even so, she narrowly missed setting the house on fire.

"Good to see someone take her to task," Rune whispered into Aislinn's mind. It was all she could do not to laugh.

"Shhhh. She'll hear you."

"I, too, am glad ye are returned." Bran straightened, laid fingers on his lips, and then placed them on the dragon's chest. "I knew ye would, for I saw it in a prophecy."

Nidhogg lowered his head and nudged both men. "Thank you. Contrary to my mate's views, your kind thoughts are well-received."

"Aye, we canna go back," Gwydion murmured. "Bran's prophecy aside, the hard truth of things is I was certain ye were dead, or else so weakened ye may as well have been."

"The thing that saved me was when Perrikus discovered a way to tap into my power." Steam billowed from Nidhogg's nostrils. "He made certain to feed me enough to not only keep me alive, but so I'd be able to help maintain life on his pitiful excuse for a world."

"What will happen without you there?" Aislinn asked.

"The world will finish dying. Without trees, the atmosphere will gradually poison even the few things left alive on it."

"Doona fear," Bran said dryly. "Perrikus will jump ship long afore that happens."

"Hell," Gywdion chimed in. "For all we know, he may be gone already."

"Aye, in search of Fionn and Arawn, no doubt," Bran added.

A lead weight settled in Aislinn's stomach. She moved between the two dragons and said, "We have to do something to get Fionn and Arawn back." Guilt about the hours they'd wasted jabbed her.

"Since it's Arawn," Nidhogg sounded thoughtful, "he no doubt took the roads of the dead."

Aislinn gritted her teeth. "Yes, Bran said that earlier. It sounds ominous. What do you mean?"

"Well, lass, he is the god of the dead—" Gwydion began.

"I know that," she interrupted. "It doesn't tell me why they aren't back yet. Or what the roads of the dead actually are."

Bran cleared his throat. "'Tis conjecture on my part, but one of the favorite tricks the dark play is to corral your magic so it bounces back at you."

"Yes, they did that to me. Once I figured out it was the tapestries and took them down—"

"Doona interrupt"—Bran eyed her—"else I'll never finish. Ye were fortunate the dark gods were lazy. 'Tis not usually something so simple as a spelled piece of fabric. In any event, Arawn knows secret ways into the halls of the dead, even from the border worlds. 'Twas the only way we could think of to subvert the dark ones' magic. 'Twas a risky choice, though. Far more dangerous than travel from Earth, since Fionn and Arawn will end up trapped in the airless void betwixt the worlds if Arawn canna locate a gateway in time."

Aislinn's gut clenched. For a moment, she thought she might vomit up her meal. "So they're either trapped where they can't breathe, or they're somewhere in Arawn's realm of the dead?"

"Yes," Dewi said. "If they made it to the halls of the dead, there's nothing to worry about. They should be here directly."

"I can't feel Fionn through the Hunter bond," Bella said.

Gwydion blew out a tense sounding breath. "That isna good."

"Aye, it argues they are far away," Bran agreed.

Aislinn thought about her bond with Rune. It extended over distance, but with limits. "How far? My bond with Rune—"

"—is different than Fionn's with Bella," Bran said. "If the bird canna sense him, he may well be trapped between Arawn's realm and the border world."

"Is there some way to go look?" Aislinn didn't like the piercing note in her voice. She'd leave in a heartbeat if she had any idea where to go.

"We can enter the realms of the dead," Nidhogg said.

"Yes, but we would need to borrow your bodies. The tunnels are too narrow for us otherwise," Dewi added.

Gwydion curved his handsome face into a scowl. "It may come to that."

Aislinn marched to Dewi and laid a hand on her scaled side. "I want to go. Will you take me?"

"If she goes, I'm going with her," Rune announced.

"Lass." Bran took her arm. "'Tis a task for Gwydion and me."

She rounded on him and jerked out of his grasp. "Why?"

"Because we command far more magic than you."

Aislinn stood very straight and jutted her chin forward. "I'm probably stronger than you with Dewi linked to me."

The dragon chortled. "You've finally realized that. Mayhap there's hope for you yet."

Aislinn felt like kicking her. Dewi was less than an unlikely ally because Aislinn still wasn't totally certain she could be trusted. Maybe Nidhogg altered the equation, though.

"Doona be stubborn." Gwydion infused compulsion into his words. "I doona wish to explain to Fionn why we sent his woman off to do a man's task."

"Goddammit. This isn't the fifteen hundreds. Even then, I'll bet the odd woman carted a broadsword."

"Stop." Bran stepped between them. "We waste time and resources. Let's map out a strategy. Once 'tis done, we shall see who implements it."

～

Fionn's lungs burned. He was dizzy from lack of oxygen. Arawn's grasp on him had long since weakened. Every time they'd turned from the void outside the border world, and made a run for the paths of the dead, they'd run up against a trap. The first time, they'd tried to power through it and been snared in something like a magical spider's web. It had taken far too much of their power to free themselves.

"Do we have enough for one more try?" Arawn's voice was the barest of whispers.

"'Tis either that or head for the *Dreaming* now."

"If we drain ourselves too much, we willna make the *Dreaming*."

Fionn tried to swallow, but didn't have any saliva. Arawn was right. They could sacrifice their immortality in this airless space between the worlds. He sent magic inward and took stock. "Aye, I have enough for one more attempt." He clung to thoughts of Aislinn. He had to survive—for her and their child. Love burned bright within him. It shored up his flagging power.

Arawn laughed softly. It came out more like a wheeze. "Aye. Now if I just had a lass to strengthen me."

Fionn gripped Arawn's arm and offered what little power he had. "We're in this together."

Arawn shut his eyes. His face was gray. "Let us pray this works. I will jump us to the entrance at the far reaches of my realm. If we are verra lucky, the dark ones willna know about it."

"Ready."

Arawn drew them through the airless void. It seemed they traveled in slow motion. Fionn's limbs ached. His lungs were raw. Blood ran down his face from ruptured blood vessels in his nose and mouth. Just when he was about to tell Arawn they had to head for the *Dreaming* now while they could still reach it, the air got infinitesimally thicker.

"Aye, and I think this will work," Arawn rasped.

They toppled out into a dark, rocky cave. Fionn hit hard because he didn't have enough magic left to soften his landing. He sucked air hungrily. "Bless the goddess. I can breathe."

"Aye. Hand over some of the water I smell in your rucksack."

Fionn was shocked how long it took him to unbuckle the pack and get it off his shoulders. It was pitch black where they were. He tried to fire his mage light, but couldn't gin up anything brighter than a paper match. He handed one water bottle to Arawn and drank deep from another. "Where are we exactly?"

"The good news is we escaped the border world."

Fionn waited, but Arawn didn't say anything further. He drank some more water and grappled in the pack for dried fruit. "Well, what's the rest?"

"We are sealed off from the halls of the dead."

"Huh? I thought this was all part of your realm."

"Sorry, I'm too tapped out to make sense. Long ago, I set aside a portion of my kingdom to confine those who were too restless to remain here. 'Tis fortified with strong magics to keep them contained."

"Can't we jump out of here?"

Arawn shook his head. "If we could, so could they—the ones who controlled magic, anyway. I believe I can free us, but not until I've rested. I haven't enough alchemy left to do much more than your pathetic attempt at a mage light."

Fionn felt anger stir, but it was as weak as his light. "Did ye know this was where we would come out?"

"Aye."

"Ye should have told me."

"Why? If 'twas the only choice left, would ye have turned it down?"

Fionn pounded a fist into his thigh. "Damn it, Arawn. If we doona return on the heels of Bran and Gwydion, Aislinn will take off hunting for me." Fear chilled him. Once he heard himself say the words, he knew how true they were.

"Sleep, Fionn. If ye canna, then rest. The sooner our magic is recovered, the sooner I can work on freeing us."

"Here." Fionn shoved a handful of dried apricots at Arawn. "Eat something. That should speed the process." Fionn placed his rucksack beneath his head and stretched out on the cold, muddy floor. A rock poked him in the back. He reached beneath himself and pried it out of the muck.

Weariness buffeted him. He doused his light and shut his eyes. Aislinn's face rose before him, pinched with worry. He was too shattered to figure out if it was a true sending or if he'd just imagined it.

CHAPTER 17

It had been light for several hours. Aislinn chafed at the delay. Gwydion and Bran had talked around whether she was to be included when they went after Fionn and Arawn. To keep from tearing their eyes out, she retreated to Marta's bedroom to retrieve a coat. She put it on and zipped it up to her chin as a hedge against the cold, blustery day. The Celts had promised they could leave by mid-morning, and it was nearly time.

"Well?" She stomped down the back stairs into the yard, with Rune sticking to her like glue.

"I say she can come," Dewi muttered. "She may have a better feel for Fionn's whereabouts than either of you."

"I doona agree." Gwydion stood in front of the dragon, his arms crossed over his chest.

"Too bad." Aislinn funneled magic and helped Rune clamber onto Dewi's back. She climbed up after him. Bella was already nestled in the junction where the dragon's neck and back came together. She fluttered into the air before resettling in Aislinn's lap.

Gwydion rolled his eyes. "What happened to women who did as they were told?"

"They went out of fashion five hundred years ago," Aislinn retorted. "Now which of you is coming with us?"

Gwydion and Bran drew a few feet away, heads bent close.

Nidhogg stamped his large hind feet, clearly impatient to be off. Steam plumed from his nostrils. The Norse dragon looked better with each passing hour. Larger, stronger, and more vibrant. Aislinn smiled at him. He twined his neck to bring his head to eye level with her. "I look forward to getting to know you better."

"And I you."

Gwydion marched to Nidhogg. "If ye would do me the honor of carrying me and mind-linking with me, I would go with you."

Nidhogg lowered a foreleg.

Gwydion shook his head. "I doona need it." Clutching his carved staff, the master enchanter used it as a pole vault. He sailed through the air and ended up on the dragon's broad back.

Aislinn stared at him. "I don't think I've ever seen you smile quite like that."

He snorted. "Aye, and 'tis been many a long year since I've ridden a dragon. That one"—he hooked a finger at Dewi—"was never overly cooperative, and she was the only one left."

"We need to leave before you say something that truly offends me." Dewi furled her wings and took off.

"Why are we flying and not using magic to jump?" Aislinn asked the dragon.

"Good question." Dewi looked over one shoulder approvingly as she gained altitude. "You're starting to think like a MacLochlainn. Did I ever tell you what brilliant tacticians they were in battle?"

"No. While I'm certain it's interesting, that's not what I asked."

"We're flying to conserve magic. It takes a lot for Nidhogg and me to project ourselves inside you and still leave some to help you in the kingdom of the dead. While we're at it," Dewi hurried on, her great wings pumping air, "there are things you must not do once you pass the gateway."

Aislinn waited, but the dragon didn't say anything further. "Are you going to tell me?"

"Don't eat anything or drink anything you find there. And don't talk with the dead. They will be attracted to your warmth and try to hold you captive. One is not a problem. If many mob you, we may have to fight our way out."

Aislinn nodded to herself. It was just like the shades who roamed Earth, unwilling to cross the veil. She buried her hands in Rune's coat. *"Did you hear what she said?"*

"You needn't worry on my account. The shades have no interest in Bella or me."

Aislinn stifled a smile. *"I was thinking more about the eating and drinking part. I've seen you pick up some of the most desiccated, disgusting—"*

"Stop right there." The wolf sounded hurt. Aislinn stroked his fur to tell him she hadn't meant anything unkind.

They flew in silence for quite a while. Perhaps an hour passed. From time to time, Aislinn glanced over at Gwydion and Nidhogg. The master enchanter looked as relaxed as she'd ever seen him. Good. Maybe it meant he'd gotten over feeling angry at her insistence she be included.

Dewi turned her head toward Nidhogg. "This gateway?" she called.

"It's as good as any other," he replied.

The dragon furled her wings and banked into a descending spiral. "How many gateways are there?" Aislinn asked.

"I don't know. Many."

"Are they physical or magical?"

"Both."

Aislinn bit her lower lip. Dewi was even more taciturn than usual. "Tell me a little more, please."

Steam plumed from Dewi's open mouth. "You're worse than a youngling dragon. The kingdom of the dead and the paths the dead roam are like the border worlds in that they exist in something akin to a parallel universe with many gateways. Unlike the dark ones' lands, Arawn's realm draws its power from Earth."

Another few circles, and they'd be on the ground. Aislinn racked her brain for what else she needed to know. Dewi would be within her, but it didn't mean she'd be talking with her. The dragon's voluminous memories and knowledge base would be available, but culling through them for answers wasn't practical. "If the gateways are magical, do they move?"

"Sometimes."

"So finding our way back out might be a problem."

"Not linked to me, it won't be." The dragon glided between two thick stands of aspen trees and landed.

Rune hopped down. Bella took flight and perched in the lower branches of a tree. A rush of wind from Nidhogg's wings buffeted Aislinn. She waited until the other dragon was on the ground before letting Dewi help her down.

Gwydion leapt nimbly off Nidhogg's broad back. The air shimmered as he summoned magic to cushion his landing. He straightened his black robes, gripped his ever present staff, and strode toward her. "No hard feelings, lass?"

"Maybe a few, but I'll get over it."

He nailed her with his intense gaze. "I suggest ye do. Once we are within yon gateway, there will be no margin for error. Ye must drive all but our objective from your mind."

"If the two of you are done tossing barbs back and forth"— Dewi's tone was laced with sarcasm—"we need to move. I've already cast the spell to render Nidhogg's and my bodies invisible while we aren't within them."

Aislinn braced herself, and not a moment too soon. Dewi slammed into her mind like a runaway freight train. "Ooph. Wonder if I'll ever get used to that." Colors brightened. A million scents bombarded her.

"I find it fair miraculous myself," Gwydion murmured. "Follow me." His body disappeared through a solid rock wall.

Aislinn stared at it and then dropped a hand to Rune's shoulder. She fought Dewi for jurisdiction over her body.

"Move, child. What are you waiting for?"

Aislinn thought about protesting that she couldn't walk through rocks, but didn't. She took a few steps forward and laid a hand on the granite. It felt warmer than she expected. She gathered magic to move herself, the wolf, and the bird through to the other side.

"Stand aside. Trust me. I won't let anything happen to you. It took us far too long to get here. We must hurry."

If Dewi had said anything else, Aislinn might've argued. For once, she happened to agree with the dragon, so she ceded control. In seconds, she was surrounded by inky darkness, and a whispery susurrus teased her hearing. Shades. Untold numbers of them. She instinctively drew nearer to Rune and fired her mage light. Powered by Dewi's magic, it nearly blinded her, and Aislinn dialed it back.

"Hurry," Gwydion urged. "I doona know what took you so long to get inside."

"It doesn't matter." Aislinn trotted after him, aware of the dragon within her. Dewi wanted to follow Gwydion and Nidhogg. If she didn't, they'd still be standing in the huge round cavern just within the gateway. Aislinn hadn't gotten a very good look, but the ceiling extended beyond the range of her vision. Limestone walls dripped water. Standing pools held a mineral smell.

It was uncomfortable playing host to Dewi. Aislinn was at the dragon's mercy, and both of them knew it. Bella flapped to her shoulder, talons cutting deep. They hurt, but Aislinn didn't say anything. The raven must be nearly as frantic about Fionn as she was.

Aislinn lost track of time as they traversed endless corridors and chambers even more vast than the first had been. Hours passed while they wandered, hitting one dead end after the next. Shades dogged them in front and behind. She was thirsty. The perpetual sound of dripping water was a fine torture, and she kicked herself for not throwing her rucksack over her shoulders before leaving Marta's.

"Daughter," hissed out of the blackness.

Aislinn spun her head around. The voice was rusty, but it had sounded a lot like her father. She ground to a halt.

"*What are you doing?*" Dewi demanded.

Aislinn felt herself lurch forward. "*Damn it, Dewi. Stop. I want to see who spoke to me.*"

"*I told you not to talk with the shades.*"

"Daughter," rasped again, nearer this time.

Aislinn whirled to face the sound. "Daddy?"

A shade detached itself from a group of them. Even with flesh rotting away, her father was unmistakable with his tall, lanky frame and blond hair.

"*We need to go,*" Dewi insisted.

"*Not until after I've seen my father.*"

"*I could force you.*"

"*But you won't. Mother protected me from the shades in Slototh's lair.*"

"Gwydion," Aislinn called. "Hold up. My father is here."

The master enchanter walked back to her, splashing through puddles. "Would Tara be with him, by chance?" Gwydion sounded interested.

"Aye, that she would." Aislinn's mother floated to Gwydion and wound her arms around him.

The master enchanter folded her against his body.

Jacob drew Aislinn close. She hugged him to her.

"Daddy, oh Daddy. I'm so sorry. I've missed you so much. We needed you, and—"

"Hush." Skeletal fingers smoothed hair back from her forehead. "Hush, Daughter."

Tara drew away from Gwydion. Breath whooshed from her dead lungs. "Ye hold that damnable dragon within you, Daughter."

"That damnable dragon"—Dewi commandeered Aislinn's vocal

chords and mouth—"is what stands between safety and your precious daughter being lost forever in these halls."

"Stop it, you two," Gwydion snapped. "'Tisn't the time."

Bella cawed. There'd been no love lost between her and Tara.

"Stop it," Aislinn told the bird. "She's my mother. I don't care what sort of misunderstandings you had in the Old Country." The bird rustled her feathers and flew to Gwydion's shoulder.

Tara hissed at the bird and made shooing motions with her hands. "Ye must be hunting Fionn," she said. "'Tis the only reason ye'd brave the halls of the dead."

Aislinn's heart sped up. "Do you know where he is?" She straightened in her father's embrace and sucked in a tense breath, girding herself for the worst, but needing to know. "Is he alive?"

"Aye, he is. And I do know where he and the other one are." Tara grinned. Her face was ghoulish, missing the flesh that would have covered her jawbones. "Never fear, Daughter. Those Celts are nearly impossible to kill."

Relief surged through Aislinn, weakening her knees.

"Tell us." Gwydion laid a hand on Tara's cheek.

"We will do you one better," Jacob said. "We will show you. Not much escapes the dead, and it's so rare anything interesting ever happens down here…" He took off with a shambling gait.

Aislinn chortled and shook her head. That sounded so like her father. An inveterate adventurer, Jacob's kiss of death had been boredom. It was foolish, but having Jacob Lenear by her side made her feel more confident about everything. "Mother."

"Aye."

"How do you know Fionn is alive?"

After an indignant volley of Gaelic, Tara sputtered, "I am still a MacLochlainn. Even in death, I feel the link to both him and that—"

"Don't say it," Dewi broke in.

The dragon was getting much better at taking over Aislinn's body parts. She clamped her jaws together. The sooner they got out of this place and the dragon left her body, the better she'd like it.

"There." Jacob patted a rock wall. "They're on the other side of this."

Aislinn felt magic race through her, courtesy of Dewi. She sent her senses along the conduit, but they ran up hard against an impenetrable barrier.

"Nidhogg," Dewi called. *"I think we can open this, but it will take us both."*

"Can you sense the Celts within?" the Norse dragon asked.

"No. But it's the only place we haven't looked," Dewi replied.

Gwydion moved next to Aislinn. He placed a hand on her arm. "Brace yourself, lass. I'll buffer their magic for you as best I can."

Power flashed through her. Her sense of channeling lightning when Dewi had helped reach Gwydion and Bran was nothing compared with the thousand-watt voltage thrumming through her body. Something cracked. Rocks poured from the walls and ceiling, and the air filled with fine dust. She shielded her head with her arms.

With a hoarse cry, the raven launched herself from Gwydion's shoulder and flew into darkness.

"Bella!" Fionn's joyous cry was the best thing Aislinn had ever heard.

"Beloved." She surged forward, but the crack in the rocks wasn't big enough for her body. She shoved her hands through and felt Fionn grip them.

"Mo croi. Arawn and I can jump out of here now that the magical shielding has been severed." He released her hands. In seconds, he was by her side with his arms around her. Bella moved from his head to his shoulder, cawing her joy.

Aislinn clung to Fionn. She reveled in the sound of his heart beating beneath her ear. She nestled her head even closer, pressing against the hollow between his neck and shoulder.

"Aye, and I could use a greeting like that as well, lass."

Aislinn lifted her head. Arawn's dark hair and dancing dark eyes were inches away. "You'll have to wait your turn."

"If I have anything to say about it, he'll never get one," Fionn growled and tightened his hands on her backside. "Now that we're free, let's jump out of here. I'd prefer to catch up in the sunshine."

"Wait." Aislinn disentangled herself. It wasn't easy, because Dewi liked it in Fionn's arms. *"He doesn't belong to you,"* Aislinn snapped. *"You have Nidhogg."*

"What?" Fionn looked at her, his blue eyes narrowed. Bella leaned her head next to his, and he ruffled her feathers.

"Nothing. Something private between Dewi and me." She turned and held out a hand to Jacob. "Fionn, you've met my mother. I'd like you to meet my father."

Jacob came forward, bony hand outstretched. Fionn shook it heartily. "'Tis glad I am to meet you. I love your daughter, sir. With your permission, I'd like to wed her."

Jacob's blue eyes twinkled. They were nearly the only part of his cadaverous body that looked the same. "You've found a version of me, Aislinn. Outspoken, bullheaded. Never lets an opportunity pass him by." He smiled and let go of Fionn's hand. "It was thoughtful of you to ask, since I've moved beyond where anyone cares what I think."

"Of course they can wed." Tara moved between them. "Aislinn is the MacLochlainn. She's bound to Fionn, just as I was."

"You escaped," Jacob pointed out. "So the binding is scarcely foolproof." He waved his hands in the air. "All that Celtic mumbo-jumbo got to be a bit much."

"Och aye, and 'tis any worse than your harmonic convergence mumbo-jumbo?" Tara placed her hands on her hips. Her brogue blended mumbo-jumbo into a Gaelic pretzel.

Aislinn laughed. She reached for her mother's hand. "I'd love to stay, truly I would. I don't have words for how much I've missed both of you."

"We can come and visit with them any time you'd like," Fionn offered.

"Not without me," Arawn said. "Remember, these halls are sacred and closed to you."

"But not to us," Nidhogg spoke through Gwydion.

"Ye've made a bit of a recovery since I saw you last," Arawn said and cracked a smile. "Come, 'tis time for us to leave. I have work to do to rebuild the fortifications you blasted through, but I havena the energy to do it today."

"A simple thank you would suffice," Dewi spoke through Aislinn. "If you could have escaped on your own, we wouldn't have had to blast through anything."

Arawn bowed slightly. "Thank you, oh queen of dragons. I would've had to destroy it myself. I was working at freeing us. Another few hours and—"

"Without the sarcasm," Dewi huffed.

Aislinn let go of Tara. She covered the few feet to Jacob and threw her arms around him. "Goodbye, Father. I wanted to tell you goodbye on that Bolivian mountain, but never got a chance. I love you."

Dead arms closed around her. Bloodless lips brushed her hair. "I love you, too. Even if it never happens again, I am grateful to have laid eyes on you one last time."

Tara's arms enfolded her from the side. "Aye, Daughter. I love you. I wish you the happiest of lives. When the bairns come, if someone might let us know, we'd be ever so indebted."

Bairns. Tears filled Aislinn's eyes. She blinked them away. Not now. No point in telling her mother she'd done something foolish and lost her first grandchild to Perrikus.

Ready? Dewi asked without the rancor Aislinn expected. Maybe even the dragon understood about the love between parents and children.

Almost. She kissed Jacob one last time and then Tara.

Gwydion drew Tara into his arms and kissed her forehead before releasing her. They spoke low in Gaelic.

Aislinn looked about. "Rune?"

"Right here."

"Yes, I'm ready," she told the dragon.

In moments, they tumbled out onto the forest floor in front of the huge boulders marking the hidden entrance to the halls of the dead. It was late afternoon from the looks of things. Fionn pulled her close. Before he could kiss her, Aislinn said, "Hold up. Dewi needs to leave first."

"Why?"

"Because I'm damned if I'll have a repeat of sharing sex with you in my head."

"I thought you were a modern woman. What happened to sexual liberation?"

"Out, Dewi. Now."

The dragon's magic oozed from her. It took a moment for Aislinn to regain the feel of her body. She twined her arms around Fionn's back and laid her head on his chest. "That's quite disorienting."

"I find it invigorating myself." Gwydion clapped Fionn on the arm. "We're all going back to Marta's."

"We shall join you presently." Fionn's blue eyes blazed with love and heat as he gazed at Aislinn. "Doona wait up for us."

CHAPTER 18

Fionn closed his mouth over hers and kissed her. Aislinn opened her mouth to his tongue and tightened her arms around him, still not quite believing he was back by her side. She barely heard Rune suggest a hunting expedition to Bella and started when the bird's feathers brushed against her face as it took flight.

Fionn's tongue sparred with hers. His spicy scent swirled around them and heated her blood. The jut of his erection prodded her belly. Her throat thickened. Emotion rocketed through her, and she pulled away from their kiss. Tears coursed down her face. "I was so frightened I'd never see you again." She snuffled.

"I was afraid Perrikus had killed you," he countered, still holding her against his body and stroking her back tenderly. "I've never felt quite so helpless or so desperate. Had I raced to your side, D'Chel and Perrikus would've snared me."

She gazed into Fionn's dear face and fought back tears that didn't want to stop flowing. "He killed our child." She sucked in a breath. "The one you hadn't told me about."

"Och, *leannán*, I tried, but ye were so—"

She waved him to silence. "I know. I've replayed that scene in

Marta's kitchen over and over in my head." She swallowed, but her throat tissue grated against itself, making things worse. "I need water."

Fionn took her hand. "I hear a stream. I could do with a rinse afore we make love."

"So long as I get to drink out of it first." She tried to joke, but couldn't latch onto the dry humor that had been a godsend since the dark gods had killed her father and her life had fallen to pieces.

"Afore ye say aught, I owe you an apology."

They walked through ancient aspens. Fallen branches and leaves crackled beneath their boots. Above it, the sound of rushing water drew her.

"For the baby?"

"Aye. I should have discussed it with you. I wasna thinking. It seemed so natural. We loved one another, were bound through the ancient stricture… Bairns seemed inevitable."

Thank God he's saying the right things. She'd worried about him being defensive. She squeezed his hand. "Apology accepted. Hang onto your next thought." Aislinn threw herself onto her belly and lowered her mouth into the fast-running brook. She drank long and deep. When she lifted her head, water ran down her chin. "I needed that. Should've brought my rucksack along. I had no idea we'd be in the halls of the dead for so long. They're enormous."

Fionn gripped her beneath her arms and lifted her to her feet. "We can talk all ye like, but I've dreamed of holding you next to me. Mayhap the talk can wait till after?" He furled a brow and winked suggestively. His face was smudged with dirt; it made him look like a latter day pirate.

"What about rinsing off?" Aislinn asked to buy a little time. She wanted to talk, needed to, but Fionn's sheer magnetism was so compelling, it wasn't easy to tell him *no,* or *not yet.*

He scanned the creek and pointed. "Look yonder to that pool near the far bank. It's enclosed enough I can warm it. Will ye join me?" He shrugged his pack off his broad shoulders and stripped tattered battle leathers from his body.

Aislinn's breath hitched. Fionn had the most magnificent build. If she didn't watch it, the sight of his naked body would drive everything else from her mind. Even bruised and marred by scrapes, the lines of his broad chest and well-muscled arms were heartbreakingly beautiful. Hard planes of muscle disappeared down his sides and into the breeches he was untying. His cock, long, thick, and rigid with wanting her sprang from its mat of golden curls.

"Will ye join me, lass?" he asked again, his voice husky with passion.

"I'd love to, but we do need to talk first, at least a little." She wound her fingers together in her lap. "If I'd known I was pregnant, I would've stayed at Marta's. To have D'Chel tell me, and then to discover everyone knew about it but me…" She hesitated, choosing her next words. "I felt like a fool and guilty as sin." She reared her head back and looked at him. "It's my fault our child—the one I didn't find out about in time—died. I'm going to have to live with that for a very long time."

She was babbling, but once she'd started, words stumbled out, gaining momentum. "I want to make love, but I feel like I don't deserve to be happy, to go on with my life. I haven't let myself think much about it, but I did a piss poor job protecting our son." The tears she hadn't shed when she got back to Marta's, tears mourning her loss, fell thickly.

Fionn gathered her into his arms and held her against him. "Hush, *leannán*. 'Tis sorry I am. 'Twas my doing for being cowardly, for not pressing ahead and telling you as soon as I knew. Even further back than that, I should have consulted with you on something so important. Och aye, my love, doona fault yourself." He cuddled her against him, whispering Gaelic endearments. "If ye'd rather, I can just hold you."

She sniffled back tears, not knowing exactly what she wanted or needed. Being in Fionn's arms felt right. She belonged there. Maybe making love to him would carve a little dent in the desolation and the loneliness she'd lived with since returning from the border world. She'd yearned for the feel of his arms and the press of his body while she'd slept alone in the back bedroom at Marta's house.

He must've been in her mind, because he unzipped her jacket and pushed it off her shoulders, and then tugged her top over her head. "I love you, *leannán*. We'll take this slowly. If ye wish me to stop, just say so." He pressed his lips against her forehead and stood back a little, gazing at her. "No matter how many times I look at you, I never get used to how fetching ye are." He bent his head and closed his mouth over a nipple.

Love for the man holding her pierced her soul. She closed her hands around his upper arms, and Fionn groaned. Aislinn undid the fastenings on her pants and slid them down her hips before she remembered her boots. She pushed his head away. "We need to get our shoes off."

He laughed softly. The sound warmed her, and she knew she'd been afraid she'd never hear it again. "Aye, lass. If we doona watch it, our bath willna happen."

She sank to the ground and untied her boots. He helped pull them off and then sat next to her to work on the lacings of his own. "Brrr," she murmured. "Ground's cold. If you could make the water warm, maybe that would be a better spot than here." She ran a hand down the side of his face and pushed his tangled blond locks aside.

He lay back, drew her against him, and shielded her body from the chill earth. His cock twitched where it was sandwiched between them. He gripped her ass and ran kisses down her neck, his breath coming fast. "Och aye, I'm not thinking. Ye must be bleeding. Would it be better if—"

"I'm all right. It's not like I was more than barely pregnant. Most of my wounding is in my heart—and you listened when I tried to talk about it. I'm fine, really I am. It's not like I miscarried a several months' pregnancy. I stopped bleeding after I Healed myself, and then Gwydion chucked in more Healing for good measure."

"If ye're certain." He cupped the side of her face with his hand; caring shone in the depths his eyes.

She pushed her hips against him. "I want you, too. Whatever it is that spins its magic between us is a two-way street. Go." She made shooing motions with both hands. "Warm the water for us."

He cut her words off with a kiss that burned all the way to her toes. She curled a hand around his erection and buried the other in his hair. More than anything, she wanted to draw him deep within her. Her body yearned for him, ached for the feel of him filling her. Her nipples pebbled against his chest. Somehow, maybe if they made love, it would help make up for all the pain and humiliation in the dark gods' borderworld.

"Ye are making it verra difficult for me to leave," he said once he came up for air.

"You don't have to," she said breathlessly. Need was so pressing, she could barely talk.

"Aye, the vision of your perfect body presenting itself for loving is too good to resist, but I need to be clean first." With a sound between a purr and a moan, he rolled into the water and yelped. "Och, but 'tis chilly. Wait till I tell you to join me. Ye'll still have to cross the cold part to get to me, but at least 'twill be better than this once ye get there."

She drew up her knees and wrapped her arms around them. A still, slow heat pounded in her core. She needed Fionn just like she needed food to eat and air to breathe. He was part of survival. When he crooked a finger at her, she made her way through icy, thigh-deep water to where he stood. "Whew! You're not kidding. It's so cold, I'm surprised it's not frozen." She stamped her feet against the sandy bottom and willed the warmer water to chase her goose bumps away. The pool was deeper than the stream had been. Water lapped around her waist.

He folded her into his arms and ran his hands down her back. "Your skin is like velvet. I tried not to think about you because it got in the way of figuring out how to escape from the dark ones, but ye were always in my mind." He smoothed her long hair over her shoulders and wove his hands into it. "I had to find my way back. I dinna wish to live without you."

She tilted her face up, and he slashed his mouth over hers. The kiss was demanding. It echoed everything she felt for him. He loved her beyond reason and wanted her with a ferocity that would shatter them both if he were denied. Fionn drove his swollen cock rhythmically against her belly. "Lass." He broke their kiss, and his voice was strained. "I must be inside you if ye'll have me. I canna wait much longer."

He slipped his hand between their bodies and pushed gentle fingers between her legs. When he rubbed her swollen nub, she pressed into his hand. She couldn't wait, either. She closed her hands around his ridged flesh, glorying in the size and weight of him, rubbed the sensitive head, and pushed her clit harder into his probing fingers.

Breath rattled in her chest. Fionn placed a hand on either side of her waist and turned her away from him. She half lay across a large, smooth boulder with warm water running over it. "I wish ye could see yourself," he panted. "Your sex is gleaming. 'Tis such a thing of beauty framed by your red curls."

"Stop talking and make love to me."

She felt the head of his cock seat itself at the opening to her body. He kept one hand on her hip and curled the other around to keep rubbing her clit. She was so close to coming, it was all she could do not to shriek at him to bury himself inside her. Her muscles clenched, desperate for the feel of him. Lust was like a live thing, clawing at her. It was hard to talk.

"I need you inside me now," she ground out. "Damn it, Fionn. Now."

He sank into her excruciatingly slowly while his hand rubbed her. Before he got all the way inside, she convulsed around him and came.

"Aye, *mo croi,* my love, my sweet, come for me." He captured her nub between two fingers and rolled it while he drew out and pushed back inside. After about six strokes, his control crumbled and he drove himself into her.

Between his cock inside and his fingers on the heart of her sex, another climax began deep in her belly. Just before she dissolved into a molten pool of heat, she felt him judder inside her. He came hard, and the spasms just kept on coming.

He didn't stop moving until the last tremor faded from their bodies. She lay on the rock, panting. Fionn pulled out of her. He was still hard. She turned and watched him rinse himself in the pool he'd warmed around them.

"That's a good idea." She knelt on the sandy bottom and sluiced water beneath her legs.

He helped her back to the bank where they'd left their clothes. She traced the line of his cock. "Making love just now was like an affirmation. They took our child, but they can't rob us of the love we bear for each other."

"I couldna have said it better myself." He smiled, his eyes lit with love and a fierce protectiveness. "We should be getting back. This was an indulgence, but one I couldna do without."

"Fionn."

He cocked his head to one side. "Aye?"

"No more bairns until we are both agreed."

He took her hands in his and looked deep into her eyes. "Ye dinna need to say that." His mouth curved into a wry grin. "I try to only make mistakes once. Not that the bairn was a mistake, but the way of his making was. It should have been something we discussed aforehand."

She pulled magic to dry herself and reached for her clothes. Dusk had fallen; the temperature was somewhere south of freezing. "There. I'm ready once we round up the animals. I assume Perrikus and D'Chel trapped you somehow. How'd you get away?"

"We verra nearly didn't. If it hadn't been for Arawn and his secret ways into the halls of the dead…" His voice trailed off. "It doesna matter. What's important is we're reunited, one with the other. The war for Earth is escalating at a pace none of us expected, but we can discuss all that once we join the others."

He whistled sharply. After a few moments, Bella's winged form separated from the darkening sky, and she landed on his shoulder. Rune trotted to Aislinn's side. A crushed rodent hung from his jaws, and his snout was smeared with blood.

"The hunting was good?" Aislinn patted his head.

He dropped the still-twitching vole. "More than good."

"Do ye want to come with me?" Fionn asked Aislinn. "I can take us all if ye'd like."

"Sure." She moved into the circle of his arms with Rune by her side and felt the familiar tug of magic. She waited for the uncomfortable sensation of being snared in someone else's working, but it never came. *Maybe it's because he and I are becoming one.* Warmth from their lovemaking still glowed in her heart when they emerged in Marta's yard.

FIONN SETTLED a hand around Aislinn's waist and drew her toward the fire the others had lit in the middle of the backyard. Nidhogg and Dewi were on one side, the three Celts on the other. Fionn assumed the group sat around a campfire, rather than inside the house, to include the dragons in their discussion. He sucked in a deep breath. "Excuse me a moment, *leannán.*"

Fionn strode to the Norse dragon and bowed until his head nearly touched the ground. "Ancient one," he murmured. "'Tis glad I am ye are returned to us."

Steam rose from the black dragon's open mouth. "I suppose you thought I was dead right along with everyone but Bran?"

Fionn straightened. "I wasna certain. Dewi searched for you. It was over a hundred years afore she returned. It dinna seem possible to effect a successful rescue after so much time had passed."

Nidhogg bent forward and placed a foreleg on Fionn's shoulder. "I will tell you the same as I told the others. We start fresh. Dewi and I are already working on repopulating Earth with dragons, but it will take a bit of time."

"'Tis a worthy goal that may well be our salvation." Fionn gripped one of Nidhogg's long, curved talons.

"In one month's time, I will have a clutch to warm." Pride rang in Dewi's voice.

Happiness for her surged in Fionn. Perhaps more than the others, he understood what the loss of her last brood had meant to her, particularly since she'd come home without Nidhogg. Dewi had gambled and lost. She'd confided in Fionn about her remorse before disappearing into the welter of tunnels beneath Taltos. If the stars aligned and she could finally raise younglings, it would lighten the guilt the dragon had carted with her since abandoning her last batch of eggs.

"The others I rousted from the Old Country never arrived." Arawn broke into Fionn's thoughts. "We were just discussing that afore ye and the lass arrived."

Fionn moved closer to the fire and held his hands toward its warmth. Gwydion, staff balanced over his knees, did the same.

Aislinn settled herself between Gwydion and Bran on an upturned log end; Rune curled into a tight ball at her feet. The light of the fire reflected in her hair, turning it into liquid flame that danced each time she moved her head. Fionn stared at her, mesmerized by her loveliness. Sucking in a breath, he drew his gaze away with difficulty. It was easy to lose himself in her beauty, and possessiveness coiled deep inside his belly. He never wanted to be separated from the MacLochlainn again. No matter what happened, she had to be by his side. It was too risky otherwise.

"Hmph. We should go find out why they dinna show up," Fionn muttered. "Though I fear we willna like the answer."

"We were thinking we needed to move away from this house in

any event," Bran said. "'Tisn't safe. We can bring a selection of Marta's journals with us."

Aislinn turned toward Bran and cocked her head to one side. "If you can bring inanimate objects when you jump, I say we need to prioritize food. Where would we go?"

"Ireland," Bran said. "We all have homes near Inishowen. Doona fash about food. 'Tis far easier to grow things there than here, and we all have foodstuffs stockpiled from past harvests."

Aislinn drew her brows together and caught her lower lip between her teeth.

Fionn moved close and hunkered between her and the fire. Its warmth seared his back. "Talk to me, lass."

"It's nothing. I guess I'm just a provincial hick, but it seems like a long way away is all. Move back from the fire before you get burned."

Fionn got to his feet and came around behind her. He buried his hands in her hair.

"It won't take much longer to get there than it took to get where we went today," Dewi said.

Aislinn shook her head. "It's not the distance. It sounds silly because there is no more *home*. I lost that when the Lemurians took Mother. Even so, it feels like I'll be letting go of the last shards of what's familiar."

"Inishowen was your mother's home," Gwydion said. "I can show you where she lived. I believe it stands yet."

"I'd like that."

"Aye, there's little enough left of your family here," Fionn concurred.

"I am her family," Rune growled from where he lay beside her.

"I hadna forgotten." Fionn bent and petted the wolf's rough outer coat and then wrapped his arms around Aislinn from behind.

She leaned against him. "If what you said earlier is right, we may not have much time for me to hunt for my roots once we get to Ireland."

Fionn felt Arawn's gaze on him. He glanced at the god of death, revenge, and terror and heard his voice in his mind. *The dark gods are stronger than they've ever been. 'Tis chancy to move the lass into the thick of things.*

"And chancier to leave her here unguarded," Fionn replied.

"Ye needn't shield Aislinn." Fionn switched to normal speech and exchanged looks with the other Celts. "We must discuss what is happening openly. None of us are immune, and it affects us all. The Lemurians were greatly strengthened by their alliance with the dark."

"Aye, and now the dark gods have shanghaied the hybrids. No doubt they have plans to marshal their power against us, too," Arawn said.

"'Tis unfortunate we doona know if there are more of the hybrids," Bran murmured. "Or the way of their making so we could undo it."

"Are there humans left in Ireland? Or did they all get marched into the vortex?" Shivering, Aislinn stretched her body toward the fire. Fionn pulled magic and drew it about her like a coat.

"There are humans all through the Old Country," Arawn said. "'Tis a lot like here. Those with magic survived the purges."

"Maybe I could convince them to work on our side," Aislinn said. "Sort of like I did here. If things are really bad, we'll need all the help we can get." She clasped her hands together in front of her and balanced her chin on them. "Besides, I want to help them all we can. They might not trust you, but I'm sure I can get them to listen to me."

"That's admirable, lass," Gwydion said, "but if we are already hard-pressed, we may not have the time."

"I'll make time." Aislinn sounded as protective as Fionn had ever heard her. "I don't want to live in a world where all the humans have been wiped out."

CHAPTER 19

"Ready for sleep, *mo croi*?" Fionn unfolded his body from where he'd been hunkered behind Aislinn, feeling stiff and sore.

The fire had burned down while they'd discussed first one strategy and then another. The consensus was they'd leave once they'd gotten a few hours' sleep. The dragons, who didn't need much sleep, agreed to keep watch. Since no one knew exactly what they faced, it seemed like wasted energy to nail down a specific attack plan. The only one who seemed truly delighted to be returning to Ireland was Dewi. She spoke excitedly about renovations to shield her youngling cave from the dark gods.

Fionn held out his hands and drew Aislinn to her feet. Tomorrow, he would bring her, the bond animals, and himself into Ireland well within the wards of his manor house. That should buy them a bit of a breather before anyone pounced on them out of hand. "I'm weary, *mo croi*. Let us rest for a bit."

She followed him up the back steps and into the kitchen. Bella rode on his shoulder; Rune padded behind Aislinn. The bird hadn't had much to say since his rescue, but he felt her relief and chiding through the tension in her talons.

199

"I'm nearly too done in, but I need to eat something." Aislinn stopped at the pot on the stove and lifted the lid. "Good. There's something left. It's so cold in here, I'm sure it hasn't spoiled. Would you like some?"

Fionn took stock of himself and realized it had been far more than a day since he'd eaten anything of consequence. "Good idea. Do you suppose I should make up more for the others?"

"Now there's a thought." Gwydion walked into the kitchen, flanked by Bran and Arawn. "We can fend for ourselves. If I had a lass to warm my bed, I'd not want to be wasting time cooking for the likes of us."

Gratitude warmed Fionn. "Thanks." He grabbed the pot and a couple spoons.

Aislinn hefted a half full mead bottle. "If we take this one, is there more?"

"Aye, lass. We can always find more mead," Bran reassured her.

"How?" She raised a brow.

"Much the same way we move ourselves from place to place."

"I have trouble jumping with anything that's not strapped to my body, and even then sometimes it doesn't work."

"Well, ye see, the way we manage the elements is different from what ye do—" Arawn began.

"Later," Fionn interrupted. "Come on, *leannán*. There's little enough of this night left as it is."

She grinned crookedly. "I suppose you're right. Lessons in magic theory aren't a huge priority at the moment."

They sat on the bed eating out of the pot and passing the mead bottle back and forth. Rune snored softly from his place in a corner, and Bella perched on a dresser with her head tucked beneath one wing. Aislinn's eyes drooped.

Fionn got off the bed and moved pot, utensils, and bottle to the floor. He doused his mage light and undressed, draping his clothes over a chair.

"No fair."

"What isna fair?"

"I like to look at you when you undress."

He snorted. "Ye could have fired your own light, lass."

"Nah. I'm so tired, all I want to do is close my eyes and sleep for a week. Besides, there's moonlight coming through the window."

"Can I help you with your clothes?"

She shimmied to the edge of the bed and dropped her legs over its side. He untied her boots and then tugged them off. Fionn held one of them up and ran a finger over a place where the leather was split from sole to ankle. "Ye're needing new boots."

"For a long time now. It's not as easy as it is with clothes, since they have to fit more precisely."

He pulled her pants over her hips and drew them down her legs. The scent of her, honey and musk, hit him right in the groin and his cock hardened. He told his body to stand down, that they both needed sleep, but his penis throbbed hungrily. It wanted Aislinn. Sleep could wait.

She closed her fingers around him. "Mmmm. Nice."

"Be a good lass and let go."

Fionn pushed her back against the mattress and reached beneath her layers of tops. Her nipples were peaked even before he rolled them between his fingers. A soft moan escaped her. He bent forward and buried his head between her legs. Her hips bucked against his face, and she twined her hands in his hair.

As he licked and sucked her sex, Fionn dropped a hand to his shaft. He kept the other one latched firmly around Aislinn's breast and tweaked her erect nipple. He jacked himself while he tongued her. No other woman had ever made him this hot. He couldn't get enough of her. Even though he'd come with a vengeance in the river just a few hours before, his cock hadn't fully relaxed since.

She thrust her pussy against his mouth. Her clit stiffened and swelled, and he sucked harder. When she came, pussy streaming with arousal, he nearly did, too. He wanted to be close so she didn't have to work to bring him off. He knew how tired she was. Fionn strung kisses up her belly. He placed a hand on either side of her head and supported himself on his arms. His cock slid inside her easily, and she locked her legs around his waist.

He tightened his groin muscles so his cock danced inside her. Tiny little movements. He did it again and again, holding himself just at the edge of coming. If he could bring her to another peak before his claimed him, he would. Aislinn dug her fingers into his shoulders. He watched her in moonlight streaming through the glass. Her head was thrown back, her throat corded with passion, her fair skin blotchy with desire. She drove her pelvis against him while gripping his shaft with her hot slickness.

"Soon, *mo croi*. Soon. I feel your climax. 'Tis so close. Let it happen." He drew out halfway and made circular motions with his cock right where he knew she was most sensitive. He was so aroused, it was all he could do to keep from coming. His balls ached with need. With a low growl, he lowered the angle of his pubic bone so it rubbed right on her clit.

Something between a shriek and a moan tore from her, and he felt the rhythmic contractions of her release. Fionn drew all the way out. Before he'd driven himself home even once, he came. Spasms shot through him so hard, the air took on a multi-colored hue.

He collapsed atop her body. Somewhere in the middle of telling her she was the most beautiful, the most perfect, the most sensual woman in the entire world, they both fell asleep.

AISLINN WOKE to the sound of the hall floorboards creaking as footsteps approached. She pried her gritty eyes open to daylight. Before she could take stock of whether the bedclothes covered their naked bodies, the door flew open.

Gwydion leered at them. "I heard the pair of you last night. 'Twas all I could do to hold myself back from joining in."

"Voyeur." Aislinn twitched the coverlet over them.

"Ye wouldna have been welcome," Fionn murmured sleepily.

"Och, and ye have no sense of humor. 'Tis long past time to be up. We all slept longer than we should have."

"Is there breakfast?" Aislinn felt hopeful. She and Fionn had polished off what was left of the barley mixture, but she'd still gone to bed hungry—at least for food. Not for other things. A soft smile curved her lips. Fionn was an incredible lover. His mouth and fingers and cock drove her to heights she'd only imagined existed. For the barest of moments, she wondered if they'd have time for one more round before they had to leave.

"Aye, and when ye get that come hither look on your face"—Gwydion grinned at her—"'tis all I can do not to give Fionn a run for his money."

"It's nice to be wanted, but you can leave now."

"You heard the lady," Fionn said. "Give her a spot of privacy so she can dress."

Gwydion slipped out the door, but not before Rune took advantage of it being open. The wolf took his leave, with Bella right behind him.

"How are you, *mo croi*? I dinna hurt you last night, did I?" Fionn laid a tender hand on her belly.

"No. Not at all." She smiled crookedly, reached for him, and cradled his erection in her hands. "I don't suppose..."

Fionn laughed. "Nay. Not that I wouldna love to, but the others are waiting. 'Tisn't fair to try their patience beyond what's reasonable."

"I was afraid you'd say that. I don't know what's wrong with me. All I want to do is fuck you and then fuck you some more." Aislinn moved to her side of the bed and got to her feet.

"It's because we're in love with each other, *leannán*. Toss me a damp cloth if ye would."

She went into the bathroom and turned on the taps, not bothering to warm the water. Once she was done with an impromptu sponge bath, she rinsed her washcloth and chucked it at Fionn. He sat on the edge of the bed. The morning light glistened off his blond curls.

He caught the washcloth and then got to his feet. "Probably better if I have running water." He pushed past her to the sink.

Aislinn rustled through Marta's clothes. "What should I bring with me? No, let me rephrase that. What am I likely to find at your house? Will there be clothes there that might fit me?" She put on black sweatpants, a green knitted top, and the black jacket she'd found at the McCloud Fishing Lodge. Her worn boots came next.

He spoke from the bathroom over the sound of water cascading into the sink. "Not sure. Bring what ye can fit in your rucksack. Beyond that, there's not much point. I'm thinking ye can do much as ye did here and find clothes in abandoned houses. Ye'll be needing boots, too. Once upon a time, I could've had a pair made, but those days are long since gone."

They worked in silence for a time. Aislinn didn't understand why she felt so ambivalent about leaving the United States. It wasn't as if they even still existed. *I suppose it's because it's the only home I've ever had.* Another, deeper truth emerged. *Once I'm in the U.K, or what's left of it, I'll be totally dependent on Fionn until I learn my way around. At least here, I'm familiar with where to find what I need.*

"I will take care of you, *mo croi*. Ye needn't fear on that—"

"Damn it." She straightened over her nearly full rucksack. "You're in my head again."

He looked sheepish. "Aye. Ye were silent for so long, I got curious."

She let out an exasperated breath. "I wish you wouldn't do that. Or at least if you do, don't talk with me about it. It makes me feel like not even my thoughts are my own."

"Are the two of you coming or not?" Dewi's voice boomed in her head.

A corner of Fionn's mouth turned down. "I could hear that from all the way over here without doing anything special. *Yes, Dewi. We're nearly ready.*"

"It's about time. For a while there, I was afraid you'd lose yourselves in rutting again."

"Och aye, and dinna I hear you and Nidhogg trumpeting your lust in the middle of the night?"

"For the best of reasons." Dewi sounded smug. *"We're making new dragons."*

Fionn grinned and pulled on jeans, a sweatshirt, and a jacket. He knelt to put on socks and boots. "She's got me on that one." He patted Aislinn's rump. "Ready?"

She stuffed a few more things into her already-full pack. "Guess so. Do you suppose there's still time to eat something?"

"We'll make time."

Aislinn shouldered her pack and strode down the hall to the kitchen. "So how does the dragon mating thing go? They're basically reptiles, so I'm guessing he fertilizes the eggs inside her."

"Aye. And then she lays them and tends them. It takes a while. She has to have a certain number of fertilized eggs afore they leave her body. Once they're laid, they take a year to hatch." Fionn held the kitchen door open, took her pack, and set it in a corner.

"I canna believe it." Bran rolled his eyes and shoved a bowl of hot cereal into her hands. "When the two of you aren't fucking, you're talking about it."

"Ye're just jealous." Fionn spooned gloppy oatmeal into a bowl and doused it with honey. "She gets a bowl already made, while I"m forced to fend for myself?"

Bran snorted. "Damn straight."

"For a minute there," Aislinn spoke around a mouthful of cereal, "you sounded nearly as modern-day as Fionn does sometimes."

"Aye, lass." Arawn came from the study, his arms full of Marta's journals. "All of us lived long enough in modern times, we learned to blend in."

"It was easier than constantly explaining why we had archaic accents." Gwydion was right behind Arawn, similarly burdened. "I think we've everything we'll need. 'Tisn't as if we can't come back here."

"Assuming the house is still in place," Arawn added.

Aislinn thought about the house she'd grown up in cracking into ruins and hastily finished her breakfast. The Lemurians were completely capable of destroying structures. Since they'd probably figured out Marta's house held a gateway into Taltos, she supposed it wasn't long for this world. As she thought about it, she was surprised they hadn't leveled it already.

"Surprised who hasn't leveled what?" Bran quirked a brow.

"Would the lot of you stay out of my mind?" Aislinn slammed her fist down on the table. "It's bad enough Fionn lives there." She shook her head, not understanding why she felt so edgy and out of sorts. "Sorry, Bran. Didn't mean to take your head off."

"Apology accepted, but ye dinna answer my question."

"I was wondering why the Lemurians hadn't destroyed this house. Surely once Fionn rescued me, they found out about the gateway into Taltos."

"Hmph." Bran drew his brows together. "Likely an oversight, except they wouldna have harmed it so long as the hybrids were here."

"Good point." Aislinn thought back to when the hybrids had disappeared and was shocked it had only been a few days. So much had happened, it seemed like much longer.

She shouldered her pack and trailed out the door after Fionn and the other Celts. Bella found her way to Fionn's shoulder. Rune met everyone in the yard.

"Where were you?" Aislinn asked the wolf.

"Saying goodbye." A poignancy reverberated through his words. Rune had grown up in this house. Maybe the wolf's instincts told him he'd never see it again.

She petted him. "Seems like both of us are sad."

"Hurry." Dewi's voice was sharp. "I don't like the feel of things. We need to be on our way."

"I agree." Nidhogg shuffled nearer to Dewi. "It will be good to return to our home."

Flames leapt from Dewi's open mouth and blasted skyward. "We would've left at dawn, had it not been for this crew of lazybones."

Fionn spread his arms. Aislinn came into them with Rune right next to her. Magic sizzled all around her. Portals opened in the air. The dragons disappeared.

"'Twill be an easy trip," Fionn said. "Look into my mind. See our destination and hold it within your thoughts as well."

"Go," Rune snapped. "I agree with the dragons. Something ominous is nearly upon us. I think it's Lemurians, but their scent is...odd."

The air wavered. Suddenly, she knew what had set her teeth on edge. The wolf was right. Lemurians. She smelled them, but couldn't see anything. "They're coming. Hurry." Aislinn threw her power into Fionn's casting to speed them away.

Just before the yard dissolved around her, a loud crash rocked the ground. The house blew sky high, sending wood and plaster a hundred feet into the air. Aislinn battled nausea that twisted her stomach into a knot. The reason she couldn't see the Lemurians was because they'd come through the Taltos gateway and into the basement. They must've used magic to mask their reptile stink, or she'd have known they were there much sooner.

With a sinking feeling, she realized they'd never give up. She and Rune had killed three of them. The Old Ones wouldn't rest until she was dead—or they were.

She clung to Fionn, heart hammering against her ribs. Rune's mournful howl sounded all around her. It was hard to get her mind around what a narrow escape they'd had. They might've been able to fight their way out of a pack of Old Ones, but not without Dewi and Nidhogg to help. *I hope the others got away safely,* she said to Fionn.

We willna know until we get to Ireland. His mind voice sounded shaken.

Aislinn wanted to ask what the worst part was for him, but thought she knew. The Lemurians had snuck up on them. They had to have been right on the other side of the gateway, or already in the basement, when she and Fionn and the others were in the kitchen trading pleasantries. The thought rattled her confidence. There was no way they could ever win this war…

Will we ever have a world where we can stop looking over one shoulder all the time?

"Probably not, lass."

For once, she didn't chide him for being inside her mind.

$\mathcal{A}$islinn peered through a portal onto endless greenery, thick with grass and trees. She smelled salt water.

"Go on through. 'Tis safe enough."

"How do you know?"

"Because I canna sense aught amiss. My manor and the lands adjacent are strongly warded."

She wanted to shriek at him that he hadn't sensed *aught amiss* back in Marta's kitchen either, but bit her tongue. She took a cautious step forward and then another.

Rune padded to her side. He nuzzled her hand. "Good hunting here. I smell game."

He has a positive attitude. Maybe I could work on mine.

She took a deep breath and inhaled the richness of damp earth and growing things. Unlike Utah and the eastern part of Nevada, which were deserts, Northern Ireland was a maritime environment. The air felt positively soggy, but it was fragrant and sweet. She turned in a circle. At about the halfway point, she stopped dead, gasped, and then clapped a hand over her mouth.

"Do ye like it?" Fionn's smile lit his entire face.

Aislinn gaped. "You didn't tell me you lived in a castle. Holy Christ, it even has turrets."

"It has a moat, too, but 'tis only for show. Magic is far more effective for controlling intruders."

"Is there still water in it?"

"Aye, but only because I like watching the ducks and swans that have made it their home. The gate still has a portcullis, but 'tis been years since it was deployed. Ye canna quite see it from where ye're standing."

Gray stone walls rose before her. They circled a central structure set on higher ground. She walked closer and examined the wall. Large blocks fit together with little mortar between them. Weeds battled ivy for ascendency; both grew several feet up the walls. She turned to meet Fionn's gaze. "Um, just what year did you move in here?"

"I had it built to my specifications."

"Yes, but when was that?"

He cocked his head to one side and drew his brows together. "Early fifteen hundreds. I included many innovations that were well ahead of the times." Fionn's voice rang with understated pride.

Aislinn stopped listening after fifteen hundreds. *Oh, stop it. I knew how old he was. It's just that seeing something like this really hammers it home.*

"Doona fash. The whole of the inside has been modernized. Not that I have electricity anymore, but there is running water from a spring, not unlike the one at Marta's house. The walls are thick enough to hold warmth from the fireplaces, and there's one in every room. I installed solar panels, so there's still hot water when the sun is out. Unfortunately, the storage batteries need an occasional boost from electricity to operate, since there are long periods here when ye doona see the sun." He turned his hands palms upward. "Electricity may be a thing of the past, but magic fills the void nicely."

Rune headbutted her. "This architectural discussion is fascinating, but Bella and I want to go exploring."

Aislinn glanced at Fionn. "What do you think?"

Fionn extended an arm in front of him. Bella hopped onto it from her perch on his shoulder. He tapped the bird's beak with a finger. "Doona be gone long. And doona go beyond the estate boundaries."

"But I like to troll for fish along the beach."

"I know ye do, but not right now. Unless things go to hell, I'll escort you there around sunset."

"Agreed. The fishing is best then anyway." Bella overflew the wolf, and he loped after her.

"Come back immediately if you sense anything at all wrong," Aislinn called after them, but neither answered. She tried to bring the geography of Ireland front and center. "Are we on that peninsula at the north end of County Donegal that juts into the Atlantic with a couple of loughs to the east and west?"

"Exactly. I have maps inside. Speaking of which, if ye're done staring at the walls, would ye like to see your new home?"

He took her arm and guided her around a curve in the walls to the central gate. She craned her head back and took in the portcullis he'd mentioned earlier. Its wooden staves disappeared far above her.

Fionn barked a command. She felt a surge of magic and realized he'd undone warding set to protect his gates, which swung open. A stone walkway spanned the moat and led to a grassy hillock dotted with wildflowers in front of broad steps rising to the front door of the manor. Assorted outbuildings sat off to both sides. Ducks paddled contentedly. Several pairs of swans swam close to them.

"What?" Aislinn looked askance at Fionn and walked closer to the birds. "Don't tell me you feed them..."

He shrugged. "Of course. 'Tis better than wasting food."

"Great. I have a spoiled wolf, and you have spoiled birds. I can hardly wait until we have actual children."

He came up behind her and swung her to face him. "Do ye really mean it, lass? Have ye changed your mind?"

Tear stung behind her eyes. "Yes, but not now. Not until it looks as if our children will have both parents to dote on them and spoil them beyond measure."

He drew her close and folded her into an embrace. He didn't try to talk, which probably meant he was just as overcome by emotion as she was. The thud of his heart beneath her ear was comforting. Without warning, he moved an arm between their bodies, swung it beneath her knees, and swept her into his arms, rucksack and all.

"What are you doing?"

"Carrying you across the threshold. Ye will be my bride. 'Tis simply a matter of getting Gwydion to recite our vows."

She squirmed in his arms. "I know you asked my father's permission. Were you going to get around to asking me to marry you?"

Fionn's eyes crinkled with merriment at their corners, and his gaze locked with hers. "I couldna imagine ye saying no, lass, but would ye do me the honor of becoming my wife?"

Happiness shot through her. She twined both arms around his neck and covered his mouth with hers.

He furled a brow once they came up for air. "I take it that's a yes."

"Yes," she exclaimed. "As soon as we can. Where's Gwydion?"

"Assuming he escaped Nevada safely, he's likely making certain his own home and lands havena been compromised." Fionn bent his head and kissed her again.

Aislinn's blood heated. Fionn's body and hands and scent drove her libido mercilessly. She couldn't get enough of him, no matter how many times they made love. She broke the kiss before she hopped out of his arms, pushed him down on the grass, and jumped him. "We need to get hold of Gwydion. Soon. Before you change your mind."

"Aye, lass. That we will. There's a chapel within his manor that would be perfect. Doona fash. I'll not be changing my mind." He rolled out from under her, got to his feet, and pulled her against him. Scooping her into his arms again, he walked briskly toward the house.

Thank Christ he didn't launch into an explanation of the MacLochlainn bond. She wriggled against him. "You really should put me down. It's a long way from here to the front door. There are a bunch of stairs, and it's awkward carrying me with my rucksack."

"What? Ye doona think I'm strong enough to carry a slip of a thing like you a few hundred feet?"

Aislinn dissolved into giggles. No one had ever referred to her as a slip of a thing with her six feet height. "We have to be serious. What if there's something bad inside lying in wait for us?"

"I would've felt it in my warding. Och, *leannán.*" He cradled her against him. "We'll have little enough of joy in the coming days. Let us steal what happiness we can afore the darkness closes and we must fight for our verra existence. I love you, lass."

"I love you, too." She settled against his chest with her arms wound around his neck. It felt right to be clasped in Fionn's arms. The rucksack's shoulder straps dug into her collarbones, but it wasn't too uncomfortable.

The stone walkway crossed the moat and then continued over unkempt grass. Wildflowers in every color of the rainbow ran rampant. The house was an enormous structure, with at least four floors, maybe five if she counted some of the tower rooms. Leaded glass windows peeked out from stone-inlaid balconies. Where the fence around the property was built from flat stones, the house had been constructed of roundish river rocks and enormous hand-hewn wooden logs. Boxes that had likely held flowers sat in front of many of the windows.

"Do flowers grow year round here?" she asked, eying the lawn.

"They do if you nuruture them with magic." Fionn mounted broad flagstone steps. She counted twelve of them before they came out onto the portico before the massive front door. Made of heavily carved wood and reinforced with metal cross-staves, it was rounded on top. "I need to set you down afore I can open the door. Doona run away." He placed her on her feet and kissed her forehead.

"Are you kidding? I wouldn't miss this for the world." She peered through stained glass side panels with sun and moon patterns, but couldn't see much.

Fionn chanted to summon magic. Once he had command of the spell, it took long minutes before he reached for the latch and pushed the door open.

"You dismantled fairly extensive warding," she murmured.

"Aye, and 'tis grateful I am it appears to have done its job." He lifted her into his arms again and carried her inside. "There, *leannán*. I have done my part to ensure a good beginning." Despite his words, he didn't make any move to set her down.

Her eyes widened. Stretching before her was a great room, like something out of a medieval history book. An enormous fireplace took up most of one wall at the end of the room. Tapestries hung on the walls. Thick woven rugs covered the floors. Wooden furniture with plump, colorful cushions was arranged in conversational groups. Cut crystal lanterns sat on occasional tables. "My God. This room could hold a hundred people."

"It has a time or two. I'm not much for entertaining, though."

"Put me down so I can look at everything."

"With pleasure. There ye go." Fionn set her on her feet, unbuckled the waist belt of her rucksack, and slid it from her shoulders.

Aislinn eyed the dust-free tabletops. "Who cleans?"

Fionn tossed his head back and laughed. "Aye, but a lass would want to know such things. I use magic to accomplish most tasks. Since I am gone from here much of the time, or I was," he corrected himself, "'twas either that, hire a stranger, or toss those abysmal dustcovers over everything."

"Where do you spend your time when you're here? This place is so huge. Surely you must have favorite rooms." She held out a hand. He set her pack down and gripped her extended fingers, drawing her right up against him again.

"I have rooms on the third floor, toward the back. Nothing elaborate. A bedroom and a study. Those rooms and the kitchen are the only ones I really use."

"I want to see." She remembered his underground bunker in the heart of the northern Sierra Nevada Mountains. It had been surprisingly comfortable and well-appointed, since he'd hogged it out from beneath a mountain. A mixture of shyness and curiosity ran through her. Fionn had quickly taken center stage in her life, yet she didn't really know all that much about him.

This is my opportunity to learn.

He tugged gently. "Come on, then. I want to share my life with you. All of it."

"You're in my head again."

He snorted. "Best get used to it. I doona know if I can resist knowing what ye're thinking. Particularly when ye get this little furrow." He let go of her hand, traced a vertical line between her brows, and picked up her pack, draping it over one shoulder. "Follow me." He mounted a staircase at the midpoint of the great room. It hugged the wall and kept going until it reached the far corner where it ended on a broad landing in front of a double door.

"Whoa. No railing." She stumbled because the risers were unevenly spaced. "This bottom floor must have twenty-foot ceilings."

"Careful." He glanced over a shoulder at her. "Nay, they're only eighteen. Still 'tis hard to heat." He pointed at an elaborate ceiling fan. "That helped, but there's naught to power it now. The upper floors are cozier." He led her through the double doors and down a wide hall, spread with Oriental carpets, to a doorway that opened to another staircase.

Aislinn glanced up and down the hall before mounting the second set of stairs. Doors opened off both sides. "What are all these rooms?"

"Mostly bedrooms. Some meeting rooms. One is a sewing room.

The garderobe started out on the main floor. I moved it to the second floor at some point and built a sewage system. Then I scrapped the whole thing when I installed modern plumbing."

She ducked through the doorway and started up the stairs after him. "Did you do most of the work yourself?"

"Aye. Too many questions if I'd brought in outside workmen. The other Celts helped, just as I helped them." He took her hand again and walked the length of another carpeted hall.

"Is there another floor above us?"

"Aye. Two in places. The manor has a basement, as well, though 'tis been long years since I've been down there." He reached out and took hold of an old-fashioned pull latch. The wooden door creaked and moved inward. He gestured her inside.

Late afternoon sun flooded the corner suite with light from two opposing banks of leaded-glass windows. A double bed piled with a duvet and pillows sat off to one side. Two armoires lined the wall opposite. A matching dresser sat cattycorner. Bed stands with antique, hand-painted glass lamps were on each side of the bed. A half-open door led to a marble inlaid bathroom with a sunken tub. Drawn by the beautiful stonework, she walked through the door, called her mage light, and bent to run a finger over creamy tiles with red and green veins. "This is beautiful."

"Italian marble. I doona think ye can find the like today."

Aislinn straightened, doused her light, and strolled to a door at the far end of the bedroom. It opened onto a cozy study with a huge mahogany roll top desk. An organizer with pigeonholes for things sat off to one side. The room was lined with shelves that overflowed with books and scrolls. The study had a homey, masculine feel that spoke of comfort and shelter.

She ran her fingertips over some of the leather-bound volumes before returning to the bedroom. A third door, next to a brick fireplace, opened onto a balcony with a magnificent view of the ocean. She inhaled the salt air, reveling in its freshness.

Fionn came up behind her and wound his arms around her chest. "If ye doona like it, lass, we can change whatever ye want."

Aislinn turned in his arms and gazed into his sea-blue eyes. "It's beautiful. I don't want to change a thing. Maybe we could drag a couple of chairs out here so we could sit and watch the sea."

His lips curved into a tender smile; he drew her back inside and shut the door. "I was hoping ye'd say that. I havena brought a woman here for a verra long time. Mayhap not since the sixteen hundreds. Once I moved to the States, I've been fortunate to lay eyes on the place a few times a year."

She overlooked his comment about other women. It didn't matter. She'd had her share of men along the way. "I know you warded it, but how did you keep vandals out over such long periods of time?"

"'Twas easy. Likely ye know such a spell. I simply made the place invisible to anyone passing by. 'Twouldn't have fooled another with strong magic, but it worked well enough, all in all."

She shook her head. "I couldn't have done something so complex. I can cast a *don't look here* spell, but I need to be around to tend it. While we're on the subject, it took me a lot to chink a hole in the wards you set in Marta's house. I got some ideas while I was unweaving them. Maybe we could talk about the mixture of earth, air, and fire you used and how I could mimic it with the magic I have."

"We could." His hand cupped her rump. "Or we could retire to the bed and never leave."

She drew back, looked down, and eyed the front of his jeans. Reaching between them, she curved a hand around his erect cock. "Maybe food first? Not that I don't want you." She rolled her eyes. "I always want you. If I listened to my body, all we'd do is fuck."

"Och aye, the voice of reason already. I hoped ye'd be so swept off your feet by desire—"

Aislinn squirmed out of his embrace and swatted him. "Food and a bath. That sunken tub looks like a hell of a playground."

"Something to look forward to. I'll hold you to it, lass. Would ye like to move to the kitchens? Ye can peruse the pantry, and I'll teach you about the magic to construct a durable ward."

"Heh. I'm not much of a cook. By that token, neither was Mother." Aislinn thought about the delectable meals Fionn had made for them in his underground hobbit hole. "You're much better at that sort of thing."

"Pick what ye want from the pantry, and I'll make it for us, then."

"Sounds wonderful." Her body had other ideas. It could care less about food. It wanted Fionn up close, personal, and buried to the hilt inside. She told her overheated libido to take a break.

He winked at her. "'Tis poor form to admit your shortcomings—about cooking and suchlike—afore the wedding, lass. Best wait and let the prospective groom find things like that out over time."

"Really?" She winked back. "Seems like false advertising, otherwise. Besides, you'd find out quick enough that if I can't chuck something into a pot of boiling water or roast it over a fire, I'm lost in the kitchen."

He turned away from her, strode to the fireplace, and tossed wood into it from a brass box sitting nearby. A sharp command and the wood caught. "There." He smiled. "Now, 'twill be warm for us when we return."

Aislinn smiled back. This small respite from Lemurians and the dark gods was welcome. In the depths of her being, she hoped it would last forever, even though she knew it couldn't. She followed Fionn out the door and down both flights of stairs. They'd just crossed the great room to doors on the far side when she heard Rune in her mind.

"We are on our way back. Open the doors." Something about his tone jolted her into high alert.

Fionn spun midstride and made a dash for the front door. He yanked it open. Moments later, the wolf and raven raced through. Magic bubbled around them, acrid and urgent, as Fionn rebuilt the wards. Bella flew to the back of a chair and curved her talons around it. Rune paced in a tight circle.

So much for any respite at all. She knelt next to Rune and sank her hands into his thick fur. "Tell me what happened."

CHAPTER 21

"Lemurians," the wolf growled. "Many of them."

"Humans were with them," Bella cawed.

"Humans as in prisoners, or humans as in helpers, like I used to be."

"Hard to tell," Rune answered. "It looked as if they were there of their own free will, though."

"They didn't notice us," Bella said.

"I don't think they did," Rune cautioned. "We were careful. There are lots of ravens around here, so Bella blended right in. I didn't see any other wolves."

Fionn trod heavily to where Aislinn sat next to Rune and lowered himself to the carpet. His jaw was clenched, and he made an effort to relax his muscles. He'd hoped they'd have at least a few days' breather, but the Old Ones must have followed them. Or maybe they were already here. "Where exactly did you see them?" He crooked a finger, and Bella flew to his shoulder.

"The empty O'Reilly manor." She dug her talons into his muscles.

"Aye, that one is to the east. Did ye check the other manor houses to the west?"

The bird squawked. "You know my hunting paths too well. We started there. Those places were empty."

"They may have looked empty," Rune chimed in, "but I thought I smelled humans. Maybe not in those falling down wrecks of homes, but in the nearby woods."

Fionn grunted and then pushed to his feet. "We'll all think better if our bellies are full." He made his way through the winding hall off the great room and down half a flight of stairs to the kitchens. Once, they'd housed banks of fireplaces. He'd replaced them with modern ovens and other appliances, all of which were worthless without power. He opened a thick door and stepped down into a cold room. Floor to ceiling shelves were lined with dried food and grains. "Come on in here," he called to Aislinn, "and pick something."

"You're sounding about as out of sorts as I feel." Aislinn scanned the pantry shelves. "Well stocked. How about if you surprise me?"

He snaked an arm around her waist and drew her close. Her warmth and scent were so alluring, it was hard to think about anything else. "If I'm out of sorts, 'tis because I'd hoped we'd have a few days to rest and regroup. Given this latest development, the only thing we'll be doing is crafting a battle strategy."

"Shouldn't you contact the others?" She pried his hand off her waist, grabbed a bottle of mead from one of the low shelves, and went back to the main part of the kitchen.

"Aye. And I will just as soon as I have something to eat underway."

Fionn settled for rice and dried herbs and vegetables. He sniffed the canisters. Many of the dried items were years old. He'd used magic to retard spoilage, but nothing lasted forever. Rune's claws clicked on the tiled kitchen floor. Thank the goddess he'd had the good sense to return. Left to her own devices, Bella would probably have taken it upon herself to do a full reconnaissance.

He'd just gotten a pan together and called a bit of magic to hold the water at a low boil when the air shimmered. Aislinn, who'd been sitting at the kitchen table nursing the mead bottle, jumped to her feet, hands raised to call power.

"Stand down, lass. 'Tis one of us."

Gwydion's form solidified. "Thought I'd interrupt the honeymoon." He swept the kitchen with his sharp blue gaze. "Convenient. I'm just in time for dinner."

"Actually, ye're a shade early." Fionn stirred the pot and turned to face the master enchanter. "How did ye find your home?"

"Untouched. But Lemurians are—"

"We already know," Aislinn snapped.

"Och aye, lass, ye're sounding a wee bit tetchy. If he's not satisfying you..." He waved a hand toward Fionn and leered suggestively.

"Stop it." She fell into a chair. "I'm in a bad mood because I'm scared shitless. I spent a whole lot more time with the Old Ones than either of you. I know what they're capable of."

"Aye, but ye killed one, too," Fionn said softly. "And were prepared to kill again when ye were their prisoner."

Gwydion pulled a chair out and sat, resting his crossed arms over its backrest. He snared the mead bottle and took a long drink. "I put in a request to convene the council so we might strategize."

"I'm guessing our kin dinna respond to Arawn's call because they were hard pressed here and couldna leave." Fionn blew out a tense breath. He'd feared as much when the others hadn't come. "When and where for the council meeting?"

"In two hours' time at our usual place."

"Did someone tell the dragons?" Aislinn asked.

"Bran was going to do that."

"Good. We're finally going to do something," Rune muttered from where he'd curled in a corner of the huge kitchen.

Fionn considered the logistics of including Aislinn and Rune. "It might be easier if—"

"If the dragon is coming, so am I," Rune broke in.

Aislinn thinned her lips into a stubborn line Fionn recognized all too well. "I want him with us. He's a part of this and deserves to have a say in what we plan. We all do, since everybody's life will be on the line."

Fionn opened his mouth and closed it again. He exchanged glances with Gwydion. The other Celtic gods wouldn't take kindly to a human in their midst, even one with magic. She'd be safe within his warded walls with Rune, but he couldn't think of a tactful way to get her to agree to remain behind. It wouldn't be so bad if she'd simply sit by his side and keep her mouth shut, but that wasn't her style.

"What?" She looked from Fionn to Gwydion. "What aren't you telling me?"

"Be prepared for some ill will." Fionn picked his words with care.

"Why? They don't even know me."

"Aye, lass, but they've known one another for hundreds, if not thousands, of years," Gwydion said. "It's made the group somewhat insular."

"I see." She got to her feet and went to peer inside the cook pot. "Looks nearly done."

Aislinn sounded hurt, but Fionn didn't go to her. There were some hard truths she'd have to come to terms with on her own. He could protect her from the dark, but not from his own people. They'd warm to her eventually—maybe—but it might take years.

She opened a cupboard, shut it harder than she needed to, and moved on to the next one.

"If ye're looking for bowls, they're to the right of the sink." He pulled spoons from a drawer and went to help her dish up dinner.

"Maybe I should go back."

"Back to what, lass?" Fionn carried a bowl to Gwydion and handed it to him.

She made a sound between a snort and a grumble. "Good question. Back to where I was living before I met you, I guess. I had an underground grotto of my own. It's probably still there. If it's not, I can find some other humans and toss my lot in with them."

"Think I'll take my meal to the far end of the house and give you two a bit of privacy." Gwydion's bare feet slapped against the tiles as he left the room.

"Aislinn." Fionn took the bowl from her hands, set it on a countertop, and took her into his arms. He smoothed her hair back from her face. "I doona want you to leave."

"I know that, and I don't want to, but if having me here will put you in an awkward position, it's not worth it." Tears glistened in her golden eyes. "Mostly, I've fought alone, but when I've had others with me, I've had to trust them beyond measure. I can't have some Celtic god who thinks I'm worthless next to me in battle. I'd have to watch both him and the enemy."

"Ye'd be by my side in battle and under Dewi's protection, as well as my own." He sucked in a tense breath. If he had his way, she wouldn't be in battle at all, but she'd never agree to that. Her spirit was one of the things he loved about her. He knew better than to try to throw a blanket over it. "Ye doona understand. 'Tis not as simple as all that. They wouldna harm you, but many will feel your place is with your own kind and not with them."

"Arawn, Bran, and Gwydion didn't feel that way." She raised her chin, as if daring him to contradict her.

"Aye, and 'tis because they got to know you, one on one. Also, they are my closest friends. They understand how lonely I've been, so they were glad for me and willing to accept you on account of it."

She laid her head in the crook between his shoulder and neck.

Fionn started to breathe again. Aislinn had a fiercely independent streak. He'd been frightened she'd take her wolf and jump back to the States.

"Things will be hard enough," she murmured. "I don't want to make them any harder."

He tangled his hands in her hair. Unbound, it streamed down her back and looked like molten fire woven through his fingers. "If ye leave, I'll follow you. I made a vow after I escaped from the dark gods that we'd never be separated again."

She wrapped her arms around him. "I'm sick of being on edge

and looking over one shoulder. I want for all this to be over so we can have a normal life together. Do you suppose it will ever happen?"

He kissed the top of her head. "I doona know, *mo croi*." His heart ached. He'd finally found the one woman for him after waiting centuries. The specter of losing her in the war that loomed filled him with dread—and a blazing anger. He wanted to kill every single Lemurian who threatened their future. Once they were gone, he'd start on the dark gods and tear them limb from limb, one at a time.

"Ouch. You're pulling my hair."

He loosened his grip on the bright strands. "Sorry, *leannán*. Shall we eat afore it's stone cold?"

She nodded and gifted him with a wan smile. "We'd probably both feel better if our bellies weren't so empty."

He kissed her forehead and handed her dish back. "Afore we discuss the physics of ward dynamics, if ye wouldna mind, I'd like to tell you about a choice Dewi made a verra long time ago. Ye already know about Nidhogg's imprisonment. What ye doona know is she abandoned a clutch of eggs to hunt for him..."

DEWI WAS PLEASED WITH HERSELF. The coordinates for their jump had been perfect. They'd come out in the large cavern just inside their cave's concealed entrance. She moved deeper into the elaborate cave system she'd once called home. From the smell of things, the outer caverns had played host to a variety of animals, and even a few humans, but they'd been deserted when she and Nidhogg materialized in the outermost chamber. He walked ahead of her. She watched while he brushed his wingtips over things and reached out to touch special pieces of treasure with a foreleg. She'd warded their hoard with the simplest of spells; it made gold and gems appear to be nothing more than broken rock.

She blew out a nervous breath. Steam plumed. For a moment,

she couldn't see because her eyes brimmed with unexpected tears. Her almost-lost-to-her mate would come to the last cavern soon. Once there, he'd—

Trumpeting shook the walls. "Goddess's teeth, woman. What have you done here?"

Dewi shuffled beside him. The deepest cave was smaller than the others. It was tight quarters with both of them standing shoulder to shoulder. She gazed at her last clutch of eggs with gold and rubies and emeralds piled around them. "I couldn't bear to throw them away."

Nidhogg twisted his long neck so he looked right at her. "You built a shrine to our eggs?"

Dewi couldn't speak, so she just nodded. Finally, she found her voice. "They were all I had left of you."

His green eyes whirled in the dim light. He picked up a cream-colored shell and peered at it. "Did you try to bring any of them to life?"

"Nidhogg. Have you lost your mind? I was gone for over a hundred years hunting you. Eggs must be kept warm." She reached for the egg, but he shook his head. "What are you going to do with it? I'd planned to clear them out once I had new ones to tend."

"I am far older than you."

Dewi crossed her forelegs over her scaled chest and waited. She knew from experience that there wasn't any way to hurry him. "So?"

"I remember when we were many."

She nodded. She at least remembered when they weren't the only two dragons left on Earth. Not that there'd been many when she was young, but she'd never understood why they'd died without reproducing.

"Our ancestors didn't have younglings for much the same reasons you and I chose not to. We assumed we had time. It turned out we didn't. The Lemurians have been here for several thousand years. At an atavistic level, they knew we would be their undoing. I believe it is written in one of their ancient prophecies, so they made a point of finding our eggs and killing the young in their shells. They were subtle about it, sneaking in when the dragon was gone and taking great pains to mask their spoor. It took a very long time before we were certain about what they were doing. By then, it was too late. You and I were the only ones left who were young enough to produce viable eggs."

"Why didn't you tell me?"

Steam poured from his mouth; he chuckled, but it held a bitter edge. "I'm guessing you don't remember how nervous you were about this clutch. I was afraid if I told you, you'd starve yourself before you'd leave our unborn younglings for even a second. I didn't expect to be gone long—only a few days. Once I returned, I planned to take turns caring for our brood until they were born."

Dewi stared at the eggs. "So after I left, those bastards came in here and killed our younglings, even before they would have died anyway?" She felt heartsick.

"No, Dewi. You're not thinking. The same spell you cast to obscure the gold must have worked with our eggs. You had so much treasure heaped over them, it took me a moment to figure out what you'd done."

He held the egg in front of his mouth and breathed fire over it. The shell blistered. Nidhogg balanced it between two talons and continued to blast it with fire.

Horrified, she lunged for the egg. It was one thing to dispose of them reverently, quite another to willfully destroy the product of their love. He shook his head and turned so his bulk was between her and their egg. The walls of the cavern flared with crimson light. Dragon scales were impervious to fire, but it got so warm in the small space that Dewi began to pant. Rage and pain roiled through her. Had Nidhogg lost his mind during the years he spent with Perrikus?

The shell cracked. It sounded like a cannon in the confined space. Nidhogg sucked flames noisily. Dewi couldn't stand it. She craned her neck and shoved her snout into the small space between his neck and shoulder so she could see. Nestled between the palms of his forelegs, the shell rocked as if it had a living youngling inside.

Her heart beat crazily. It wasn't possible. If the eggs had life in them, she would have known it. She was their mother. She gripped Nidhogg's shoulder with her talons hard enough to rattle his scales. He didn't react. All his attention was focused on the egg in his hands. It rolled from side to side. Another crack formed at right angles to the first one. Nidhogg breathed steam over the egg, bathing it in damp heat. A scaly red foreleg poked out.

Dewi couldn't breathe. Her eyes flooded with tears. Where they fell, they added to the gemstones piled at her feet. "How?' she gasped.

"Our eggs go into a kind of stasis so long as they're far enough along. I wasn't certain how developed the younglings were, but at least this one looks as if she'll make it. Here." He turned and handed the partially open shell to Dewi.

Her forelegs trembled. "Should I help her?"

"No, just keep her warm. If you reach out with your mind, you can encourage her." His jaws parted in a soft smile. "It's how I knew her sex. I'll start on the rest. Remind me, how many eggs did we have?"

"Fifteen." Dewi blew on her daughter, her heart bursting with joy. She wanted to ask Nidhogg a million questions, but they could wait.

Another tiny foreleg emerged. The shell opened farther. It took all Dewi's control not to insert a talon and help the small dragon. Because she'd never been around younglings, she knew very little, other than they grew fast. Within a month's time, they'd have an impervious coat of scales. Of course, they'd keep growing for years after that, adding layers of scales as they did so.

"You can do this, darling," she crooned.

"Yes," a tinny voice chirped. *"I can."*

Dewi thought her heart would melt. Miniature forelegs gripped each side of the opening and pushed. The shell gave way; Dewi stared at her firstborn. The little dragon was red like her. Intense blue eyes whirled, and the little one craned her head in all directions. *She's going to be just like me. Tough and curious.* Dewi folded her close and murmured wordless endearments while bathing her with steam.

Eight of the fifteen eggs yielded living younglings. Five males and three females cavorted amidst the piles of gold and gems under Dewi's watchful eye. All the females were red; one male was black, one copper, and three green. As far as she was concerned, they were more beautiful than any treasure she'd ever seen.

Nidhogg had left a while ago to bring them fresh meat. She heard him lumber through the outer cave system. Good. She was hungry. He came into view carrying a dead goat in his mouth and another under one foreleg. He dropped the one in his mouth. The younglings converged on it. They made adorable hissing noises as they tore at the hot meat.

"This one is for us." He bit off a chunk and handed it to her. "I will hunt more once the sun goes down. Lemurians are close. They can smell our brood and are probably beside themselves with rage because they missed a dragon clutch."

Dewi tore into the meat and then handed it back to him. "How did you know fire would resurrect our brood?"

He ripped off another hunk of meat and chewed thoughtfully. "I wasn't absolutely certain. Fire was the way of our original birthing, though." He shrugged, his scales clanking together. "We had nothing to lose, my dear, and everything to gain. We have little enough time before the dark engages us in a full scale onslaught."

Maternal protectiveness surged. "Surely you aren't considering having our children fight anyone."

"Once their scales harden in a month, they will be as lethal as you or I. Perhaps more so since they are smaller and more maneuverable." Steam puffed from his mouth. "You haven't been outside. The place reeks of Lemurians. I think I may have smelled one of the dark gods, too."

The air off to one side took on a shimmery hue. Bran stepped from a portal. His copper eyes widened and he raced forward. "Young dragons." He bent to stroke one. It turned from its meal for long enough to bite his finger. "Feisty." He straightened and looked from Dewi to Nidhogg. "These must be from the last batch of eggs. How in the goddess's name—"

"It's a long story," Nidhogg said. "I have an extensive memory, and I got lucky. This isn't a social call. Tell us why you're here."

"The council meets in two hours' time. We would have you in attendance."

Dewi shook her head. "We can't leave our brood. Do you suppose the council could meet here?"

Bran smiled warmly, lighting his face from within. "I doona see why not. I'll get moving and let everyone know."

Dewi heard him murmur half to himself as his body disappeared from sight. "Dragons. Mayhap we shall win this war after all."

CHAPTER 22

*A*islinn stepped into Dewi's cave with Rune by her side. Bran had stopped by for long enough to tell them about the change of venue for the council meeting—and the baby dragons. "Where do you suppose everyone is?" She blinked to get her eyes accustomed to the dim light of the cave.

Fionn closed off his working and their portal winked out. "I doona know, but we are a shade early. Ye couldna wait to come once ye heard of the younglings, especially after I shared Dewi's sad story."

Aislinn bit back a sharp retort. She didn't fully understand why the prospect of baby anythings was so appealing. *Maybe it's because new life means hope some of us will survive.*

Or maybe it's because I wanted to share Dewi's joy. Aislinn had been horrified when Fionn told her how the dragon had gambled and lost everything. No wonder she had such harsh, bitter edges. *It's a good lesson to me that I should never judge others.*

"Doona be hard on yourself, *mo croi*—"

"Out of my head. Out. Out. Out." She flapped her hands at him.

"I want to see the babies, too." Bella launched herself from Fionn's shoulder and flew deeper into the cave system.

Aislinn strode after her, tripped over a good-sized rock, and called her mage light into being. Her eyes widened. "Surely all this can't be gold." She pointed at piles of shiny coins, bars, and nuggets.

Fionn chuckled. "What else would it be? They are dragons, after all. 'Tis their hoard. I wouldna be surprised to find gemstones among the mix."

She bent to touch a nugget as big as her fist, straightened, and cupped her hands around her mouth. "Dewi."

"Keep coming. You have to pass through three large caverns. We're in the last one."

Rune padded ahead of her. She called him back. "There's no love lost between you and Dewi. Best let me go first."

"Surely she wouldn't think I'd be a threat to her pups." The wolf sounded hurt.

Aislinn switched to mind speech through the Hunter bond. *"Not if she was thinking clearly, but new mothers sometimes don't."*

A narrowed portion of tunnel opened up. Aislinn stopped dead and clasped her hands together, buffeted by amazement. Dewi was crouched on the floor, with younglings racing around her. Gwydion, who'd left before them so he could bring more fresh meat, hunkered next to a goat carcass. The small dragons ran up and down his robes and over his lap to get from their mother to the carcass. A red one sat in his hand, practically nose to nose with him, and the master enchanter crooned to it in Gaelic.

Aislinn stepped to Dewi's side. "They're wonderful. And big. I had no idea dragon eggs were large enough to hatch something this size." The black youngling attacked her pants and pulled itself toward her torso with sharp little talons. "May I touch him?"

"Of course. Young dragons grow very fast. They're twice the size they were when they hatched, and it's only been a couple of hours. So long as we give them as much fresh meat as they can eat, they should grow to half my size their first month."

"What are their names?"

Dewi huffed. "They will name themselves when the time is right."

Aislinn reached down. The small dragon curled talons around her fingers and crawled into her hands. His tail spilled over the edge. He reared on his haunches; a flurry of question words like *who* and *what* tapped the edges of her mind. Maternal protectiveness rushed through her, followed by deep grief for her own child. "He's trying to talk to me. Can they talk so young?"

"Of course. They can talk while they're still in the shell." Dewi paused. "I'm not certain, but at least some of them should be linked to the MacLochlainn just as I am."

"Pretty." The dragon pulled a lock of her hair. *"Just like fire."*

She focused on the small creature in her hands. *"Thank you."*

"What is that?"

It took Aislinn a moment to understand the youngling's whirling eyes were focused on Rune. *"A wolf that is bound to me."* She glanced at Dewi. "May I? Rune won't hurt him."

Steam boiled from Dewi's mouth. "Yes. I am over whatever animosity I felt for your bond animal." She turned her head, and steam enveloped Aislinn. "How could I be anything other than joyous today?"

"Thanks, Dewi. You'll have to tell me how you managed to hatch them after so long. Bran tried to explain, but it didn't sound like he really understood." Aislinn bent slightly so the baby dragon and Rune were snout to snout.

"Thank you." Rune inclined his head toward Dewi. "The truce extends to both sides."

The youngling touched the wolf's fur. *"Where are your scales?"*

Rune switched to mind speech. *"I don't have scales, little one. Few creatures do. You are one of the lucky ones."*

The little dragon preened in Aislinn's hands and then leapt to Rune's back. *"I like it here."*

Aislinn straightened and looked around. Fionn had settled next to Gwydion. Both Celts were stroking dragons. It seemed as private a moment as she was likely to get, so she sidled close to Dewi. *"Fionn told me about the choice you made. It must've been incredibly lonely and difficult all those hundreds of years without either your children or your mate. I'm sorry—"*

"Thank you, Daughter. You needn't say more, but your sentiments are appreciated." Dewi bent close and puffed more steam around Aislinn.

When she could see again, Aislinn asked, "Where's Nidhogg?"

"Coming." Heavy footsteps followed his voice. "I hadn't planned to hunt until after dark, but I wasn't certain when everyone would arrive, and the little ones were hungry. Hmph. Could've saved myself the trouble. The outer cave is filling with Celts, and it seems they've all brought food for my brood."

"Our brood," Dewi corrected him.

The black dragon lumbered into the room and dropped a sheep carcass next to Gwydion's goat. He picked up the remains from their earlier meal and tossed it to one side. Nidhogg chortled; steam rose from his nostrils. "At this rate, we'll need to excavate another cavern just for bones."

"Where is everyone?" Aislinn craned her neck around.

"I told the Celts to stay in the first cavern. It's largest," Nidhogg replied.

Fionn pushed to his feet. He picked his way carefully over to Aislinn and took her arm. "Shall we? There are many ye have yet to meet."

"I don't know." She tapped Dewi's side. "Do you need me to stay in here and babysit?"

"Thank you for offering, but no. You run along. The younglings will follow after us. Nidhogg said there's plenty of meat out there." She snorted. "It doesn't take much to keep them happy at this age. So long as they're eating, they stay out of trouble."

Aislinn bit her lower lip. She wasn't looking forward to meeting a roomful of potentially hostile Celtic gods.

Gwydion slipped past her and Fionn. "Doona fash, lass, I'll not let them carp at you. At least not too much."

"Besides"—Fionn tugged her toward the rounded opening leading to the tunnel to the next cavern—"most will be in an excellent mood once the younglings race in. Nothing like a good omen."

"Tell me." She fell into step next to him. "Everyone's been nattering away about Dewi's brood bringing hope. What's that all about?"

"I doona have time for the whole legend now, but the short version is no matter how much blood spills on Earth, the return of dragons signals a promise of better days to come. We may still see much carnage, but with dragons fighting by our side, we should turn a corner soon and reclaim Earth for ourselves."

"So they're kind of like Hope in Pandora 's Box?"

He turned his head and smiled. "Aye, lass. Ye understand. Even more than that, though, dragons have a direct connection with the earth's magnetism and healing waters. Because of that, they have a strong influence over how cosmic forces flow through and influence the land."

She rolled her eyes. "Who would've guessed? Apparently Mother didn't know about that legend. Dewi annoyed the crap out of her."

Fionn grunted. "Tara fled Ireland because the dragon had all the subtlety of a steam engine. Remember, as far as she was concerned, your mother belonged to her."

Aislinn squeezed his hand. Fionn was right. Dewi was about as understated as a sledgehammer. A giggle threatened to erupt. She swallowed it. Maybe if she kept a low profile, no one at the council meeting would notice her. *Yeah, fat chance of that.*

The murmur of Gaelic got louder. She groaned inwardly and hoped the discussion wouldn't take place in her mother's tongue. While she could follow if they spoke slowly, she'd need Fionn to translate if the discussion got heated, which it was sure to do. She couldn't imagine a room full of Celtic gods agreeing easily on anything.

Rune caught up to her. The little black dragon was still on his back. "Good job." She patted Rune's head. "Maybe when he grows up, he'll let you ride him."

"Very funny," the wolf shot back and pulled ahead.

A collective gasp surged from the unseen crowd. She heard the Gaelic word for dragon—*arach*—and the one for wolf—*cú faoil*. *Probably as good a time as any to show myself.* She straightened her shoulders and walked into the last cavern. It was so bright from multiple mage lights, she shielded her eyes with a hand.

A harsh voice asked if it were her wolf in Gaelic. "Yes, he is mine through the Hunter bond." She answered in English and made her voice loud enough to carry. Low profile be damned. She'd show this crew she wasn't about to be bullied.

"There's my girl," Fionn murmured low into her ear.

"Well," she turned her head and whispered back, "it kept the Lemurians off my back. It ought to work with these bozos."

Rune, small dragon in tow, was making the rounds. The Celts seemed nearly as entranced with him as they were with the two-foot-long black dragon. A flurry of claws over rock sounded behind her, and the seven other baby dragons piled forward. She heard their mind voices filled with curiosity about *visitors* and *food*. Aislinn stepped aside to let them pass, followed by Dewi and Nidhogg.

Fionn leaned toward her, grinning. "They're impossible not to like."

"No kidding. They're all the best things about babies rolled into one: curiosity, innocence, belief everybody loves them."

"Doona mistake them, *leannán*. They can be quite aggressive, even at this tender age. And they are verra canny at sorting out friend from foe."

"How come you know so much about dragons? These have to be the very first younglings you've seen."

"Aye, they are, but I've read a lot of history. Dragons have always held a fascination for me. Dewi and I got close once she was certain both Nidhogg and her clutch were lost to her, because she needed someone to talk with."

No wonder she wanted to hang out in my body while he and I made love. Aislinn did her best to shield her mind. For once, it seemed Fionn was elsewhere, because he didn't react to her thoughts.

A muted boom sounded from one end of the crowded room. Aislinn jolted and snapped her head toward the noise. She scanned the sixty or so Celts for the source of the noise, and her gaze landed on Gwydion. His staff was raised; light streamed from it. "I call this council session to order," he said first in Gaelic, then in English. "We have a guest among us today, other than the charming dragon younglings, that is." He lowered his staff. When he drew it upright again, a green dragon clung to its rich carving and made its way to his shoulder. "So, please translate your comments, or simply speak English. We all understand it."

"'Tis a MacLochlainn," someone muttered.

"Aye, I smell her blood. Why canna she speak Gaelic? Her mother was from these parts."

"Tara raised me in the United States. She taught me a little Gaelic, but there wasn't anyone else to practice it with. I will work at learning your language."

Fionn wove his arm around her waist and tightened it.

"The business of the day is to craft our war strategy," Gwydion spoke sharply, "not bemoan a lack of linguistic skills."

"Aye, agreed," a voice shouted.

"The new dragons change everything," someone else called out. "How long afore they will be large enough to fight for us, Dewi?"

"One month," Nidhogg answered.

"Ye are returned." A woman dressed in flowing blue robes strode forward and stopped a foot from Nidhogg. She inclined her head. "I would know how this has come to be. We thought ye were dead."

Dewi moved forward. "I was on Perrikus's border world, saw the opportunity, and rescued him. The details are best saved for another day. We have more pressing matters to discuss." A small gout of flame rose from her nostrils. "As I suspected, my attempt worked this time because I had help to divert the dark ones."

"Enough, Dewi," Nidhogg said from behind her.

"I wasn't going to cast stones," she protested.

"I see," the woman in blue robes cut in smoothly. "'Tis glad I am ye are returned to us." She bowed to Nidhogg again. "And gladder still to see your brood."

"Thank you." Nidhogg pointed a taloned foreleg at Gwydion. "Proceed."

"I'm open to discussion on this point"—the master enchanter picked up Nidhogg's prompt—"but it seems to me our primary task is to stall the war until the young dragons reach maturity."

"And how do ye propose to manage that?" A tall, thin Celt with dark hair that fell to his waist stepped forward. "Lemurians are arriving in droves. I dinna know there were so many on Earth."

That's because they've all been hiding out in Taltos. Aislinn kept her thoughts private. She wondered what else the Celts didn't know about the Old Ones. Not that she knew everything, but her proximity to them for three years had yielded a bevy of information.

"I am certain the Old Ones are aware the brood has hatched." Arawn stepped from a shadowed alcove.

"Aye, and are castigating themselves for not destroying the eggs," Bran added. "Goddess knows they had enough time."

"They may not be so quick to attack," the Celt with long dark hair said thoughtfully, "in light of there being two dragons that will fight to the death for their brood. And all of us, of course. Plus, I made a point of alerting the Sidhe and fae."

"What about the other elder creatures?" Gwydion asked.

"Not yet."

Should I? Aislinn clamped her jaws together. Once she jumped into the fray, there'd be no way to back out unless the Celts told her to keep her mouth shut. She twisted out from under Fionn's grip on her and walked forward briskly. "May I have permission to speak?"

Gwydion furled his brows. "Aye, lass."

"She isna part of our council," the woman in blue robes

protested. "She has no right to speak here. Besides, 'tis not her battle."

"Oh, really?" Aislinn set her hands on her hips and glared. "Seems to me it's everyone's battle. If we lose Earth to the dark, none of us will have a place to live. By the way, who are you?"

"Andraste."

"No wonder," Aislinn cut in before the robed woman could say more. "Goddess of victory. It's not surprising you wouldn't want me, a mere human, at your war council."

The woman raised blonde brows in her ageless face. "Who are you to speak thus to me?"

"I'm sorry if you think I'm being disrespectful." Aislinn bit her lip and turned her attention back to Gwydion. "I shouldn't let my anger sidetrack me. There are two things I want to get out on the table. The first is I was, um, conscripted by the Lemurians when it was to their benefit to make humans believe they were on our side."

"Why would they bother?" Andraste asked. Her tone made it clear humans were of so little value, they were scarcely worth taking seriously.

"I've thought about that. What I came up with was they wanted to shape and mold our magic—and make certain we wouldn't band together and use it against them." Aislinn glanced about, but no one seemed in a hurry to shush her. "I worked closely with Metae, a highly placed Lemurian, for the better part of three years. I have some understanding of how the Old Ones think."

"Yes." Rune trotted to her side. His amber gaze moved from one Celt to another. "My bondmate was able to outthink the reptile scum. Her wits allowed us to escape from Taltos when they would have held us. We killed three of them."

"I got lucky," Aislinn muttered. "It could just as easily have gone the other way. Besides, Rune killed two of the three."

Andraste cocked her head to one side. "How is it they did not simply link with your mind and snuff out your life?"

"Because I can shield myself against them. Besides, they have a sort of group intelligence. It's nearly impossible for them to make decisions on their own without conferring with two or three others."

Fionn moved to her side. "'Tis one of the things they use the dark gods for: marshaling resources and moving forward. Otherwise, they mire themselves in endless discussions. Have any of you seen or felt one of the five remaining dark ones here in Inishowen?"

"I thought there were six," someone said.

"Aye." Gwydion pointed his staff at Aislinn. "The lass incapacitated Slototh. He's no longer an immediate problem."

A collective breath whooshed around the room; all eyes turned toward her. Aislinn stood straight.

"Got lucky twice, eh, lass?" A look of grudging admiration shone from Andraste's green eyes. The goddess shoved heavy blonde hair over her shoulders. "It seems I've misjudged you."

"Thank you." Aislinn inclined her head and hurried on. Things were going so well, she wanted to make her next pitch while she had everyone's attention. "The second thing I wanted to point out is you're overlooking a valuable ally in humans. They will be more than willing to fight alongside us and will greatly swell our ranks."

"They doona trust us, lass," someone said.

"No, but they'll trust me. I rallied thousands back in the States."

CHAPTER 23

Fionn kept a protective arm around Aislinn. They sat against a curved wall in the brood chamber in Dewi's cave with dragons curled in their laps—three in his, two in hers. He didn't know where the other three were, but assumed they were with Dewi. The council was still haggling in the far chamber, but Aislinn had been close to asleep on her feet after hours of discussion. When she'd stumbled against him for the umpteenth time, he'd excused them and led her to the relative quiet in the back of the cave system. She'd fallen asleep nearly as soon as her head slumped against his shoulder.

He stroked one of the red dragons. She pushed into his hand. The dragons had closed in once they were settled, no doubt drawn by something warmer than the sandy cave floor to lie on. The council had the seeds of a plan in place, unless something had changed since he left. Basically, everyone was going to return home, but quietly, placing invisibility wards about themselves and their manors and lands. Fionn was in full agreement with that part. If they played their cards carefully, they just might be able to run out the clock and let the younglings grow enough so they could fight, rather than needing constant protection.

The next part of the plan carved worry furrows in his brow—and fear into his soul—but Aislinn had been insistent about rallying the humans. She'd have to be sly about it so as not to alert the Lemurians or, goddess forbid, the dark gods. He had several ideas, but each held its own precarious set of pitfalls. Fionn shook his head. He was grateful she was asleep; it gave him time to think.

Rune and Bella moved toward him. He placed a finger over his lips in the universal sign for quiet. *"Are they still going at it?"* he asked Bella.

"Yes. They can't figure out how to split up the baby dragons. Dewi and Nidhogg don't wish to be separated from any of them until they are old enough to defend themselves."

Fionn didn't blame them. After the miraculous resurrection of half the eggs, he could see why neither adult dragon wanted their young scattered hither, thither, and yon. One of the Celts—Fionn couldn't remember whom at the moment—had asked why the other eggs couldn't be salvaged, but Nidhogg hadn't had an answer.

Aislinn stirred against his shoulder. "Can we go home yet?"

"Let me see if there is aught we need to know. Rune is here. Ye can lean against him." Fionn moved the small dragons gently from his lap to Aislinn's. The wolf nudged one that was in danger of falling off. It dug its tiny talons into his fur.

"Take care of things here," Fionn cautioned Rune and Bella and then got to his feet. "I'll be back soon."

He half-jogged down the rocky path to get some circulation back into his legs and feet. It hadn't been very comfortable sitting against the wall of the cave. That Aislinn had been able to sleep told him how exhausted she was. The sound of raised voices drew his attention.

"There you are." Dewi pointed a foreleg at him. "I was just about to hunt you down. Are my children with you?"

"Five of them. I assumed ye had the remaining three."

"We do," Nidhogg's deep voice rumbled.

"We have come to agreement"—Gwydion moved to Fionn's side and placed a hand on his arm—"but it requires your assent."

Fionn steeled himself for an impossible demand. He made an effort to keep his voice neutral. "Aye, and what is it ye need from me?"

Dewi nailed him with her whirling eyes. "The two choices it comes down to are Nidhogg and I remaining here with Celts guarding us round the clock, or all of us coming to stay with you."

Fionn exhaled in a whoosh. What they were asking wasn't nearly as impossible as he'd feared. "I doona see a problem with that."

"There's one more bit she dinna tell you," Arawn said.

"Mmph. Are ye going to tell me, or keep me in suspense?"

"We picked your manor because it has the largest amount of ground surrounded by a defensible perimeter," Gwydion said. "That being said, ye'll need help watching for incursions from the dark and keeping a much more extensive set of wards in place than ye likely have now. Bran, Arawn, and I will come to stay with you. Ye have the space. There are rooms in that rambling manse ye've probably not laid eyes on for centuries."

"I need to check with Aislinn about all of this, but I'm sure she'll—"

"It's fine with me." Her sleepy voice rang from the back of the cave. She paced forward, her arms full of dragons. "I don't see how it's possible, but they've doubled in size just since I went to sleep. Ooph. Pretty soon, all I'll be able to carry is one."

Smoke plumed from Nidhogg's nostrils. He lumbered toward her, bent forward, and held out his forelegs. "No. Soon, you'll not be able to carry any of them." He gathered the four dragons from her, nestled them next to his black-scaled chest, and then scanned the cave with his whirling green gaze. "Where is—?"

Aislinn pointed at Rune. The little black dragon was curled on his back right between the wolf's shoulder blades. "They seem to have taken a shine to one another."

Bella flew to Fionn and landed on his shoulder cawing. "Aye." He murmured and reached to ruffle her feathers. "Looks like we can go home now." He held his arms out to Aislinn. She walked into them and leaned against him.

"What do you want to do about him?" She gestured toward the dragon asleep atop Rune.

"I'll take him. Nidhogg's hands are full." Dewi plucked the little dragon from the wolf's back. It squirmed and squealed until she bathed it with steam.

Fionn listened to the small dragon's mental protests and laughed. "Eight of them, eh? My quiet country manor is about to turn into a three-ring circus."

FIONN WALKED arm and arm with Aislinn down the third-floor hallway. They'd stopped by the kitchens and carried an assortment of edibles with them. Bella flew ahead. She pecked at the door to Fionn's rooms. Rune had been unusually silent since leaving the dragon's cave. Fionn knew the wolf well enough by now to understand something was bothering him.

He unlatched the door and gestured everybody through. Bella flew to her perch. Fionn set dried fruit and nuts on one of the bedside tables. He knelt and took the wolf's head between his hands. "Are ye willing to tell us what's troubling you?"

"I'm glad you asked, since I was just about to." Aislinn set mead and the cook pot from earlier down on a table. She hunkered beside the wolf and stroked his fur.

"It's nothing." The wolf shook himself from head to tail tip, dislodging their hands. "The younglings are so vulnerable. I don't want anything to happen to them."

"Aye." Fionn cocked his head to one side. "I was thinking 'twas something like that. Dragon magic is strong. The small one who spent all that time with you has already set you to do his bidding."

"But my bond is with Aislinn," Rune protested.

"That is but one type of bond. Dragons bind you with loyalty. They may be verra young, but the little dragons are canny. They understand they canna fend for themselves yet, so they inspire others to ensure they survive."

"I'm not sure I like the sound of that," Aislinn said. She stood, snatched a handful of dried apricots from the bedside table, and munched on them.

Rune whuffled softly. "I will take care not to listen to everything the little ones say. That small male is a charmer."

"They all are, big or small. Dewi manipulated me three sides from Tuesday before I figured her out," Aislinn said.

"Aye, and then she got far more real with you. Grab a seat. We need to talk a bit afore we rest. By the time we waken tomorrow, the others will be here."

Aislinn pulled a chair over next to the food. Fionn was glad to see her eating. Already thin, she looked as if she'd been losing weight.

"Talk." She gestured with one hand. "I'm so tired, my eyes are crossing."

He straightened from his spot next to Rune, dragged a chair next to Aislinn, and sat in it. "Unless I miss my guess, we'll be under attack verra soon. Are ye still determined to round up what humans ye can?"

She nodded. "They can help us. It doesn't feel right to not give them fair warning of the firestorm that's about to descend."

"Bella and I saw a few humans right after we arrived," Rune said. "So there are some close by here to start with."

"Great!" Aislinn exclaimed and then glanced at Fionn. "Is it a safe bet they'll have at least one of the five gifts?" He nodded. "Excellent. That will save me the time of checking each one I meet."

"'Tis possible many work for the Old Ones, just as they did where ye came from."

"I'd thought of that. They did a hell of a good job hornswoggling us back in the States. No reason they wouldn't have done the same thing here."

Rune padded over to Aislinn and said, "I should be able to figure that out."

She fed him an apricot. "What? You can smell Lemurians on them?" The wolf grunted.

Aislinn placed a hand on Fionn's arm. "Can we use my Seer gift like we did last time to pinpoint where to find them?"

Fionn flinched from her direct golden gaze. "Aye, we could. 'Tis far more dangerous here, though."

"Why?"

"The Lemurians know we're onto them. When you and I marshaled those thousands of humans, we still had the element of surprise on our side."

"Hmph. Hadn't thought about that angle. Do you have any better suggestions?"

"There isna much time—"

"We have a month. That's a whole lot longer than we had in Nevada when we rounded up everyone to go after Slototh." She let go of his arm and narrowed her eyes. "You don't want me to do this."

No point in lying. "Ye're correct. I doona wish you to be at risk."

Her golden eyes darkened to amber, so he knew she was angry. "I don't want any of us to be *at risk*, but that's not realistic. You can't put me in a box. After a while, you wouldn't respect me anymore. Worse, I wouldn't respect myself for caving in to your irrational need to protect me."

Fionn recognized truth in her words. Ashamed, he dropped his gaze. "It's just I doona wish to lose you, lass. I've been alone forever." He draped an arm around her shoulders and pulled her against him, but her body was stiff and resistant.

"No." She ducked from under his arm and turned to face him. "We can get lost in lust for each other, or we can talk. This time, we need to talk."

"All right." He folded his hands in his lap.

"What?" She snorted. "Back to American English. Did I upset you that much?"

He shook his head. His feelings were such a muddle, it was hard to make sense of them. He thought for a moment and then selected his words as if he were walking through a minefield. "Yes. American English because I don't want anything to creep into this conversation that might make for misunderstandings. We're all products of our environments. You have to understand that modern ways, where women are seen as equal partners in all things, are but a small part of the years I've lived…"

She crossed her arms over her chest. "Did you like it better when we shuttled between the bedroom and kitchen attached to a ball and chain?" She drew her brows together. "What about Joan of Arc?"

"Lass, er Aislinn. Take a few deep breaths. Hear me out before you let your temper get the better of you. Can you do that?" At a tight nod from her, he went on. "Not that Joan of Arc has anything to do with us, but had she been born in current times, she would've ended up in a mental institution. She was a religious zealot. Her actions had nothing to do with her sex, but everything to do with her being burned at the stake. If she'd been a man, they would have burned him, too. You can't imagine how bloody those times were."

Aislinn made shooing motions with both hands. "You're right. I don't want to talk about her."

He inhaled deeply. "Wise of you. Moving on, then. I was raised to revere and protect women. I love you more than life itself. It goes against the grain for me not to do everything in my power to shield you from harm."

"Yes. I get that. What if your shielding gets in the way of me being who I am?"

Compassion nearly choked him. He swallowed around thickening in his throat. "Who would you have been if the dark gods hadn't killed your father? Who would you have grown into if the

Lemurians hadn't taken your mother away and forced you to fight for them?"

"We'll never know those things." Her voice softened.

"No, we won't." He reached for her hands. She gave them to him. "I want to offer you a chance to have a carefree life. The life you might have had if—"

She pulled both hands free, raised one, and laid a finger over his mouth. "I can't live like that, buried in *what-ifs*." She got to her feet, stood in front of him, and balled her hands into fists at her sides. "I spent the months between when Daddy was killed and the Lemurians took Mother feeling sorry for myself. I was so mired in self-pity that it was hard to take a crap. I took long drives while there was still gasoline, hoping I'd find some little community that hadn't been touched by Lemurians or dark gods. I was going to move Mother there, so she could find a way back from madness."

Tears welled and dripped down Aislinn's cheeks. Fionn reached for her, but she took a step back. "I'm not done." She blinked furiously; a muscle twitched in her jaw. "Yeah, it's too bad I got cheated out of my young adulthood. Nothing I can do will ever change that. I need you to love who I am"—her damp eyes flashed a challenge —"not who I could have been if I hadn't been forced to be an adult before I was totally ready.

"So, either you help me find the humans here in Ireland—and maybe in the rest of the U.K., while we're at it—or I'll do it by myself."

"You won't be by yourself. I'll be with you." Rune got up, padded over, and stood by her side.

"Thank you." She unclenched a fist and dropped a hand to rest on his head.

Point taken. Fionn's heart swelled with love and pride. He'd gotten truly lucky. The MacLochlainn was wise as well as beautiful. "I do love you, Aislinn. I'll help you any way I can." He blinked back tears of his own. "If it means I only have you by my side for a short time, I'll find a way to come to terms with it. Though, I swear I'll throw my body—and my magic—between you and whatever threatens you. Nothing you say or do will ever drum that out of me."

"Fionn—"

He shook his head. "Now I'm the one who isn't quite done yet. It tore me to bitter shards inside, knowing you'd been captured by D'Chel. After listening to you, I recognize it as selfishness, but I wanted to spare myself that kind of agony again."

"How do you suppose I felt when Dewi whisked me back to Marta's without you?" she demanded. "And then when Gwydion and Bran showed up without any clear knowledge of where you were, or even if you were still alive? I'm not proud of this, but I wished you'd been the one to return. I wasn't glad or joyful to see either of them." She lowered her voice. "I should've been falling all over myself to see anyone from our side. We'll need every single one of us, and then some, before this is over."

He got to his feet and opened his arms. She closed the gap between them and twined her arms around him. He stood for long moments, breathing in the smell of her and reveling in the feel of her body against his. His cock swelled, but he ignored it.

"I want to begin first thing tomorrow." Her voice was muffled against his shoulder.

"Aye, lass, and we shall do just that. Your idea about tapping into the Seer magic is excellent. I'm thinking we should begin across the Irish Sea, mayhap in Northern England, or even Scotland."

She tilted her head back to look at him. Her eyes were still damp, but her mouth curved into a tender smile. "Hey, the brogue is back. I was beginning to miss it."

"Well, 'tis a bit of an improvement. As I recall, at the beginning, ye hated it."

"Only because it made me sad about Mother. Why not begin with the humans close by?"

"Because that's what the Old Ones will likely expect. 'Tis what they'd do, if I read them correctly."

She nodded slowly. "It is what they would do. Their hive mind mentality starts from a central core and moves out."

A corner of his mouth twitched downward. "Aye, then, 'tis glad I am I've gotten something right here. Do ye want another few mouthfuls afore we lie down for the night?"

"I don't think so." Aislinn stood on her tiptoes and kissed him lightly before turning away. She went to the bed and flipped back the covers. Dust rose. She sneezed. "Didn't have those cleaning genies up here, eh?"

"Sorry." He gathered the quilt, went to the door to the balcony, opened it, and shook out the duvet's velvety fabric. He glanced at the angle of the sun. It was late afternoon; they'd spent nearly an entire twenty-four hours at the council meeting. Balancing the quilt over one arm, he pulled the door shut. "That should be better." He quirked a brow. "Don't ye want to take your clothes off afore ye get into bed?"

"Nope. Took my boots off, though." She flashed him a grin. "It's cold in here. That fire you lit went out hours ago." She pulled sheets and blankets over herself.

"So it did." He chucked some wood into the fireplace, lit it with magic, and then walked next to the bed. "I can warm you until the fire takes over." Fionn peeled off his jacket and wool shirt. His skin pebbled from the chill air. He bent to untie his boots and then toed them off. The only thing left were his worn jeans. He slid them down his hips, aware that his cock was still hard.

"No shorts?"

"Ye wanton hussy. Ye're supposed to be asleep."

"What, and miss the show? You're nearly as good as the Chippendales guys."

"And when would ye have seen them? Ye weren't old enough to frequent nightclubs afore things went to rat shit."

She winked lewdly. "False ID."

He slid under the sheets and drew her to him. "If ye're too tired, lass, 'tis fine. There's always the morn."

"Um-hum, we can do it then, too. Right now doesn't have to be fancy, but I'd like to feel you inside me."

She kicked a leg over his hip and rubbed herself against him. Already stiff peaks, her nipples poked his chest, even through her clothes. He dropped his hands to the waist of her pants and hunted for a zipper or buttons before realizing all he had to do was push the elastic downward. She wriggled her hips to help.

"It's good," she panted. "All I need is one leg free." She rolled onto her back and pulled him atop her.

His breath caught in his throat. He supported his weight on his arms. With her red hair fanned around her and her face blotchy with lust, Aislinn was the most beautiful thing he'd ever laid eyes on. He wanted to kiss her, but he wanted to watch her, too.

She spread her legs, reached down, and guided him inside. He sank into her easily, gasping as her damp heat closed around his shaft. She rocked her pelvis against him and locked her legs around his waist. He bent his head and closed his mouth over hers. Unlike their previous lovemaking, this was full of gentle movements. Tiny muscle flutters sent jolts of electricity to heat his blood. Somewhere in the midst of things, he felt her tighten around him again and again and knew she was coming. With a mind of its own, his cock joined her in release.

Sleep took them both while he was still buried deep in her body.

CHAPTER 24

The scrabbling of tiny claws outside the door woke her. Aislinn opened her eyes to sunlight pouring into Fionn's bedroom.

"Let us in. We want to play."

Fionn rolled over and groaned. "May as well get up."

"See?" She eyed him and winked lazily. "It's a good thing we got other things taken care of before we fell asleep."

"No kidding. Nothing like bairns to ruin your love life."

"I thought you wanted a houseful of our own."

He chuckled. "Aye, and mayhap I'll be rethinking that one."

The clawing at the door escalated. It shuddered against its frame. A moment later, it popped open with the black dragon clinging to the latch. *"Told you,"* he broadcasted proudly. *"All I had to do was pull it."*

Fionn got to his feet and tugged a robe off a hook on the back of the door. He scooped the adventuresome dragon up and moved it so they were nose to nose. "Now look here, youngling. Ye must learn to knock."

"I did." The dragon had a high, piping voice. It blew a puff of smoke in Fionn's face.

Aislinn stifled a giggle. What a good chance to see Fionn's parenting skills—or lack thereof—in action.

He tightened his jaw. "Aye, and ye dinna wait for me to open the door."

"You took too long." More smoke.

Fionn rolled his eyes. "Stop that. It doesna matter how long ye must wait. There's such a thing as manners…"

The bedsprings shifted. Aislinn glanced to the side expecting Rune, but the rest of the youngling crew were crawling onto the bed. A red female led the pack. She strolled across the covers and curled on top of Aislinn.

"Plucky little things, aren't they?" She stroked the dragon's head. It leaned into her. One of the green ones hissed and snarled, trying to snare the choice spot for itself. Aislinn pushed herself to a sit and stuffed pillows between her back and the elaborately carved headboard.

"Gutsy and totally unprincipled." Fionn put the dragon on the floor and tightened the sash of his robe. "Dewi!" he bellowed.

"You needn't shout. I'm right outside. If I remember correctly, I'm near your quarters. Open your balcony door."

Fionn strode across the room and threw the door open. Aislinn craned her head, but couldn't catch a glimpse of Dewi's long neck. *Makes sense. She's not tall enough to reach the balcony. Hmph. Maybe we need to move to the second floor.*

She pushed a few dragons out of the way and dropped her legs over the side of the bed. One of the red ones tried to get into her lap again. "You're very sweet, but I'm leaving. It's time to get up."

"But we just got here." The red dragon's chant was picked up by seven other voices.

Aislinn straightened her sweat pants and pulled them back on. She would've liked to rinse off in the bathroom, but didn't especially want an audience. The floor was cold. She hunted down her socks, slipped them on, and clumped across the room to the open door.

Fionn was leaning over the balcony talking with Dewi and

Nidhogg. "…better control over your younglings. 'Tis deucedly unsettling to have them burst into my verra bedchamber."

"Dragons aren't like other creatures," Nidhogg said. "They're independent from birth."

"They told us they were going into the house," Dewi added. "Obviously, we couldn't follow them. I figured it was safe enough."

"Safe's not the point—"

"It's all right." Aislinn moved to his side and placed a hand on his arm. "No harm done. We'll be leaving once we've eaten anyway, and the little ones can have the run of things."

"Leaving?" Dewi sounded annoyed. "Where? Your job is to protect my brood."

Annoyance flared. Aislinn's gut tightened. Damn the dragon anyway. She was insufferably highhanded. "They're your children, Dewi. It's *your* job to protect them. I'm not adverse to helping when I'm here, but I have other things to do."

"Oh. That." A small gout of fire burst from Dewi's open mouth. "I was certain Fionn would talk you out of it."

She gritted her teeth together. "What passes between us is none of your business, and I'm not going to stand out here, where anyone within fifty miles could listen in on our conversation." She spun and stormed back into the bedroom.

The hum of Fionn's voice rose and fell for a few moments before he came inside and shut the door. "Ye shouldna let her get to you."

"I know." She pinched the bridge of her nose between thumb and forefinger. "I want to clean myself up. It may be the last bath I get for a while."

"We like water."

"Yes, water," seven more voices chorused.

Aislinn rolled her eyes. "Rune."

The wolf got to his feet, displacing the black dragon. "I know what you're about to ask me, and I'm not—"

"Please," she cut in. "If you and Bella could entertain them for the next half hour, I'd be in your debt forever."

Rune opened his jaws; his tongue lolled. "By my count, you already are."

"This will be fun." Bella left her perch and flew from youngling to youngling, pecking at them. "Out the door, little ones. We're going downstairs."

The last Aislinn saw of them before she closed—and bolted—the door was the black dragon clinging tenaciously to Rune's back. "Whew! Even if we get lucky and the Old Ones don't attack, it's going to be a long month."

Fionn blew out a breath. "It wouldna be so bad, but they're the size of bobcats already. By the time ye and I return, they'll be as big as small ponies."

"Look on the bright side. When they get big enough, they'll be forced to stay outside with their parents."

"Let me get the water going." He kissed her gently and then moved into the bathroom. "The thing that would keep them out of the house," he said over the sound of running water, "is girth. That willna happen for quite some time. They grow upward first and then fill out."

"Hmph. Too bad." She shucked her clothes, walked into the bathroom, and looked at the tub. "Takes time to fill, huh?"

He whistled. "You have the most incredible body. I can't think of a better way to while away the waiting, than—"

Aislinn's blood heated at the raw lust in his eyes. She took a deep breath before desire got the better of her. "Nope. We're going to talk. I was too tired last night. I do remember you said we were going to Scotland, or maybe it was Northern England."

"You remember right. We'll get travel packs together and leave as soon as we've eaten and I've had a chance to check in with the others."

"Shouldn't we search first with Seer magic? Seems like we'll be wasting time, otherwise."

"Nay. 'Tis better if we do that once we're there. I doona know just how sharp the Lemurians are at picking up on the varieties of human magic—"

"Pretty adept," she broke in. "They're the ones who taught us about the five gifts and helped determine who had which."

Fionn dropped a hand in the water. The air around him shimmered as he summoned magic. "There, lass. Ye can get in. I'll add more water, but ye may as well get started." He held out his other hand and helped her navigate the tiled steps into the sunken tub. "Soap and shampoo are in those porcelain containers. Back to the Old Ones... I'd feared as much. So if we go throwing out megawatts of Seer magic, they'll likely figure we're up to something and drop everything to attack."

"You're probably right. Do you have a more specific destination in mind than Scotland? It's a pretty big place. Not by U.S. standards, but you know what I mean."

He untied his robe and pushed it off his shoulders. It puddled on the floor. He stepped into the water and sat on the tiled floor of the tub. Apparently deciding the water was deep enough, he reached across her and turned the tap off. "There's an old castle in Penrith."

"That's Northern England."

He smiled. "Aye, lass. Good ye know your geography. 'Tis only a few leagues south of the Scottish border."

"Why there?" She tilted her head back, wet her hair, and lathered shampoo through it. The liquid soap smelled delicious, like wild lavender.

"Because one of us used to live there. Lean against me, lass."

Wonderfully knowing fingers massaged her scalp. She gave herself up to being cared for. Once her hair was washed, she soaped his body, loving the feel of his golden skin stretched taut over hard planes of muscle.

"You're not making this easy." Her breath hitched. "All I really want to do is drag you back to bed and fuck you until neither of us can walk."

Fionn grinned at her. "I thought that was supposed to be my

line." He curved a hand around his submerged erection. "'Tis here for you whenever ye want."

She leaned into him and wrapped an arm around his shoulder. "I love you."

He bent his head and kissed her. The kiss was gentle and tender and full of promise. When he broke away, he said, "I love you, too, Aislinn. I'd love you even if ye weren't the MacLochlainn."

"What if I weren't and there was another—"

He laid a finger over her lips. "I'd figure something out. Nothing will ever separate us, shy of death." Emotion thrummed beneath his words.

Joy took root and bloomed deep within her.

All too soon, the water cooled enough it was time to leave. Feeling refreshed, she dried off and dug through her rucksack for something warm and practical to put on. Arms closed around her from behind.

"I'll see you downstairs, lass. I want to talk with Gwydion and the others and get something started for breakfast if they havena already." He tweaked her nipples and started for the door.

"But you're naked."

"Ye noticed. Good." Fionn shot his ten-thousand watt grin over one shoulder and bolted out the door.

"Well, it is his house," she muttered to the closed door. "He must have clothes stashed lots of places."

It took her a while to dress and repack her rucksack with what she thought she'd need. She looked ruefully at her boots. Maybe Fionn would have some sort of shoe glop she could use to glue the gaping rents in the worn leather.

"Rune. How's it going?"

"There's a reason I never fathered pups. Although, small wolves mind their elders. Bella and I are trying to herd them outside so their real parents can take care of them."

"I'll be down soon."

Rune didn't answer. She shouldered her pack and let herself into the hallway, taking care to latch the door. She looked about for a key to turn the bolt from the hall side, but didn't see one. The dragon horde could do a lot of damage if they were left to run wild through Fionn's manor house. *I'll have to tell Gwydion and the others to keep a close eye.* She snorted. No matter what she said, she had a hard time envisioning any of the Celtic gods as strict disciplinarians when it came to the younglings. They were far more likely to over-indulge what they saw as an unexpected gift.

She looked around the empty great room as she moved down the second set of stairs. It really was elegantly appointed, with huge wooden beams crisscrossing below its high ceiling. The tapestries looked like heavy silk, and the rugs appeared to be old and hand-woven with an inch-thick nap. Dragons and unicorns cavorted across the dark carpets. A man with a flute, probably Pan, held court on one of the tapestries in the midst of a crowd of centaurs.

Aislinn shook her head. "It's like walking through a museum," she murmured and pushed the door leading to the kitchen hallway open.

The buzz of voices reached her. She rounded a corner and went down a few steps and into the main kitchen. Smaller rooms opened off it that probably hadn't been in use for centuries, like the buttery.

Gwydion, Arawn, Bran, and Fionn sat around the kitchen table. An oak oblong, it could have accommodated twenty. Fionn had traded his earlier nudity for battle leathers. They hugged his tall, well-muscled form.

Gwydion looked up. "Top of the day to you, lass. Come eat."

"I smell coffee."

"In the silver pot on the counter." Fionn got to his feet and poured her a cup. "We got lucky. I dinna think I had any left. Rune snuffled it out afore he and the herd left."

Aislinn giggled. "Herd, indeed." She took the steaming mug from Fionn and sniffed appreciatively before taking a sip. "Is there any milk?"

"Powdered."

"I'll pass." She set her mug in front of an empty place at the table, got a bowl, and dished up a cereal mixture from a large pot. "Oatmeal?"

"Aye," Arawn said, "with a bit of barley and dried fruit and nuts. I did mix powdered milk in with it, but ye canna taste it—at least not much. And honey. There's honey in it, too."

"Sounds great." She settled at the table. "Anything I don't have to cook myself is always wonderful."

"Hear that." Bran elbowed Fionn who'd sat back down. "The lass actually admitted she doesna like to cook."

"Truer words were never spoken." Aislinn flashed him a grin and tucked into her food. Voices ebbed and flowed around her speaking Gaelic. She caught some of the conversation, but far from all of it. She took a sip of coffee. It was perfect: hot and strong and bitter. "Where did Rune and Bella take the younglings?" She glanced around at the men.

Arawn snorted. "Does it matter, so long as they're not underfoot? They were unbelievable pests while I was cooking breakfast. One actually fell into the cook pot."

"Heat doesn't bother them, does it?" Aislinn asked in between bites.

Arawn shook his head. "Nay, but it slowed me down since I had to take the little devil over to the sink and hose him off."

"There would've been hell to pay if ye'd burned our breakfast." Fionn tried to keep a straight face, but burst out laughing.

Gwydion joined in. When he could talk again, he looked from Fionn to Aislinn. "We need to map out a strategy afore ye leave."

"Aye." Bran got up and refilled his mug with tea leaves and hot water. "If ye find willing humans, will ye transport them back here?"

"We'd almost have to," Aislinn said. "If they're to fight with us, they need to be here."

"Not necessarily, lass," Arawn cut in. "'Tisn't as if there aren't Lemurians on the other side of the Irish Sea as well. Once we know with whom we collaborate, we can coordinate telepathically."

"It's too far." She set her spoon down and thought about whether she wanted another helping of breakfast. Deciding in the affirmative, she got to her feet and scooped more into her bowl.

"In the States, ye would be correct." Fionn held out his bowl to her. She filled it, too, before sitting back down. "Magic is stronger here."

"That could be convenient." She bit her lower lip, thinking. "I really haven't experimented with my own magic since we got here. Otherwise, I might've realized that."

"Depending on how many willing volunteers we find," Fionn said around a mouthful of cereal, "our best bet would be to bring some with us, but leave enough there to fight our enemy."

"That would be the catch," Gwydion muttered. "Humans have never been especially fond of us."

"'Tis a safe bet the Old Ones have done their damnedest to capitalize on that distrust," Bran added.

Aislinn thought about her near brainwashing at the hands of the Lemurians. She nearly pulled her sleeves up to look at the faint remains of tattoos they'd stenciled into her as a tracking device. "It will be easy enough to figure which ones have been corrupted by the Lemurians," she said. "All we need to do is look for the tattoos. We were planning to have Rune sniff them out, but this is better."

Fionn snapped his fingers. "Brilliant, lass. I'd nearly forgotten about those tattoos, even though 'twas I who removed them from you."

"What's this all about?" Gwydion asked. His spoon clanked against the bottom of his bowl, and he set both aside.

"The Lemurians tattooed the inside of both my arms," Aislinn explained. "They told me it was a way to focus and strengthen my magic, when it was really a way for them to always know where I was."

"Hmph." Bran settled his arms across his chest. "'Tis winter. Mayhap not so easy to see someone's arms."

"Not at first," she agreed. "If we find someone who says they want to ally themselves with us, we can ask about their experiences with the Old Ones, and Rune will be able to smell if they've spent time with them."

Speaking of Rune... "Rune. We need you and Bella in here."

"On our way."

The wolf loped in from the far end of the kitchen, followed by Bella. "Quick," the wolf said. "Close the door. Maybe it will keep them out for a few moments."

Aislinn shot to her feet, but she was too late. The scrape of claws on tile heralded eight bouncing dragons. Once they were in the kitchen, half of them took wing. She settled back into her chair. "Great. They've learned to fly already."

"Watching them grow is like time-lapse photography." Bran laughed and held out an arm. One of the green dragons perched on it. Steam billowed from its jaws.

"Like with any babies," Aislinn said, "we should enjoy them. They won't stay small—or innocent—for very long."

"Truer words were never spoken." Fionn pushed to his feet. "Have ye had enough to eat?"

She nodded and got up. "We probably should go."

A red dragon landed on her shoulder. "You can't go. Mother says we need you here."

"Yes, Dewi would say that. Never fear, little one. We'll be back before too long." The dragon huffed steam and flapped about the kitchen.

Aislinn glanced at her feet. "Fionn, do you have something I can patch my boots with?"

He shook his head. "Nay, and mine would be too big for you. We'll have to hunt you down a pair somewhere. Can't have ye going barefoot."

"I doona see why not." Gwydion spun so he faced away from the table. His perennially bare feet stuck out from beneath his robes.

"You're used to it. Mine would get cold." She shouldered her pack and met Fionn's gaze. "Is your travel pack ready?"

"Aye. Follow me. We'll leave from the great room." Bella landed on his shoulder with a whoosh of feathers.

"Bye, everyone." Her mouth twitched into a smile. "Hold down the fort. There's nothing wrong with making Dewi and Nidhogg parent their brood." She clucked to Rune and followed Fionn out of the kitchen, up the stairs, and into the manor's main room.

CHAPTER 25

*I*t was such a short distance, the jump was over within minutes. Aislinn started through the portal, but Fionn grabbed her arm.

"Wait. I need to see if 'tis safe." He fanned magic about and held his breath. Travel to any location hadn't been truly safe for years—not since the dark gods kicked open the gates between the worlds. Though Fionn hadn't realized it at the time, the dark ones' alliance with the Lemurians was the leading edge of the demise of modern life.

About all Fionn had done in the intervening time was shuttle from the U.S. to his country estate, so he knew woefully little about how the rest of Ireland, England, and Scotland had fared. The Celts didn't pay much attention to humans, but he wasn't about to spell that out for Aislinn. No doubt, she'd already figured it out herself, without him tossing it in her face.

Fionn sent his enhanced senses twirling along the paths his magic had opened. Nothing overt bounced back at him, and he sheathed his power. No point in drawing undue attention to them. "All right, lass."

She walked out onto a grassy swale. The skies were gray and it was raining. She swung her head from side to side, taking in the ruins of Penrith Castle. While far from the best-preserved castle in the area, most of its primary walls were still partially standing. She turned to face him with Rune by her side. The wolf's ears were pricked forward; his tail swished.

"What now?" she asked.

"Sidhe used to live in the barrows beneath this castle, but I canna sense them."

"There is nothing living close by," Rune confirmed. "Nothing human, anyway. I smell game and birds."

Aislinn's eyes narrowed. "How long since you were here?"

"Before the world turned upside down," he admitted.

"Hmph. That explains what happened to your friends." She pulled her jacket hood up. "What we need is shelter so we can find out who's here now. How about over there?" She pointed across a wide swath of asphalt with large cracks in it to a brick building.

"It might work. That used to be the train station."

"For whatever reason, it's still standing. Let's go." She jogged across the street, zigzagging to avoid the worst of the potholes.

Fionn wanted to tell her to stand back and let him go first. Instead, he clung to her like a shadow, damned if he'd let anything happen to her.

"Crap." She rattled a padlocked chain on the front door.

He snorted. "Ye dinna believe 'twould be sitting wide open just for us." He focused magic on the four banks of numbers. They twirled and the metal hasp snapped open.

Aislinn stared at him. "That's rather convenient. You'll have to teach it to me."

"Aye, and I'm just full of interesting tricks." He quirked a brow and mock bowed. "After you."

She pulled the length of chain out of the door handles and went inside. Surprised families of mice scattered in every direction. Rune pounced on one fleeing rodent. Bella snapped another up in her beak.

Something harried the edge of his attention. It felt wrong, like shielded power. Fionn dragged Aislinn behind him.

"What are you doing?" she asked.

"Hush, *leannán*. We're not alone."

Magic senses on full alert, he tapped into earth power and felt Aislinn do the same. Good. They'd need to defend themselves—and damned soon—or his instincts weren't worth a crap. Aislinn called to Rune in mind speech. The wolf shot to her side, growling low. Bella flew to Fionn's shoulder.

He thought about asking if the wolf or raven sensed anything, but didn't want to divert his attention. A rustling susurrus from the far end of the station stood the fine hairs on the back of his neck on end. He twirled to face the sound and repositioned Aislinn.

She moved to his side. "I can't fight from behind you. Do you know what—?"

A resounding crack nearly deafened him. The floor splintered in half a dozen places, and Bal'ta poured out. Minions of the dark, they stood between five and six feet tall. With their sloping foreheads, matted hair, and ropy muscles, they looked like apes, except for their eyes, which glowed an unholy orange. Fionn pulled lethal magic and chucked blow after blow at them. He wasn't too worried about killing them—so long as there weren't an endless number. That they'd been able to cloak their presence until the last possible moment was a huge concern, though.

I canna think about that now.

Rune darted forward, intent on launching himself at one of the creatures. Fionn took care to direct his magic elsewhere. Bella pecked out eyes. It was one of her favorite tricks. Blind opponents were no longer a threat. He heard Aislinn panting beside him. The wolf buried his teeth in a carotid artery. Blood geysered several feet into the air. Satisfied he'd disabled his opponent, Rune moved to another.

Fionn's blood pumped hot and fast. Adrenaline hummed along his nerve endings. He'd always liked the whine of battle, with its coppery blood smell and the dying screams of his enemies. He frowned and heaved more magic. Three Bal'ta keeled over. If he weren't so worried about Aislinn, he'd almost be having a good time. The ape-like enemy had no magic of their own, so they had to kill the old-fashioned way, up close and personal. He nimbly side-stepped a flail one of them chucked at him. The studded ball grazed his cheek, but didn't hurt.

"Look sharp," he told Aislinn.

She ducked, narrowly avoiding a cudgel. "I've fought them before." It sounded as if her jaws were clenched together.

He lost count of bodies and time, but the light slanting through the glass station doors was fading. Finally, no more Bal'ta emerged from beneath the abandoned railway station. Fionn straightened, but didn't drop his guard. Rune's fur and Bella's feathers were coated in blood. He glanced at Aislinn. Her hair hung around her torso. She'd had it in a braid, but most of it had escaped. There were smudges beneath her eyes, and her face held a haunted look. Her hands were still raised in front of her.

"I think 'tis all of them, lass, at least for now. One thing is certain: we canna remain here. Their masters will be along to tally up the dead."

"Fine." Though she tried to hide it, her lips trembled. "Get us out of here."

He whistled. Rune and Bella came as fast as they could. Fionn opened a gateway and jumped them to Loch Lomond in Scotland. It was a common enough location; he hoped it would be one of the last places the dark—or the Old Ones—would hunt for them. At least they could wash the blood off, breathe a bit, and figure out their next move.

Night was falling as they stepped through the portal onto the overgrown shores of the loch. He scanned the bank for problems and then reminded himself it had been wasted effort in Penrith. Either the Old Ones or the dark gods—it didn't really matter which—had hidden the Bal'ta so effectively, he hadn't been able to sense them until he was right on top of them. That didn't bode well.

"Do you think it's safe?" Aislinn hung back.

"Aye. Safe as anywhere. Come on through. We must stop somewhere to regroup, rest, and eat. If we canna do it here, we may as well give this up for a lost cause and return to Inishowen."

Rune jumped into the loch. Bella clung to a large branch that overhung it and dipped her plumage to clean it. Aislinn shucked her rucksack, fished out a water bottle, and took a long drink. Fionn did the same, wishing he'd thought to bring a bottle of mead. "That was damned unsettling." He wiped water off his chin.

"The worst of it was I had no idea they were there until the floor cracked open. It's like my magic was on strike." She shuddered. "I don't think we can afford to lollygag around. Let's deploy Seer magic and see who we can find."

Fionn didn't agree with her. The last thing he wanted to do was use a large amount of magic. The dark had spies everywhere. He blew out a tense breath. They'd come across the Irish Sea with a purpose. Aislinn was right that they wouldn't accomplish it sitting on the shores of the loch.

"Look..." Her voice was soft. "I understand it's a risk, but I don't see any other way. It's either that or go home."

"Hmph. We're beginning to think alike. I'd come to the same conclusion. If nothing else, your Seer gift may tell us what's happened here. Turn your pack over and sit on it." He patted a flattish area on the lakeshore. Once she was settled, he did the same and sat next to her. "Ready?"

She nodded. He linked to her mind and guided her fledgling talent. Aislinn had only discovered she had Seer magic quite recently. It was the hardest of the five human magics to direct and control. Visions pummeled him. Most notably, a large group of humans was on the far side of the loch. Having established that, he molded Aislinn's magic to give them information about the past few months. It didn't take long to get more than he needed. Fionn cut the flow of their combined power and gathered her shaking body into his arms.

"Perrikus was here. Who was the other one? It had to be another of the dark gods. He looked a lot like D'Chel, except for his eyes."

"Aye, lass, 'twas Tokhots."

"He's the trickster, isn't he?"

He held her against him. "Um-hum. At least that explains the shielding at the train station. I dinna believe the Lemurians were capable of something that sophisticated. Watch out for Tokhots. Doona let his blood, or saliva, or anything from him get anywhere near you."

"Why? I understand the dark gods are dangerous, but—"

"His blood is deadly poison. So is Majestron Zalia's, if she should happen to show up."

"I stumbled across her once. She didn't notice me, but being near her scared the holy crap out of me. That's Perrikus's mother, isn't it?" she asked.

Fionn nodded tersely.

Aislinn moved out of his embrace. Her lips were set in a thin line, and she looked grim. "Let's pay a visit to those humans we saw on the far side of the lake."

He opened his mouth to ask if she were certain she was rested enough, but shut it with a clack. She wouldn't appreciate mollycoddling. What he wanted to do was take all of them back to his estate. That would be prudent, but...

"We're not going back."

"I dinna say aught—"

"You didn't have to. I can see it in your mind. If I called up my mage light, no doubt I'd see it written all over your face as well." She got to her feet and slid her pack over her shoulders. "Ready."

Fionn grabbed a handy branch and hauled himself upright. He grabbed his pack. Rune and Bella understood and gathered close. Aislinn shot Fionn an odd look when he reached for his magic and said, "They're just on the far side of the lake—or I guess it's a loch. I thought we'd walk."

"Doona ye wish to get there soon? 'Tis a large loch. It would take hours to walk to the far side. Mayhap two. More if the lakeside track is washed out."

"Oh." She wove her magic with his. "Let's go."

Fionn brought them out about half a mile from where they'd sensed the settlement. He hoped it would be far enough away that they'd at least have the element of surprise. Goddess only knew what the Lemurians had done on this side of the Atlantic. Christ! He hadn't even known they were here until recently.

He felt Aislinn throw wards up and did the same. They walked through thick underbrush, making as little noise as possible. He pulled a bit more magic to muffle the sounds of cracking branches and sucking mud. He felt Rune's energy, and Bella's, too, but couldn't see either animal.

"Halt!"

A light shone so brightly that Fionn shielded his hands with his eyes.

"I feel your ward. Show yourself." The voice had such a strong Scottish burr, it took Fionn a moment to decipher the words.

Before he could stop her, Aislinn took a few steps forward and dropped her warding. She held out both hands, fingers spread wide in a self-deprecating gesture.

"You're human." The figure behind the light sounded surprised.

"What did you expect?' She squared her shoulders. "Now, if you'd lower that light, or shutter it somehow, maybe we could talk."

"Someone is with you. I must see them also."

Aislinn looked over one shoulder. Her expression spoke volumes. It told him to either get with the program or go back to Inishowen. With a great deal of misgiving, Fionn loosed his ward.

A long hissing sigh came from the lantern-bearer. "Celt. You've got a hell of a nerve to show up here. Where were you when we needed you, eh?"

"Fionn came with me to help you," Aislinn said. "We wish to speak with as many of you as we can."

"We don't wish to talk with him. If it were you alone, maybe. The Celts didn't lift a finger to help us when the Old Ones mowed through our ranks like so much crabgrass."

Aislinn half-turned. "Is that true?"

Fionn shrugged uncomfortably and said in perfect American English, "I don't know for certain. Remember, I've been in the States for the past few hundred years." He could tell from the line of her jaw that he hadn't heard the last of his pathetic attempt to sidestep responsibility for his kin.

"What magics do you hold, human?" The light moved off to one side, but Fionn still couldn't see behind it. He considered focusing magic, but the human would feel it, and he didn't want to do anything to annoy the man further.

Aislinn sucked in a breath. "All of them."

"Bullshit."

"No, it's not. Once upon a time, I thought I was a Mage with weak Seeker skills. Rune—" she whistled and the wolf trotted to her side "—taught me I was both Hunter and Healer. Fionn showed me I had Seer ability. I'm still learning about my Seer gift. It's not easy to control."

Another figure melted out of the darkness and joined the first. Fionn felt magic as they spoke telepathically to one another.

"We invite you and your bond animal to talk with us," the first man said after a few moments. He moved the light so his form was visible.

Aislinn started forward with Fionn behind her.

"Not you, Celt," the second man snarled.

Fionn grabbed Aislinn's arm. She tried to pull away, but he held fast. "She isn't coming without me. We were just set upon by Bal'ta in Penrith. They were shielded so well, we weren't aware of them until they were on us. Once we arrived here, we used her Seer gift mixed with my magic and discovered two of the dark gods are close by."

"What's the woman to you, Celt?" one of the men sneered.

"She will be my wife. She is bound to me through an ancient covenant that links the kings of Ireland to my house."

"What hogwash." The other man made a face and spat in the dirt.

"It really is true," Aislinn said. "It's not important, though. Soon, we shall have to deal with far worse things than we have faced so far. We must stand together if we're to have any chance of success."

"If we lose Earth, and we may well," Fionn cut in, "her blood will be on the hands of all who refused alliance against the dark."

"You should talk. Maybe not you, but your kinfolk who left us to die."

"I apologize for their poor behavior."

Bella flew from a nearby tree and landed on Fionn's shoulder.

"What's that?" one of the men asked. "Your familiar?"

"The raven is linked to me much as the wolf is bonded to Aislinn. It is a variant of the human Hunter bond."

Bella cawed menacingly and fluffed her feathers.

"Maybe we should hear them out," the first man muttered.

"I'm not so certain. They could be spies for those oversized reptiles," the second retorted.

Rune growled. Aislinn dropped a hand to rest on his head. "You're upsetting my wolf. He killed two of those oversized reptiles. They're called Lemurians."

"So they told us," the second man muttered.

"We thought that whole thing about them living under some mountain in the States was a crock," the first cut in.

"It's not," Fionn said. "The four of us have been there. Look, either take us to where the rest of you are, or make a decision not to so we can leave. Time grows short—for all of us."

The second man moved in front of the lantern and beckoned. "Walk ahead of us. I don't trust you enough to have you following."

"What if we feel the same way?" Fionn asked.

"Then we are at a stalemate and you may as well—"

"Oh, stand down, both of you. The testosterone is so thick, I can smell it." Aislinn walked toward the second man. "Just show us where the path is, and you can follow along after us."

Fionn kept hold of Aislinn's arm and walked by her side. The men had accused them of being spies. What if it was a projection and they were walking right into a trap?

CHAPTER 26

It took everything Aislinn had to control her fury. Fionn and his friends had been kind to her, probably because she was the MacLochlainn and linked to both Fionn and Dewi. She could easily see the haughty group of Celts that had convened in the dragon's cave telling local humans they were on their own. She unclenched her jaw and inhaled a steadying breath. Fionn had looked guilty as sin when she asked if he knew anything about the human's accusations. And he was doing his damnedest to distance himself from the U.K. by speaking Americanized English.

Get a grip, her inner voice snapped. *I need to be on top of my game, not mired in anger.*

A substantial structure emerged from the mist. She couldn't see all of it, but it looked like a medieval castle. "What's this?" she asked Fionn.

"Castle Balloch. It was built in the early twelve hundreds and reconstructed around eighteen hundred."

"I didn't ask for a history lesson. Have you been inside it before so you know the layout?"

"Yes."

The one word had a terse, bitten-off quality. She knew Fionn well enough to understand he was worried about what the two humans were up to.

"Say," she called over a shoulder. "What are your names?"

"Names have power."

"Well, you know mine and Fionn's and Rune's." She kept her voice cheery and non-confrontational. "Trust needs to be a two-way street."

"Keep quiet, woman. We are nearly there. Decisions will be made then regarding who trusts whom."

Rune growled and headbutted her leg.

"What?"

"Not certain. Something doesn't smell quite right to me."

Fionn tightened his grip on her arm. He'd obviously listened in. *"Keep us apprised,"* he told Rune.

Aislinn came to a stop at the outer stone wall. One of the men channeled magic, and a panel swung inward, revealing a huge courtyard. The castle lay ahead of them, a looming silhouette outlined against the night sky. The men moved around her, trading the lantern for mage lights. In the increased illumination, she noted both men had shoulder-length red hair. One was her height, around six feet, the other a few inches shorter. They jogged across gravel-strewn dirt to the base of a tower, where one tugged on a door that opened onto stairs winding upward.

The men darted inside. "Hurry it up, now," one called back at them.

She leaned into Fionn. *"What do you think?"*

"Ye know what I think. 'Tis your call, lass."

Rune's hackles stood up along his back. After a momentary hesitation, he launched himself after the humans.

"Guess that decides it," she muttered. "I'm not letting him go in there alone."

She counted as she climbed the circular stone staircase set into the sides of the tower. At two hundred, a landing opened off to her left. One of the humans motioned her through into a hallway. Her nose twitched. The stone smelled old and damp. Something she couldn't quite get her mind around pricked her senses and set her teeth on edge.

In only a few steps, the corridor led into an enormous chamber. Hundreds of humans milled about. Many were eating. Some sat in small groups, talking. Everyone's clothing was sturdy, serviceable, and had been patched many times. Her heart went out to them. These were her people, even though they might not see it that way —not yet, anyhow. How could the Celts have been so callous?

Aislinn balled her hands into fists to quell her nervousness. No matter how precarious her position was amidst all these strangers, this was what she'd hoped for. Enough people to make a difference. She scanned the dimly lit room, but she couldn't locate Rune. Mage lights bobbed; they were the only source of illumination. Fionn's solid warmth was welcome where he pressed against her side. It wasn't as hard as she'd feared to box up anger at his kin and lay it aside.

"Well, well, well," a voice boomed out.

The crowd parted to let someone through. The din of voices and clatter of eating utensils faded.

Something clicked. Aislinn raised her hands to pull magic. "Travis," she hissed. "I was hoping I'd run into you again. What have you been up to since you sold me out to the Lemurians?"

"She's lying." Just as tall and skeletal as ever, Travis strode to stand within a few feet of her. His civet rode on his shoulder. "It was her who threw me to the dogs. Look what she's with." He pointed at Fionn. "Celts can't be trusted, and neither can humans who consort with them."

"I need one of you where Seeker magic is primary." Aislinn spoke loudly enough for her voice to carry. "Seeker magic holds the key to truth. I invite you to test the truth of my words against his."

"Totally unnecessary." Travis waved a dismissive hand and pushed disheveled blond dreadlocks behind his shoulders. "I do need a few of you, though, to toss this sorry lot into the dungeon."

He narrowed his brown eyes. "Don't even think of trying to escape. Before we ran the Old Ones off, we shielded the lower levels."

"Listen to me," Aislinn said evenly. "Travis is a spy turned by the Old Ones. He set me up so they could trap me."

"If that's true," someone called from the depths of the room, "how is it you're here?"

"I rescued her." Fionn radiated menace. His blue eyes looked like ice chips.

Travis rolled his eyes. "What tripe." He started for Aislinn.

Rune launched himself out of the shadows and drove Travis to the ground. The civet screamed. Bella left Fionn's shoulder and flew straight at the cat.

In the split second before the room erupted in mayhem, Aislinn jumped onto a table. "I have no reason to lie to you. Come on." She made *come hither* motions with both hands. "Seekers. Test my words from where you stand."

"Don't listen to her," Travis wheezed. "She's a witch. She'll ensorcel you—"

Rune's growling and snarling drowned out the rest of his words.

"Like hell I am. Besides, the Seeker gift is immune to such tricks. I first met Travis back in the States when he and I fought for the Lemurians." A gasp rose from the crowd; Aislinn forged ahead. "In those days, the Old Ones convinced us they were on our side, and we were all fighting against the dark gods. Fionn and I have discussed this. We're still not certain, but we believe the Lemurians conscripted humans to make certain we wouldn't rise against them before their power was consolidated. They're a dying race. It's why they joined forces with the dark gods: to reinforce their flagging power."

Aislinn scanned the crowd and took a deep breath. At least they weren't rushing toward her. Rune seemed to have Travis under control. Bella was baiting the cat, dive-bombing it and then flying just out of reach. "How am I doing so far, Seekers?"

"What you've said is the truth." A blond man stepped forward with a dogged expression on his face. He was medium height and solidly built, with a barrel chest and broad shoulders.

"Would you like to hear more?"

A rustling chorus of *yesses* started in the back of the room and surged forward.

"Once we figured out the Lemurians had sold us a bill of goods, Travis fought with a group of humans and Celts in our first campaign to go after a dark god. I managed to disable Slototh. After the battle was over, Travis left with a group of Hunters, except he didn't stay gone long. The Celts and I and our bond animals were strategizing which dark god to target next when Travis materialized in our midst. He wove a tale of Hunters being under attack. Of course, we went to his aid. He manipulated the jump magic with the help of Regnol, his Lemurian mage lord, and—"

"She lies. Do not listen to her."

"No." A woman detached herself from the crowd. "It's you who aren't telling the truth. Your words ping sour against my Seeker gift."

Travis struggled against Rune. The wolf's jaws descended, hovering over his throat.

"You'd better behave," Aislinn said, "or I'll tell him to kill you."

"If he doesn't, I will," Fionn growled. "After that trick Travis played on us, he deserves to die."

"The rest of what happened, please," the female seeker demanded.

"There isn't much left to tell. I sensed I'd been separated from Fionn and Rune and panicked. Regnol showed up, told Travis he'd done an excellent job, and hauled me beneath Taltos to await punishment for killing Metae, my Lemurian mage lord. I'm certain the Old Ones were none too happy about the two my wolf killed, either."

"Travis must be newly arrived among you." Fionn's gaze swept the crowd. "How long has he had to share your secrets with the enemy?"

"Too long," someone muttered.

Six men hurried forward. They formed a circle around Rune and Travis. "Would you call your bond animal?" one asked. "We have our own ways of handling traitors."

"Rune."

The wolf backed away from Travis. The men parted to let him through, and he loped to Aislinn, jumping onto the table to join her.

"Well done." She stroked his head and then turned toward Fionn. "What will happen to Travis's bond animal?" She didn't feel the least bit bad for Travis. He'd cooked his own goose, but she'd always liked the civet.

"That depends entirely on him," Fionn answered. "Most often, if the human is corrupt, the bond animal cannot be salvaged, either, because of the depth of the connection." He whistled; Bella flapped to him and landed on a shoulder.

Aislinn surveyed the room from her perch on the table. "Is there anyone else among you that you don't know well? Or haven't known for a long time?"

"Not an easy question to answer," the woman with the Seeker gift said. Curly dark hair fell to her shoulders. She was buxom, but not very tall. "Some of us are local and have known each other forever. There's a group from the Highlands, another from beyond Hadrian's Wall on the other side of what used to be the border. There are even a few from the coastal areas and southlands."

Aislinn remembered what her wolf had said. "Do you mind if Rune wanders among you? He's good at sniffing out Lemurian taint."

"Some will smell like Travis," a man pointed out. "Those of us who've sat and talked with him."

"Or me." A slight blonde with hair past her waist came forward. Color stained her thin cheeks. "We did a bit more than sit and talk." She pounded a closed fist into her other hand. "Bastard. If I'd known…"

Aislinn considered telling the woman she was far from the only one Travis had charmed into bed, but when she caught the expression on Fionn's face, she changed her mind.

"If your wolf knows, let him have at it," the Seeker male said.

Murmurs of assent rolled forward like a wave. Rune lost himself in the crowd.

The men hauled Travis, kicking and screaming epithets, to his feet. Fionn pushed his way right next to Travis, doubled up a fist, and socked him in the nose. A loud crack sounded; blood poured down Travis's face. Fionn drew back to hit him again, but one of the men got between them.

"Hold."

"I'd like to kill that sorry bastard."

"Yes, we all would. But first we want to stretch him over the rack. A little pain should wrench the truth out of him."

Fionn moved out of the way, giving her a clear view of Travis. If she hadn't been watching carefully, she would have missed the subtle contortion in his jaws. She hurled herself off the table and shrieked, "He has cyanide under a false tooth. Don't let him swallow it."

The men closed around Travis. After a scuffling struggle, one of them bellowed, "Got it."

Another yelled, "Thanks," as they hauled Travis out of the room.

The civet screeched its displeasure. Someone cornered it, picked it up by the loose fur at the back of its neck, and carried it away.

Fionn closed his arms around her. "How did you know about the poison?"

"Because I used to have the same thing hidden under one of my teeth." She swallowed hard. "Once, I almost took it."

His arms tightened around her. "Thanks be to the gods, you didn't."

Rune made his way back to her side. *"No other spies as best as I can tell. The one who smells strongest is the woman who admitted sharing his bed."*

"That's a relief." Fionn let her go.

"It looks as if you've saved us from a huge mistake." The blond man with the Seeker gift walked briskly to her, hand outstretched. "My name is Daniel."

Aislinn took his hand. "Nice to meet you. I am Aislinn, and this is Fionn."

"You sought us out for a reason. What is it?" The man stared hard at her out of green eyes.

"The battle for control over Earth is heating up," Aislinn said. "It may well be heading into its endgame."

"We know that," Daniel murmured. "No one else has come to warn us. Why you? And why now?"

The line of Fionn's jaw tightened. He lifted his chin. "Aislinn is only recently arrived here. I'm not proud of my kin. We have a long history of underestimating humans, or ignoring them entirely." He took a breath. "Aislinn taught us—or at least she taught me—that you're a valuable ally."

"Yes." Aislinn jumped into the conversation. "The more of us who are working together, the stronger we are. We would like it if some of you returned to Ireland with us."

"And then we would come to wherever the fighting is worst to support you," Fionn added.

"Can you make that promise in good faith?" Aislinn turned her head to lock gazes with Fionn.

"Bran, Arawn, and Gwydion will come with me. If the four of us set an example, others will follow."

"Arawn as in god of the dead and revenge?" Daniel asked, his eyes widening.

"The same, though he's really not so daunting as all that." The corners of Fionn's mouth twitched. "Could you gather everyone so we might forge a plan?"

AISLINN KNELT next to Rune and stroked his rough outer coat.

Fionn was using magic to do a final check of the hundred or so men and women who were coming back to Inishowen with them. He was also checking for arm tattoos. "Not that I don't trust you," he'd told the wolf, "but it's better to be safe than sorry."

Rune reassured him there wouldn't be any hard feelings. "If we both make a mistake and someone slips through, everyone will blame you," the wolf added with understated lupine humor.

Aislinn bent and kissed the tip of Rune's snout. When she raised her head, she asked, "How soon did you realize Travis was here? Truth, now."

Rune laid his head in her lap. "As soon as that man opened the door at the bottom of the steps."

"Is that why you took off and didn't wait for me?"

"I wanted to locate Travis and get myself into position to protect you from him."

She felt the hot prick of tears, and her throat thickened. "Still, you should've said something."

Rune leaned into her hand. "If I had, you'd have held me back."

Aislinn winced, knowing truth when she heard it. *I'm as overprotective of him as Fionn is of me.*

She glanced at Fionn standing in a corner of the room. Magic buzzed around him and the volunteers. She closed her eyes for a moment. It really had been a stroke of luck that led them to this group. Amongst them, they had links to just about every human left in the U.K. The ones who weren't coming to Inishowen were heading back to their home communities to rally support and get ready to fight. They'd settled on a telepathic frequency and a communications schedule. All in all, she couldn't have hoped for a better outcome.

Fionn strode back across the room to where she sat. As usual, Bella was on his shoulder. "Are ye ready, lass? I've told them where to jump so they'll come out within the grounds of my manor."

She got to her feet. "What? That's the end of the American English?"

He rolled his eyes. "For now. I've apologized sufficiently for the Celtic gods' oversights. It feels safe enough to sound like one again."

"The next time that council of yours gets together—"

He shook his head. "'Tis not a time to be holding grudges. Let us hope there *is* a next council meeting. 'Twill mean there are enough of us left for a quorum."

Rune moved between them. Fionn channeled magic. The walls of Castle Balloch dissolved, and Fionn's bedroom rose around her. Aislinn shook her head hard when she looked out the window and was greeted by the feeble light of dawn. No wonder she felt tired. They'd been gone the better part of twenty hours. She looked longingly at the bed, unbuckled her rucksack, and set it on the floor.

Rune whined just before the hall door flew open. "You're back." Looking more harried than usual, Gwydion stomped in without waiting for an invitation.

"Aye, and about a hundred humans will begin arriving soon. Is something amiss?"

"Ye could say that." Arawn crowded behind Gwydion, with Bran close on his heels.

"Aye," Bran muttered, his coppery eyes radiated worry. "Two of the baby dragons are missing. Dewi and Nidhogg are running amok out there, setting fire to everything in front of them."

"If you two had been outside, you'd have smelled the smoke," Gwydion said.

No rest for me or any of us. Aislinn squared her shoulders and turned to face the Celtic gods.

CHAPTER 27

"Where are the other six younglings?" Aislinn asked.

"Locked in the kitchen and caterwauling their tiny heads off," Gwydion said. "If we'd taken a firm line with the brood from the get-go, we'd never have had this problem."

Aislinn bit her tongue. She'd said something to that effect before they left for Scotland, or maybe she'd just thought it. Instead of rehashing might-have-beens, she asked, "How long have the two been missing?"

"Hours," Arawn said succinctly. He pushed farther into Fionn's bedroom. "Goddess's tits, you two were barely off when Dewi decided to do a nose count and came up short."

"What have you done to locate them?" Fionn crossed his arms over his chest. When Aislinn glanced at him, she saw worry lines etched in the corners of his eyes.

"Everything," Bran said.

Fionn made a come-along gesture with two fingers. "Could ye elucidate *everything*? Mayhap I'll come up with something ye might have missed."

"We searched the house and grounds with magic and our five senses—" Gwydion began.

"Aye, all the way to the sea," Bran broke in, "since we know how fond the younglings are of water."

"While ye were about it, did ye hunt for traces of the Old Ones or the dark gods?" Fionn asked.

"Aye, of course we did." Arawn sounded affronted. "The whole countryside stinks of Lemurians. There were hints of the dark ones, as well."

Fionn launched into an abbreviated version of the Bal'ta attack in Penrith and finding evidence of Perrikus and Tokhots.

Gwydion blew out an aggravated sounding breath. "This isna good," he muttered.

"Did you try reaching the baby dragons with mind speech?" Aislinn asked.

"I would've thought one or both of their parents would have tried that first," Gwydion said defensively.

Aislinn wasn't so sure about that. What she did expect, though, was for Dewi to blame this whole catastrophe on her and Fionn leaving. "Um, the brood seems to be able to talk among themselves. Have you asked the other younglings if they know anything?"

The master enchanter's eyes widened, "Nay, lass. That's one thing we havena done."

"And a brilliant suggestion," Arawn added. He poked Fionn in the arm. "I'm starting to see why ye are so taken with the MacLochlainn. She's smart as well as stunning."

Aislinn was already on her way out the door, with Rune right behind her.

"I can talk with them, too," the wolf reminded her.

"Good. Maybe you can settle them down. If they're as wrought up as Gwydion described, it might not be easy to get anything worthwhile out of them."

She ran into Gwydion's warding when she tried to pull the latch on the kitchen door. It stung, and she yanked her hand back. Aislinn reached with her mind and recoiled. What a complex piece of work. It would take her hours to unravel it. She raced back into the great room and ran headlong into Fionn, displacing Bella. "I can't get past the wards."

The raven resettled herself on Fionn's shoulder and squawked her outrage.

"'Tis why Gwydion sent me after you," Fionn said. He tapped the bird's talons. "Stop fussing. Ye're not hurt, just surprised."

Aislinn tried to follow Fionn's magic as he untangled Gwydion's casting, but he worked too fast. The second he had the door open, she sprang through and was practically mowed down by baby dragons. A quick head count confirmed one red and one green were missing. Two of them took wing and headed out the open door. "You are not free," she spoke sternly. "Get back in this kitchen. We need to talk."

One listened, the other didn't.

Rune sprang on the red one and carried it back, writhing between his jaws. *"I am not hurting you. Stop it,"* the wolf admonished the young dragon.

"Good advice." Aislinn used her mind voice. *"All of you just stop it. If you minded better, we wouldn't be in this predicament."*

By the time the other Celts got to the kitchen, she was on the floor with all six of the younglings ringed around her. Rune suggested feeding them, and Fionn had dug strips of dried meat out of the pantry.

"How did ye do that?" Gwydion exclaimed. "When we tried to settle them, they flew around the room like modern aircraft."

"Mother's touch, I guess," Aislinn said. "Hush. I was about to try to see what they know."

"Lost," the black dragon wailed. "They are lost."

"Lost where?" Aislinn asked gently.

"They wander in the dark," a red dragon cried.

"Does that mean they're still alive?" She held her breath.

Rune leaned closer. Bella left Fionn's shoulder and landed in the midst of the brood.

"We think so," the black youngling—apparently the brood's alpha—replied.

Gwydion folded his body accordion-fashion until he sat next to Aislinn. "Do you think you could find them?" he asked the rest of the brood.

"Mother could," a red dragon offered.

"Or Father," the black dragon said. "He is wise and brave. He can do anything."

Aislinn turned to Gwydion. "Do we know where either of them are?" He shook his head. "Okay." She grabbed hold of a chair and hauled herself to her feet.

"Where are you going?" Fionn blocked her egress from the kitchen.

She put her hands on her hips. "I'm going outside to call Dewi. She has to come. I'm the MacLochlainn."

"She'll commandeer you to go with her and search."

"Fine." Aislinn blinked. Her eyes felt hot and sandpapery. "It's for a good cause. You need to stay here to meet the humans. They should be here any moment."

"I doona think much of—"

"Too bad. The brood thinks the other two are still alive. If they're right, we got lucky, and I aim to take advantage of that." She swept past Fionn and stormed out of the kitchen, with Rune right behind.

"What a little spitfire."

It was hard to determine just who'd said it, except it hadn't been Fionn. The look in his eyes had been perilously close to murder. She wondered if he'd truly scoop her up and lock her away to prevent her from leaving.

"If he does, all bets are off," she muttered and sped across the great room and out the front door. The minute she got outside, smoke burned her eyes and stung her lungs when she breathed. It was hard to fathom just what could be burning, since everything was perennially damp.

Aislinn cupped her hands around her mouth. "Dewi." She

switched to mind speech and cried the dragon's name again. Squinting against the smoke, she scanned the skies. Long minutes passed. She was just about to call again when dark forms emerged from the smoky canopy and circled to land.

"I was beginning to wonder where they were," Rune said. He whuffed from the smoke.

"Hmph. I suppose I was, too, but I'm not looking forward to this."

"If she gives you a hard time, I'll bite her."

"Save your energy. Her scales might break your teeth."

The dragon screamed and cursed before she was even on the ground. By the time she had her feet beneath her and lumbered toward Aislinn, she'd progressed to the predictable, "This is all your fault. It you hadn't left—"

Something snapped. A thin, brittle anger filled her. "Stop it," Aislinn shrieked. "Just stop. We're wasting valuable time, which is the same thing you've been doing lighting the countryside on fire. Your brood thinks their missing siblings are still alive."

"That's exactly what I've been trying to tell her." Nidhogg made his way to them. "We must clear our minds so we can locate them. Anger clouds everything."

"Good. At least one of you is being rational," Aislinn muttered.

Fionn chugged up beside them. "I'm ready to leave. I'll ride Nidhogg."

"What?" Aislinn just stared at him. "What about the humans?"

"They've begun to arrive already over by the stone bridge next to the moat. Arawn and Bran are taking care of them. Gwydion is closeted in the kitchen with the dragons."

Fionn watched Aislinn run out of the kitchen, incredulous that she was about to undertake something so dangerous on her own. Arawn's good-natured teasing didn't help matters. Good Christ!

The woman would go into the jaws of Hell itself if she got her dander up. "Come on, you two." He pointed at Arawn and Bran.

"What about me?" Gwydion asked.

"You're babysitting. Try to do a better job this time. Your wards seemed to keep them in."

The master enchanter blew out a breath. "All right. I'll resurrect them as soon as you're out of here." A cacophony of discontent rose from the dragons. Gwydion shook his staff at them. "If any of you aren't interested in growing up to be dragons, I'd be glad to practice turning you into toads. Do I have any takers?"

Fionn raced out the door, gratified to feel Gwydion's spell seal it once Arawn and Bran were through.

"What do you want us to do?" Arawn asked.

"The humans need to feel we care about them. You can show them to rooms. Help them get settled. Apparently, those of us who live on this side of the Atlantic hung them out to dry."

"Aye," Bran said. "I'd heard much the same." He shrugged. "Old habits die hard."

"Old habits," Fionn said through clenched teeth, "were formed when humans dinna have magic of their own. We must alter our views. They are partners in this war. Worthy ones, at that. They nearly dinna let me inside Castle Balloch on account of how poorly we've treated them."

"I canna say as I blame them," Arawn said and gestured toward the gates. "Look over there. I daresay they're beginning to arrive already."

"Excellent. I'll just introduce you two to whomever emerges first, and then I'm leaving with Aislinn and the dragons."

He caught up with Aislinn just about the time Dewi's temper had blown itself out. After making a bold statement about riding Nidhogg, he remembered himself and bowed to the Norse dragon. "That is, if ye'll have me as a rider."

"Of course. And your bird, as well."

Fionn felt heat rise to his face. He'd all but forgotten Bella.

"I'll remember that," the bird said acidly.

"Stay out of my head," Fionn snapped. "If ye doona behave, I'll leave ye to tend to the younglings." Bella clacked her beak shut right next to Fionn's ear. He glared at her.

"Help me get Rune up onto Dewi," Aislinn said. "Let's not waste time bickering."

The wolf clambered up Dewi's scales with both of them pushing and a bit of a magical assist. Aislinn followed and settled the wolf in front of her.

Fionn vaulted onto Nidhogg's back. He hadn't ridden a dragon in centuries, not since Dewi had flown him a place or two. Despite his worries about finding the younglings in time to save their lives and the delicate logistics of extricating them from whoever had kidnapped them, part of him looked forward to the beat of Nidhogg's powerful wings.

Dewi spread her wings and launched. Nidhogg's leathery wings unfurled.

"Do ye know which direction to begin searching?" Fionn asked as they gained altitude. Cold wind rushed by him. It felt welcome after the overheated kitchen and everyone strung tighter than piano wire.

The dragon switched to mind speech. *"Not yet. Let me deploy magic. Now that I'm not caught up in Dewi's fury, mayhap I'll sense something."*

"Oh, so now you're blaming me."

"I'm not blaming anyone. Join your power to mine and help locate our younglings."

Fionn moved Bella to a more protected place between his spread legs and the dragon's neck. The bird's talons had dug deeper and deeper into his shoulder as wind buffeted them. *"While we were across the Irish Sea, we sensed Perrikus and Tokhots."*

"I feared as much," Nidhogg replied. *"The Lemurians aren't stealthy enough to have snuck up on our children and made off with them. Even*

young as they are, they would have noticed something was amiss and kicked up a terrible ruckus."

"Are ye certain?"

"You asked for a reason." Nidhogg sounded uncharacteristically sharp. *"What is it?"*

Fionn wasn't sure how to couch the answer without offending the dragon. By the time he was done hemming and hawing, Nidhogg said dryly, *"If you were going to infer that our young may not have noticed the difference between our energy and the Old Ones' because we are both types of reptiles, save your breath."*

Fionn felt embarrassed. *"Don't mind me. I'm grasping at straws."*

"Birds are descended from dinosaurs," Bella said sarcastically. "They're a kind of reptile, too. It doesn't mean we're stupid."

Fionn rolled his eyes. Bella was in a snit; only time would cure it. "Hush," he told her. "Let the dragons follow their magic."

They flew in large circles for a while. It began to drizzle. Water ran down Fionn's face and beaded on Bella's feathers as he gazed at the countryside. At least the many fires were smoldering and going out. Nidhogg banked; his wings bit the air. Fionn hunkered in his seat and hung on. He wanted to ask the dragon what he'd found, but didn't think it wise to distract him. *Och aye, likely I'll find out soon enough.* Adrenaline hummed along his nerves as he readied himself for the fight to come.

Fionn still wore the battle leathers he'd donned for their trip to Scotland. The tanned hides were wet and cold where they clung to him. He pulled a small amount of magic to warm himself. The air ahead of them got darker and darker. At first, Fionn thought they were flying into the heart of the storm, but the atmosphere felt thick and wrong somehow.

Lemurians. The wrongness was Lemurian magic. Fionn chided himself for not recognizing it sooner. The Old Ones knew they were up here. *"We're flying right into the enemy's lair,"* Fionn warned.

Nidhogg trumpeted. Fire roared from his mouth. "Yes. No more need for mind speech. They know we're here."

"Ye sound pretty chipper."

Nidhogg craned his neck so he was almost facing Fionn. "I am. All those years I was imprisoned where no matter what I did, it didn't make any difference… Unless you've been there, you have no idea how sweet freedom is. Even if we don't manage to save my younglings, we'll make those bastards sorry they were ever born."

"We need a strategy."

"We have one. Dewi and I have been conversing privately. You can use your powers to jump from my back to the ground once we are in the thick of things. Aislinn will do the same, along with her wolf. Dewi and I are most effective providing support from the air."

"Do ye have any idea how many Lemurians are down there?"

"Many."

"Dark gods?"

"Yes, I sense them, as well."

Fionn's heart hammered against his chest. Finding Aislinn before the enemy did might not be easy. They'd have to come out at the same place, or damned close. An idea took root. "Fly close to Dewi. I'll bring all of us down together."

"That could work if we fly in a circle nose to tail. Then you could use the channel our bodies make for safe passage."

Fionn snorted. "Safe is relative. Wait. I have an even better idea. Backtrack."

"I don't think so."

"Nidhogg. If Aislinn and I come out in the middle of fifty or more Lemurians plus a dark god or two, we're dead meat. We'll never find your younglings. We need to be stealthier. Put us down—or let me jump us—to a place we'll at least be able to get our bearings and craft an attack plan."

The dragon wheeled. In moments, the air grew clearer. Dewi flew near. Nidhogg didn't seem to be circling to land, so Fionn called to Aislinn, "I'll jump us down."

She nodded across the air between them. Fionn stroked Bella. "Do ye wish to be included, or will ye fly on your own?"

The raven spread her wings and took off.

Fionn battled momentary anger at the bird's high-handedness and then shoved it aside so it wouldn't get in the way of his casting. He called magic and wove strong wards into his spell, taking care to test them. They needed to be invisible until they determined their next move.

A savage protectiveness settled in his mind, clouding it. What he really wanted to do was jump them back to Inishowen, where Aislinn would be sheltered, and return with one of the Celts to figure things out here. Her presence made it hard for him to focus on anything other than making certain no harm befell her. He set his mouth in a determined line. Shy of locking Aislinn up, he knew she'd never stay put. Her independence was a two-edged sword and one of the many things he loved about her.

He clamped his teeth together and loosed the spell to bring them down.

Aislinn stopped holding her breath when her feet landed solidly on the ground. She'd rather have cast her own jump spell, but understood the wisdom of them forming a unit. Fionn's arms closed around her. She leaned into him for the barest moment before she scanned their surroundings. A rolling plain stretched ahead of them, dotted with the occasional cottage. Standing puddles gleamed dully in the gray light of the rainy day. She reached for Rune through the Hunter bond. The wolf materialized by her side, last to emerge from the portal. "Do you know where we are?" she asked Fionn quietly.

"Aye. Still in Ireland, but toward the south and inland."

The portal shimmered and disappeared.

"We need cover," she said.

"I've warded us."

Aislinn thought about that. "It might work here, but not when we get closer to the Old Ones."

"Never mind that. Did Dewi tell you aught about where her younglings are?"

"Yes. She even showed me. I had to join her mind because I

couldn't see through the murk. There's an enormous castle that's crawling with Lemurians. The younglings are deep within it."

He blew out a breath. "Amazing they're still alive. The Old Ones must be using them as bait to draw us."

"There has to be at least one of the dark gods involved. This has the stink of their maneuverings."

"I agree. Unfortunately, so did Nidhogg." A muscle jerked beneath Fionn's eye. "I'm going to put out a call for reinforcements."

"We can't afford to wait. Every minute—"

He ran a gentle hand down the side of her face. "We willna wait, lass. The others will come as they can." He shut his eyes. Magic heated the air as he cast a telepathic sending. A corner of his mouth turned downward. "At least this way, there will be someone to pluck our bones from the dust."

A frisson of fear marched down her back. She straightened her shoulders. "Let's get closer and see if we can't sneak into the castle. Rune and Bella might be particularly good for that." The wolf grinned at her, his jaws lolling.

"At least someone thinks I'm good for something." Bella flew from behind a boulder and landed on Rune's back for a moment before taking off again.

Aislinn glanced from the bird to Fionn and back. She didn't ask what was wrong. They couldn't afford to divert their attention from the task at hand. They moved forward at a brisk pace until they reached the perimeter of darker air.

Fionn stopped and turned to her. "The River Boyne is to the east. It isna far, and there will be high marsh grasses to give us cover. The river leads straight to the castle."

"If it's like most river bottoms, the ground will be uneven. I don't think we should do anything that will delay us. Dewi and Nidhogg are up there somewhere." She gestured. "They're waiting until we storm the castle to provide a diversion. Once we come out with the younglings, they'll get us out of here somehow."

His drew his brows together. "Is there aught else ye decided with Dewi?"

She shook her head. "We didn't really decide anything, other than they'd wait until they sensed us…" Her voice ran down. Now she heard the words out loud, she knew how exposed they'd be. "I may have a better idea. Do you know the castle I'm talking about?"

"Aye." The word seemed torn out of him, as if he guessed what she had in mind.

"Jump us there."

"That isna smart. No better than it would have been to go directly from the dragons' backs into the thick of things. We'll be vulnerable coming through at the far end of our traveling spell— and likely captured. They'd be able to sense our magic afore they could see us. 'Twould alert them to our presence."

"Well then, bring us out in the dungeon. At least there won't be as many Lemurians there."

"Ye doona know that. They like underground places. Remember Taltos."

"Okay." She put her hands on her hips. "You think of something."

"I did. If we'd begun walking when I suggested it, we'd be at the river by now and swallowed in ground fog and marsh grass. Hell, we'd likely be at the castle wall. 'Tisn't far from here."

"What other outbuildings does the castle have? Stables? Shops?"

He cast an approving look her way. "Aye, ye just may be onto something. There'd have to be a blacksmith shop. The Old Ones are not enamored of iron. I doona care much for it myself, but so long as I do not spend overmuch time around it…"

"What about the dark gods? Do they have the same problem?"

Fionn shrugged. "I doona know. My guess is they're sensitive to iron like us."

She frowned. "What do you mean, sensitive?"

"'Twill burn me, though not badly. If there is enough, it can dampen my magic, which is a far greater problem." He shook his head. "'Tisn't important. Give me a moment so I can recall the way the castle grounds are laid out."

"What's it called?"

"Castle Trim. 'Tis on the River Boyne. The waterway wends beneath the castle." Fionn whistled for Bella, but the bird didn't come.

"Bella. You're holding us up," Aislinn sent and then added, *"Rune needs you,"* as further inducement. The raven flew slowly toward them.

"I don't know what happened between you," Aislinn muttered to Fionn, "but fix it, now."

He snapped his fingers. Bella landed on his shoulder, head cocked at a defiant angle. Aislinn wanted to throttle the bird, but it wasn't her bond animal. Fionn murmured low to the raven in Gaelic and then gathered magic. Within seconds, stone walls rose around them. Fionn hadn't been joking when he'd said they were close to the castle.

Barely breathing, Aislinn warded herself and Rune. Fionn piled wards atop hers. She glanced about; they were indeed in the ruins of a blacksmith shop. Dusty piles of metal littered the floor and hung on the walls. Long cold fire pits sat along two walls with an assortment of primitive-looking tools. Everything was blackened by centuries of soot. A low, sloping roof had partially collapsed at one end of the structure. Mice and rats scuttled away from them.

"At least we're alone."

"Mayhap not for long. They have to be expecting us."

"Which way is the castle from here?"

Fionn didn't answer. He picked his way through the shop. It looked as if he were hunting for something. A spell shimmered around him to muffle noise. Through its indistinct borders, she saw him chuck things aside. He called, *"This way. Quick,"* and yanked hard at something embedded in the floor. She drew in a whistling breath. A wooden trap door. How had he known? Aislinn hurried to his side.

He gestured her and Rune through and whispered, "These old castles always had a warren of underground passageways for use during sieges. Ye'll need your mage light, but keep it dim."

The smell of damp and mold enveloped her. She nearly slipped on slick stone steps. Partway down, she heard the trapdoor close and hoped Fionn was able to secure it. Beady eyes shone in the beam of her light. Rats. Hundreds of them, from the looks of things. A strong rodent smell mingled with everything else. The steps disappeared into standing water. At least it didn't look like a sewer. She huddled on the last above-water step and waited for Fionn to tell her which way to go.

He was by her side in a flash. "Can ye swim?" He spoke right into her ear.

"Of course."

"Good. Ye may well need to. I dinna know this would be flooded. The castle proper is to our left. Mayhap three hundred yards."

"How will I know what to look for?"

"Ye canna miss it. The foundations run deep."

She continued down the steps, feeling stupid. A structure as substantial as the castle she'd seen in Dewi's mind must've been built on something sturdy, or else it would have fallen down long since. When water hit her knees, she ran out of steps. Aislinn turned and slogged through the passageway against a mild current. The curved walls were low and coated with thick green slime; she had to duck her head in places.

She shivered. The water was cold enough to make her feet and legs ache. She ran a small stream of magic downward to warm herself. Rats paced them, but didn't close in, maybe because of Rune, who swam by her side. *"Are you all right?"* she asked him.

"Yes. Water's not my favorite, but at least this is fairly clean."

Huge stanchions rose out of the murk. *Holy crap.* She snorted. *No way could I have missed them.* High-pitched shrieks filled the passage-way. Claws and leathery wings brushed against her as flocks of bats exited upward in a rush.

"Now all we have to do is locate a set of stairs." Fionn's voice sounded in her mind. *"No doubt there will be more than one."* He hesitated. *"I hope no one was keeping an eye on the bats. They're an ancient early-warning system."*

"The Lemurians aren't smart enough."

"Mayhap not, but the dark gods are. Huzzah. Found some stairs. We're not going to be picky about this. Over here."

Aislinn hastened toward him and started up stairs that were in much better repair than the ones leading downward from the black-smith shop. Looking almost modern, they spiraled around a sturdy central post. A landing was just ahead. She came out onto it, glanced back to make certain Rune was behind her, and ran into something.

Damn! I thought things were going too well.

She stared at a miniature portcullis blocking a stone-inlaid passageway. A rusted padlock secured chains that wrapped around its latticed wooden grillwork, effectively disabling the pulley system. A bevy of rats chittered at her from the other side. The landing vibrated as Fionn came up behind. The intensity of his energy heartened her. She could have managed alone in this creepy, underground warren of byways, but it was better with Fionn by her side.

"Hmph. Not much point in mind speech. The rats and bats will drown out most anything we might say." His voice buzzed against her ear. "Besides, we need to conserve our power. I can break the lock, but it will draw enough magic to attract attention if anyone is looking."

"We don't have much of a choice. Do you want me to do it? The chain is metal."

"I can manage. Iron is only a problem if it surrounds us or if I have to touch it for verra long." He shrugged. "For all I know, the chain is something modern, like aluminum. Get behind me. If ye sense aught amiss, take the wolf and jump back to Inishowen."

"I'm not leaving without you and the dragons."

Fionn blew out a frustrated-sounding breath. Magic bubbled

around them as he focused a mixture, which was mostly fire, to cut through the chain. It glowed red hot just before a length clanked heavily on the ground. She fanned magic to see if anyone was coming. She didn't know how the castle was laid out above them, so it was difficult to tell for certain, but she didn't sense anyone near. Aislinn allowed herself to hope they'd avoided detection.

"Cut your magic. Help me with this."

She sheathed her power instantly and unwound lengths of chain. She tried to be quiet, but metal against metal and stones made noise. "Should I shield the sound?"

"Nay." A terse, bitten-off quality to that one word discouraged further conversation.

She focused on the corridor beyond the gate, intent on being ready the second she felt anything like a Lemurian draw near. Her nerves jangled with tension; her stomach was sour. At least the rats —never her favorites—had scattered after the first loud clang of metal on the stone floor. *Maybe that's not good, either.* She hoped they hadn't scuttled off to tell the Lemurians—or, God forbid, the dark gods—they had company.

Fionn shoved the gate up a couple of feet and shinnied under it with Bella. He held it while she and Rune scrunched beneath. Once they were all on the other side, she started up a stone-inlaid corridor.

Fionn grabbed her arm. He spun her around, pulled her against him chest-to-chest, and spoke right into her ear. "They know we're here. So do the dragons. I feel fire energy. Dewi and Nidhogg are strafing the castle from above. I will go first. Ye will do as I say. No heroics like ye did on Perrikus's world. Do ye understand, lass? I canna protect us if I am worried about what ye will do next. It breaks my concentration."

"If they know we're here, why haven't they come for us?"

"'Tis an excellent question. I doona know, but I fear we shall find out—sooner rather than later. Mayhap the Old Ones have summoned one of the dark gods, and they're awaiting further instruction afore they move against us. 'Tisn't as if they fear we will get away. They know we've risen to the bait and willna leave without the young dragons."

"How will we manage against twenty, or thirty, or fifty of them?"

Fionn's face hardened; its planes bespoke grim determination. In the glow from her mage light, he looked like the thousand-year-old warrior he was. His eyes glittered menacingly. In that moment, she wondered if she knew him at all.

"Getting cold feet, lass? There is still time for you to leave."

She felt out of her league. What did she, a young woman raised in modern times, know about bloody, brutal warfare? She'd be much better off—She balled her hands into fists. "Stop it, Fionn." She wriggled against him, but he held fast. "You're good. Damned good. I almost didn't notice your compulsion spell until after it snared me."

He tightened his arms around her until they felt like metal bands. "Ye are my life, my heart, *leannán*. I wouldna want to live should something happen to you. Ye are not immortal, yet I am selfish enough to wish to see ye grow old and die by my side."

"I'm not leaving."

"Hush. Fighting is my life. 'Tis the only life I've ever known. Ye are strong and brave and beautiful, but ye doona have—"

Rune barked. Fionn sprang apart from her, hands raised to call power. Aislinn did the same. She'd been close to capitulating, to telling him she'd return to Inishowen and wait. It didn't matter whether he was still weaving compulsion, the anguish in his words had settled into her heart. Fionn loved her beyond wisdom or reason. That love drove him, and she couldn't fault him for it.

The sound of footsteps hastening toward them jolted her heart into high gear. If it was Lemurians—and it practically had to be— they'd be shielded. The only way she'd killed them before was in personal combat. She started to remind Fionn of that when four of the impossibly tall aliens came into view. They were in humanoid form, with long, thick, fair hair swirling around them, but the skin hidden beneath their flowing golden robes was scaled. The Old Ones switched from male to female, seemingly at will; Aislinn had never truly understood the magic that fueled their transformations.

She ducked a lethal blow that flew at her, warded herself, and chucked killing blows as the Lemurians closed on them. "We have to get past their shields. Otherwise, we'll wear ourselves out for nothing."

"No shit, *leannán*."

Rune took to the shadowy edges of the corridor, with Bella on his back. Understanding, Aislinn diverted a stream of power to create a *don't look here* spell about him. She couldn't tell Fionn what they were up to without alerting the Lemurians.

He clucked to Bella in mind speech.

"Don't," she panted. "Wait. There will be an opportunity. When it comes, go for their throats."

Magic blazed from his hands, lighting the high-ceilinged hall-way. Rune was past the Old Ones and turning around. Bella launched herself from his back. The wolf targeted one of the Lemurians. He leapt on the alien from behind and buried his teeth in its carotid. Bella latched onto another's shoulder and pecked holes in its neck, right over the major vessels. Greenish blood geysered.

"Now," Aislinn shrieked. She poured magic into her ward and hurled herself at one of the two remaining Lemurians. Its magic pounded against her ward; cracks formed, but the ward held. She was inches away, so close she could smell the metallic reptile stink of her opponent, but she couldn't penetrate its shielding. Her ward was weakening. Panic formed a knot in her belly. There wasn't enough magic to protect herself and drill through his defenses.

"I've got him." Rune snarled and drove his body sideways into the Lemurian she'd been struggling with.

Aislinn sidestepped just in time to avoid it falling right on top of her. Rune was on its back. Understanding slammed home. The Old One's shielding was directed in front of them, not behind. It was why the wolf and raven had been able to kill the first two. She yanked her knife from her belt and drove it deep into the Lemurian's neck. Its blood burned where it splattered her.

Gasping for breath, Aislinn straightened, ready to help Fionn. He was cleaning a wicked-looking silvery blade on his leathers. A feral grin split his face as he re-sheathed it. "We learned something," he said between harsh, raspy breaths.

"Yes. Take them from behind." Aislinn knelt and drew Rune into her arms. "You are the best, the bravest, the most amazing—"

"Stop it. I did what needed doing. Let's get moving."

"The wolf speaks true." Fionn turned to Bella where she perched on a dead Lemurian, feasting on its eyeballs. "Well done, my lady."

"Thank you." She plucked an eye out, held it in her beak, and flew to his shoulder. *"You're forgiven."*

Aislinn snorted. The bird had reverted to mind speech because her beak was busy. "We must be getting close if they sent a greeting party. Do you think we should try for mind contact with the young dragons?"

Fionn shook his head. "Not yet. Let the Old Ones believe their kin killed us, at least for a few minutes."

"You're not thinking." She strode to his side. "They already know these four are dead because they've checked out of the hive mind."

"That may be, but I still doona wish to send our magic any farther than we have to. At the moment, there's only one way to go." He pointed straight ahead. "Unless we get to a choice point, there's no reason to stir things up further."

CHAPTER 29

Fionn moved forward at a brisk pace. Aislinn walked beside him, with Rune next to her. No need to be stealthy. The Old Ones knew they were here. He sucked in a ragged breath. He'd nearly had a heart attack when Aislinn had gone toe-to-toe with the Lemurian, but there wasn't any other way to kill them, unless he could come up with a surefire way to dismantle their shielding. He replayed the feel of it in his mind, and an idea formed. Fire wasn't the ticket. The reptilian aliens had been forged in fire, much like the dragons. Earth just might do it. Lots of earth power, with just a smidgeon of air woven in.

They'd gotten lucky this time. Four Lemurians against four of them. The odds wouldn't be as favorable once they got closer to the dragon younglings.

"I have an idea how we might disable their wards…" He launched into a description, but before he finished, she cut in.

"I don't have enough magic for that. Just keeping myself warded drains me."

"Good to know." He didn't like the next part, but didn't see any way round it. "I will test my theory on one of their wards. If it works, ye must kill and kill quickly as soon as ye can get through their shields. If the three of you tag team, we might stay alive."

"Agreed," Rune and Bella said in unison.

"As soon as I'm done with one Lemurian, I'll move to the next. If we sow enough confusion, mayhap we can get them to retreat."

She snorted. "You're assuming they'll just stand still and let us mow through them. And that a dark god or two won't show up at an inopportune time."

"Nay, I'm assuming nothing of the sort. Ye must remain vigilant and hold your warding in place while ye kill."

"What about Rune and Bella?"

"They'll have to be damned careful. Or else remain right next to one of us, within our wards." Breath whistled through his teeth. He shook his head. "That would mean they couldn't kill with the alacrity we're going to need."

"Mother says you're coming to get us."

"Goddammit!" Fionn slammed a fist into his thigh. "Did ye hear that?"

Aislinn nodded. "If we did, so did everyone else within earshot. Dewi's trying to comfort her younglings, but she doesn't think."

"Of course she does, but only of herself." Fury boiled so hot, a red haze settled over his vision. Damn the fucking dragon to hell. He took a steadying breath and then another. He wouldn't do any of them any good if he gave in to his rage. Killing Dewi wasn't an option. He hoped Nidhogg had gotten his mate under control, but the damage was already done. He also hoped at least a few Celts had heeded his desperate message and were even now on their way to help.

"Mother says you're coming to get us," a voice mocked from the darkness ahead of them.

"Shit! It's one of the dark gods." Aislinn moved closer to him. Tension radiated off her.

"Keep moving. He's by himself." Fionn latched on to the concentration that had always made him a worthy adversary. Feral energy smoldered deep within him; it burned bright, anxious to be unleashed. Now was a time for action, not for hoping or cursing.

"Of course I am. And I have excellent hearing. Welcome to my castle." Tokhots came into view. Long dark hair was pulled back from a beautiful face with high cheekbones and a sculpted chin. Fine dark eyes shone with anticipation. A crimson robe made of a silky fabric accentuated the perfect lines of his body. Like Perrikus and D'Chel, he was sex incarnate. Fionn didn't bother to check for a full-blown erection. All the dark gods wanted to fuck Aislinn. Why should this one be any different?

"Last I checked, this castle belonged to the Irish government," Fionn snarled.

Tokhots tossed back his perfectly-shaped head and laughed. The musical sound could have lured men to their deaths. "And last I checked, Celt, the Irish government had fallen, along with every other organized human structure on Earth."

"If you're the greeting party"—Aislinn sounded as if she were talking through clenched teeth—"take us to the baby dragons."

Tokhots rolled his eyes. "What a handful two of them are. I can only imagine how it was with all eight. No wonder it was so easy for us to, um, borrow a couple."

Dewi shrieked epithets into Fionn's mind. He shook his head. *"I don't mind if you listen, but you have to shut up."*

Tokhots laughed again. "Their mother. She's quite a piece of work."

"Yes," Aislinn said silkily. "Enough of a piece of work to steal Nidhogg from under your very noses."

"I am in a good mood, human. Watch it. Things can change quickly." The dark god moved closer. His lascivious gaze swept over Aislinn.

Her breath hitched.

Damn! Tokhots had spun a sexual net. It wasn't Aislinn's fault she was aroused. The dark ones used sex as a means of control.

Fionn stepped between them. "She's mine. Leave her be."

"Maybe we should ask the lady who she'd prefer. I can smell the heat from her sex from here."

"The baby dragons," Aislinn hissed. "You can fight over me later."

"I suppose we could." Tokhots nodded. "It might be amusing. D'Chel informed me you belonged to him. Now that I see you for myself, I believe I'll give the old chap a merry go."

"Like I said…" Fionn pushed Aislinn behind him. "She's mine."

Tokhots rolled his eyes. "You're not even in the running, Celt. We'll have sent you scuttling to the *Dreaming* long before her fate is decided."

"Fine." Aislinn shoved in front of Fionn and stormed past Tokhots, with Rune right behind her. "I'm not going to stand here while the two of you argue over me like I'm some prime cut of beef."

"Sprirted," Tokhots murmured. "I like that in a woman. It's so much fun to watch them beg after I break them."

"You mean after you kill them with your poison blood," Fionn snarled.

Tokhots shrugged. "It is rather the same thing, don't you think?"

Fionn judged his chances. He itched to take Tokhots on in single combat, but they were so evenly matched, they'd trade blows for days. Better to follow Aislinn and see what they faced. He tried to push past Tokhots; the dark god feinted and blocked the passage. Fionn went the other way. With the grace of a prize fighter, Tokhots blocked him again.

Fionn rolled his eyes. "Oh please. I'm not in the mood for your games."

"I'm the trickster. Playing games is what I do."

"Fine. Go back to the comics."

"I'm surprised at you, Celt. Marvel named their characters after us, not the other way around."

"Are ye going to let me pass?"

"I'm thinking about it."

Fionn stared down the dim passageway. He couldn't see Aislinn anymore. He twitched the shoulder beneath Bella's talons. The raven didn't need a second invitation. She flew at Tokhots, beak open and talons extended. In the split second the dark god diverted his attention, Fionn swept past him, snapped up the raven as he went, and returned her to the relative protection of his ward.

When the blow came from behind him, as he'd known it must, it nearly knocked him off his feet. "Temper, temper," he called over one shoulder. "What? Ye're a sore loser?"

"Damn it, Celt. Turn around and fight like a man."

"Sorry, I havena the time."

"You like to play games. We could have some fun, you and I. Why, if you wanted to, you could even join up with us. Of course, you'd never have our power—"

"Save your breath...and your compulsion. I doona even like most of my fellow Celts all that well. I'm not interested in making new friends."

"Now who's the grumpy one?"

Another bolt of power hit Fionn's back. He broke into a run. He still couldn't see Aislinn, but her energy trail had just disappeared around a bend in the corridor. Something shifted in the air currents behind him. He spun, intent on protecting himself and Bella, but Tokhots was gone.

"Aislinn, wait," Fionn called. "He's gone." She didn't even slow down, so it took him a few minutes to catch up to her. "What are you doing? Why'd you run off?"

"Two reasons," she panted. "The main one was I needed to put some distance between myself and that lecherous bastard. I can't think when they send out those *fuck me* vibes."

"The other?"

"We need to hurry. Every instinct I have says if we don't get those babies out of here, either the Lemurians or the dark gods are going to kill them. I've passed a few branching passageways. I think it's time to have the younglings tell us where they are."

"I'll find them." Fionn threw his mind wide open, searching. Fortunately, the dragons had a unique energy signature. "This way."

He motioned them forward and then cut hard right down a side corridor. "Not far now."

"Even I can feel them." She lowered her voice and pointed to a closed door. "They're in there."

AISLINN STOOD in front of the door with Rune by her side and girded herself for a second go-round with Tokhots. She'd been desperate to get away from him. Each of the dark gods she'd had the misfortune to meet in person—Perrikus, D'Chel, Tokhots, and Slototh—made her want to throw her clothes off, lie on her back, and beg them to take her. The tender nub between her legs still felt hot and swollen. Her hypersensitive nipples rubbed against the rough fabric of her top. She felt dirty and used, even though he hadn't laid a hand on her.

"No time like the present." Fionn pushed the door open and strode inside.

She followed him and instantly wished she hadn't. The baby dragons were in a cage in the middle of the room, surrounded by about thirty Lemurians, Tokhots, and Perrikus.

The auburn-haired god inclined his head. "We meet again, human." His green eyes flashed a challenge. "I see you recovered from our last meeting. Too bad. I thought I'd killed you along with that brat of yours."

Fury coiled like a snake in her innards. She got a firm grip on her temper. If ever she needed a cool head, it was now.

"What are you waiting for?" Dewi screeched into her mind. *"Get my children."*

"Come get them yourself. Try that trick you used when you linked us in the halls of the dead."

"Not a good idea," Fionn muttered. "Ye canna control her."

Aislinn's gaze swept the room. She waited for the jolt that meant Dewi had joined her. It came with a force that nearly knocked her off her feet. While she tried to get her bearings looking through Dewi's eyes, all hell broke loose. The dragon commandeered her body and threw herself at the pen where the younglings were. Lemurians mobbed them. Fionn pulled magic and worked furiously to neutralize the Old Ones' wards.

"You've got to help Fionn," Aislinn screamed at Dewi. *"We need to kill everyone in here. Then we can get your young."*

"No. We're going to get the younglings and leave."

"I'll fight you every step of the way. We are not going to abandon Fionn, Rune, and Bella. It doesn't work like that. You don't throw your allies to the dogs."

"But they're my children."

"Fionn is my husband—or he will be. Rune is my bond animal. It's sort of the same thing."

Magic pummeled her. It bounced off shields Dewi erected and maintained, without breaking a sweat.

"You're strong, Dewi. Lend your magic to help us all."

Aislinn breathed a ragged sigh of relief. Maybe her last plea got through, because it no longer felt as if her body was being torn in two. Dewi sent power spiraling across the room. A Lemurian fell in its tracks, gurgling in death throes.

Fionn ducked and wove his way to her side. "Got her under control, did ye? I'm impressed."

"Shut up and help me kill this scum. Opinions are a luxury," Dewi spoke through Aislinn.

Like it had been every time Dewi shared her body, Aislinn felt like a spectator. The dragon didn't use Aislinn's magic at all. She killed effortlessly, with an atavistic power strong enough to break through the Old Ones' warding. Aislinn wondered just how strong the dragons were. If Dewi's current demonstration was a bellwether, she and Nidhogg could take on entire armies and come out victorious.

Rune and Bella joined the melee. As soon as Fionn neutralized a shield, one of the animals closed in with a killing blow. In less than fifteen minutes, half the Lemurians were dead. The rest cloaked themselves in magic and faded from the room, which didn't surprise Aislinn. She'd never known them to stand around and embrace death. She grimaced. They'd been quick enough to send humans on risky missions. Never mind that the whole thing had been a sham. Part of her wanted to race out of the room and run down the cowards who'd left, but she was tethered to the dragon.

Tokhots made a dive for the wooden pen that held the younglings. He yanked it open, grabbed a dragon, and tossed the other to Perrikus. "You want to play, momma dragon? Let's have some real fun." He twisted the dragon's foreleg.

Aislinn heard a bone snap. The youngling bellowed in pain, bent its head, and bit the dark god's hand. Aislinn swallowed a sick horror. Surely only a drop or two of blood wouldn't hurt—

"No," Dewi shrieked. "Nooooooo." She raced forward, heedless of Aislinn's body. Cuts opened where she careened off solid objects. The room spun wildly out of control. The dragon shifted back to her own form with Aislinn locked inside.Dewi drove her talons through Tokhots's neck. He crumpled to the floor. She pulled her child away from him and cradled it against her, crooning. The youngling nestled close, but Aislinn sensed its life energy ebbing. Sadness filled her. The young dragon's bite had been small, almost experimental; it couldn't have exposed the youngling to enough of Tokhots's blood to kill it. Fionn's words played in her head. *Deadly poison*. She knew she was deluding herself. If she'd been in her own body, Aislinn would have cried.

Tokhots stirred. Dewi kicked him with a powerful hind foot, followed him across the room, and sank her talons into his chest.

"Did you kill him?" Aislinn asked.

"Probably not. But he'll be out of commission for a while."

"You touched his blood. Why didn't it kill you?"

"The short answer is I tangled with Majestron Zalia years ago. I became very ill, but Nidhogg cured me and I developed immunity to their poison."

Aislinn pushed out a tense breath. It emerged as dragon steam. *"I think we should kill Tokhots if we can,"* she persisted, *"while we have the chance."*

She felt the dragon's internal struggle. Dewi didn't want to take the time. She was focused on the youngling dying in her arms. The dragon bent close to Tokhots's prostrate form, opened her mouth next to his—careful not to touch him with her lips—and breathed fire down his throat. The god screamed, but it came out a gurgling retch. Dewi moved nimbly out of the way. *"You got part of your wish,"* she told Aislinn. *"He will burn from the inside out, but it probably won't be the death him."*

"Thank you. Suffering isn't as good as death, but I'll take it."

"Prepare yourself. I'm going to separate from you and take my child to Nidhogg. If anyone can save her, he can."

"What about the other youngling?"

"Do the best you can." Dewi's mind voice was surprisingly gentle, as was her exit from Aislinn's body.

Fionn stomped across the room and stood in front of Perrikus. "Ye killed my bairn. I ask you for the one in your hands."

"Ask all you like, Celt. I'm not giving it up. Maybe it will make the same mistake its sister did."

"No, I won't." The dragon writhed defiantly.

Aislinn strode to Fionn's side. She met Perrikus's green gaze, grateful he wasn't running his *fuck me now* fountain. "You're the only one left." She made a sweeping gesture with both hands. "You gambled and lost. Give us the youngling."

"Never."

Rune and Bella rushed the dark god from behind. While he fought to stay on his feet, Aislinn jabbed her knife into the hand curled around the dragon. As she hoped, Perrikus's fingers loosened. The dragon howled and jumped to her; its talons clung precariously to her clothing. She wrapped her arms around it. "You're safe now. Shhhh. Safe. Just hang on in case I need my hands to fight."

The air shimmered. Power erupted all around her. Celts poured through portals in full battle regalia, poised to fight.

"Och aye, and ye are a wee bit late, but welcome." Fionn grinned.

Perrikus's form wavered.

"Hey, there. Not so fast, you old pirate," a Celt cried and made a grab for one of the dark god's arms. Another Celt closed to help. Magic sizzled as they wove a spell to force Perrikus to remain where he was.

Tokhots's body made a bubbling, whooshing sound and burst into flames.

Aislinn stared at it. "Die, you bastard," she muttered, glad something had finally happened.

Tokhots had lain there groaning for so long, she'd started to wonder if Dewi had lied to her. Maybe the seeds of dragon's fire took time to percolate. She drew back a foot and kicked him hard in the groin through the flames. If felt so satisfying, she did it again.

"Kick him some more," the dragon in her arms crowed.

Aislinn smiled grimly and cradled the green male against her chest.

"Ye can leave, MacCumhaill," someone said. "We've got things covered."

"There are a bunch of Lemurians you might want to chase down, as long as you're here," Aislinn said.

"Gladly." A Celt with dancing blue eyes and black braids looked enthralled by the prospect. "They're naught but trouble."

Fionn strode to her side. Bella flew to them and landed on his shoulder. Rune padded over, snout stained with Lemurian gore. Aislinn bent to pet him. "You didn't bite Tokhots, did you?"

"No, not after what happened to the baby dragon. Even without that, I remembered what Fionn told you earlier about the dark one's blood being poison."

"I know better," Bella cawed.

Aislinn looked at Fionn. "How come only two of the dark gods have poison blood? Or do you even know?"

He nodded. "Tokhots's blood wasn't always poison, but he challenged Perrikus a verra long time ago, and Majestron Zalia cursed him."

Aislinn rolled her eyes. "I suppose they would have their own internal struggles. Sharing power probably isn't something that comes naturally to any of the dark ones. Majestron Zalia is their de facto queen, right?"

Fionn nodded. "None of this is verra pleasant, but ye would do well to remember." He hesitated. "If Tokhots had fucked you like he wanted to, he would've killed you."

"Hmph." Aislinn held the dragon close. It blew steam onto her hands, warming them. "That's quite a curse. Bet he has a hard time coming up with bedmates."

"'Twas the idea." Fionn shot her a grim smile. "What good is a curse if it doesna ruin something special?"

"I'm free now. Take me to Mother and Father." The little dragon hesitated, and then added, "Please."

Fionn furled his brows. "Mayhap he's learned something from all this."

"We can sort that out later. I'm going to jump Rune, myself, and little no name here outside."

"We'll be right behind you." Fionn's smile was laced with tenderness and hope.

Her heart swelled, overflowing with love and gratitude. Tears were close to the surface. "Thanks for sticking by me. I know I'm prickly and not the easiest—"

"Hush, *leannán*. Ye needn't apologize for who ye are. I love you."

Joy blazed bright inside her. It began in her belly and traveled all the way to her fingertips and toes. She pulled magic, visualized Dewi and Nidhogg, and asked her casting to take them there.

CHAPTER 30

The two dragons sat nose to nose on a broad expanse of unkempt lawn in front of Castle Trim. The rain had stopped, but gray clouds hung heavy in a gunmetal sky. Dewi and Nidhogg keened in archaic Gaelic over the small body stretched between their forelegs. Aislinn's happiness winked out. The youngling must have died. She hurried over with the one in her arms and Rune at her side.

"Dewi. I have someone here. He's missed you."

The dragon shook her head. Tears flew everywhere; they turned to gemstones where they landed. A small fortune in rubies, emeralds, and diamonds surrounded both dragons. "Don't bother me. I'm in mourning."

Nidhogg raised his whirling green eyes and drew in a breath. "One yet lives. I hadn't dared to let myself hope. Beloved, Aislinn saved our other child."

Dewi twined her long neck so she could look at Aislinn. Bottomless dark eyes, so like the Lemurians' it was unsettling, zeroed in on the green dragon in Aislinn's arms. She felt the dragon's magic, tentative at first, sweep over the youngling.

"I really am all right." The green dragon pushed away from Aislinn's chest and sat on its haunches, still balanced in her hands.

Dewi's eyes whirled so fast, it was hypnotic. She folded Nidhogg's forelegs around the youngling they'd lost and bent to take her living child from Aislinn. "Thank you, MacLochlainn." Her tone was formal. "In the end, you did not fail me."

"Any success we had is because you helped Fionn and me and the animals kill so many Old Ones. Setting fire to Tokhots helped, too." Aislinn bowed her head. "I am sorry for your loss."

"As am I," Rune said.

Fionn walked to her side, Bella on his shoulder. He, too, bowed. "My condolences to both of you. If it weren't for Tokhots and his lethal blood, we would have saved them both."

"I should've taken care of that bastard millennia ago," Nidhogg growled; flames blasted skyward. "He came by a few times while Perrikus held me prisoner and did his court jester routine, mocking me."

"We may have killed him." A spear of hope flared in Aislinn's mind. "I saw him burst into flames."

Nidhogg shook his head. "He'll be back in some other form. You cannot kill them any more than you can kill these Celts. They go to the *Dreaming*. I don't have any idea where the dark gods go to mend themselves. We can incapacitate them, sometimes for centuries, but they always pop back up again."

Dewi crooned to the green dragon in Gaelic. He wriggled in her arms.

Nidhogg held the dead youngster against him. "I will lay her to rest. At least she named herself before she died. That is important for our kind."

"Will you tell us?" Fionn looped an arm around Aislinn's shoulders.

"That is something she can tell you, even in death," Dewi replied. "Show them, Nidhogg."

The black dragon unfolded his forelegs. The youngling still had red scales, but many had turned to gold. As Aislinn watched, the transition rippled slowly down her body. "Her name is D'Or," Nidhogg said. "No matter how many younglings we produce, she will always be my golden child."

Aislinn met Dewi's gaze. "If you want to go with Nidhogg to bury your youngling, Fionn and I will see that your son gets back to Inishowen safely."

"It's kind of you to offer." Dewi bent her head to the child in her arms. "Would you promise to behave if we did that?"

The green dragon's head bobbed up and down. "Yes. I like Aislinn."

"What about me?" Fionn furled his brows.

"I don't know you," the dragon piped up, "but I like the wolf."

Rune whuffled in an approximation of lupine laughter. He head-butted Fionn. "Beat you out again. Must be my handsome coat and—"

"Enough." Fionn untangled himself from Aislinn and buried a hand in Rune's ruff.

Aislinn held out her arms. The green dragon spread its wings and floated down to her.

Nidhogg glanced at Dewi. "Are you ready?" She nodded.

The black dragon turned to Aislinn. "Just so you know, we do not bury our dead. They return to the fires where we were first forged. I cannot tell you where that is, only that it will be two days before we return."

"We'll make certain the others are safe." Fionn stroked the dragon in Aislinn's arms. "He looks like he weighs over fifty pounds. Would you like me to carry him?"

"Sure. It's amazing. One of them is as heavy as four were a few days ago."

"No one asked me." The green dragon scented the air. "Maybe I want to ride on the wolf."

"Good to know we haven't totally quenched his spirit," Aislinn murmured. She placed a finger beneath the dragon's snout. "You can ride on Rune after we're back in Inishowen. For now, Fionn can carry you." She raised her gaze to Dewi and Nidhogg. "Safe journey. I look forward to your return."

Dewi's jaws parted. Steam rolled upward. "I believe you mean that."

"I do." Aislinn stepped closer to Dewi's bulk. "It's like any partnership. We had to get used to one another. We'll still have our misunderstandings, but I think we trust one another now."

The dragon nodded thoughtfully. "Yes. Trust makes all the difference. Say…" Her whirling gaze caught Aislinn's golden one and held it. "I will lay another clutch soon. Perhaps you'd be willing to tend them for me from time to time. It takes nearly a year before they hatch. Egg nannies are worth their weight in gold."

Aislinn thought about the piles of treasure in the dragon's cave. Once upon a time, before the old world fell apart, she would've been entranced by the gold and gemstones. They didn't mean much anymore. "I'm honored you'd trust me to watch over your eggs. I'll help any way I can."

"Come." Nidhogg spread his wings. Dewi did the same. In moments, the dragons were airborne.

Aislinn turned to Fionn. "I wonder why they didn't jump to where they were going."

"Probably because they want to make certain to keep their destination hidden. No matter how carefully ye shield yourself, magic leaves a trail. Adva, D'Chel, and Majestron Zalia are still on the loose. Mayhap Perrikus, too. He's wily. Until I talk with the other Celts, I willna know if they managed to corral him for a bit."

"Shall we go home?" A smile tugged at her lips. She liked the sound of *home*. Wherever Fionn was would be their home, now and always. It could be his manor house, or it might be a cave, or a deserted building, or an open field. The important thing was they were together.

Bella cawed raucously. "I like that idea. I want to sit on my perch, put my head under a wing, and sleep for hours."

~

FIONN BROUGHT them out on the rolling green land in front of the gates to his manor. Night was falling. While he felt sad for the youngling's death, they'd come through nearly unscathed. Relief whooshed through him. He'd never stop worrying about Aislinn, but he couldn't lock her in a box like a valued treasure. Her spirit would wither and die, and she'd stop being the woman he loved.

A magical net settled over them. "What the fuck?" He batted at its strands.

Rune snarled; Bella quorked. Aislinn just looked exhausted.

"Oh, it's you. Sorry." Three humans walked out the main gate and chanted to dissolve their casting. One of them—a tall, slender, thirtyish woman with shoulder-length red hair—shrugged. "Better to be safe than sorry, I always say."

A dark-haired man eyed them. "We were given guard duty on the north side of your manor."

"Let me down." The dragon wriggled out of Fionn's grasp, spread its wings, and floated to the ground. It craned its neck in all directions and started for the sea.

"No so fast." Aislinn raced after it, scooped it up, set it on Rune's back, and said, "Take him inside to where the others are."

"What if I don't want to go?"

"Too bad," Rune mock snarled. "You just became my responsibility. If you even think about getting away—"

"I can fly." The green dragon smirked.

"So can I," Bella piped up. "Which means I'll hunt you down if you try anything funny."

"You have to land sometime," Rune said. "When you do, I'll make you sorry you were ever born." He trotted through the manor gates with the youngling sitting on his back muttering imprecations.

Fionn looked after Rune's departing form and rolled his eyes. He extended a hand to the humans. They shook it by turns. "Doona fash about the net. No harm done. I'm glad to see someone's keeping an eye out."

"Those little dragons are a mite headstrong." The woman's mouth twitched, as if she were suppressing a smile. "We're taking turns watching them, too."

"Impetuous, stubborn. Yep, they're quite the handful. Thanks for standing watch duty. I'll take a turn once I've had a few hours' rest." Aislinn shook hands with the three humans. She looked at Fionn. "I need food and then sleep. Right now, I'm about as useful as tits on a boar."

"Well now, we canna be having that." He twined an arm around her waist.

She leaned into him, and they walked side by side across the bridge and up the stone walkway.

"Why don't ye go to our rooms? I'll just snare a bit of food and some mead from the kitchens. That way, ye willna get caught in whatever drama the younglings are hatching up."

"Good idea. I'll run us a bath."

He grinned. "Even better. I dinna want to say aught, but both of us stink."

Aislinn laughed. The sound warmed his soul. "Yes, we smell like Lemurians. I smelled like them for years, so long I nearly got used to it."

By the time Fionn made it out of the kitchen, nearly an hour had passed. Gwydion, Arawn, and Bran had insisted on a full report. While the Celts caught up, the green dragon held court; his version of events was so inflated, it made Fionn laugh. To hear the youngling tell it, the dark gods were ten feet tall and breathed fire that incinerated everything in its tracks. The other six dragons were ringed around him in thrall.

Rune followed Fionn out of the kitchen and up the stairs,

muttering about how he wasn't cut out to tend pups. Bella rode on the wolf's back and commiserated with him.

"Quiet now," Fionn cautioned both animals. "Aislinn may well be asleep."

He pushed the door open quietly. Bella flew to her perch. Rune padded to a corner and lay down. Aislinn was curled on her side in the bed. Her mouth was half open; she had dark smudges beneath both eyes. Wet hair splayed around her on the pillows.

Fionn set the food and liquor on a nearby table and latched the door. He stripped off his stained and worn battle leathers and left them in a heap. They needed to be rinsed out and hung to dry. He tiptoed into the bathroom. *Good.* Aislinn hadn't emptied the tub. He bent and tested the water. It was tepid, which was good enough. He soaped himself, rinsed, and opened the drain.

Fionn wrapped himself in his robe and crept back into the bedroom. A gentle smile curved his lips. He was glad Aislinn was still asleep. She hadn't had a decent rest since well before they'd arrived at Inishowen. He uncorked the mead bottle. Its rich, pungent scent filled his nostrils, and he drank deep. He looked at the food, decided he wasn't all that hungry, and took another draught from the bottle before setting its cork back into place. The liquor burned a trail down his throat to his stomach, warming him. The room was chilly, but building a fire would make noise. He compromised by pulling magic to warm the air around the bed.

He slipped under the covers, trying not to disturb her, but the bedsprings creaked. She rolled toward him, eyes at half-mast and held out her arms. He wrapped his around her and cradled her head on his shoulder. "Och, lass, I love you to distraction. Ye are everything I hoped for and waited for all my life."

She giggled. "Bet you say that to all the girls."

He snorted. "Not even close. Can ye allow a man—your man—to make a declaration of love without poking fun at him?"

She nodded against his shoulder. "It feels kind of overwhelming."

"What does?"

"Everything. I've never loved anyone before—except my parents and Rune. This is different."

"See?" Bella cawed sleepily from her perch. "*She* includes her bond animal when she talks about love."

"This is a private conversation. You're not supposed to be listening in." Fionn raised his head off the pillows to glare at the raven. "Sorry." He gathered Aislinn against him. "Ye were saying?"

"It will sound corny, but you're as elemental to my existence as eating and drinking and breathing. When I thought you were lost in the border world, it felt as if my life had ended." She moved back so she could look at him. "Is it the MacLochlainn bond thing? Is that why you feel so important?"

"Ye know the answer to that one, lass. Look at your mother. She was linked to me through the bond, and she fell in love with another and ran like hell."

Aislinn grinned. "Oh, yeah. I hadn't exactly forgotten that, but I'm not firing on all cylinders right now, either."

"Probably neither am I. What's between us is new. 'Twill ripen and mature. Just like with you and Dewi, trust grows in stages. Over time, 'twill strengthen our relationship—and our love. Ye'll be less, um, prickly."

"Does it mean you'll be less protective?"

A laugh bubbled up from his belly. "Nay, lass. Probably not. 'Tis the warrior in me. We shield what's ours. 'Tis hardwired in."

She dropped a hand between them and curved it around his half-erect cock. It stiffened instantly at her touch. Her golden eyes glowed warmly, her lips parted. She snaked her other hand around his neck and drew him down so he could kiss her.

He settled his lips on hers and ran his tongue across the seam between her lips. She opened her mouth, and he sank his tongue inside, tasting her. Her tongue sparred with his, and then she withdrew it and nibbled his lips. Fionn's groin tightened in anticipation. He'd never had such an instantaneous response to a woman before; she filled him with insatiable lust. Even so, he held himself back and drew his mouth away from hers. "Are ye certain, *leannán?* I was going to let you rest."

She tossed a leg over his hip and pressed her hot, passion-slick center against his thigh. The musk of her arousal nearly drove him mad. Her hand tightened around his shaft. With an inchoate moan, he pushed back the covers and strung kisses down her neck and chest. He maneuvered her onto her back so he could capture a wonderfully hard nipple in his mouth. She had the most beautiful breasts he'd ever seen. High and full, they were tipped with strawberry circles. He tongued one, moved to the other, and then back again. She buried the hand that wasn't busy with his cock in his hair and arched her back. Little panting gasps told him she was just as hot as he was. Fionn didn't fully understand why he wasn't face down and asleep. They hadn't had enough sleep for a long time, and it had been an exceedingly difficult day. All he could think about was sinking himself inside her wonderful pussy and feeling her close around him.

His cock jerked in her hand. If he didn't watch it, he'd come before he even got inside her. He let go of her nipple and gazed at her. "How would ye like us to be?"

She rubbed fluid that had leaked from his cock around the head and then put her fingers in her mouth and sucked on them. "Mmm. Sweet. You taste so sweet." She gifted him with an impish grin. "It's a hard choice. It always is with you. I want to do it all. Fuck you, taste you, touch you. How about this?" She slid from beneath him, flipped over, and got to her hands and knees.

The perfect globes of her ass separated, showing him everything. Red curls, spiky with her juices, gleamed in pale moonlight streaming through the window. Fionn's breath hitched. Presented to him like that, her sex was incredibly arousing. He moved behind her, curved his fingers around his shaft, and guided himself home. Her muscles clenched tight as soon as he was inside and then fluttered as she released and tightened over and over. He threw back his head, closed his eyes, and gave himself up to the ecstasy of the moment. Sensation knifed through him, so sweet and hot it set fire to every nerve in his body.

She butted him with her hips, and he laughed. Obviously, she wanted him to move.

"I can do you one better, lass." He reached between her legs and rubbed her swollen nub. Holding firmly to the center of her sex, he drew his cock out and drove himself into her long and slow. Fionn plumbed her again and again. He focused on her and remembered to breathe. If he didn't, he'd speed his strokes until he drowned her in semen. It would happen soon enough anyway. His balls snugged tight against his body, aching for release.

She clamped down on him, muscles rippling against his shaft. Her hips bucked. She cried his name and her fingers clawed at the sheets.

"Aye, *mo croi*, come for me. That's right, come for me." Somewhere in the midst of her climax, his body got the better of him. He passed beyond control, and his cock got so hard, it felt like it was about to burst. Semen arced into her, one spasm blending with the next until he was certain he'd keep coming forever.

Fionn stayed on his knees, gasping for breath. He'd never had orgasms like he had with Aislinn. Climaxes that lasted beyond reason, that left him feeling euphoric and wrung out and exhilarated all at the same time. He pulled out of her body. His cock was still hard, and it shone with their combined fluids.

She collapsed beneath him, panting and laughing. "You are the best lover," she said between breaths. "And it just keeps getting better."

He lay on his side next to her and opened his arms. She scooted into them. "I feel the same way about you, *mo croi*. Ye take me so high, we snatch a piece of the heavens when we make love."

She snuggled close. In minutes, the pattern of her breathing told him she was sinking into sleep. He moved his head at an angle so he could watch her. He wanted to savor the moment and lose himself in the tenderness he felt for the incredible woman drowsing in his arms.

Fionn sighed. He'd be back to strategizing and problem-solving soon enough. They were far from out of the woods. The Lemurians had obviously bred like rats. Goddess only knew how many of them had infiltrated Earth. And then there were the hybrids and the dark gods... Sleep tugged at his eyelids. There'd be time enough later to figure everything out. For now, he had Aislinn. She was so much more than he'd ever hoped for, he still couldn't believe she was his.

Aye, the gods truly smiled upon me, for she and I found one another. 'Tis more than enough. With his arms around the woman he loved more than life itself, Fionn let sleep take him.

You've reached the end of *Earth's Blood*. This story concludes in *Earth's Hope*, book three of the *Earth Reclaimed Series*. All three books are available in e-format, audio and paperback. Read on to sample the first chapter of *Earth's Hope*.

ABOUT THE AUTHOR

Ann Gimpel is a USA Today bestselling author. She's also a clinical psychologist, with a Jungian bent. Avocations include mountaineering, skiing, wilderness photography and, of course, writing. A lifelong aficionado of the unusual, she began writing speculative fiction a few years ago. Since then her short fiction has appeared in a number of webzines and anthologies. Her longer books run the gamut from urban fantasy to paranormal romance. She's published over 50 books to date, with several more contracted for 2018 and beyond. A husband, grown children, grandchildren and three wolf hybrids round out her family.

Keep up with her at www.anngimpel.com or http://anngimpel.blogspot.com If you enjoyed what you read, get in line for special offers. Sign up for Ann's newsletter on her website or her blog.

EARTH'S HOPE, CHAPTER ONE

*D*ewi's blood-red wings cut through cold, blustery air. Day edged into evening, and the western horizon would soon be awash in the muted tones of a winter sunset. The dragon traveled without thought, following Nidhogg's dark bulk as he flew in front of her. For a time, she'd kept pace with her mate, the Norse dragon god, but the sight of their dead child cradled in his forearms smote her, and she'd dropped back to where the dark gods' treachery didn't smack her dead in the heart. Perrikus and Tokhots had kidnapped two of her younglings. One was safe, but the other had bitten Tokhots and succumbed to his poisoned blood.

Fire burst from Nidhogg's mouth, followed by steam. His grief was shifting to anger. Too bad hers couldn't do the same. Dewi rotated her head atop her sinuous stalk of a neck. Today she felt every single one of her better than two thousand-year life span, and her mistakes haunted her. Life had been simpler before mankind developed a fondness for machinery and electronics. Back then, everyone still believed in magic and treated her with the reverence that was her due as the Celtic dragon god, but the world had changed. Humans no longer jumped when Celtic gods—like her— snapped their fingers.

Smoke burbled past her double rows of teeth. Not that the electronic age was a problem anymore. The dark gods had joined forces with Lemurians, alien beings from the lost continent of Mu, and stripped the planet of all human life they couldn't turn to their advantage. They'd done a damned thorough job of it too.

Dewi was falling behind, so she flew faster. Not fast enough to pull in front of Nidhogg, though. It was pathetic, not dragonlike at all, but Dewi clung to sanity by a thread. If she didn't watch it, despair would get the better of her, and she'd set the countryside below on fire.

"What are you doing, woman?" Nidhogg trumpeted.

Dewi's eyes snapped open and she looked around. Lost in her thoughts, she'd veered off course to the east. "Sorry," she called and flew faster until she drew alongside the coal black dragon who'd been her mate for millennia. He turned whirling green eyes awash in pain her way. Dewi shook her head and said firmly, "This is my fault. I should've—"

"Stop." He narrowed his eyes. "We can't go back. You think I don't feel guilty for what happened to our child?" More fire streamed from his nostrils. "I was so spellbound to have you by my side again, I deluded myself into believing nothing wicked would befall us. How could it? Hadn't we paid enough?" Bitterness underscored his words.

"Hush, love." Shaken out of her own sorrow by Nidhogg's distress, she sent healing magic across the air between them.

"We will find time for talk," he said, "but now I need your help crossing the barrier into our borderworld."

"Of course." Dewi wove magic around them, strengthening the air currents beneath their wings. She'd been overjoyed and astonished when Nidhogg breathed life into dragon eggs she'd turned into a shrine. Between delight at being reunited with Nidhogg after his centuries of imprisonment, and the sudden reality of eight baby dragons, she hadn't fully settled into motherhood. The small dragons were so endearing—and unexpected—she'd coddled them, denying them nothing.

In hindsight, she should have been more vigilant. While her back was turned, the dark gods had filched two of her precious brood from beneath her nose, with help from the Lemurians. Thank the goddess Fionn and the MacLochlainn had stepped in and saved one of her purloined children. They'd tried to save them both, but had been too late. Aislinn—the MacLochlainn—might be headstrong, but she was courageous and loyal. Dewi hadn't thanked her enough, something she'd remedy just as soon as they returned to Fionn's manor house in Inishowen.

Dewi peered through the gathering gloom of the dying day. She couldn't see across the barrier quite yet, but she knew what lay beyond it. Dragons had been forged in a fiery world. Long ago, most dragons raised their young there, but she and Nidhogg—and the eight younglings he'd resurrected from their egg casings—were the last of their kind. New eggs percolated in her belly, but it would be weeks before they'd be ready to incubate, and a year beyond that before they hatched.

"Pay attention!" Nidhogg's deep voice held an uncharacteristically sharp note. "Your mind is wandering."

"I said I was sorry." Steam curled from her mouth. "This isn't easy. I want to be back in Inishowen with our other younglings."

"You think I don't?" More smoke followed his words. "Would you have us pile one sin atop another? We must honor our lost child by bringing her home."

Dewi didn't answer. Each of them was so mired in grief it was a miracle they were able to be civil. She pushed more power into her spell. They were close to the magical barricade separating Earth from the dragons' homeland. The air darkened and developed an iridescent glow. Power tinged with an electrical jolt zinged off her wingtips; the air smelled singed with a hint of ozone. "I haven't been here since we lived in the Old Country," she murmured.

"That long?" At least the funereal quality had left his voice. "Why?"

The anger that had eluded Dewi earlier slammed into her like a runaway train. Fire boiled from her belly and erupted through her mouth. "Because," she snarled, "there were hundreds of years when I was convinced I was the only dragon left alive. Why would I want to return to our world—unless I planned to die?"

"You gambled when you tried to free me that first time." Nidhogg's tone was soothing, gentle. "In your place, I would have done the same."

"I may have gambled, but I lost," she moaned. "I tried my damnedest to liberate you from the dark gods, but I wasn't strong enough, and I abandoned my clutch of eggs when I went after you. It was a hell of a choice. You or our children. In the end, I lost both." She shook herself from nose to tail tip, and scarlet scales rained from her hide.

"I love you for trying to save me." He turned his head and gazed at her. "You did rescue me. It just took a few hundred years longer than you'd hoped." He hesitated through a couple wing beats. "I've never been so happy to leave anywhere as I was to escape that wretched borderworld Perrikus calls home. Ruler of power and energy, my ass. Petty despot, more like. He only kept me alive to siphon my magic, so he could keep his pathetic excuse for a world from withering. That idiot D'Chel didn't help matters. He'd stop by my prison and gloat until I wanted to smash his face in and shove those perfect teeth of his down his throat."

"How did you know dragon's fire would reanimate our eggs?" she asked. "If I'd known it was that simple, I'd have done it long ago."

"I didn't. Not for certain. I'm much older than you, Dewi." He blew a gentle tongue of flame her way. "It's entirely possible I'm the oldest living creature on Earth. I hold bits and pieces of things, images that float in my mind. We had nothing to lose."

Dewi thought about the shrine she'd made of her clutch when

she returned without Nidhogg after her first rescue effort. She'd mourned so deeply, the eggs were surrounded by mounds of precious gemstones from her tears. "I suppose you're right," she murmured and stopped. No reason to admit she'd also kept the eggs as a reminder of her own fallibility.

"Brace yourself." Nidhogg's wings beat so fast they became a blur. Dewi shuttered her inner eyelids across her corneas. The dragons' world was a place of heat and light. Moments later, familiar smells buffeted her, singeing her lungs until she inhaled deeply, breathing past the pain. A charred landscape spread beneath her, beautiful in its barrenness. Red, orange, and black scorched dirt stretched in all directions.

Dragons could go for long periods with no food and little water. Their home world had only a single spring, and it had always proven sufficient for the dragons and small herds of wildebeest-related ungulates they fed on. Most of this land was a continuous string of volcanoes ringed around caves. The spring was deep within the cave system. Double suns were just falling beneath the western horizon, turning the sky a deep crimson, like a bloody gash across the world. Soon the only light would be from the ever-present fires.

"We will offer our daughter to the flame," Nidhogg said and inscribed circles in the thick, smoky air as he headed for a stark volcanic crack. Dewi followed him down. Some part buried deep within her welcomed the barren world, recognized it as part of her making. Nidhogg touched down, and Dewi joined him on the cracked, dry ground of their borderworld. He held out their daughter's body.

Dewi took her child and clasped the small dragon close. She would have grown up to be golden; even in death, her red scales had continued to change color. Dewi bent her head and brushed her jaws over her youngling's scaled head. "I'm so sorry," she said. "So very sorry. I wish I'd had time to get to know you."

"She would have been special," Nidhogg broke in. "Just like her mother."

Tears gathered, welled, and spilled into the dust. Pearls, diamonds, rubies, and emeralds sparkled at Dewi's feet. She gazed into Nidhogg's eyes. "I will always blame myself for this. Just like I blamed myself for making the wrong choice and leaving our eggs to search for you." She blew out steam and fire-streaked air. "We'll move beyond this, but those bastards will not get any more of our children."

"I hope you're correct." Nidhogg narrowed his spinning green eyes. "We've thrown down the gauntlet. Not just you and me, but the Celts and humans like Aislinn, humans with power. The bond animals are in this too."

"I suppose they are." Dewi thought about Rune, the wolf bonded to Aislinn, and Bella, the raven bound to Fionn. Hunters bonded to animals, infusing them with magic, or drawing out latent power that was already there. Human magic came in five iterations: Hunter, Mage, Seeker, Healer, and Seer. Most humans had two magics, one primary and one weaker, but Aislinn held all five. Fionn did too, just like all the Celtic gods.

"Dewi." Nidhogg laid his snout alongside hers. "There's never been a war without casualties. You may not come through this. I might not. Certainly, people we love will die."

Dewi bristled and clutched her child closer. "No more of my children. Not on my watch."

"No matter how vigilant and well-intentioned you are, it could happen." He straightened. "We fight to save Earth. We have no choice. Tomorrow is far from a certainty. Hear me when I tell you I welcome death as a free dragon. Dying by inches over hundreds of years in that stinking pen on Perrikus's world was agony. No matter what comes to pass, it won't be worse than that."

Alarm sluiced through her, and she shifted so she faced him. "You can't die. I just got you back."

Compassion streamed from his eyes. "I feel the same way about you, Dewi, my love, my heart. Remember they said we'd never last? That the Norse dragon god and Celtic dragon god would be at each other's throats?"

Dewi nodded. "Now that you mention it, yes, I do remember." She snorted and smoke rose above her head. "Proved them wrong, didn't we?"

"Yes, love. We did." He held out his forelegs for their daughter. "Let us pray and send her to her rest."

The sound of his chanting in their ancient language rose and fell around her. After a time, he kissed their daughter and handed her to Dewi one last time. Nidhogg didn't have to talk. He glanced at Dewi and then at the jagged crack at their feet, which belched sulfuric fumes. Dewi joined her voice with his for the final stanzas of the lament for the dead. Once they fell silent, she hunkered forward and dropped their daughter's body into the bowels of the dragons' borderworld.

No matter what Nidhogg says, I am never burying another of my young.

Never.

"Come." Nidhogg's deep voice rumbled next to her. "So long as we are here, we should visit the caves and make certain the everlasting spring still flows." He spread his wings and beat the air with them.

Dewi had been ready to teleport into the caves, but flying was better. They'd be able to lay eyes on their world, assure themselves it hadn't been disturbed. Not that it was likely. Wards wrapped their borderworld, powerful magic that would incinerate anyone who wasn't a dragon.

Dewi took to the skies; once airborne, she scanned familiar landmarks and felt a bittersweet tug. Humans would never understand the attraction of the dragons' home. Neither would the other Celtic gods. She'd always felt she lived two lives, particularly once she believed she was the last dragon. Longing rose in her like a hot tide. If she had a choice in the matter, she'd bring her children back here and settle in with them and her mate. Let the humans and Celts sort out the mess with the dark gods. She could raise another clutch of eggs, and they'd be well on their way to repopulating the Earth with dragons…

Nidhogg circled to land, touching down in a flurry of dusty, reddened dirt. Dewi blew steam to clear her nostrils and lumbered near where he stood.

"We could bring the younglings here—" she began, but he silenced her with a harsh look. Fire plumed from his open mouth.

"The same thought crossed my mind, but we will not do that. How could we live with ourselves if we turned our backs on honor? More importantly, what kind of lesson would that teach our children?"

Shame burned hot and viscous in her chest, and Dewi looked away. "Once our younglings are a month old, the Celts will want to use them in battle."

"They would be within their rights." Nidhogg's tone was devoid of inflection. "Our children will be capable of fighting once their scales harden." He shook his head, and steam flew in all directions. "No one gets an exemption, Dewi. Not me. Not you, and not our children."

"I'll be chained to the eggs in my body once I've laid them. I don't know how I'll manage being stuck in our cave in Ireland knowing how thin a margin we hold."

"I've been thinking about that." Nidhogg raised his snout. "You will hold the eggs within you. Until the outcome of the coming battles is more certain, we will need you in battle."

"But how can I do that?" Dewi stared at her mate as if he'd lost his mind. "Last time we produced a clutch, the eggs came when they did. I couldn't have stopped them anymore than I could have turned back time."

"It's numbers. So long as you have fewer than fifteen fertilized eggs within you, you control when they emerge."

Dewi rolled her eyes. "Why do you know that and I don't?"

He shrugged, his black scales jangling against one another. "Maybe because I paid attention when the females got together. What this does mean, though"—he eyed her meaningfully—"is no more mating. We can't risk creating more eggs."

"Not sure I like that," she muttered and clanked her jaws together. "Let's get going with the caves. We've already burned up the better part of a day getting here, and we told Fionn and Aislinn we'd be back in two."

"I don't like the not mating part, either." Nidhogg winked broadly. "But it will create an incentive to plow through to the other side of things and secure Earth once and for all."

"I heard the tail end of that." Arawn, Celtic god of the dead, terror, and revenge, strode out of the mouth of the cave system. Black robes cloaked his tall, slender frame. Black hair hung loose to his waist, and his dark eyes glittered dangerously.

Dewi puffed smoke in surprise. "How did you get here? This world is closed to all but dragons."

"I'm surprised ye have to ask. The Halls of the Dead link to every borderworld, even this one." Arawn narrowed his eyes. "It got me around the problem with your ward system."

"So I suppose a better question," Nidhogg cut in, "would be why you felt the need to intercept us."

"Neither of you have been to these caves for a verra long time," Arawn spoke deliberately, enunciating each word until Dewi felt like strangling him.

"Your point?" she snapped.

"A handful of dragons yet live—"

"That's scarcely possible," Dewi huffed.

"Hush, dear." Nidhogg straightened his spine until he hit his full eight-and-a-half-feet height and shifted his gaze to Arawn. "I suppose you're going to tell us why you kept their existence a secret."

The dark-haired god shook his head. "Nay, I will let them tell you that themselves. I merely wished to prepare you. They are here at my behest and have remained so out of deference to me. I saw no reason to alert our enemies to their existence after Perrikus imprisoned you." A rare smile split Arawn's gaunt face, displaying very white, very even teeth. "I must return to Inishowen. I presume I will see you there soon."

"Thank you." Nidhogg inclined his head.

Dewi gnashed her teeth, not believing her mate was actually thanking Arawn for his deceit. "You could have told me," she gritted at Arawn. "I can keep secrets."

"Unless ye'd been taken," Arawn pointed out. "And tortured."

"Damn you, you arrogant Celtic ass," she sputtered. "I suffered terribly."

"Aye, but ye dinna die." The god of death's dark gaze flashed menace. "Enough. We all made sacrifices, and I fear we are far from the end of them." He raised his arms skyward, shimmered, and was gone.

"Get hold of yourself." Nidhogg nudged Dewi with his shoulder. "Let's get moving. I want to see which of our kin remain."

"Traitors, the lot of them," she hissed.

Nidhogg pivoted on his powerful hindquarters until he faced her and grabbed one of her forelegs with a taloned foot. "You will hear them out," he pronounced. "Only a fool makes judgments without facts."

Ouch.

Shame nudged anger, not totally displacing it, but at least making room for something beyond indignation. She yanked her foreleg free. "I promise to listen, but if I don't like their answers—"

"Neither of us will take action without consulting the other." He skewered her with his gaze. "Agreed?"

"Agreed." She aimed for neutrality, but a sullen undernote crept beneath the word just the same.